Readers love the Sinners Series by RHYS FORD

Sinner's Gin

"This is a sexy, fast-paced, hurt/comfort, murder mystery with… scorching hot sexy times!"

—Gay Book Reviews

Whiskey and Wry

"It's one thing to write a great book. It's a whole other level of talent to write song lyrics, too, and Rhys delivers."

—Happy Ever After, *USA Today*

Tequila Mockingbird

"The author has done it again with a complex intriguing story line that explodes from the beginning and never slows down…"

—Guilty Indulgence Romance Reviews

Readers love the
Sinners Series by RHYS FORD

Sloe Ride

"*Sloe Ride* is rife with mystery and intrigue. If you're looking for unconventional characters and action, Rhys Ford's books would be a perfect match for you."

—Fresh Fiction

Absinthe of Malice

"It made me laugh, it made me angry, it made me irritated and at times, I was gutted. But in the end… it made me smile and be grateful I got to go on this journey with the guys."

—The Novel Approach

Sin and Tonic

"Rhys Ford has with mere words created a magical, at times rambunctious, blue bleeding family that loves deeply and fully."

—Love Bytes

By RHYS FORD

Published by DREAMSPINNER PRESS
www.dreamspinnerpress.com

RHYS FORD
TEQUILA MOCKINGBIRD

Published by
DREAMSPINNER PRESS

5032 Capital Circle SW, Suite 2, PMB# 279,
Tallahassee, FL 32305-7886 USA
www.dreamspinnerpress.com

This is a work of fiction. Names, characters, places, and incidents either are the product of author imagination or are used fictitiously, and any resemblance to actual persons, living or dead, business establishments, events, or locales is entirely coincidental.

Digital ISBN: 978-1-63216-014-0
Mass Market Paperback ISBN: 978-1-64108-192-4
Trade Paperback ISBN: 978-1-63216-013-3
Mass Market Paperback published August 2019
v. 1.0

Printed in the United States of America
∞
This paper meets the requirements of
ANSI/NISO Z39.48-1992 (Permanence of Paper).

This book is dedicated to Lisa Horan, my sister in coffee, words, and sleepless nights spent talking and laughing. This one is for you, pookie, because you wanted Con's story so badly. Love you.

ACKNOWLEDGMENTS

TO THE Five: Lea, Penn, Jenn, and Tamm. Always and forever *breaks out in cheesy song*. My love also to my sisters, Lisa, Ree, and Ren. I treasure each and every one of you.

To everyone at Dreamspinner who polishes up the coal I give them into a beautiful diamond. I send you all a huge thank-you—Elizabeth North, Grace and her fine editing team, Lynn, Julianne, Mara, Ginnifer, lyric, Shannon, and everyone else there. Soooo many thank-yous.

And once again, my Beta readers and the Dirty Ford Guinea Pigs. You guys keep me sane, talk me off the ledge, and most of all, believe in the stuff that comes out of my brain. Thank you. God thank you.

Lastly, to everyone who ever thought about picking up a guitar, drumsticks, or any other instrument to make music. Whether you know it or not, you keep our lives moving at a steady beat. I could not write without music. Nearly every single word in every single document I've written has had a soundtrack forged in someone else's heart, mind, and soul. There is not enough gratitude to give you for that so I can only say well done and keep going.

PROLOGUE

You cracked me open,
Sucked out my filthy core,
Held my heart in your hands,
And gave in when I begged for more.
—Begging Again

"FUCKING HELL," Forest spat as he fell back into the garbage again. The damned Dumpster's sides were too tall. Or he was too short. Either way, he couldn't get the hell out of the thing, and his arms were now shaking from the numerous times he'd tried.

The last thing he wanted was to be there in the morning. Someone would find him, and that someone would bring down the cops on his head. Cops meant social services, and *that* meant he'd be spending a good amount of time fighting to get out of plastered walls and plastic suburbia.

He'd rather die in the Dumpster.

He just didn't know if he could try to get out again. He hurt so damned much.

Mostly—this time—it was his face. It definitely was his jaw. Or maybe his cheek. Whichever. He just knew he hurt. He tried to remember who told him to always trust guys in a minivan, but Forest couldn't recall where he'd gotten that information. Whoever it'd been, he'd kick the guy's ass whenever he found him again.

Because apparently guys in minivans with those happy little sticker children on the back glass *really* didn't want to pay for their hand jobs ahead of time.

Now Forest was in a Dumpster because minivan guy thought it would be fun to toss him in there when he was done beating the shit out of him, and he still didn't have more than fifty cents on him.

Fifty cents did *not* go a long way when someone needed food. Even dog-food tacos cost two for a dollar, and tax ate up a nice piece of the money pie all on its own.

"Yeah, Mrs. Whatever-the-fuck-your-name-is, tell the principal I'm stupid," Forest muttered as he glared at the Dumpster's too-high edge. "Go hungry for a bit, bitch, and you learn math real fucking quick."

He heard a door slamming—a heavy, thick-sounding door—and he froze, hating himself for holding his breath because it was stupid and doing so made his chest hurt. There were bruises there too, Forest was sure of it, and his back wasn't doing too good either. From the familiar throbbing along his spine, he was going to be pissing blood as soon as he had to take a pee.

Something slippery under him gave, and Forest went down, biting his tongue when he hit the hard floor. He tasted blood—for the third or fourth time that night—and the light from the streetlamps spun, leaving trails of stars on his eyes.

Swallowing at the salty taste in his mouth, he sighed. "Fuck me."

A SCRATCHING sound caught Franklin Marshall's attention. It shouldn't have. Not in the middle of San Francisco's Chinatown, where the rats grew fat and happy on some of the best cuisine from the other side of the Pacific. No, this sounded different than a rat or any other kind of vermin he normally found in the middle of the night when he was dumping out the empties from his recording studio.

This sounded oddly human. Not so much the scratching but the murmuring noises accompanying them.

And it was coming from the open Dumpster at the end of the alley.

The Sound was a legacy of a hippie co-op he'd once been a part of. As his former lovers shaved their beards, or armpits as the case might be, and drifted off to respectability, he'd remained behind, mixing records for young artists with more talent than money and certainly with less sense than most. A decade ago he'd finally gotten sick of the restaurant next door changing hands more often than a five-year-old girl changed her clothes, and he'd bought the place out, called it Marshall's Amps, and turned it into a lounging coffee shop where he could get a good cup of Big Island coffee whenever he wanted.

With the bad-restaurant-roulette gone, the vermin population had dropped dramatically, but every once in a while, something—or someone—came creeping around, and Frank was forced to move whatever or whomever it was along.

He was too tired to care. All Frank wanted was to toss the trash out and go pack a bowl.

And at three o'clock in the morning, rousting an undesirable from a Dumpster was sometimes quite dangerous, and Frank knew he wasn't getting any younger. There was only so much more damage an aging hippie musician could take before he'd have to start begging one of the studio guys to come help him change a lightbulb because he'd gotten the shit kicked out of him by a crackhead.

He put the bottles into the recycle bin and set a box of leftover pizza on the café table he'd set up under his RV's awning. Ever since the city banned smoking within spitting distance of anything or anyone, he'd given up living in the apartment over the studio and instead opted to toss his bag of bones onto a queen-sized mattress in an old motor home. Owning a building was a headache and a half, but owning a parking lot smack-dab in the middle of Chinatown more than made up for the hassle. Especially since he'd found he rather liked living in a quasi-gypsy state.

It was a long, cold walk to the Dumpster. Set in the tiny alley between his building and the street-front strip of stores backing the private parking lot he'd parked his motor home on, he'd agreed to let the stores use it for their daily trash on the condition they kept it as clean as they could. Still, people had to eat, and they tossed their leftovers into the Dumpster without thinking to close the lid to keep scavengers out. Frank really hoped it was a possum like last time instead of some old man looking for something to eat.

He needed to go grocery shopping, and short of giving a homeless guy a half-eaten jar of peanut butter and a spoon, he had nothing in the RV for a handout. Sure, he could have sacrificed the pizza, but there was going to be a nice tight bowl of Tai before he crashed for the night, and his stomach might catch a second wind by then. Leftover pizza came in handy for second winds.

His sneakers squeaked on the rain-damp blacktop, and as Frank got closer, it became apparent his vermin didn't walk on four legs and certainly wasn't an old man. Not by a long shot. Instead, the Dumpster appeared to be hosting a different kind of scavenger—one in the form of a rather scrawny preteen boy.

And like the possum he'd scared the shit out of the last time, the boy froze to a dead stillness when he heard Frank approach, the faint lights from the street beyond catching his eyes and turning them a demonic gold when he cocked his head to spy on Frank over the lip of the battered green bin. If anything, the boy's hiss certainly was more possum-ish and less grumbling homeless guy looking for aluminum cans to cash in.

Frank cleared his throat and called out to the boy, "Hey—"

That single word spurred the boy into action, and he grabbed at the Dumpster's edge to hoist himself up. Either he was too short or the rhino covering the interior of the bin was too slick because the boy couldn't get traction, and he slid back down the side, landing in the—hopefully—mostly paper trash around him.

"Fuck!"

As swear words went, it was an elegant growl—fluid and heartfelt with a tinge of bitterness to flavor its edges.

It also sounded way too world-weary to come from such a young boy.

Because as Frank drew even closer to the Dumpster, he caught sight of the golden hummingbird of a boy trapped inside the steel bin and instantly took back a few of the years he'd given him.

But then he poured all those years—and more—back into his assessment of the boy's dark, liquid eyes.

As kids went, this one was scrawny—dirty-chicken scrawny with a side of bone—barely enough meat on his frame to do more than move his lanky limbs. A mop of tangled, dirty-blond hair covered most of the boy's face, but what Frank could see straddled the line between delicate and masculine. Sitting on the verge of puberty, the kid should have been fuller in the face, even a bit chunky around the middle as his body stored up fuel for that impressive height jump from child to man.

When that jump came for this kid, his body wasn't going to have anything to feed his growth. There was barely enough energy stored in his flesh to leave his skin supple, and Frank winced at the crackle of dry skin on the boy's downy cheeks, a telltale sign the kid wasn't eating.

As if the jut of his breastbone and rib cage through the thin fabric of his filthy T-shirt wasn't enough of a clue.

There was a lot of dead in the kid's gaze. Dead and suspicion, with more than a few ladles of fear. All that was wrapped up tight with ribbons of challenging aggression. Frank would have been more cautious if it weren't for the bruises blackening the right side of the kid's face or his swollen lip turned deep purple where something had cut it.

Even in the wane of the streetlamp light, anyone with sense in his mind and eyes in his head could see the boy'd taken more than a few knocks from life on his chin. And from the chunk of enamel missing in one of his front teeth, he'd taken more than one blow to the mouth too.

"Do you need some help there, kid?" Frank called out loud enough for the boy to hear him over the rustle of paper and debris. The kid ignored him and continued to flounder, grabbing at the lip for another attempt.

Another struggle to get out of the bin and the boy hit bottom again, a flailing bundle of arms, legs, and curses strong enough to fuel Moses's drive out of Egypt.

"Here, give me your hand," Frank said, reaching into the bin. "You're too short. You're never going to get out of there without some help."

"Fuck off, old man. I'm fine." The kid growled and shoved as much of his ratted-together hair out of his face as he could manage.

"Okay, so you're fine." Leaning over the edge of the Dumpster opening, Frank looked down into the bin. Despite being a day after pickup, the Dumpster was fairly clean. "Tell you what. I'm going to toss in this wooden box for you to sit on while you think about how to get the fuck out of there and walk away. If you want to shut the lid when you're out, that would be appreciated. I don't like thinking someone's cat might get into one of these things and get turned into a smashed meat pancake because it was open."

He grabbed one of the discarded shelving boxes the clothing store left stacked up near the Dumpster and tossed it in. The kid jumped back, lifting his feet out of the trash. Glaring up at Frank, he pinned himself against the far wall, coiled up tight, as if waiting for an attack that only Frank knew would never come.

"Now, I'm going to head off to bed. There's some leftover pizza I'm going to leave out on the table. Grab something to eat and go home, kid." Large drops of water began to strike the Dumpster's open lid, rumbling a deep percussion through the thick black plastic.

"Yeah, like I'm going to fucking eat something you leave out—"

"It's up to you, kid." Frank shrugged, scratching at his thick graying beard. "Just see if you can close the lid. If not, I'll do it in the morning."

He walked away. He had to. The boy's eyes were burning into him, stealing past the lazy haze of his apathy toward children and his resolute stance on people getting a few handouts, but lifelines were something a person had to braid themselves. Walking away from the kid should have been easy. Even if he couldn't shake off the wince of pain when the boy pressed his back into the Dumpster or the whimper when he'd landed on his back amid the piles of discarded plastic bags and tissues.

Frank put one foot in front of the other and entered the RV, closing the door behind him with a firm *snick*. After digging out the chartreuse and orange bong he'd gotten from a friend's little girl, he sat down to pack in a bowl before he allowed himself to sleep.

Not that he thought he'd be *able* to sleep with the image of the boy's haunting face floating behind his eyes.

He was drawing out his first gurgle of smoke when he heard the Dumpster cover slam shut, the lid hitting the bin's rim with a singsong chime. He'd regret leaving the pizza, especially since he really didn't think the kid would chance eating it. There'd been talk around the neighborhood of more than one street kid getting roofied and fucked after being given food by strangers.

Bad enough people poisoned cats and dogs. Did they have to go after the kids too? Frank thought as he finished up his hit. The rain struck, drowning out even the pull of his inhale through the bong's skunky water, and Frank sighed, wondering if he was going to be hit with a raging case of the munchies just because all he had was peanut butter and possibly—now—soggy pepperoni pizza.

When Frank woke up in the early afternoon, the rain was still intent on sliding the city into the bay, and he smacked his lips, tasting a serious need for a toothbrush and possibly a cigarette. Just not in that order. Grabbing his smokes from the RV's slender kitchen counter, he headed outside to shiver under the awning. Having forgotten about the boy, he stared at the empty box of pizza sitting on the café table outside his door.

Two quarters on the lid were the only evidence left of the kid's existence—that and a note scrawled on the inside the box. The pen the kid used seemed like it was on its last legs or perhaps had higher aspirations on being a tattoo machine for all the ink it leaked. Still, the uneven scrawl was easy enough to read, even if it was a bit misspelled.

"Money's all I got, but next time I'm around, I'll give you a blow job, 'cause I took the rest of it and it was a lot. Thanks—Forest."

"Well, shit and Jesus Christ, kid." Frank frowned as he read the note. "What the fuck has the world done to you?"

IT BECAME a game of cat and mouse—although Frank wasn't sure if he was supposed to be the cat *or* the mouse, but it definitely was a game of some kind because not long after the Great Pizza Incident, he found himself lurking in the parking lot hoping the Dumpster kid would show his face again.

Frank left food out and got notes in return—sometimes accompanied by small trinkets, like a beaded bracelet or a Golden Gate keychain. He wore the bracelet, and the tiny metal icon now hung from the RV's rearview mirror. After a month and a half of chasing the blond kid's trail, Frank came out of the Amp's back door with a bag of In-N-Out he'd meant to leave for the boy when he found himself staring at a very filthy Forest sitting at the same café table they'd exchanged food and notes on.

If anything, the kid looked even worse than the first time Frank'd seen him, and the overly hungry look on Forest's face made his stomach clench in sympathy. There were frozen burritos he could microwave. The Double-Doubles in the bag were going to the kid, even if Frank had to shove them down Forest's throat.

"Here," Frank said, tossing the bag to the boy. "Have some dinner."

"I don't take handouts," Forest growled as he dug into the bag and pulled out one of the thick cheeseburgers. "I told you I'd do you for the food."

"I'm not into little boys." Frank groaned when he eased into one of the chairs.

"But you keep giving me food," the kid pointed out through a mouthful of meat and fries. "You gotta want *something*."

"Maybe I just don't want you out on the street."

"Yeah right, because everyone's just lining up to take other people's kids. Whatcha want? Blow or hand?" Forest yanked at the air with his fist. "I'm better with my hand. I can't throat it right, but I'm working on it."

The kid's words hit Frank hard, and he blinked, unsure about what to do with the lump in his throat. "Tell you what, kid. How'd you like a job? I need some help in the studio."

CHAPTER ONE

Drowning in tears,
Soaked too long in my salt.
This is what I am.
This is what I should be.
Something that never ends.
But I want to be more than me.
—Blue Notebook 3/8

"MORGAN! TEAM One ready?"

Captain Leonard's query rattled through Connor's earpiece. The rough gravel in the man's voice came from a cigar habit he'd had instead of any defect in the equipment. Leonard's aggression boiled out through his voice, shotgunning his orders to the TAC team through a mic. A cancerous spot on his lung took him off the street, but he'd recovered more than enough to kick their asses. Leonard was also the first one to pull a rookie up and walk him gently through training.

Connor'd been that rookie once, and while parts of his ass were still smarting from some of his fuck-ups, he had to admit Leonard knew what he was doing—especially when they were going in blind to a dilapidated RV doubling as a meth room.

"Team One ready," he replied into his headset, tapping Roberts on the shoulder.

The early-morning hours brought in the fog, its misty air drawn toward the cooling city's hills. With the damp came a steep of smells unique to Chinatown. Somewhere close by, a small back-alley factory made *li hing mui*, and the wind carried the preserved plum's scent of anise and sugar through the area's tight weave of buildings. The light crackle of nightlife continued off behind them, hidden by the brick buildings surrounding the nearly empty parking lot they were about to descend upon.

Its sole occupant, a swaybacked RV from the seventies, sat at the back of the lot, its tires flat and wispy grass growing up through the cracks in the asphalt around it. A couple of swap-meet tents provided a kind of lanai area, and someone'd set up a few mismatched plastic chairs around an upended wire spool, its flat surface marred with cigarette burns and candle wax. The RV's original door'd been torn out at some point, with a larger one framed in. Instead of the standard flimsy aluminum ladderlike steps leading up, a sturdy set of wooden stairs led up to the RV's front door.

The wind picked up again, and Connor held his team in the shadows, waiting for Leonard to give him clearance so they could crack open the RV and find who they'd come for.

"On your call, then," Leonard growled. "Bring 'em all back out, Morgan."

"Like they're my babies, sir." Connor grinned even though Leonard couldn't see him. "Moffatt, Evers, you're on point. Davis, Clark, cover six. Roberts, time to break it down."

They went in slowly, circling the RV until they got to the front. Keeping to a tight pattern, Con motioned Roberts to slam through the RV's door. He'd had the barest of thirty minutes to pull the raid together, pulling up the manufacturer's schematics for the ancient motor home from someone's Facebook page. It wasn't a lot to go on, but it was the best they could do—especially since the informant told them the meth was moving out that night.

If the CI was to be believed, it would drop enough ice into SF's streets to kill off a brontosaurus, and they had to move *fast*.

Leonard opted for a launch raid, hoping to catch the RV's owner, Franklin Marshall, unaware. Based on the lack of lights coming from the RV's dirt-clouded windows, either Marshall was asleep at three in the morning, or he'd covered the windows with tinfoil to block anyone from looking in.

Either was a possibility, as was the man having an arsenal inside despite his lean arrest record. Con's team planned for the worst-case scenario and hoped for the best. It was far better than trusting humanity's kindness and burying one of their own.

They worked silently—a small team of six black-clad officers stealing through a dimly lit parking lot. Hours of training and practice helped with their synchronicity, but nothing beat working a raid. Connor stepped in time with Roberts, keeping his weapon aimed up over the man's head as the smaller man swung a black battering ram into the RV's door.

It burst in, a scatter of old plastic, wood chips, and metal. The team poured in, and Con's heart began to skip its curious, familiar beat, a pounding of excitement in his chest. There was nothing to compare to the feeling of that first whiff of danger or the sound of boots on the floor when they came in. The press of his team around him, then the explosion of their bodies separating to break down a house's interior, working back to back to secure the area.

The motor home was no different. The shatter hit and they were through, deep murmurs of voices and then the hush of their breathing amid the periodic orders Con barked out to his team. He'd handpicked each one, culling through the applicants until he was satisfied he'd go into a dangerous situation with his ass and back covered.

Adrenaline hit his bloodstream hard and fast, amping up his senses as he ducked away from the splinters coming at him from the remains of the door. While the RV was a long straight space, there were nooks and crannies within its enormous rectangular shape. A bathroom took up a bit of the side, and a quick glance at the back showed a thick curtain of beads—both areas potentially dangerous for their raid, especially since the space was tight and there wouldn't be a lot of room to maneuver.

Con broke off Evers and Moffatt to the back, keeping Roberts with him for the front. At some point in the RV's lifetime, probably soon after its weary carcass was dumped in the parking lot, someone'd converted the driving cab to another lounging or sleeping place, but a partially drawn tie-dyed curtain blocked off a clear view of the area.

The rest of the RV was empty, and if there was a shit-ton of meth in the vehicle, they'd probably find it hidden under platforms or in walls. It was going to be a long and tedious hunt, and Con wanted to secure the RV before they dragged it off to the yard to be broken down—because nothing said surprise like finding a drug dealer hiding in the bathroom of an impounded motor home.

"Clark, Davis—bathroom's yours." Connor waved them off. "Mind your Qs."

He kept his own quadrant clear, pressing back to back with Roberts as they moved to the front of the RV. Their boots clunked on the faux-wood floor. It was strangely spongy beneath Con's feet, and he pondered if the drugs were in caches beneath the floor, because as they inched forward, the RV rocked and swayed under them.

That supposition would have to wait until they got the RV dragged away. For right now, his sole focus was on finding the man who'd parked the RV so many years ago, then decided it would be a good place to stash poison—a poison Connor Morgan had no intention of ever letting onto his city's streets. They'd hit the building next. The RV was too small to cook meth in, but Marshall owned the brick building beyond the parking lot.

Lots of space there to cook up a chemical stew strong enough to rip a man's brain apart.

Something was off about the raid. The niggle of off nipped at Connor's mind, and he scanned the interior, looking for something—anything—to tell him what he was bothered by. The RV wasn't clean by any stretch, not a sparkling eat-off-the-floor kind of environment, but neither was it packed to the gills with papers or rotting garbage. If anything, it looked like an aging hippie's sanctuary, complete with a cardboard poster of a topless Janis Joplin at an old Haight-Ashbury event. Several lit candles lined the kitchenette's counters, flickering erratically from the wind coming through the now extinct front door.

There was an odd scent Connor couldn't quite place lingering in the air, and for a second he passed it off as some type of incense, but it *bothered* him. There was a heavy raspberry or floral odor, but something wafted underneath that—a curious odd tickle of a scent Con *knew*. Only when he spotted a man's bare foot peeking out from under a corner of the rainbow-swirled curtain did he realize it wasn't patchouli scenting the air.

Con saw the man's foot poking out from behind the curtain just as his brain clicked on what he was smelling, and someone's footsteps jostled the RV enough to send the candles toppling over, igniting the propane in the built-up space.

"Evac!" Con yelled into his headset. "Get out!"

He didn't have time to give his team visual cues to hit the open door. A fireball erupted from the kitchen's gas stove top, and the cop part of his brain kicked in the RV's details. From their initial recon, the team was sitting on at least two long propane tanks, and if either one was full, the RV would blow sky-high once the flames ate through the lines and exposed the whole fucking mess to the open air.

Connor grabbed at the man's foot and yanked, pulling him clear of the bed and into the open.

Unresponsive, the man was a dead weight in his arms, but Connor couldn't risk checking the man over. The fire spread, the gases thankfully thinned from the team's break-in, but the tanks were still a worry. Hefting the barefooted man up over his shoulder, Connor

was the last to peel through the door—then the concussion blast of the RV's demise hit his back, and he
went flying.

Connor and his rescue hit the pavement hard, and
Con rolled, wrapping his arms around the unconscious
man's limp body. Debris flew over them, and Connor's
head echoed from the rocking pings of things hitting
his helmet. The heat of the blast covered them, scorching the air around them, and Connor felt gravel bite into
his cheek as they tumbled. His limbs would ache from
the uncontrollable cartwheels of their blast-propelled
bodies, and he vaguely heard himself grunt when they
bounced on the pavement, only to bounce down hard
again.

His elbow went tingly when they struck and rolled
to a stop. He lay there, smelling the acrid scent of his
gear cooking on his body and sucking in as much non-
fire-filled air as he could. Training for a fire kicked his
brain into automatic pilot, and he'd expelled as much
of his breath as he could when he'd jumped out of the
RV. Without oxygen or propane in his lungs, it was as
large of a fuck-you to the fire's touch as he could give
it at the time.

It did, however, leave his chest screaming for air,
and his ribs shuddered painfully when he drew his first
full breath. Stars clouded his vision, and Connor forced
himself to roll off the man's body, feebly calling for
a med team to find him in the parking lot. His head
still sang its song of sixpence from where he struck
the parking lot, but other than his aching muscles and
possibly singed eyebrows, Con was relatively sure he'd
emerged unscathed.

It was just going to take him a moment before he
could stand up long enough to take a full inventory.

"You okay there, Morgan?" Davis crouched over him, her hands busy at the fastenings of his vest. She sounded far away—almost as if underwater—and Connor frowned, wondering if he'd somehow gotten his headset shoved down into his ear or if his hearing was blown out by the blast. "Can you hear me, Lieutenant? How many fingers am I holding up?"

"Yeah, just… not a lot of hearing yet." Connor slapped Davis's hand away from his face. "And you pick *now* to flip me off?"

"Seemed like as good a time as any, sir." She grinned at him from under her helmet. "Need some help up?"

"No, I've got it." He rolled over, wincing at the pricks of pain along his back, but for the most part, all his parts seemed functional. There was blood on his hands and a trickle of it winding down his face from where he'd scraped it. "Get to Marshall. See how he's doing."

"Yeah, about that, sir." Evers popped his head over Davis's shoulder. "You need to take a look at this."

The medic crouching next to Connor's rescue wasn't working on Marshall—and it was definitely Marshall lying there in the pool of melon-hued light cast from one of Chinatown's streetlamps. Connor recognized the man from his driver's license photo even with the gray streaking his heavy, long beard. He'd been younger in the photo.

And considerably much more alive.

His arms were slack, lacking even the tension of muscles drawn against the pain of overextension. Flung out like an insect smashed against a wall with a fly swatter, Marshall's body lay still and quiet, his slight potbelly hanging flaccid above worn gray sweatpants, and his chest, thick with a salt-and-pepper pelt, sported numerous holes. Deep holes Connor suspected punched right through the man's chest and out his back, giving him the appearance of being riddled with numerous grotesque nipples.

The EMT brushed off his hands and began walking to his rig, not even stopping as he patted Connor on the shoulder and said, "Congrats, Lieutenant. You've rescued a dead man."

FOREST HEARD the *wrong* in the air. He liked leaving the windows open a bit, even after Frank chastised him about burglars and lung damp from whatever came in off the bay's waters. The sounds felt wrong— abnormal for the area. The neighborhood had a certain rhythm in it, one Forest knew as much as he did the sound of his own breathing.

Mostly asleep, he labored in the depth of his slumber, his mind sorting through the sounds around him. Voices were deeper, not like the chatter of clubgoers cutting through the parking lot to get to the BART, and certainly not the Asian food workers starting their day in the curve of an early morning to prep for a long, busy day feeding tourists and locals alike. These voices were serious, hammering at his quiet. Then a boom shook the air.

And Forest smelled the taint of fire licking at the edges of his world.

It smelled close—too close for his liking—and he fought the long threads of sleep wrapping over him. The coffee shop was a possibility, but none of the alarms had gone off, and the studio's wiring was new, revamped in the last renovation bug Frank had up his ass.

Then the screaming panic of sirens shot through his open window, and Forest finally opened his eyes to see hell had come to visit.

He stumbled over his drum kit, barking his toes on the set of Rotodrums he'd been tuning earlier. Trying to pull on a pair of jeans as he made it to the back wall of his studio apartment, Forest banged his elbow on a counter and nearly slammed into one of the barstools he used to sit at the kitchen counter and eat. Frustrated and smarting, he yanked away the curtain from the slender back wall window and stared down into the parking lot where Frank Marshall first found him.

Frank's RV was on fire, and from what he could see, the cops standing around it were doing jack shit to help the man inside. It definitely was a slice of hell served up on a knife, because his heart imploded under a thrust of pain cutting through it.

"No no no." Fear did silly things to a person, Forest knew that. He'd thought fear was something he'd left behind in that Dumpster years ago, but it lingered there, waiting to reach out with its cold, slithery fingers to yank at his teeth until their roots ran cold in his gums.

He couldn't lose Frank. He never even imagined that being a possibility in his life. In Forest's mind, the scruffy old hippie would always lurk nearby, marinated in pot and glory days when San Francisco was about love, not pixels, and always with a word or two about how he played Perdie's Filmore rendition of "Memphis Soul Stew."

"Fucking cops. Goddamn it!" Forest couldn't see the second-story landing when he pulled open his front door. His eyes burned from a mingle of smoke and tears, but he went down the back stairs without even thinking about putting on shoes. He didn't even feel the small pebbles under his bare feet or how cold the night turned since he'd fallen asleep after drumming a session for a has-been rock band.

Because the world was trying to yank away the only family he'd ever found to love him, and suddenly the past decade slipped away, and Forest was once more that scared, skinny twelve-year-old kid Frank found trying to get out of a Dumpster.

Forest hit a wall before he could reach the engulfed motor home. Some part of him realized the wall was a man. His cock certainly knew it was, and his mind registered an enormous amount of muscle, large encompassing hands, and flashing bright blue eyes. Dressed in body-hugging black and wearing a thick vest with SWAT written across his chest, the wall smelled of embers and cop.

Even as his heart lay in the ashes fluttering about on the parking lot under his torn-up bare feet.

"You've got to let me go!" he yelled at the cop. The man held him, immovable and steady. Forest tried shoving at the man's chest, but all he got for his trouble was a jarring rattle in his teeth and spine. He stared into the man's hard, handsome face and pleaded. "Dude, please. That's my dad in there. My *dad's* in there. Please. If it were your dad—"

"I'd want in there so verra bad," the cop replied softly, and some small part of Forest's brain registered other things about him—the small block letters on his chest spelling out his name as Morgan, the Irish strung through his rumbling, deep voice, and how good the man's hands felt rubbing at Forest's shoulders and back to soothe him. "But he's already gone. I pulled him out before the whole thing went up. He's gone."

Forest went frigid—as if he'd turned into the cold, hard ground Franklin Marshall would eventually be buried in. The roar of the fire masked the sound of a gurney being wheeled toward a waiting ambulance, its lights and sirens dark and muted. No one lit up the skies for a dead man, the streets wouldn't shriek with the hope of getting Franklin to the hospital in time, and Forest crumbled, his legs unable to hold up the heavy weight of his breaking soul.

The cop caught him. The Irish rock who'd kept Forest back from the flames wrapped his bulky arms around Forest's body and held him, murmuring softly through the smoke smothering them so only Forest could hear. "I've got you now. I've got both of you now. We'll find out who did this to your da. I promise you that. I promise."

CHAPTER TWO

You know I love you, yeah, Mick?
Yeah, why?
Because your damned dog is stealing all
* of my socks.*
Nah, that's me. My feet get cold sometimes.
Don't you have your own socks?
Yeah, but it makes me feel like you're rub-
* bing my feet.*
Then I probably don't want to know what's
* happened to my underwear.*
—Doing Laundry with Kane

CONNOR DIDN'T know why he was here. It wasn't for coffee. God knew there were enough java places in San Francisco to pretty much support Columbia's bean trade—if Columbia was still *in* the coffee business. From the looks of things on the street and the raids he'd been in on, it seemed Juan Valdez and his

donkey had moved on from picking beans to process-
ing coca leaves.

But there he sat with the engine off in his Hummer
and staring at Marshall's Amp coffee shop.

The long rectangular two-story building held the
coffee shop and the studio next door, two apparently
legacy places according to some of the other cops in
his division. Marshall's Amp was relatively new—for
San Francisco, anyway—with only a little more than a
decade under its belt, but the Sound—apparently *that*
place had seen some legends come through its doors.

Tucked into the wide end of Chinatown, the
two-story brick building seemed a bit out of place
amid the surrounding shops. The street ran to fami-
ly-run jewelry stores with constant sales and smaller
discreet holes-in-the-wall catering to generations of
local Asians. A few restaurants—mostly noodle hous-
es—served up traditional foods, their kitchens spicing
the fog-damp air with a blend of savory aromas.

The neighborhood was a great place to people
watch—even at seven in the morning.

He'd even brought a travel mug of Major Dicka-
son's he'd brewed at home with him. To a coffee shop.

A florist shop opened up early, setting out long tubs
of fragrant blooms, splashing color against the dreary
gray rainy morning. Connor could smell the sweet powder of carnations above the more delicate fragrances, a
soft undertone of roses catching on the wind. An awning protected the flowers from the inclement weather,
and from under the shadows, the store owner, an old
charm bracelet of a Cantonese woman, bobbed about
as she arranged her displays, her tiny face bright with a
smile for anyone passing by.

Gentrification moved in on the fringes of the area, blending a bit of urban with traditional Chinese and the remains of San Francisco's hippie days. A pair of young blonde women jogged past Connor in matching vivid green yoga pants, their sports tanks wicked with sweat. Both were pushing running strollers, and they expertly maneuvered through the sparse morning sidewalk traffic, keeping in pace with one another while carrying on a lively conversation.

He should have been locked onto their asses, following the flow of a gently rounded curve jiggling in time with each stride. They both seemed to have miles of lightly tanned skin, definitely a product of a salon, considering San Francisco's meager sunlight allotment over the past six months. Connor should have had a smile ready when the blonde closest to him smiled flirtatiously as she went by.

Instead, he felt *nothing*. Nothing at all. Not even a telltale crinkle of desire along his cock or a tightness at the back of his throat when lust rose up from his belly. No, Connor just watched them go by, his attention drifting back to the staircase going up the side of the studio's outer wall to a doorway on the second floor.

There was no question about it; he'd lost his mind.

It also was a pity he couldn't stop staring at the parking lot where an old man'd lost his life, and Connor'd found himself holding the man's son, unable to let go of the blond even after his sobs turned to shuddering hiccups. Something happened to him that night. He still wasn't sure what it was, but every second of that dark, stormy night replayed in his mind whenever was most inconvenient.

Like in the middle of the night when he was lying naked in bed and listening to the rain hit his newly shingled roof.

If only he could get the idea of holding Forest Ackerman out of his head—because there was *no damned good reason* that man should be in his head.

"What the fecking hell am I doing here?" Connor muttered and reached for the keys still dangling in the Hummer's ignition.

He'd run Forest Ackerman's record—as illegal as *that* was—but what he'd found didn't surprise him. A sealed juvenile record he'd left alone, and other than a few disorderlies for participating at slam-fests in the parking lot behind the Sound, Forest appeared to live a clean and stable life. Franklin Marshall, on the other hand, had a long list of petty priors—mostly centered around protests and pot, with a curious addition of assault on a man who'd been arrested for trying to pull an unidentified juvenile male into his car.

It didn't strain Connor's brain to figure out who the kid in the guy's car had been.

"Okay, enough time wasted, Morgan." His fingers brushed the cold metal keys again, and then Connor froze, catching sight of a long-legged blond man coming down the set of stairs from the building's second floor.

He'd *wanted* to drive away. It was his damned day off, for God's sake. There were things that needed doing on the old house he'd bought—important things like laying down a floor *everywhere* or even painting, because the painting never ended. He was living in two rooms at the moment, the kitchen and a side bedroom, both of which were in midrenovation themselves, but Connor couldn't force himself to start the Hummer's engine.

Not with the flash of gold hair, pretty face, and lean body coming down the stairs.

Nothing made sense anymore. His world—his organized and orderly world—lay in bits and chunks around him, and Connor was left with the feeling he spent more time trying to gather up its scattered remains than trying to make sense of the life he'd been living. He'd been building a puzzle using all the wrong pieces, because it was coming out so very different from the picture on its box.

Somehow, Forest Ackerman was a part of that puzzle, and for the life of him, Connor couldn't figure out how or why.

Whatever was going on, it obviously dulled his senses, because Connor didn't hear the black-and-white pull up next to him and nearly had a heart attack when the patrol cop inside it honked his horn to get Connor's attention.

"You okay there, Lieutenant?" The man had to crane his neck a bit to see up into the Hummer. "Spotted you on the drive-by, so I wanted to make sure, you know? Waiting for someone?"

"Yeah, I'm good," Connor responded with a tight smile, then held up his cell phone. "Pulled over to the side to talk to my da. Done now. Thanks."

"Yeah, wish more people would pull over before getting on those things. See you later, sir." The uniform smiled, waved, then drove off, leaving Connor holding his phone up like an idiot.

Sighing, he banged his forehead on the steering wheel, muttering darkly, "This is what it's come to? Lying about talking to my father? Jesus H. Christ.

"Just turn the key, Con," he urged himself. "Go home. Finish demoing the wall in the kitchen. Fucking do some laundry, if you have to. Just turn the bloody key."

The Amp's windows were shrouded from steam, condensation forming from the interior's warmer air hitting the cold glass. While Connor spoke to the uniform, Forest'd disappeared, probably into the coffee shop to get something to drink before he started doing whatever the hell it was he did in the Sound besides drumming for stray bands.

"Aw, fuck it," Connor muttered as he dumped his coffee out onto the street and tossed the travel mug into the back seat. "I'd rather have a latte anyway."

"YOUR COP is back."

Forest looked up toward the counter, nearly scalding himself on the espresso machine. Jules, the Amp's coffee shop manager, smirked at him and winked, her curly brown hair bobbing about her face as she jerked her chin at the buff, tall man taking up most of the air in the shop's dining area.

It was bad enough he was gay in an industry where gay wasn't a bad thing, but dating other musicians was like playing Russian roulette with a fully loaded gun. The last thing Forest wanted to complicate his life was lusting after a thoroughly straight chunk of muscle with a badge. He didn't need a massive cop whose thick black hair seemed to grow wildly out of control before he hacked it back with a ruthlessly short cut—an orderly cut lasting only three days. Sure, he was grateful for Morgan's support following Frank's murder, but Forest wanted nothing else to do with Lt. Connor Morgan. Or everything to do with him. Either way, it would lead to nothing but madness, and Forest had enough insanity in his life as it was.

He'd just recently been able to go a full day without crying about Frank's murder, and only now began to fully hate all the paperwork, lawyers, and stupidity that followed close on the heels of discovering his adopted father left him a bunch of money, a few properties, and a shit fuckton of headaches. Connor Morgan did *not* need to be added to his pile of shit to worry about.

"He's not my cop," Forest replied, keeping his voice as steady as he could, but he couldn't help watching Lt. Connor Morgan eat up the space around him.

And Forest *hated* what the man did to him—because he found himself looking for Morgan every morning when he came down for coffee, and the little chirrup of glee in his chest was getting a bit too loud to ignore every time he spotted the lieutenant coming through the Amp's front door.

Connor Morgan showed up at the most inconvenient times, usually when Forest just stumbled downstairs after an all-night session running beats over his kit for other musicians. Since Frank's death, he'd thrown himself into his work, keeping the studio's time booked tight and working the drums when needed.

In the three months since Frank's murder, Lieutenant Morgan of the SFPD's SWAT division appeared to have gotten very fond of the Amp's lattes. He also really liked Jules's double-chocolate cake donuts, because he always bought four at a time with his coffee and ate two of them as he waited for his drink to be made. The way he ate sugar should have been a crime—and also made him fat—but no, Connor Morgan merely stood at the end of the pickup counter and mouth-fucked pastries as Forest tried to ignore the Irish cop's broad shoulders, flat stomach, and tight ass.

Not that Forest watched the man lick chocolate ganache from his fingers and from the corners of his lips.

But he had. And the disappearing chocolate frosting entranced him because it took him a few seconds for an alarming beep to penetrate his brain before he realized he'd scalded his soy milk beyond recognition.

"Fuck." Juggling the milk pitcher, Forest found someplace amid the staff mugs to put it down and searched for a cold rag to wrap around his steamed fingers. "Ow. Ow. Shit."

He couldn't find a towel, and what made things worse, the shop was full of customers—paying customers—so he couldn't really yell across the floor for Jules to come help him.

"I so don't need this." Forest threw his gaze up to the ceiling and wished God would quit fucking with him. "Really, Dude?"

"Here, give me your hand. Let me see to you." As if the Irish roll of the man's voice wasn't enough to send shivers through Forest's nipples, the damned erotic masculine smell of Connor Morgan did him in with one whiff. Whoever thought green tea in a cologne was a good idea should be flayed and left out for the seagulls to eat their eyeballs.

And Forest would do the flaying too—as soon as he licked every inch of the man's muscular body.

"You're not supposed to be back here," Forest muttered, trying to sound more like the owner of two thriving business and less like a tongue-tied loser. "Customers—"

"Most customers don't have EMT training." The rolling burr hit again, raking its delicious claws up Forest's back. "Now let me take a look at that."

He'd look stupid fighting the man off, especially since Morgan *was* a cop and probably used to carrying babies out of burning buildings. Forest immediately regretted thinking about a burning anything as his mind seized up on the memory of smoke and melted plastic. Frank should have been there to scold him about scalding his fingers, because he'd have to keep time with a speed metal band in the afternoon, and drumming was hard enough at that rate without adding first-degree burns to the mix.

Connor either didn't see the tears in Forest's eyes or did the manly thing and ignored them, concentrating mostly on scooping some ice into a plastic bag. After wrapping the bag up in a bar towel, Connor balanced the makeshift pack on the back of Forest's hand, keeping it steady with the press of his palm.

"I could have done that," Forest snarked. "Where'd you get your EMT certificate? With a piece of bubble gum?"

"If I had the gum, I'd give it to you so you had something to keep that smart mouth of yours busy." Connor chuckled.

"I'd need more than gum to do that."

Forest winced, hearing the innuendo in his words, especially when Connor's deep blue eyes narrowed and his sharp focus shifted from Forest's hands to his face. It was a glare sharpened on life's whetstone, giving Forest an idea of what the man might look like as he came through a door behind a black battering ram.

Or even on his knees between Forest's legs and working up a sweat tearing apart his ass with a thick, long Irish cock.

"Are you warm?" One of Connor's ice-chilled hands drifted up to test Forest's forehead. "You're turning red. Do you have a fever? Getting chills, maybe?"

"Maybe it's the ice," Forest lied. "I'm okay. Really. Jules will have your ass for being back here."

"Really? Because she's the one who told me to come check on you when we saw you foaming up your hand with milk." Connor's fingers were warm on Forest's wrist, and Forest wondered if the man knew he was stroking at Forest's pulse point. "Can I trust you to hold the ice pack there while I go see if there's burn ointment in that first-aid kit on the wall?"

The man was way too close. He filled every inch of Forest's awareness, stretching out to touch even the darkest corners of his soul. Connor was too much—too vibrant—too fucking male for Forest to wrap his mind around. The only thing he wanted to do was fall into the sweet promise of Connor's brogue and forget everything pressing in on him. He needed the cop to be away from him—anywhere away—away from lingering over his skin or so near Forest could feel Connor's breath on his face. It was just too much and made Forest feel guilty for forgetting about Frank's death—even if it was only for a moment.

"Look, I'm fine. I'll do it," Forest insisted, edging away from Connor and responding with the only thing he knew he could use to drive someone off, his sharp tongue. "You want to help me out? Go find out who put a fucking bullet into Frank's head."

The cop jerked his head back, and from the shocked expression on his face, Forest could have punched him straight in the mouth and gotten the same reaction. He wanted to apologize. The words were at the edge of his tongue, but something insane seemed to be nesting in his brain, and instead of *I'm sorry for being an asshole*, something much meaner came out.

"You guys have been about as useful as tits on a fish, dude." Forest tried to yank his hand away from

Connor's grip. "Fucking hell. Let go, dude. I can do it myself."

The man held on. Even through the violence of Forest's harangue, the cop held him in, keeping his fingers wrapped tight around Forest's arm. It was a brief, unsuccessful struggle, and short of screaming for help, Forest should have felt trapped.

He hated being trapped. It reminded him of different times. Back before the apartment over the studio, before Frank lured him in and called him son. The clench of Lt. Connor Morgan's hand around his wrist should have thrown dark memories into his face—of being slammed up against walls, the pain of his empty stomach folding in on itself, or having his jaw ache from being used. That was how trapped usually felt—staked through his body with a metal pin as he fought to get free. Even when he'd known it was useless, he still fought.

This time—this man—didn't serve all that up on a silver platter to him. Instead, the damned hand around his wrist made him feel—cared for—tended to. It made Forest want more than that simple touch, and he kind of maybe hated Connor Morgan for making him feel that way. Fighting the man off should have been like breathing—something he did automatically—but with Connor, he couldn't quite make that break.

And throughout it all, Connor Morgan's deep-ocean gaze never left his face.

Sighing, Forest gave up and wilted against the counter. "Really, man. What the fuck do you want from me? You come in here every other day, and it screws with my brain. I don't know what to do with you. It's not like you say anything about… my dad, and the inspector they assigned to the case hasn't even called me back. I left a fuckton of messages, but nothing. I just want to know what the hell they're doing—"

"What's his name?" Connor asked softly, still holding on to Forest's wrist. "The inspector. What's his name?"

"Her. Um…. Devorsky? Something like that. I wrote it down from what the uniformed cop told me, but I probably spelled it wrong."

"I don't know her." The cop frowned, his dark eyebrows closing in over his strong nose. Those fingers began anew, stroking away the cold. "But I'll see what I can find. She should have called you. At least to take your statement. I'm sorry—"

"Look, I'm sorry. I was a dick," Forest rubbed at his face with his free hand. "I just don't know—"

The window behind them blew in, an explosion of glass and sound. Forest's heart pounded once, a scared, fluttering tight beat. Then he found himself on the floor, the blue-eyed cop's body stretched over him. Connor's weight pinned him down, and his fight-or-flight response kicked in. Forest squirmed, unable to see what was going on.

A rat-tat of gunfire sprayed the air, and there were screams—so many screams—too blended and horrifying for Forest to pick out individual voices. The panic burbling in his stomach flowed up his throat and hit his face before spreading out to his spine. People were dying out there, lying in their own blood, and he lay safe behind a bank of short refrigerator units with a man he'd just lusted for pressing his crotch into the curve of Forest's ass.

"Jules!" Forest twisted around under Connor. "I've got to find Jules."

"Lay there," the cop ordered as he got up into a crouch. Forest wondered numbly where the gun Connor had in his hand came from and when the lazy Irish burr had suddenly hardened into a rough-edged bark of authority. "Don't move."

The buzz of bullets seemed to have ended, but the burn of sound continued to echo in Forest's ears. For a short moment, he debated getting up, but the heat of Connor's hand on the small of his back remained, a searing reminder of the order he'd been given.

"God, scared shitless and I'm fucking hard," Forest whimpered, resting his forehead on the floor.

With his head down and close to the floorboards, Forest got a good look at the underside of the Amp's bakery case. Sniffing, he inhaled a sting of pine-scented cleaner and sent a mental thank-you to his night crew for mopping thoroughly. Then he turned his head, saw the carnage of the Amp's dining room, and threw up all over a pool of blood.

CHAPTER THREE

The Devil's waiting for me behind that door.
She's got my heart, lay waste to my soul.
Nothing I do can make her let me go.
Hard to touch a heart as black as coal.
—Devil's Waiting

THERE WAS so much blood. Forest could taste it
in the air.

But what was more frightening was the silence—a
still, weighty silence where he could hear every little
shiver of the dying.

Outside the Amp, the world somehow stopped
turning. No wind-blown leaves, and the flicker of the
sun through the trees produced nothing but cold shadows. Forest heard *everything* in that sickly quiet. A few
feet from him, a man struggled to breathe, his lungs
gurgling and bubbling as he sucked in air through newly pierced holes. There was no telling where all the

blood came from—or who it came from. All Forest knew was it made its own special noise, a squicking wet pop when he pulled his hands up from the floor.

"Forest." Connor's voice shattered the quiet, and the world took a breath. The noise—all the ugly, glorious noise—flooded back into it and it began to turn, once more ignoring the death splattered all over its face. "Are you okay?"

"Yeah," he gulped, and a new fear stroked his spine. "God, how—Oh God, Jules."

Because he didn't know where to start or who to reach for first. The man's chest stilled, and he crawled quickly over, ignoring the new squicks his hands made or the slide of his knee through a puddle of vomit and blood. He didn't know who to help, the man whose chest lay splayed open like an eighth-grade frog experiment or the gray-haired woman lying slumped against the bakery case, her temple turned crimson with blood.

"Check that guy there. Check his breathing." Connor's bark broke the ice of Forest's fear. "See if you can press your hands over his wounds. Stop the bleeding."

"He's not breathing." Forest didn't know where to put his hands or whether or not the sluggish flow of blood cooling along the man's side was something he should be worried about. "I don't think he's—"

"Switch with me. Jules is over there. You go help her. Just keep her company." The cop was next to him in a second, an enormous mountain of calm amid the chaos. "She's going to be fine."

It was as if the coffee shop suddenly came alive, now that its predator was clear of the area. The more ambulatory began to stir, and Connor directed anyone who could walk or function. A couple of men—regulars if Forest remembered right—moved from person to person to help Connor assess the injured. Shakily getting to his feet, Forest lurched off balance, and Connor's hands came up to catch him.

"I've got you, Forest," Connor promised. "I won't let you fall."

There was that hug again—the same one—the same kind of never-ending safety he'd felt when Connor'd held him after Franklin's death. In the middle of the horror, Forest hugged back, then let go, taking some of Connor's strength with him.

"Thanks." The cold set in when he broke from Connor, but his heart settled, catching only a riff of excitement when he spotted Jules lying on the ground under a table. "Jules. Oh shit—"

"Hey, boss." Her eyes wandered to where Connor crouched. "My arm hurts like fucking shit, and I'm checking your boyfriend's ass out. It's a really fucking incredible ass. If that's the last thing I see, I'm totally good with it."

"Not my boyfriend," he replied automatically. Her arm looked bad, dangling uselessly from her shoulder. Anything he might have learned from the safety videos Frank forced them to watch each year flew out of his mind, and a cold settled into Forest's chest. His gums tightened over his teeth from the fear burbling up inside him, but Forest swallowed the sensation down, forcing himself to focus on the one person he'd come to count on just as much as he'd trusted Frank. "Don't die on me, Jules. What the fuck am I supposed to do without you? Who's going to keep me company while I'm waiting for some stupid band to get their shit together to play?"

"Pretty sure your cop counts as company," Jules snorted, then winced. "I'm not going anywhere. Might pass out, though. It really hurts, Forest. And I can't die. Who the hell is going to make that man donuts?"

He missed anything else Jules might have said under the scream of emergency vehicles pouring into Chinatown. The thick morning traffic would mean a sluggish response, even if there were somewhere for drivers to pull over in the district's tiny streets. He tried to remember if the parking lot was empty when he'd come down for his own coffee, but for the life of him, Forest couldn't recall anything other than Connor's long, hot body on his back as the cop protected him from the gunfire and the whimpering screech of constant pain coming from the injured around him.

Forest hadn't really thought about his life until he'd first seen her lying slumped against the café table. Jules—the manager of the Amp—was the only person he really could call friend, and even then, they'd never done anything together other than walk to the street fair every other Saturday to gorge on street food. They sometimes held hands, mostly because she needed help stomping over the uneven cobblestones while wearing high-heeled boots, but he'd welcomed the touch. So few people touched him—other than casual lovers he'd picked up while playing in the studio or subbing in for a live show when someone's drummer went missing. No, Forest couldn't remember the last time someone'd just touched him for the sake of it—for the pleasure of feeling their skin glide together.

Other than Connor Morgan. He still burned in the places where *that* man touched him, and he felt a pang of guilt for having naughty thoughts when he should be focusing on Jules and her pain.

"Hold on, Jules." He held her hand and squeezed— just like when they held hands and picked at the mounds of exotic fruits, looking for tarantulas or a new flavor to bring into the shop. She'd always returned the light pressure, her nose wrinkling when he reminded her he was gay and couldn't ever really be in love with her.

Except this time she didn't squeeze back.

"YOU HAVE a gun," Forest mumbled, his words nearly lost in the swaddle of Connor's leather jacket.

Shock turned the young man's lips nearly white, his brown eyes burned dark in his pale face. Connor's thick black leather hung from Forest's shoulders, making the lean, muscular man seem boyish. When he'd forced his jacket on Forest, Connor'd been taken aback by the power in the man's arms and chest. Too used to the sheer bulk of his siblings and the other members of his team, Forest's sinewy musculature proved as much of a shock as the gunfire storm hitting the Amp.

A storm fierce and brutal enough to leave four people dead in its wake.

"I'm a cop. We carry guns," Connor said. He'd tucked his weapon into the shoulder holster he normally kept hidden under the jacket he'd given Forest to wear. It felt odd to wear it openly—brazenly so—but Forest needed the warmth a hell of a lot more than his Glock. "You okay? I'm going to talk to the inspectors, and then I'll be right back."

"I'm okay. I'm just… cold inside."

Connor got a brief nod from the musician, and the barest of sighs slipped its way out of Forest's leather cocoon. The blond looked lost and more than a little hurt, even though he'd come out of the fray intact. If one could count surviving the slaughter of innocent people intact.

Connor reminded himself to keep things cool between them. Even as some part of him wanted to take hold of Forest's shoulders and stop the other man from shaking, Connor kept his arms to his sides. Touching the blond would be a mistake—he just didn't know what exactly it would do to him, and Connor wasn't so sure he wanted to find out in front of a sea of blue and badges.

There was barely anything left of the Amp's dining area and even less of its customers.

"Stay here out of the wind," Connor said, gently moving Forest toward his Hummer. "Roll the windows up and turn on the heater if you need to, okay? I left the keys so you can do that, and if you fall asleep, don't fight it. Just nap. I'll be back as soon as I can."

"I don't think I can sleep. Too much—I couldn't *do* anything for them," Forest whispered, but he let himself be handed up into the Hummer's spacious seats. "Jules—"

"She's going to be all right. Let me follow up with the guys here, and I'll take you over to the hospital," Connor promised. He was an old hand at soothing away nightmares. It was a pity that this one just happened while they'd been awake. "They're going to be working on her for a bit, so you won't be able to see her anyway. The EMT said she was good, just a puncture through the arm, but the docs will want to anchor the bone. I'll get you over there before they even get her out of surgery, okay?"

"Okay." The stillness in Forest's once-lively brown eyes punched a hole into Connor's gut, and he awkwardly patted the blond's leg. Forest's lashes fluttered, and he slid down into the seat's cradle, pulling his knees up to his chest. "I'll be fine."

He didn't want to leave Forest there. Not alone. Not shaking from a bone-deep chill born from having Death's fingers brush against him. And certainly not when his tears were frozen up inside him, unable to break past the wall of fear some asshole built up around Forest with a spray of hot bullets and cold-blooded murder.

"I'll be right back," Connor repeated, as much to reassure himself as Forest. "If you need anything, call over to me."

All he got in return was a nod, but it would have to do. Closing the door, Connor patted the window and walked over to where his sister Kiki paced off the scene outside the coffee shop.

Of the two girls in the Morgan brood, his flame-haired sister Kiki was probably the more serious of Connor's sisters. While Kiera might have been on her birth certificate, Connor couldn't remember a time when she hadn't been called Kiki, a nickname bestowed on her by a two-year-old Quinn, who'd disliked their mother's choice of names for their first sister.

It wasn't until much later they'd discovered it wasn't a mispronunciation of Kiki's name but instead Quinn's random brain pulling up a Chinese word for inner strength and energy—something he thought his ginger-topped, fussy sister possessed in spades.

The chubby toddler quickly became a lanky teenager, then a formidable woman who took up the badge along with most of her brothers and proceeded to kick her ass through the ranks. Now an inspector, Kiki stood shoulder to shoulder with her partner, Senior Inspector Henry Duarte, her hands waving about as she spoke in quiet tones, reconstructing the event in order to pinpoint where to begin their investigation.

Duarte, an older Hispanic man with a fat mustache and rolling wit, chewed on the end of a pencil as Connor approached. He nodded to the eldest Morgan sibling, his hound-dog eyes thoughtful while he took in the scene, looking from the street back toward the decimated coffee shop.

"Con," Duarte grunted in greeting. "How you doing, *mijo*?"

"Doing okay, Henry. You caught this one, then?" Connor shoved his hands into his pockets, trying to ignore the cold wind chewing its way through his bones. "You and Keeks?"

"Oh, don't call her that. You'll get her all spun up." The inspector rolled his eyes when Kiki turned on her boot heel to head over to her brother. "Ah, too late. Here comes the banshee."

"And you tell *me* not to spin her up," Connor muttered.

"Hey, big brother. Come to check up on me like Kane does with Riles?" Kiki's red mane fought desperately to escape the hair ties she used to pull it back into a double ponytail. Gentle curls softened her vulpine features, but nothing could take the edge out of her Morgan-sharp gaze.

"That would be difficult, *colleen*," he teased his sister with a slow smile. "Considering I was here before it all happened. What kind of inspector doesn't know her witnesses before she shakes them down?"

"I haven't gotten the list yet." She joined Duarte in a visual reckoning of the area. Pointing to a scatter of casings going from one end of the sidewalk to the other, she gestured with her cell phone, taking a panoramic of the scene. Frowning, she looked at him over her shoulder. "What are you doing down here? Kind of far from home, are we, big brother?"

"*We* are…." Connor searched for an explanation for being in the wide end of Chinatown in the middle of the morning. "Visiting. I know the owner of the place. Places, really."

"Forest Ackerman?" Duarte read off from his notes. "That the guy you poured into your Hummer?"

For all his apparent laziness, the senior inspector caught even the smallest of details—including, apparently, Connor's rescue of Forest from the uniforms, EMTs, and forensics people crawling over the sidewalk and coffee shop.

"Yeah, that's the guy." Connor nodded. "His dad caught a few bullets in the parking lot back there. Then someone set his RV on fire—with his body still in it. It's been a rough few months."

"Rough is a good word," Duarte agreed, nibbling on his eraser again. "Even better words? Drug deal gone wrong, and the family's drinking from the shit river because of it."

"Marshall—the father—was a casual pot user. Nothing harder than weed. A few hits for acid and rec stuff back in the White Rabbit days, but nothing recent." He rattled off from what he remembered of Marshall's rap sheet. "Ackerman's clean. I'd know if he were on drugs, Henry. I'm kind of trained for that sort of thing."

"Sometimes we don't always see what's right in front of our faces, Morgan," Duarte replied softly. "Or under our noses. Mind where you step. Fuck up my scene, and I won't care who your father is. I'll beat your ass redder than your sister's hair."

"Duly noted, sir." Connor snapped the man a quick salute, watching Duarte amble away before nudging his sister with his elbow. "He's a good partner for you."

"Yeah, like I don't know Dad had him picked out for me like some guardian angel disguised as a basset hound puppy." Kiki snorted. "Since I've got you here, Con, how about if you walk me through what happened?"

"Don't really know a lot. I was inside. Behind the counter. Forest scalded himself, and Jules—the manager—asked if I'd go help him get something on it."

"I'll get back to the manager. What did you see? Did you get a look at the shooter?" Kiki pointed out the trail of casings. "He was using something on auto—semi or full. Maybe something modified or black market."

"I was shoving Forest under the counter so he didn't get his head blown off," Con reminded her. "By the time I got up and had my weapon out, the guy was gone."

If Kiki's scowl was any indication, his answer didn't seem to satisfy her question. "Recognize the weapon? Maybe shoot something like it before?"

"I'm a SWAT cop, Kiki. Not Eliot Spencer," he drawled. "I can't just pull the make and model of a gun out of my ass just because I hear it being shot. If I had to guess, I'd say AK because it was a higher tone, and the casings are bigger than you'd find in an M16. Casings will tell you at least what you could be looking at, but you just might find it's some AR or even an AK variance. Those are harder to control too."

"And here you said you didn't know shit."

"I couldn't promise shit, brat," Con replied. "AKs are harder to control on full auto, and ARs are easier to get ammo and parts for. If he was in a car and moving, it would explain why the spray is all over the place. All of this doesn't matter to Jules or anyone else shot up by this asshole."

"Jules is the manager, right? I guess she knew you from before because she asked you to look after her boss. Or she just sniffed out that you were a cop from her finely tuned badge-dar?"

"Beforehand. Remember? I did the raid on the RV. I've been checking up on Forest to see how he's been doing. He kind of took a kick to the teeth that night."

"Were you guys friends before then?" Kiki returned to taking pictures, but Connor could tell her attention was fully on him.

It was a skill they'd both learned from their father, Donal—a misdirection of the eyes gave a witness or suspect a false comfort, a sense of safety to spill their secrets because their interrogator didn't seem to be listening. It took Connor about ten years to catch on to his father's tricks, and he'd spilled many a damaging secret before he learned to keep his mouth shut when Donal looked away to do something else.

Being a good older brother, Con'd informed the younger Morgans, but Quinn—the fucker—seemed to have caught on as soon as he was weaned but didn't see fit to let his older brothers in on the deal until way too many punishment chores were dished out.

Seeing Kiki pull a Donal made Connor smile, then frown when he realized she was trying to pull one over on him.

"What are you asking me, Kiki?" he pressed. "Can't a man have friends?"

"Seems kind of odd, Con," she replied with a shrug. "Unless you're working on something you can't tell me about. Else why would a SWAT lieutenant come back every couple of days to a place where he'd been on a raid? Just to check up on a dead man's adopted son? The guy's an adult, not a little kid. He can't need much comforting beyond an *I'm sorry about your da, man.* So spill, what's going on?"

"Nothing. Really. I come by and grab some coffee once in a while. See how he's doing." Connor pressed his lips together and exhaled hard. "His dad was murdered, Kiki. Imagine how we'd feel if that happened to Da?"

Kiki went silent, and Con knew his words struck deep. "Fair enough. Go on, then. What about the raid?"

"Shit to hell and gone the moment we got out of the truck. We entered the RV after a short investigation from a tip. Someone had a CI say Marshall was doing a heavy meth trade in his motor home. Come to find out, not only was the guy clean, but Horan down in forensics thinks he was shot about an hour before we got there."

"So a false tip led you to a dead guy?"

"That false tip led us to a dead guy in an RV full of propane. Captain doesn't know how to slot it—murder or cop-killer trap. Maybe the shooter turned the gas on so it would blow, or Marshall was interrupted while he made dinner and the burner went out in the struggle. We won't ever know, *colleen.*" Connor shrugged. "Someone—maybe the shooter—left candles burning. The whole thing sparked. I didn't know he was dead until after I'd pulled him out and handed him over to the med guys. It was a shitty bust all around."

"What did the CI say afterwards?"

"He's to the wind. After that night none have seen him. Captain's a bit pissed, but there's nothing to be done about it."

The squeak of wheels on the road caught Connor's attention, and he touched his sister's arm, alerting her to one of the coroner techs moving toward them.

Kiki took a step back, moving out of the man's path as he pushed a sheet-draped gurney past them. She ran her hand over one of the truck's rails, silent in her contemplation.

Connor dropped his head in respect for the dead passing them, lightly touching the St. Michael's cross and wings hanging from a leather thong about his neck. "*Solas na bhflaitheas tar éis an tsaoil seo ar do shon.*"

"Light of heaven after this world for you," Kiki repeated in a soft murmur. They stood together for a moment, watching Death pass them by, before Kiki turned back to her brother. "I hate that this is our family's business, Con, but at the same time, I don't want anyone else doing it."

"Best to take up the sword yourself and defend the village than complain of the wolf that steals your children." Con cocked his head and stared down at his sister.

"Is that what you're doing there? With Ackerman in your car, Con? Defending the village?" Kiki eyed him.

"When I'm done with you, brat, I'm taking him to the hospital so he can sit with his shop manager," he replied. "Catch up with him there. Or talk to him later. He's a bit shook up right now."

It was a good enough explanation for why Forest was in his Hummer, certainly one that should have quelled his sister's curiosity—it just wasn't explanation enough for the butterflies beating themselves to death in his belly or why the sight of his jacket around Forest's shoulders tickled at some primal spots in his cock and soul.

Or even why he'd never known those spots existed before he'd held Forest in the middle of an ashen rain.

"Con?" Kiki's voice penetrated the haze of Connor's thoughts, and he jerked his attention away from the blond man curled up in the Hummer's passenger seat. "I'm going to need to talk to him."

"He was on the ground, Kiki. I know. I shoved him there and told him to stay put."

"And he listens so much to you that he wouldn't even look?" She eyed him. "Better than most of the sibs, then."

"Kiki, you look me in the face and tell me that you'd get up if I shoved you to the floor and told you to keep your head down." Her gaze met his, challenging him, but Connor stared her down, and she looked away. "He stayed where I put him until the shooting stopped. If he saw anything, it was probably the floor, but after we make sure Jules is okay, I'll have him around for you."

"Think this is connected to Marshall's death?" Kiki swept her hand around, encompassing the scene in a fluid motion. "Can't be a coincidence. No such thing as those."

"Sometimes there are," Connor replied softly. "But in this case, no, I don't think there are."

CHAPTER FOUR

Hands on my skin, their filth working in.
I can't feel anything but pain.
Why won't this ever end?
Too hard to breathe.
Too worn to care.
Pushing sharp knives in my soul.
Bleeding inside, still too tired to cry.
—Bleeding Tired

HE WAS scared. Down to his bones scared, and no matter how hard he wrapped his arms around himself to get warm, Forest couldn't reach the core of cold lodged in his belly. He'd given the cop back his jacket when they'd come to the hospital, and after sitting for a few hours in one of the many waiting rooms near the surgical ward, Forest wished he hadn't insisted the cop take it from him.

Especially since Connor Morgan seemed to disappear for half an hour at a time, only to come back with a worried look on his face.

Curling up over his thighs and hugging his shins seemed to help, but it didn't leave Forest with much of a view other than the hospital's black-speckled linoleum floor. Around him, families ebbed and flowed, some chattering away as if no one was dying a few feet away, bleeding out on unseen surgical tables while their loved ones shivered from the overly enthusiastic air-conditioning.

And try as he might, Forest couldn't remember ever actually being in a hospital for anything other than the cops or CPS dragging him into the emergency room to check him over for damage. Once Frank took him in, he hadn't seen the inside of a hospital again, although he'd seen doctors and dentists, since Frank'd taken periodic checkups quite seriously.

"Fuck, who the hell is going to tell me when it's time to get my teeth cleaned?" he muttered at his knees, hating the tears falling from his eyes and soaking into his jeans. "Dad took care of all that shit."

"Here, sit up and drink some of this," Connor ordered, and a hot cup of coffee appeared under Forest's nose. "I got you something to eat too."

Taking the cup, Forest inhaled its steam, coughing slightly at the bitter in its aroma. He sipped at the sharp opening in the cup's plastic lid, wincing at the sour sweetness of the hospital's blend and Connor's heavy hand with the sugar. Food turned out to be a couple of microwaved green chile and bean burritos, their molten innards leaking out from cracks in the tortillas and spilling onto a scallop-edged paper plate.

"I'm not hungry." Forest wasn't feeling the love for his stomach at that moment, especially since it'd been nearly an hour since they'd last heard from someone official about Jules's whereabouts. He put the plate down on the empty chair next to him. It stayed there for about a second before Connor picked it back up and put it firmly in his lap.

"Eat something. Now," Connor growled. "Actually, before I forget, put this on and *then* eat. You're going to make yourself sick."

The much-missed leather jacket settled on his shoulders again, and Forest numbly let Connor take the coffee cup from him. Connor's holster was empty, a dark slash of black leather against his broad shoulders and back. The man's chambray shirt was old, an obviously well-worn garment used to hugging the Irish cop's muscular form. Small white patches dotted Connor's chest, areas rubbed down from his holster, and a thumbnail-sized splash of pink on one of its tails turned out to be nail polish.

Forest wondered about the woman who'd stained Connor's shirt, leaving behind a small territorial mark to claim him as her man. Any thought about the unknown and mysterious woman disappeared from Forest's brain as Connor began to roll up his shirtsleeves to reveal his thickly muscled forearms and strong wrists. A satin-brushed gold ring on his pinkie gleamed dully under the hospital's fluorescent lights, its wide surface engraved with fluid Celtic designs Forest thought looked like animals of some kind.

"On, Forest. The jacket," Connor repeated. "Now."

He was about to argue—just for the sheer fuckery of it, but one look at Connor's face stopped Forest in midbreath, and he tucked his hands into the jacket's sleeves, sliding it on.

The scent of Connor's faint cologne and the musk of his skin swaddled Forest immediately, and he reluctantly took the coffee back, wishing its bitter scent wouldn't drown the Connor out of his nose. Stewing in the lingering heat of the man's body, Forest sighed and felt the coldness in him melt, slipping away under Connor's ad hoc gesture.

Despite not knowing anything more than he had a few seconds ago, life felt so much better, and he risked another sip of his coffee, not even caring there was enough sugar in it to turn the burned brew into caramel. The burritos—he thought as he eyed them squatting and oozing on the plate—they would have to wait until he had enough courage to choke them down.

"Fucking pretentious shit," Forest lightly scolded himself. "Couple years back, you'd have kicked someone's ass to have that much food."

He was about to thank Connor when the jacket's inside chest pocket began to sing an almost familiar song. It took a second for Forest to realize the music was coming from Connor's cell phone, and then another second passed by in a burning arousal when the man reached into the jacket and pulled the phone out. Forest felt every centimeter of the man's bare hand sliding over his chest, and the pinch of his nipple where Connor's ring rubbed didn't seem like it would ever subside.

"Eat," Connor ordered again. Then he sat back in the chair, thumbing the phone on to answer it. The cop listened for a second, then another, before a frown clouded his handsome face. "No, I'm at the hospital. Shit, across town. What happened?"

"If you've got to go—" Forest began, but Connor shushed him, waving him off. The hand not occupied by the phone settled on Forest's thigh, inches from his already tightening cock. Suddenly developing a very healthy interest in the cooling burritos, Forest picked one up, shoved its end in his mouth, and listened to the rest of Connor's conversation.

"Do you need me there?" Another pause, but Connor's eyes flicked over Forest's face. "No. It's complicated. If you guys don't need me... look, I've got to stay here, K. Talk to me. Is Mick okay? Did they get the guy?" Forest counted off five breaths before Connor spoke again. "Good for him. Tough fucking son of a bitch. The guy'll be hurting. He'll have to go someplace for treatment, it sounds like. Okay. You let me know if you need something, and don't let Mum bully you into taking him to their place. Stand your ground, man, or she'll be moving in before you can even blink. Talk to you later."

Connor hung up his phone and sighed, rubbing at his face tiredly. Forest chewed and swallowed, the beans sticking in his throat on the way down. Connor picked a cup up off the floor and sipped, making a grimace before handing it over to Forest. "Here. I think this one's yours. I didn't put sugar in one. Guess I gave you the wrong cup. I can change the lid over if you want."

"No, I don't mind." Forest shook his head and exchanged the coffees. He put his mouth on the lid, slightly disappointed he couldn't actually taste Connor above the sour. "Everything okay? Do you have to go?"

"Everything's good. My brother's—boyfriend, I guess you'd call him—he was attacked, but he took the guy down. Beat the shit out of him with one of those sidewalk magazine racks." Connor tapped at the bottom of the cup with his ring. "You don't fuck with Miki. He'll hand you your ass before you even realize your pants are down around your ankles and the wind's bitten your balls off."

"Sounds kinda hard core," Forest said softly.

"Really?" Connor laughed under his breath and took a sip of his coffee. "Because I was just thinking the same thing about you, *ghrá*."

THERE WERE rushes of people around them, intruding on their oasis. It was hard for Forest to hear the crying children wandering about the waiting area while their parents spoke in hushed tones about death and the living. He'd never sat vigil for someone before—didn't know what he was supposed to do other than wait. And lust for the man sitting by his side.

As if Death weren't enough to fight off, the world had to go and throw Desire into the fray as well.

Forest tried not to hear any of their whispers, but they slithered into his mind, wrapping his fears up in bloody red bows. His fingers refused to remain still, finding the different tones in the chair's arm and then its support bars before moving on to the flat of a small table next to him.

"That's a Celtic beat you've got going there," Connor remarked, catching Forest in midroll. "I hear a lot of it with my family. Irish, you know. They like a rolling drum. Usually while yelling at one another. It's like living in a battlefield sometimes. Did Marshall—your da have any other kids?"

"Just me and Frank." Forest didn't feel like dumping more hospital coffee into his belly, but the bean burrito had already started a rave in his guts, and the only thing that could possibly quiet it down was to drown it in the acidic brew. Most of the time his small talk centered on music, alcohol, and the probability of a quick fuck in a motel. He had no idea what to do with Connor Morgan, so he seized the one opening he saw available to him. "So you have a big family, then?"

Talking seemed preferable to sitting there in silence, mulling over how the other man's palms would feel on the small of his back, and Forest already caught himself staring at Connor's hands. A man's ass—he understood staring at an ass—but hands apparently were his thing too.

"Huge. Legion." Connor's smile softened the hard angles of his face and curved his generous mouth up into a bow. "My parents took 'go forth and populate the Earth' as their own personal motto. Didn't mean to, but, well, apparently Da only needs to look at my mum and she gets pregnant. The one after Quinn was supposed to be the last, but that one turned out to be two, so that upped the numbers a bit."

"So, what, four? Five?" Forest guessed.

"Eight." He chuckled when Forest choked on his mouthful of coffee. Pounding lightly on Forest's back, Connor worked the air back into his lungs. "After the twins there was a bit of a lull, and I guess Mum thought she'd seen the worst of it. Then *bam*—three right in a row. I'm pretty sure my mother said enough and was done. You'd like her. Fierce. She's the one you go to when you want someone beaten up. My da's the one you talk to when you're lost. Good man."

For all they'd been family, he knew Franklin had faults, and he couldn't remember a time when he'd spoken of his adopted father in the hushed, rolling reverence the cop used when talking about his father.

"Shit, that's a lot of kids." Forest winced, hearing himself. Unable to think of anything to backpedal his awkwardness, he went back to sipping his coffee. It was cold and if possible even more bitter with each passing swallow. "Sorry. I suck at this."

"Waiting?" Connor studied his face, and Forest shifted in his chair, uncomfortable under the man's assessing gaze.

"Small talk," he mumbled back. "I'm a drummer. I'm used to waiting. All we do is wait while the precious guitarists and lead singers talk about their harmony line and if the lyrics say what they truly mean."

"Oh, I so know what you mean. I know a couple of musicians. They babble a lot. It's like listening to two magpies discuss how they're going to divide up a piece of bread." Connor's grin was a flash of bright white in his tanned face. "You're doing fine at the small talk. It's shite and a half waiting for the doctor to come out. Worst thing in the world, really. Even if you know someone's going to be okay, it's a worry."

THE WAIT was over. For someone, anyway. The double doors blocking off access to the surgery ward opened, and a tired-looking Bengali woman in a white coat emerged. Smiling in the general direction of the waiting area, she called out in a softly accented voice, "Who is here for Jules Desmond?"

Forest stood up.

But then so did four other people at the far end of the room, including a brawny young man in old jeans and a faded T-shirt advertising an Irish pub near one of the piers. His eyes were red and a bit swollen, his nose rough from being wiped, but the look on his face—a

blend of expectant and fret—slipped into confusion
when he spotted Forest responding to Jules's name.

"Wait, who the hell are you?" the man snapped,
stepping closer to Forest.

He was surprised to see other people waiting for
Jules—people he'd assumed belonged to one of the
other victims. It shouldn't have been a shock—Jules
spoke endlessly about her boyfriend, Randy, and how
he loved her, or about what she did with her friends on
her days off. His mind *knew* these people existed, but
apparently it refused to believe people weren't as alone
in the world as he was. With Franklin gone, he didn't
really have anyone left in his life, other than a few loose
friendships and the coffee shop's staff.

A response to the man was forming in the back of
his brain when Connor moved in between them, blocking the way.

"He's her boss. From the shop." Connor caught
Randy's growl and threw it back at him, forcing the
man to take a step back.

"Oh, Forest, right?" The man's attention shifted
between the doctor and Forest. "Sorry, it was really
nice of you to come. Really. Most bosses wouldn't
have. It means a lot. Things have just been—"

"Shit," Forest supplied. "Yeah, I get it. It's all
good—"

"Yeah. Really. I'm sorry. Things are just a bit
tense." He waved at the doctor. "Let me see what she's
got to say, and I'll be right back."

Forest stood there, rooted in place as he sifted
through his emotions. Everything came at him too hard,
too fast, and he swallowed, needing to look away from
Randy's head bending slightly so he could hear the
much shorter doctor while they spoke. Randy's smile

nearly wrapped around his ears, and as the doctor disappeared back into the depths of the surgical ward, he turned to the cluster of waiting people and enveloped as many of them as he could in a fierce group hug.

Their elated voices drowned out the murmur of the hospital, stealing away the power of beeps and shushing noises coming from the air-conditioning units. Even the faint whoop of a siren creeping through a bank of double-paned windows drowned under the sound of Jules's friends celebrating her prognosis—while Forest stood and watched.

"I've got to get out of here." Forest turned, blindly searching for an exit out of the room—hell, he'd want an exit out of the city if it meant he didn't have to examine why the edges of his eyes burned or how his throat suddenly felt as if he'd swallowed a sour tennis ball. "Thanks for bringing me. I can catch a cab or—"

"Hey now, none of that."

He might have been lost, but Connor was there, guiding him around with a pair of strong hands closing down over his shoulders. "Come on, we need to get some food in you. That burrito was crap, and I know a diner that makes a mean stack of pancakes. Go wash your face while I go make sure they have my number to call in case someone needs something."

Forest wanted to scream at the cop—anything to take away the fear and loneliness pressing up from inside him, but Connor's fingers were gentle, stroking at the ridge of his collarbone with a lingering promise of something more heating his skin. He either wanted to shove away everyone or simply fall against Connor's solid body—he wasn't sure which until the reasonable part of his mind whispered *liar*. He knew which one he'd want—it was just that the wanting itself was probably as insane a thought as he'd ever had.

Straight Irish cops smelling of coffee, green-tea cologne, and a fog-kissed day did not cuddle fucked-up blond drummers who'd suckled at any teat or cock offered up to him because he needed *someone* to touch him—anyone—because it made him feel alive.

"Sure, yeah." Forest scrubbed at his face, unsurprised to find it gritty from tears and street dirt.

"Good," Connor replied with a wink. "You go on, then, and when you come out, you'd best be ready to eat. Because I've got a banshee for a mother, and I'm not using her to get you to eat some dinner."

CHAPTER FIVE

Shaking your ass down Broadway
Walking tight down the ole street line
Got a wink for the boys
Nasty smile that's just fine
Boy you've got some balls
Teasing cock as you go by
Better get some man to love you
Before you lose that sexy shine
—Hustle and Wink

FOREST'S PLACE was a shit hole. No other way to put it. What should have been written off as a small crack in a wall barely large enough for a Cockney caterpillar and his wife to squat under was being passed off as a suitable place for a young man to live in.

God, it pissed Connor off, because the man seemed very content to live in the cramped squalor, even when there wasn't enough room for Forest to turn around in without banging his elbows against the studio's four walls.

The diner, sadly, was under renovation, and Connor refused to send Forest off without something in his belly. Too many hours had passed since Connor first got out of his Hummer to get a cup of coffee, and the bean burritos they'd choked down were a faint memory for their aching stomachs. While there was something to be said about the outside staircase being steep enough to satisfy a leg day at the gym, the rest of it had little to cheer about.

Other than the long-legged blond currently trying to unearth a skillet Connor could use to make pancakes.

Connor unloaded the groceries they'd grabbed on to the kitchenette's small counter. Behind him, Forest rattled about in the cabinets. Having already liberated a serviceable spatula, he'd gotten a list of kitchenware to hunt for so Connor could cook for him.

What Connor *really* wanted to do was tear the whole damned apartment down and start over, because he couldn't even breathe in the tight space—or imagine Forest living in pretty much a refrigerator box with window cutouts.

"How long have you lived here?" Connor frowned at the pair of car jacks he'd just found holding the sink up. Cranked up as much as they could go, the jacks were placed diagonally under the counter, wedging an assortment of bricks and wood scraps up against the metal sink's bowl.

"Since I was thirteen? Kinda? Frank lived in the RV, but I lived up here. We'd eat together mostly." Forest's voice echoed in the depths of the cabinet. "This used to be a storeroom. Well, it kind of still is. The rest of the second floor is for the coffee shop's stuff and where we store a lot of the Sound's equipment if we're not using it. The shower kicks ass, though. Good pressure. Not so much in the kitchen, though."

That didn't surprise Connor one bit. Judging by the grit and impressions into the wood, he guessed the jacks weren't a recent development. Someone—probably Forest—used strip silicon to seal the gap between the sink and kitchen counter, the press-in tape glaringly white against the counter's brown-speckled avocado tiles.

Other than Forest's gold-streaked hair, it was the brightest spot of color in the whole place.

No, Connor revised his opinion. *That* dubious achievement probably belonged to the vividly stained red-and-black drum kit dominating most of the living space. The drums' golden bands gleamed, even in the soft light coming from the kitchen's overhead lights, and their tops showed definite signs of wear. A plastic milk crate stood on its end, open side up, and inside it, several empty coffee cans sprouted a bristled hedgerow of drumsticks.

It was the only new thing in the apartment by far, and probably shook the place when Forest really got going on it.

The walls were a unique putty yellow a cream paint only gained with age and constant cigarette smoke. Since Forest didn't smell like he was a three-pack-a-day addict, the wall color was probably a legacy left to him by his adopted father—and based on the depth of the stain, a daily visitation of tobacco farmers intent on smoking their entire crop.

The walls were mostly bare, although at one point there'd been posters or paintings—their absence now beige scatters of pale on the sickly yellow walls. Two battered doors led off to a bathroom and a closet—and from what Connor could see, while the tub and toilet sparkled as much as they could, there was only so much bleach and scrubbing powder could do when a sledge-hammer should be used instead.

And the less said about the institutional short-loop blue carpet or the studio's drab mauve curtains, the better.

A sagging queen-sized futon was almost an after-thought, a tangle of bedsheets and pillows holding the promise of Forest's scent if Connor could only some-how casually stroll over to them and put them to his face.

The idea of wanting *that* scared Connor in places he didn't even know he had—and since he made his living going through doors where hell waited for him, he thought he'd found every single place he *could* stash fear.

Connor needed something to draw him away from the unfamiliar stirrings in him. Seizing on the obvi-ous to distract himself, Connor commented on the red-black elephant sitting in the room. "That's a lot of drums you've got there."

"What?" There was the distinct sound of someone hitting their head on the cabinet, then Forest swearing in what sounded like Italian. He emerged from his hunt rubbing his forehead and clutching a small Teflon skil-let. "My drums? Yeah, it's a double kit—Yamaha PHX. Best thing I've played on. Great tone. Really loud, but I can buffer it down if I want. I've got another set like it downstairs in the…." He trailed off, setting the pan down on the small bar counter separating the kitchen-ette from the rest of the apartment. "And I'm talking about shit you've got no clue about."

"Not a single damned idea, but still, it's good to hear you talk about it." Connor nodded to the tall barstools set against the wall. "Pull one of those up here. You can talk to me while I cook."

"If it isn't music, there isn't a lot I can talk about," Forest said, setting a stool down. Hooking his foot over a rung, Forest balanced himself on the seat and leaned on his elbows to watch Connor break eggs into a large Tupperware bowl. Forest stared at Connor from across the counter and picked chocolate chips out of the bag Connor bought to make pancakes with, popping them one by one into his mouth.

"Tell me about Frank." Connor tossed a handful of shells into an empty grocery bag. "I know he was your foster dad for a bit, then adopted you. You were his only foster kid. Seemed kind of weird—a single guy adopting a thirteen-year-old kid."

"Cheap labor. Kind of like getting a mail-order bride 'cept he found me in the Dumpster outside." Forest studied Connor intently, then said, "I'm guessing you ran me through the system, so you figure, considering what I got arrested for, Frank was fucking me or something? He wasn't. He was weird and maybe not really a dad, but he was better than what I had."

"Your juvie record is sealed—" Connor began to protest, but Forest cut him off, his brown eyes alive with a fire Connor'd not seen in him before.

"Dude, you're a cop. Of course you're going to run me, and Frank too. Juvie records are open for review unless there's a formal request to seal them—and you usually need cause for that. They're so fucking wide open, they make Cartman's mom look like a damned nun."

"I didn't look." Connor hated the hard skepticism Forest had on his face. "I could have broken it open, yeah, I admit that, but you don't need that kind of betrayal. Anything you did in the past—if it's something you need to share with someone, it should be on your own time, by your own choice. Any truth—past or present—should be yours to share. No one should take that choice from you. So, anything you want to say?"

"Is that why you're here? Because you think there's shit on me, and you're trying to scrape it off?" Forest cocked his head, his face nearly hidden behind a shock of blond hair. "'Cause we're not friends. Hell, I don't even know what we are. You come by almost every fucking day now, but we don't talk or anything. And it's not like you want a piece of ass—or at least my ass."

There was a battle going on inside Forest. Connor could see it being waged right on the man's handsome face. The tension in his body ran down his shoulders and into his hands. Connor watched it spread, seizing up Forest's long limbs and finally into his face, where a tincture of fear tightened his mouth. Something—everything—was holding the young man back. It wasn't the same as the skepticism Connor often saw in Miki's eyes. No, this was different, a deep-seated trepidation born of something dark in Forest's past.

Connor ached for the man in front of him because he could see the damaged little boy cowering inside Forest. Frank might have pulled Forest out of the deep icy waters he'd been drowning in, but Frank did next to nothing to chase away the cold burrowed into Forest's soul. Its desolation resonated, creating ripples of unease most would shy away from.

He was going to give Forest that chance to warm up inside—because if it helped alleviate the bewildering heat growing in himself, Connor was all in. He just hoped he didn't lose himself in the process.

"No, I wouldn't say we're friends," he admitted. "But I don't know why not. I don't even know why I'm here. How's that for sharing. I don't know why I'm by for coffee—I don't live around here, but it's not that bad a drive from work. I can't tell you why I need to see you, to make sure you're okay. Sometimes I think I'm crazy for coming by, but if I don't, it bugs me—gets under my skin like bugs eating me alive. So there you go. My share."

"Fuck, so it's like you're my stalker, but you don't know why?" Forest's mouth quirked into a half grin. "That's weird. Really fucking weird."

"Told you, no idea why." Connor tried to shrug it off, but the unease lingered.

His life'd been simple—uncomplicated even. For as long as he could remember, he'd known what he wanted to be, who he'd wanted to be. Hell, he even had an example of that man in his father. Being a cop was as natural to Connor as having black hair or blue eyes. He just didn't *think* about it. His life plan'd been all laid out: college, police academy, a house, then wife and kids.

He'd been on track—until he'd wrapped his arms around the man sitting across the counter from him, and suddenly Connor found himself floundering in a snarl of suffocating dreams. Now all he wanted was something he couldn't grasp. The knowledge of it hovered just out of his sight, like a ghost slipping in and out of a haunted mirror, visible only out of the corner of his eye but gone when he looked straight at it.

"I suck at it. I get nervous and then shit pours out of my mouth." Forest shook his head.

"Anything. No judging," Connor promised.

The tired in Forest's body broke through, and he sagged. Spreading his hands on the counter, he stretched out his arms and worked his shoulders back and forth as if trying to loosen some of the tightness in his body. "I'm not good with people."

"You seem pretty good with me. And with Jules," Connor pointed out softly.

"You kidding? People scare the shit out of me. I mean, I try to hide it, but hell, it's always right there. Jules—the guys who come to the Sound for gigs—hell, I don't even want to think about how much you freak me the fuck out." Forest pointed to a cabinet behind Connor. "There's some Jack in there. Can you hand me the bottle?"

"How old are you again?" Connor teased as he re-trieved the whiskey. It sloshed about, a third of it already gone.

"Dude, I'm twenty-three, and I went through puberty around musicians. You think this is going to be the first drink I've ever had?" Forest took the bottle and opened it, setting its cap down on the counter. "Want some? There's glasses behind you."

"No, I've got to drive." He pointedly looked at the futon behind Forest. "I don't think that's big enough to hold us both."

Forest took a healthy mouthful of whiskey, swallowing it as Connor slid bacon strips into a skillet. The meat sizzled a bit, and Connor turned down the gas until the flame was low so the bacon wouldn't burn.

A few minutes and a couple of mouthfuls later, Forest began to talk.

"I fucking never know what to say. Like now, what do I tell you? Do I tell you that, yeah, I fucked guys for money when I was a kid, and Frank took me in because he'd gotten a wild hair up his ass one night to save the world?" Forest's words were mingled with a heavy dose of disgust. "Or do I talk to you about how fucking hard it is to hear someone else talk about how great their family is, and I have no idea what to say about mine? Frank was my dad because he *wanted* to be. Sure, he wasn't, like, the greatest, but I knew I had someplace to crash and food to eat whenever I wanted something. More than I had before. Shit, my mom didn't even show up for any of the hearings when Frank asked to adopt me.

"And some asshole—some fucking asshole killed Frank, and for what? No one knows. And why someone shot the Amp up to shit? 'Cause between that and Frank, I'm beginning to think I should just burn the whole fucking place to the ground and run away. That's all I've got to talk about. There's nothing else I can do. Shit, I don't even know where to start."

"Do you know what you want to do?" Connor poked at the bacon with a plastic spatula, checking if the strips were ready to be flipped. "I mean, life-wise. You happy with owning a coffee shop and a music studio?"

"Don't own them yet. Probate. Lawyers need to see if anyone's going to crawl out of the woodwork and want keys to my kingdom." Forest snorted, waving the now half-empty bottle about. He stared at Connor for a long moment, long enough to make Connor wonder if he had something on his face. "You know what I want? I want someone like you. Someone like you to love me, but—hold up, you've got a squillion brothers. Any of them like you but gay?"

"Two, but the one that's like me is—married. Very married, even if he doesn't realize it yet, and to a musician, actually." Connor didn't want to mention Miki, or Damien for that matter. It would bring the conversation out of the tight intimate something they'd started, and he wasn't ready to fall out of its odd warmth. "The other gay one is—well, *so* not much like me. I don't think he'd be what you were looking for."

"So, shit. I'm out of luck, then." Forest rested his chin on the bottle, looking forlornly at Connor through his bangs. "Too bad I just can't have you. Make things a hell of a lot easier, but Gay Rule number one, don't fall in love with a straight boy. Only shitty things can come of it."

"Yeah—no, you can't have me." The bacon popped, and a speck of hot oil seared the back of Connor's hand, pulling his attention away from Forest's whiskey-dappled lips. "Tell you what. You shouldn't be drinking alone. Pass me the bottle there, Forest, and damn wherever I might end up sleeping tonight."

IT WAS torture. Torture plain and simple. Forest couldn't think of any other word for it. He'd been hungry before, so hungry his stomach felt like it was wrapped around his spine and twisting into a knot. He'd been beaten so badly he couldn't breathe or see anymore, his eyes swollen so shut he couldn't even cry out of them, and every shuddering inhale he took was another stab of pain down his entire body.

None of that compared to the insane anguish of having Connor Morgan sitting next to him eating pancakes and bacon while asking about how Forest got into drumming.

If there was a God, He'd have struck Forest down dead in between a mouthful of buttery eggs and the piece of sourdough bread they'd had to crisp in the oven because Forest's toaster somehow grew legs and walked away.

"God, the toaster." He froze, a forkful of eggs poised at his open mouth. "It wasn't my toaster, was it? The RV—"

"It wasn't your toaster," Connor reassured him. "There was a candle lit. A couple of them, I think. That's what took the propane buildup out."

He should have felt relieved, but a sliver of panic lodged itself into his brain, leeching its poison into Forest's thoughts. "Then why the fuck did someone call you guys in to raid the place? They could have gotten you all killed."

"Yeah, that's kind of been something we've all been wondering." The cop took a sip from his glass, its whiskey-soaked ice cubes clinking against one another as he set it back down. His startling blue eyes pinned Forest in place. "You sure you wanna be talking about this?"

If the man's mouth, face, and hands weren't enough to drive him crazy, the Irish in his voice was going to do Forest in. His dick seemed primed to the man's rolling accent, so Forest took another long swig from his glass and sucked in an ice cube to chew on. His cock ignored the cool rush of crunchy ice on Forest's teeth and proceeded to do its own happy jig when Connor continued to speak after Forest nodded.

"Your da was already gone when we went in. There's that. So either someone wanted us to find his body, or they wanted to take us out with him." Connor studied his plate for a moment, picking through a mound of fried potatoes until he found a caramelized onion chunk. With the stabbed onion on his fork, he bit into it, chewing as he spoke. "You already talked to the inspector—the first one—not my sister, right? She told you all of this."

"Kind of," he said, shrugging. "Mostly she talked about how he was trafficking meth. Frank didn't do that kind of shit. Sure, he got stoned off pot, but that's about it. Shit, he hated taking aspirin because it was made of chemicals. He had to be convinced not to smuggle in raw milk for the coffee shop."

"You miss him, huh?" The cop's attention flicked back to Forest, and the tingle of attraction fired up again, trailing down Forest's belly. "Was he a good da to you?"

"Better than what I had before...'cause I didn't have anyone before," he said, pushing his half-empty plate away. He'd eaten more in the past half hour than he had in the past two days, and his stomach rebelled at shoving any more into it. "Frank was... kind of, like, just there. He'd tell me kind of what to do, how to get what I needed. Shit, when he found out I liked the drums, he hooked me up with all kinds of guys to teach me."

"What about school? No college?" Connor chewed another mouthful and glanced at Forest's plate. "You going to finish that?"

"Hell, no. You want it?" At Connor's nod, he pushed the plate farther over.

"Thanks," Connor said as he scraped Forest's left-overs onto his plate. "So, school?"

"Yeah, school," Forest snorted. "I went. Kind of. I pulled a GED as soon as I could, then got out. College isn't something I wanted to hook up into. I could barely go to high school. My head's too busy. Too much damned noise, you know?"

How could he tell the cop about how he'd sit in class and hear the tap of feet on the floor and get frustrated from the lack of pattern? Even the scrape of markers on a whiteboard shattered his focus, especially when his history teacher bent over to pick up a dropped pen. The man's ass had been extraordinary, and Forest couldn't remember how many times he'd prayed for an earthquake to jostle the markers to the floor during a test.

Frank got it—the lack of focus on things Forest couldn't get to stick in his head—and he'd been understanding when Forest trotted home a report card with a full range of the alphabet. He'd been great at math, aced the two business classes he'd taken, but the rest of it was crap. Even the music classes were a struggle from the moment he walked through the door and found his teacher had a fierce disdain for blues rhythms.

Forest watched in silent amazement as Connor reached for the pan of fried potatoes and helped himself to another two spoonfuls. "Hungry?"

"It's been a long day," the man grunted. "There wasn't any sign of meth in the prelim lab tests, and the only Marshall we could shake out of the grapevine turned out to be a guy who'd been popped for possession a few days before. So either it was a case of mistaken identity or something else. I'm guessing something else because someone went through a hell of a lot of trouble to murder your da and then either hide it or cause some major shit around it. The question is, who did it?"

"You said the guy who tipped you guys off is missing. Think he knows?"

"Don't know," Connor replied ruefully. "I'd like to tell you we'll find him, but guys like him crawl back into the sewers like roaches when the lights are on."

"Yeah, I know how that is," he mumbled. There'd been a time when he was a roach. Now Forest wasn't exactly sure where he stood in the sewer food chain, but the light didn't bother him as much anymore. "This other inspector—the not your sister one—is she even looking?"

"Truthfully, downstairs is a crime scene now too, but it's Kiki's. You're better off with her and Duarte." Connor pointed to the frying pan in front of him. "Eat some bacon at least. You look like you need a couple of pounds on you."

"Dude, I'm too full. Not even one thin mint hungry," he complained back, pulling up his shirt to pat his stomach. "If I'm lucky, the whiskey'll just go around it and get me drunk."

He didn't miss Connor's glance at his stomach nor the man's nostrils flaring. Tugging his shirt back down, Forest wondered if Connor thought he was hitting on him. Unable to think of anything to say, he reached for his glass and drained it, letting the whiskey burn through him.

"You can take the futon," Forest offered, glancing over his shoulder at his living space. "I can move some of the kit to the side. I've got a roll of foam and a sleeping bag in the closet. I can crash on that."

"Nah, I'll take the floor." Connor stood up and began to stack the dishes. Forest reached to help, but the man shook him off. "I'll go wash the dishes, and then we can polish off that whiskey. Maybe I'll even teach you some Gaelic."

"But—"

"Let me do this, Forest," the man rumbled. "Just this once, let someone else help you."

"What? And get used to that?" He tried to laugh it off and moved to take the plate from Connor's hand, but the man gently pushed him back onto the barstool.

"Yeah, maybe you should," Connor murmured. "Maybe it's time you learned what it's like to be taken care of."

CHAPTER SIX

*Kid's good, Miki. Young but good. Frank's finally
    got a decent drummer in here.*
Yeah, Dave. He's okay.
*Keeps up with me fine. He could be your drum-
    mer after we hit it big and I go raise llamas
    or something.*
*You're not going anywhere. And who the fuck in
    their right mind wants to raise llamas? They
    look like they'll bite your head right off.*
—Conversations at the Sound

THE LONG-GONE morning after the shooting,
pancakes, and unrequited lust, Forest had woken up
alone. Alone with two empty whiskey bottles, an empty sleeping bag smelling of Irish cop and bacon. His
dick was rock hard, and it clearly remembered being so
close to that cop but having nothing done to it.

But Connor Morgan was a ghost, or at least that's how it seemed to Forest over the next couple of weeks.

There were text messages—small notes long enough for Forest to know Connor was alive, but hardly conversation. Especially since they mostly revolved around how the shop was getting fixed up and that Con'd fielded his sister Inspector Kiki's questions about the day of the shooting for him.

Oh—and to call him Con. *That* was the cherry on top of Forest's shit sundae. He didn't *do* platonic. Hell, he could barely pull off casual acquaintance without shoving his foot in his mouth. *Con* texted at least once a day, and Forest hated the little jump of his heart when his phone pinged him with a message. And he didn't even want to think about the happy dance he'd experienced when the cop said to call him Con.

Like a damned twelve-year-old girl. Next, he'd be writing *i*'s with little hearts instead of dots.

"Wait, he doesn't have any *i*'s in his name—and why the hell am I even thinking shit like that? Get your head in the game." A glass shard of reality shoved through him, driven in by his own words. Alone. He certainly was that. "Frank's not coming back, dude. Just own this shit. You're on your own in this."

The *this* was Marshall's Amp, and the shit was definitely what was left of it after being used for target practice.

So he dragged himself down to the coffee shop on Sunday afternoon and stared at the remains of his inheritance.

The bakery case was shot—literally—and he stood in front of the wait counter's remains while trying to make sense of the drawings the contractor gave him to choose from. The familiar *ching-ching* of the Amp's door hitting a short string of bells jerked Forest's attention away from the plans, and he cracked a smile, the first one in forever it seemed, when Jules came through the door.

"Shit, it is good to see you." The plans hit the counter's single standing surface, and Forest crossed over the floor, ready to hug her, when he stopped a few inches short. "Um, hi!"

"God, you suck at people," Jules said cheerfully, enveloping him in a hug and banging his ribs with her cast. "Hug me, you asshole." He got a mouthful of hair and another bruising embrace before Forest could even think about peeling himself away. "What are you doing here on a Sunday?"

"What are *you* doing here on a Sunday?" He relaxed into Jules's hug and sighed. "God, I am so fucking glad you're okay."

"Yeah, I'm good." Laughing, she let him go and looked around, taking in the stripped-clean interior. "Wow, gutting the place?"

"Sorta had to," Forest replied, rubbing at his side, where he was sure he'd end up black-and-blue from her cast. "One of the espresso machines still works. Want one?"

"Yeah," Jules replied, picking up the proposed plans. "Can I take a look? That is, if I still work here. Randy told me you were at the hospital and that he was a jerk. He should have made sure you stayed. I love him, but sometimes I think he's more socially inept than you are."

"Yeah, I love you too. Go sit down at the one table we've got left. I'll bring you some coffee."

It took him a bit to juggle two large cups of espresso and the bag of Oreos he'd brought down with him from his apartment, but after a one-sided salsa around a broken cabinet, Forest made it to the round table Jules spread the plans on. She had a purple Sharpie, tapping at the plans with it as she stared at the drawings.

"Did you agree to this yet?" Jules looked at him when he got near. "And oh God, oh God—real coffee. My mom uses instant. And not, like, good instant like Vinacafé. Sanka instant. With Sweet'N Low. She doesn't *believe* in sugar. Like it's a unicorn or something."

"You're staying with your mom?"

"She insisted." Jules made a face, then gave Forest a rueful smile. "It made her feel better. I got released from maternal custody yesterday. And we'll talk about why you didn't visit me in the hospital for my short vacation afterwards, but now, answer the question—did you agree to this yet?"

"Do you still *want* to work here?" He slid into his own chair and took his first sip of coffee for the day.

"Why wouldn't I?" She stared at him, then waved her cast at him. "This? Are you kidding? How the hell could you have seen this coming? Besides, the insurance company paid for everything, and they had the nerve to ask me if I was going to sue you because you didn't have bulletproof glass. Where the fuck do they think we work?"

"Mrs. Li died," Forest said gently. "It's why I couldn't come see you. I went to go get flowers from her stand, and they were packing everything up—her family was. I just… couldn't, you know?"

"Oh, honey, I'm sorry." She leaned over the table, clasping his hands with hers, and squeezed as much as the plaster would allow her to. "I totally understand. God, you must have known her as long as you knew Frank."

"She hated my guts, you know? She hated my damned guts, but when they told me she was dead, I just couldn't take any more of it. I even told Con that." He refused to cry, even going so far as to lean his head back and blink, but the tears came anyway. "Fucking hell. This is so stupid. I can't stop crying over this crap, and fuck, I don't want to do any of this. Not the coffee shop. Not the studio. I just want to play the drums and write music."

"Well, I can help with one." Jules picked out a tissue from her backpack and wiped at Forest's face like he was a toddler. "You know jack shit about the coffee shop and what it needs. Do you trust me?"

"Are you kidding? I'm wondering why Frank didn't leave you the damned shop to begin with." He rubbed at his nose. "Do you want to buy half of it? A partner or something? You practically run the place. Okay, you do run the place. I just sneak in to steal coffee and sign the bills once in a while."

"You're serious."

"As a fucking heart attack. We get along fine. I'm the first one to say I don't know what to do with these plans. How the hell am I supposed to rebuild something if I don't know what's going to work?" His hands were shaking, and Forest had to put his coffee down. "There's already lawyers and shit picking at me. Might as well have them do something to sell you half the business."

"Not being one to look a gift horse in the mouth, but make sure I only own 49 percent. Keep a controlling interest. I love you. You love me in your own weird little Forest kind of way, and I know you're sincere, but never ever hand over all of something you own. Always keep control of it in some way." She used a tissue on her face, smearing her mascara on her fingers. "And shit, I came here to ask if I still had a job, and now you're trying to sell me half of it."

"Anything, so long as I don't have to figure out what the hell to do with the banquettes." Forest read down the list of things to be replaced. "I don't even know what that is."

"The booths." Jules laughed. "Okay, I'll take these and look things over. Now how about if we sit here, and you tell me all about your guy, Con."

VERY LATE Sunday afternoon, Forest found himself still without a coffee shop but with a reasonably chipper shop manager slash friend poring over the notes she'd made about the Amp and what she wanted to do with it—providing Forest ponied up the cash instead of waiting for the insurance company to get off its ass and pay the bills. They'd already gone over the proposed plans, and she'd tanked most of the designers' suggestions, pointing out none of the names on the bottom of the blueprints actually worked in a coffee shop.

"You know, we should go all retro and do a sixties theme," Jules mumbled around her pencil. "Kind of like a tribute to Frank."

"If this place became a tribute to Frank, you'd end up wearing camo pants and tie-dye shirts." Forest snorted as he steamed milk for his coffee. "And does air freshener even come in skunkweed?"

"No no no, less Humboldt and more mod," she complained. "Mod is cool."

"Frank hated the mod thing. Said they all went on to become faux skinheads just to stay relevant." Forest shrugged away Jules's outraged gasp. "Hey, take it up with him when you see him. I had to listen to him rant about how mod wasn't about the working class and was some jacked-up, pretentious offshoot of beat poetry elitists. And you never wanted to get him started about new punk."

"Well, I love the mod look. Your take on history is jacked up, there, sweetie."

"Better than what I was taught in school," he replied. "Not all of us had apple pie and Thanksgiving dinner families like you and Con."

"You guys are so cute." Jules caught the nickname before Forest could even wince at saying it. She grabbed at his wince and ran with it. "You sound all sweet talking about him."

"It's his nickname. People have nicknames. *You* have a nickname," he pointed out. "If anything, I'm the weird one 'cause I don't have one. And he's not... he's just a guy who was there when the shooting happened. Nothing else."

Even if he'd promised to be something else, something more, but Connor's words meant jack shit because, other than the texts, Forest might not have even known the man was alive.

"Okay, so wait, he pretty much saved your ass, took care of you, then made you dinner." Jules tapped off her points on her fingers. "And afterwards got drunk with you, then slept on the floor and was gone before you even woke up?"

"Yeah, pretty much," Forest agreed from across the room as he steamed more milk for their refills.

"Does he know you were a whore? Not that it matters, 'cause you were, like, twelve. Really. What the hell were you thinking?"

"Fuck, Jules. Come on, trying to carry things here." He stumbled on the same broken cabinet he'd been stepping around for about a week—or at least that was the lie Forest told himself when he pitched forward into a lurching stop. Sliding away from Jules's penetrating gaze, he sat down and mumbled, "I was thinking I wanted to eat."

His phone rang, a roll of music from a band he'd once loved and whose remains were smeared all over a blacktop in Los Angeles following an accident. Forest almost slid it over to voicemail, not wanting to deal with any of Sound's crap, but a quick glance at the number heated up the simmering want he'd started for Connor Morgan.

"Shit, I—um—I've gotta take this," Forest mumbled and pushed his chair back quickly. He heard it fall but didn't care. All he wanted was to find someplace quiet so he could listen to the roll of Irish coming through the phone or maybe even spit back a few *where-the-fuck-have-you-been*s he'd been storing up since he'd last seen Connor Morgan.

Forest hit the button to answer the phone, and one damned word undid him.

"Hey," Connor rasped.

Any bitching out he had planned was shot. A single drop of Irish cop whiskey growl, and Forest had to prop himself up against the remains of the back counter, or he'd have been on his knees begging for more. It was back to heart-dotted *i*'s and wondering how the man's long, thick fingers would feel stretching him apart. He didn't even like getting his ass played with, and Forest found himself fantasizing about Connor holding him down and peeling him open with those rough, graceful hands.

"What are you doing?" Connor's voice broke through Forest's thoughts. "Tell me you've at least eaten some lunch."

"No, working on coffee shop shit. Jules is here. I've decided I know crap about retail, so I'm kind of handing things over to her to fuck up."

"Good to have a partner in the fucking… up." That last word came too late, barely on the heels of the one Forest focused on.

"Hey, you should come by and take a look at what the designers came up with… and um, Jules too. You drink a lot of coffee. Maybe from a customer's point of view." He saw a bread knife pinned to the wall by a blade magnet when he glanced at the kitchen cut-through and wondered if he could somehow hold the knife up long enough to fall on it. "Shit, you're probably doing family things, right? Sunday stuff? No worries. We can—"

"Nah, it sounds like something fun. I like doing stuff like that. I'm restoring a Victorian I bought. That kind of stuff interests me." Connor's deep purr made Forest rethink the whole fall-on-his-sword thing. "Give me a little bit. I've got to talk to my da, and I'll be right there. So I'll see you soon."

"Sure, won't be soon enough," Forest murmured back. Hearing himself, he curled into the edge of the wall, hoping its hard edge would lend him its strength, considering he'd lost his spine somehow. "Not soon enough, you know? Jules might be gone. Um… but I'll be here. I'll wait."

He hung up, then contemplated the espresso machine's power cord, debating if it could make a good loop to hang himself with. Sighing, Forest settled for hitting his head with the edge of his phone and grumbled to himself, "Jesus. What the fuck, dude? You've made out with rock stars, did all-nighters with hard-core musicians, and you've come to this? Spooging over a fucking cop? Jesus H. Christ."

"You talking to yourself over there? Or are you having phone sex?" Jules called out, startling him. "'Cause if you are, I want to listen! Maybe even record it. You're hot. I could make some bucks on the video."

"No, no phone sex, but shit, I need help. I act like I'm an idiot around him. I can't wait for him to lose interest in whatever the fuck he thinks he can save me from and go away. Then everything will go back to normal." He again meandered back to the shot-up dining area. "Come on. Let's go over this stuff so I can give it to the designers this week. Sooner I get this place fixed up, the sooner customers can come back."

"Customers like Lt. Connor Morgan?" Jules wiggled her eyebrows at him, grinning when he flicked a bit of her curls away from her shoulder. "Because, you know, if I had to worry about one customer coming, it would be him."

"God, why do I want you back here?" Forest grimaced.

"Because I'm your friend." She winked. "And who else is going to tease you about crushing on a straight cop? Teasing you about it is just a perk—kind of like taking vacation days. I don't always do it, but when I do, it's sublime."

CONNOR'D SPENT his entire life carving himself into a man his da would be proud of. As life went on, it seemed Connor dogged Donal's every step, matching the Irish-born cop stride for stride. They shared a love for the job—even as a kid, wearing the blue and a badge was all Connor had ever wanted. He'd stayed up late at night to watch his father come in after a long shift, peering through the window, then sneaking downstairs to watch him take off his gun belt and lock up his weapon for the night. He'd seen his parents dance in the kitchen and laugh over a shared midnight meal, catching up on their day and basking in each other's humor.

He'd grown up wanting that... thinking one day he'd come home to a little boy and a woman who'd kiss him on the mouth while teasing him about his big feet. There'd not been a moment he'd doubted his future. Not the uniform. Not the badge. Not the woman. Then suddenly his future tilted, and Connor couldn't find his feet underneath him.

So he did the only thing he knew to do during one of those times: reach for his da.

He just didn't know if his da would reach back.

If Connor had to be honest—so fucking brutally honest—he'd have said the biggest fear he had in his life wasn't death. Death just meant leaving things unfinished. What frightened him the most was the look on his father's face when Donal suddenly realized the son he'd raised wasn't the man he'd wanted him to be.

When he was young, hearing his father say "I'd have thought better of ye, Connor boy" killed him. There were blackened nuggets in his soul, dusty, foul stones of disappointment and regret Connor couldn't step around without feeling dirty. Each of those moments burned to ash inside him had come from a certain look on his da's face, and the shame of those nuggets weighed heavily with every breath he took. Especially since he wasn't going to be the son Donal Morgan expected, not the firstborn who'd one day step into his father's shoes, and Con knew it would kill him even if life went on around him. He would die from the depth of his failure.

"I've fallen, Da." Connor snagged a bottle of Irish whiskey from the study's shelves and joined his father on one of the room's couches. He'd asked his father for some time during a Sunday family gathering. They'd finally gotten rid of the threat of a cold-blooded killer hunting Sionn's lover, Damien, and the Morgans were doing what they did best—eat, argue, and drink. "Fallen in love, I mean."

"And that's got you worried?" God, his father looked so happy. Donal's face lit up when he smiled, and to Connor, it always felt like his father's happiness warmed the family, broad sweeps of sunshine pouring over cold mountains. He would be dimming that light, and his gut grumbled from the sour pouring into it. Donal must have seen something on his face, because his da frowned slightly as he poked at Connor's arm. "What's wrong? Is she married? What's her name?"

Connor wondered how Quinn and Kane made speaking the truth look so easy. They'd both done it together, sitting at a Sunday dinner table and casually dropping a gay bomb all over the roast chickens their mother'd made that afternoon. From what Connor remembered, he thought nothing of Quinn's postscript mention of his homosexuality. Kane's had come as a surprise because he'd never imagined having two gay—or in Kane's case, bisexual—brothers. Now he was sitting on the other side of that line, and saying those words—such oddly damning words—aloud made him appreciate how strong his younger brothers had been.

Because he was scared shitless to speak the truth he'd been avoiding the fuck out of for the past couple of weeks as a madman stalked his family, and he tried to be as nonchalant about checking up on Forest as he could. If saying out loud what he thought made his heart clench, he couldn't even imagine what he could say to the drummer about why he'd been avoiding him.

If confronted, Connor would have made up some bullshit story about a man named Parker targeting his family's loved ones, but that would leave so much of Con open to be picked at, and he couldn't risk those wounds being opened at a time he needed to focus.

It would have also meant he would have had to acknowledge what he was about to share with his father—Parker had been going after anyone connected to Damien. His assault on Miki proved that, and attacking Sionn's pub manager proved it didn't matter how nebulous a connection was, Parker would exploit it, and Connor couldn't risk putting Forest in that sick bastard's line of sight.

Because Con would have had to admit there *was* a connection between them, and he hadn't been ready to even think about it out loud.

Until right now, and not to the man who'd drawn him in with a fierce vulnerability and brown eyes. No, the first time Connor spoke about his growing attraction to a blond drummer, it would be to the man who made him and could potentially break him as well. And he would do it in the womb of his family's home—in the safety of a room he'd come to so many times before to work out his anger or confusion.

"His name is Forest, Da. Forest Ackerman." The *his* stung. It was out. A pretty demon with unknown powers to scald him and flog his soul clear off his body. Stumbling over his tongue, Connor continued, working his fingers together into a knot. "I met him on a case and, well…."

Donal Morgan was many things, but dumb ranked nowhere on that list.

"But… he? You said he."

Connor couldn't look at his father, but when Donal's hand touched his thigh, he looked up to stare into his da's perplexed face.

"But, Con, yer not gay."

"Yeah, I know, Da." He picked up the fine Irish whiskey he'd set on the table near the couch and took a hefty mouthful. It burned the edges of his gums, and his tongue tingled and sparked under the fiery liquid. Swallowing was difficult because he had harder things to do besides get drunk—one of which was break his father's heart. "I know. Fucking hell, don't I know that, but here I am. In this."

The silence nearly killed him, and Connor wondered how long it would take to die from alcohol poisoning before Donal finally exhaled. After taking the bottle from Con's hands, he set it down and then yanked Con into a suffocating bear hug.

"Well then, I guess we'll work through this," he murmured. "Ye and I… we'll find a way to make it work. Because yer my son, and I'll be damned if ye shouldn't be happy in love."

CHAPTER SEVEN

Wings under my skin,
Fighting to break free.
I need a razor to cut them out,
So I can live as I'm meant to be.
A drop of music, a sip of wine.
Watch the sky when I fall.
I'm sure I'll be fine.
—Falling

HE WOULDN'T cry. Connor'd promised himself that, but it was hard going, especially when his father pulled back and gripped his shoulders tightly. Shaking, Con let go of the dank, foul fear he'd held in his lungs, and Donal reached a hand up to cup his face, his broad fingers tapping Con's cheek.

"Yer trembling, son. Why?" If Connor thought his father's disappointment was his greatest fear, it was nothing compared to the pain in Donal's eyes when he whispered, "Did ye think I'd stop lovin' ye for this? Did ye really think so low of me, Connor boy, that I'd walk away from ye because of who ye are? Have I done such a bad time of it being yer da?"

The tears came then, hot and silent, as Connor pressed his mouth together and grabbed his father back into a hug. He couldn't speak. It was too much effort to get around the emotions clotting his throat with their thick, viscous tendrils.

"No," he choked out, but the word was barely audible over his clenched-back crying. "No, Da. I just don't… I didn't know what. This is all fucked up, and I don't know what I'm doing with this. I never wanted *this*. I don't *want* this now, but here it is, and I'm drowning in it. I want this fucking shite to go back to wherever it came from, but I can't stop from thinking about him—worrying 'bout him, and it's making me crazy."

"Let's be talking first about why ye'd think I'd be disappointed, Con." Donal pulled back and wiped his eyes, smearing away the tears his son'd brought to his face. "What were you thinking, boyo?"

Connor's face ached, pressure from the vent of emotions inside him. There were too many threads of whys and why-nots in his mind, reasons he'd felt he failed his father in this one thing Donal asked of him— to be a man like Donal—to be someone others could look up to, a man who'd pick up the family's burdens on that one horrific day when they'd need him the most.

And the words came, pouring from him as if he were a five-year-old confessing to eating the last donut, a horribly heavy and dense donut he'd baked solely to anchor himself in life.

"I needed to be you, Da," Connor heard himself whisper. Every word grated in his throat, raking barbs through his heart and soul before bleeding off his tongue. "I don't know when, I don't know why, but there it's been. In me. All this time. Everything I do— everything I am."

"Oh, Connor boy, I never meant for you—" A look of horror crept over Donal's face. "Are ye a cop because ye think that's what I'd want for ye? Please tell me—"

Connor gave his father a rueful look. "Maybe. In the beginning of it all."

"Ach, Connor." Donal said something in Gaelic, too low and too soft for his son to hear. "I'd never have wanted any of my children to take up the badge if they didn't want it."

"I was a little boy, Da," he explained. "And you came home wearing a uniform and carrying the world. How could I *not* want to be that man? Be you? And yes, I probably wanted to be a cop because you were one, but I love it. It's who I am. It's the part of me I don't question."

"But ye question this man in your life? That ye love him?"

"I don't know if I love him. Maybe. Maybe I'm just… I don't know." Connor collapsed back into the soft couch, rubbing his face in frustration. "Everything's gone cattywampus and upside down. I had a plan—career, house, and then a wife. Children. And now…."

"No one is saying ye can't have those things. Well, except for the wife. This Forest boy might be having a problem with that," Donal teased as he ran his hand through his son's hair.

"I don't know if I'm ready for that. For this."

"I'm going to ask ye a question, and I want ye to think about it before ye answer," Donal said gently. "Is he the first man ye'd thought about this with? To be with?"

Connor leaned into his father's touch, a comforting, firm hand on the back of his head. They'd sat so many times in the same position, often in the dimly lit study while his father watched footie games on the television or while working on his reports. Donal's touch anchored Connor as much as his dreams had, a forever kind of tether to the world around him.

He'd feared he'd lose that touch, that anchor, when he'd spilled his secrets to his father, and now in the light of a Sunday afternoon, Connor found himself adrift, even with his father holding him steady and firm.

"I'd watch Rafe," Connor admitted softly. "When we were in school. Something about him. Before we were really close, and he was just Sionn's friend, I'd watch him. I used to tell myself it was because he was... lost, because he needed saving of some kind, but now I don't know."

"Rafe's a handsome boy," Donal replied. "A bit of a fuckup, but he's worked hard to be back on his feet. He's had a rough time of it from the start."

"I couldn't fix him, Da. And we tried." Connor shook his head at the years of frustration he'd had with Rafe in his life. "But he was the first, I think. The first time I wondered, but then I put it all away. I couldn't... think on that. There were women—and I love women. I love the way they smell and feel on me and how their skin tastes on my tongue, but there's been times when I've wondered—when I've thought about how it would be."

"Lately?" his father asked. "Before yer Forest? Or just about him?"

"About Miki—but just for about a second, Da," he confessed, shunting his gaze away from his father to stare at the opposite wall where their lives played out in framed photos. "I wondered how it would be with him—just for a few moments when Kane introduced him. Something about him kicked me in the gut, and I had to take a step back. I'd never touch him—he's Kane's—but it was there. That wildness about him. I could see why Kane wanted him, and I'd never had that before—that recognition of *why* a man would touch some part of me."

"And now Forest." Donal sighed and rubbed at Connor's head once more before sliding his hand down his son's back to pat at his shoulders. "Ye can't let him go, then? Do ye even *want* to?"

"He haunts me, Da. Worse than a sunburn I cannot wait to heal but at the same time tightens my skin so I can't *not* feel him. I see him, and I want to touch him, to hold him, because I don't think he's been held enough or been told someone cares about him. He's had a shite hippie who took him in off the streets and who probably loved him but didn't *give* him any kind of self." Connor pulled himself away from the wall of family and friends. "He's not had any of this, and I want to give it to him. I want to lie in bed with him when it rains and listen to the water hit the roof. I find myself wondering how the coffee foam on his lip would taste on my tongue or if I could make him smile by blowing a raspberry on his belly. It's not just want, Da. It's *need*. I *need* him. And for the life of me, I fucking don't know what to do with that. I wanted to be like you, Da. And I don't know—"

"All I want is for ye to be Connor," Donal cut in and looped his arm around Connor's shoulders, giving him a quick squeeze. "Ye don't *need* to be me. I don't want ye to be me. I want ye to be the best *Connor* ye can be. That's the man I raised, not this Ken doll ye've built around yerself."

"And if that means I want to be with a man? Then what?"

"Then ye're with a man." He shrugged. "What difference does it make who ye love so long as ye love? That's what I told yer brothers. That's what I'm telling ye. Are ye telling me they're less of a man than ye because they love who they love?"

"No, I'd fucking kick anyone's ass who said so," Connor spat back.

"Then why aren't ye letting yerself have as much of that right to happiness as they do? Why won't ye fight for yerself as much as ye'd fight for yer brothers?"

Connor sat, silent and stunned. He'd die for any of his siblings, but he was especially close to Kane and Quinn. Hell, his knuckles still bore scars from being bashed into bullies' teeth for taunting Quinn during school. His awkward, brilliant young brother deserved to smile every day. He'd just never really thought he deserved that same pleasure.

The revelation—such a small tidbit of truth—took Connor's breath away.

"Is he gay?" Donal patted his son's back and reached for the abandoned whiskey bottle. After taking a swig, he handed it to Connor. "Does he know you feel this way?"

"Yeah, he's gay." Connor took the bottle from his father when it was offered and took a mouthful, knowing he'd fit on the couch or one of the spare beds if he needed it. "And no, I haven't told him."

"Then I'll tell ye what I told ye the first time ye'd come to me to tell me ye wanted to ask Amy Patterson out to a dance." His father nodded and patted Connor's thigh. "Be respectful, be honest, ask sweetly, and hold yer head up if he says no. But yer my son, and knowing the man ye are, Forest would be a right idiot to say no to ye, and if he's that stupid, then he doesn't deserve ye. So go forth and ask for him to be in yer life, Con."

"And the family? What do I tell—"

"Ye'll do nothing. Ye'll say nothing or everything if ye want to. Ye don't owe anyone—including yer kin—any explanation for where yer heart lies," Donal informed him. "If I'd had done that, ye wouldn't be here, boyo, because let me tell ye—if ye think yer mother's a pain in the ass now, ye should have seen her back when I first met her. Follow yer heart, because no matter where it takes ye, the journey is worth it—especially if it's love."

MORE THAN an hour passed, and Jules made a show of looking at her wrist. Forest caught her at it for the third or fourth time before tapping her hand and whispering, "You don't have a fucking watch, remember?"

"He's late," she sniped back. "I want to see him before I head back to my mom's for dinner, but then I'm heading home. She's doing the whole church thing with the priest coming over. Randy's doing penance for being an ass to you. She got a load of avocado in, and he's chopping it up for the fire pit. I promised I'd be home so I could rub all over his sweaty, manly body."

"And while gay, I am still grossed out." Forest pulled a face, then yelped when Jules kicked him in the shin. "I've been dripping sweat after a gig. It does not feel sexy."

"I've seen you, and yeah, it's not attractive. *You* look like a drowned rat—a dumbo rat named Bon Bon or something, with your ears sticking out of your hair." She laughed at him. "Randy's different. He glistens, and there's sawdust on him. It's kind of sweet. I like showering with him when he's like that."

"And the mental image just crumbled upon the introduction of the vagina." This time Forest dodged the blow, jerking his leg out of the way. "Besides, you can't wash with that cast, right? It's got to be all wrapped up."

"Yeah, it sucks. Like wearing a sarcophagus on my arm." Jules waved it about. "It's not dead! Just resting! Seriously, he's kind of late for 'be over soon.' Maybe he blew you off?"

"Nah, I think he lives up the hill or something. You know it's a bitch to get past Ghirardelli. He wouldn't do me like that. He's a nice guy," he said. "I got the feeling his family doesn't raise shitty kids. Maybe you get one fuckup, and then they set you out on the iceberg because you've shamed the clan. They've got enough of them. I don't think anyone'd notice if one goes missing."

"Anyone gay? Maybe he can hook you up? Or, you know, he could take a walk on the wild side with you."

"Yeah, went over that. Apparently no." Forest laughed. "Very straight, and the gay ones are either taken or broken."

"Straight, huh?" Jules asked, picking up a fingertip of foam from her new coffee. "So then tell me, why is he standing out there looking like he's about to ask you to the homecoming dance?"

Forest turned to stare out of the Amp's remaining picture window. Connor stood there, in the damp foggy afternoon, looking like a handful of sex and want dressed all in black and a leather jacket so buttery smooth Forest could still feel it against his skin. He barely heard Jules get up or felt when she patted his arm, but suddenly he was alone with the man he'd lusted over since the first day Lt. Connor Morgan came in to order a cup of coffee.

He took a step toward the black-haired Irish cop, unsure if he was going to punch the shit out of him or steal a kiss so fiercely deep, it would get him punched in return. The phone call had only whetted his appetite, and he still smarted a bit under his skin from the back and forth of his emotions. There was too much going on—too many pieces and parts left up in the air from Frank's death and then the attack on the coffee shop. He was drowning, and for some reason, Connor Morgan'd thrown him a lifeline.

Raising his hand to say hello, Forest took another step toward the front door. Then the walls came tumbling in, and any thought Forest might have had about stealing a kiss was lost under a tidal wave of bricks and pain.

A FEW cups of coffee, some hastily gulped down food, and Connor was back on the road. He'd had a short conversation with himself—very short—about texting Forest to tell him he wouldn't be there.

It was a very short conversation.

He didn't even bother to answer himself.

The parking lot behind the Amp was mostly empty, a few cars parked in defiance of a sign announcing the space as solely being for customers of a now blown-out coffee shop. As if by some unspoken suspicion, the spot where Frank's RV once stood remained wide open, the black smear marks on a nearby concrete slab nearly washed away by the bay's intermittent rains.

Connor stared at the blackened lines, wondering how Forest could stand waking up every morning to a view of his father's murder scene. Hell, he still felt guilty about finding the man, even though Frank Marshall was long dead before Con hit the RV's front door.

"Fuck of a lot stronger than me, Ackerman." Shaking his head, he got out of the Hummer and keyed the alarm.

An icy wind sliced up the street, cutting through the neighborhood with a howling vengeance. Even with his jacket on, Connor felt its bite. Then he turned the corner and found the man he'd come to see sitting down with a cup of coffee in his hands, his lips turned up in an enigmatic smile but the faint hint of laughter touching his soulful eyes.

Something hit him, grabbed him in the chest and stomach, then twisted Connor around. Seeing Forest lightened the press of darkness he'd not realized he'd been carrying, and the dread of walking up to his father—the fear of not being the man he'd thought he wanted to be—lifted away, leaving behind an effervescence he could feel in his heart.

"*Shite*," Connor slurred the word, feeling it roll around on his tongue. "I'm in love with a man."

Forest spotted him, and the smile tugging at the man's mouth became broader and solely his. Connor grinned back and, out of the corner of his eye, caught an odd movement—a red-and-black blur where one shouldn't have been.

The van hit the front of the Amp, slamming through its remaining window and plowing into the dining area. The brilliant spark of light shimmering in Connor's chest burst, and a foul sickness bloomed up into his throat. Around him there was screaming, something harsh and wild coming from a feral animal, and his ears rang with the horror in its cries.

He took a step toward the building and realized the screaming was his and his alone.

There wasn't a question about who to go to first. He was in the building, climbing through rubble before his throat realized he'd screamed it raw and bloody. Glass shards and steel ribbons blocked his way, and Connor caught something on his temple, a heavy chunk of debris cutting him deep enough for blood to drip into his eyes. He tumbled forward, smearing the blood with a swipe of his hand, and spotted Jules moving sluggishly a few feet away.

Her cast was busted open, exposing the metal pins piercing through her arm, but for the most part, she seemed fine. Blinking at Connor, Jules tried clearing her throat, spitting out a mouthful of dust, but only a squeak came out when she spoke. The panic in her eyes was enough to spur Connor into action, especially when he realized Forest was nowhere to be seen.

"Get out if you can walk," he shouted at Jules. Nodding, she struggled to get to her feet. Using a chair to brace herself, the woman toddled out of the building's damaged front, stepping carefully through the trickle of debris still coming down from the broken wall.

The initial sting of cracked stone on his hands smarted, but a flash of a Converse logo buried under a pile of wooden chunks drove Connor to dig faster. He couldn't tell if he'd been at it a minute or a moment—either felt like an eternity, especially when he couldn't find the man he was looking for. The logo turned out to be a flyer, something printed on a sales postcard, probably slid through the Amp's mail slot, and Connor's heart sank, a hot, prickly stone cutting through his soul with its sharp-edged fear.

Hands bleeding, he went to work on the larger pile of crumbling red brick, then through the crackle of falling stones. A faint noise lifted away any pain shooting through him. It was a murmur—a golden dip of something precious he'd not quite held in his hands but coveted beyond reasoning.

And in typical Forest fashion, it was laced with profanity and a healthy dose of mad.

"Fuck—" Anything else Forest might have said was buried under the sound of crushed stone sliding from the table he'd slid under when the van hit. Rising out from under the protection of sticky laminate and oak, the drummer emerged, his gold-streaked hair turned white from dust and mortar. He spotted Connor and smiled, off-kilter with a peek of a skewed canine behind his full lips. Winking as he stumbled free of the pile, Forest said in a shaky voice, "P-p-please, Raoul. I can give you stars. Just drop the refrigerator on my head one more time!"

Connor climbed, falling forward and reaching for the man at the same time. His arms ached from the strain of moving heavy beams and enormous chunks of brick, but none of that mattered. The next breath he took was cold with the hint of rain from outside coming in, and his exhale frosted the warmer air near Forest. His hands shook. Then he smeared blood and dirt over Forest's cheeks when Connor cupped the man's face in his palms.

Connor'd never felt this kind of fear before. Certainly not the true spine-rippling terror he'd had just moments ago. He thought he knew the sink of terror. After all, he'd taken fire while huddled with his team in a raid gone south and experienced moments of stuttering pain when they'd almost lost Brigid after she'd given birth to his youngest sister, Ryan. He thought he'd known fear when he'd found Quinn on the roof of their school's highest building, his brother's face wet with tears and his feet balanced on the edge. There'd been a rush of heart-stopping jerks and starts during those moments—nothing like the deep blackness swelling up to consume him as it had a few moments ago. Connor couldn't seem to find his lungs, no matter how hard he pulled air in to sustain himself. With the anguish fading away, he was left with a shaking truth carved out by his fear's unforgiving blade.

He'd been scared of losing the man who'd shaken off life's beatings as if they were raindrops during a light spring drizzle, and Connor knew he couldn't—wouldn't—risk losing Forest ever again.

Forest tasted of sweetness and coffee, a hint of tang from something he'd eaten, a whiff of citrus on his tongue. Connor needed more, and he pulled the man in closer, needing the length of the man on him. Delving deeper, Con found more than sweet in Forest's mouth. There was a sensual, velvety darkness with promises of pleasure and maybe a hint of pain from the nip of Forest's teeth on the edge of Con's lip—then Connor realized he'd taken the man into a deep kiss and had no intention of letting go.

Their world became a tight space, heated not by the sun but from their bodies pressed in tightly together. Forest's hands trembled at Connor's waist, his slightly cold fingers sliding into the warmth under Con's leather jacket and then around to caress the small of Con's back.

It was so very different an experience. Discounting the dust caught between their lips or the singsong wail of sirens circling closer like sharks to bloodied waters, Forest felt different, tasted different, and in ways Connor couldn't wait to explore.

Forest's cheeks were slightly rougher than a woman's, although not by much. The slight burr of a scruff felt good on Connor's work-roughened palms, tickling more than just his hands. His cock stirred in its denim prison, aroused by the small stroking circles Forest's fingers were making on Connor's hips. Pressing in, Connor suckled and tasted his first kiss, experimenting with the touch of his tongue on the roof of Forest's mouth and then along the slick polish of the man's teeth.

The taste of him—of *Forest*—filled him. Connor needed more. Wanted more. He wanted to find someplace soft and dark so he could explore every inch of the man's body, if only to feel the texture of Forest's skin on his lips. He'd known pleasure, but in that moment Connor wondered if he'd even begun to understand it. Temptation teased him, flirting with the seductive pull of Forest's length, and then a small, husky laugh escaped the man's mouth, and that resonance—a puff of air carrying a dollop of sound—poured into Connor's body, and he was finally complete.

Connor couldn't find his English. Instead, a guttural crawl of Gaelic flowed from his mouth and spread over Forest where Connor's lips touched his skin. The man's hands dug into his sides, and Connor loved the sheer strength of them, a tumble roughness he'd never had before. There was a solidity to their touch, a whispering pledge from Forest's muscular body that he was able—and more than willing—to take anything Connor could dish out. And perhaps even give Connor back more than he could ever imagine.

They'd kissed for only a hiccup of an eternity when Forest drew back and moved his hands out from under Connor's jacket. He took a breath, then clutched at Con's biceps, wrapping his fingers around Connor's thickly muscled arms. As Forest rested his forehead on Connor's chest, Connor cradled the man to him, thankful for the table Forest found to hide under, grateful for his father's love and assurance he could love anyone he wanted and still be the man Donal would be proud of, but most of all astonished at the reality of Forest in his arms.

"By all that is holy, I am in love with you," Connor whispered into Forest's tangled blond hair. His mouth stung from their kisses, but his fingers itched to explore. There was so much to discover between them, and Connor wondered if he could bring more than a wisp of a smile to Forest's mouth.

"Whoa. Did you just kiss me?"

"Aye, I did."

"Did you mean you'd catch me?" Forest whispered, weaving slightly in Connor's embrace. "If I fell?"

"Yes." He frowned at the man. Forest's brown eyes were blown out to black, and he blinked under Connor's intense stare.

"Good, good. 'Cause I think I've got a concussion." Forest nodded. Then a green cast spread under the blush of his cheeks. "So I'm going to pass out right now, and I might really need that catch you promised me."

CHAPTER EIGHT

Working in deep
End of the line
Black river at my feet
Red fire down my spine
Getting harder every day
To hold on to what is mine
—Working In Deep

"Kiera Joyce Morgan, if you don't get out of my face, I'm going to—"

"Going to what, Con? Punch my face?" Kiki inspected her brother's scowl, then gave him one just as fierce. "See? I can do Big Bad Connor Morgan face too. Except the difference is I know you're not going to do anything other than spit and growl at me."

"I'd risk the suspension," he snapped, pacing another length of the waiting room to distance himself from his younger sister.

"You might," Kiki agreed with a nod. "But you won't risk Da being pissed off about it."

He couldn't shake Kiki. Not without causing a scene or earning himself a black mark on someone's ledger. Rubbing at his face, Connor mumbled through his fingers, "What do you want, Kiki? I told you everything I know."

"Really? Because I don't seem to get it." She rounded on him, poking her finger into his chest. "I want to know why you left a family thing to go down to an old crime scene. And—"

"And it's none of your business, *Kiera*," Connor said flatly.

She must have finally realized he meant business, because his little sister took a step back, dropping her hand down to her side.

"I told you I was standing outside when I saw something moving out of the corner of my eye. I didn't have time to think about what that was, and no, I don't know what the fuck is going on. I didn't see who started the van. I didn't see who locked its steering wheel in place, and I sure as fuck don't know why someone would do this to Forest. What I *do* know is that it's none of your fecking business about why I was there or why I'm here now. So step back a bit, *colleen*, because there's nothing more I can give you."

The smell of the hospital was making him sick. The not knowing what was going on ate away at Connor's patience, and he'd locked horns with the doctor in charge more times than he could count. If he pushed the man one more time, Connor was fairly certain he'd be marched off the floor and out the hospital's sliding glass doors before he could blink.

"How about if you let me decide if you've got nothing more to give me?" Kiki stood next to him, her hands on her hips. It was hard to reconcile the gun-toting, badge-wielding inspector with the frizzy-haired little girl he'd once carried on his shoulders so she could see the dragons at a Chinese New Year parade over the thick crowd. "I'm going to do my job, Con. It'll be nice if you help me with that."

Kiki was right. Connor knew she was right, but it didn't mean he liked it. Talking to his sister would mean taking his eyes off the doors, and Con wanted to see the doctor's face when he walked out, because in that moment before he searched for Forest's next of kin, the plain truth of the situation would be plastered on his features.

"Make it quick, Kiki." His sister stood in front of him, and Con was doubly glad she'd gotten her height from their mother, because he could see right over her head. With one eye on the doors and a drifting attention area around Kiki's face, Connor said, "I don't know when they're going to be done with him."

"I'm not going to talk to you like you're a civvie, Con. I need to know your impressions—especially about Ackerman. Okay?" Kiki didn't wait for her brother's consent, calling up her case notes with a tap of a stylus on her tablet's screen. "Let's start off with Ackerman. No past history of drug arrests, although his adopted father was a known pothead. Medical marijuana license issued to Franklin Marshall, and he apparently debated opening up a dispensary but never followed through."

"And?" Connor frowned. "What's that got to do with Forest?"

"Do you think there was any validity to the drug tip you guys got on Marshall? From what I can tell, you've been around Ackerman a lot in the past couple of months. You'd have had time to observe any traffic."

"I think the strongest thing he does is booze," he said, shrugging. "His apartment's clean of pot stink, and there wasn't any paraphernalia lying around."

"So you've been in his place? Above the studio? Could something have been hidden there? Maybe you didn't see it."

"There's barely enough room for a flea to turn around in that shit hole." The door bumped out, and his heart seized on that slight ripple, but it was only the air-conditioning kicking in. "Most druggies will use at home. I came through the door first after the shooting, so he wouldn't have been able to stash anything from me. Not enough time. There was nothing there, Kiki. Not even a whiff of pot."

"He's listed as a professional drummer. You think a musician isn't going to take something if it's offered to him?"

"I'll be sure to ask Kane and Sionn that next time I see them. They might want to be on the lookout for Miki and Damie's stash," Con shot back. "What are you leading around to, Kiki? That he's involved in some shit Marshall left for him? Because I haven't seen it."

"Let's talk about the van, then—stolen from a Canadian couple who drove it down from Vancouver." She consulted her notes. "Talk to me about the first thing you thought when you saw it."

"Truth? I thought someone couldn't park." He stopped to recall what was on his mind when he'd seen the van jump the curb. "I didn't think it would keep going. There's a cash machine across the street from the Amp that's got a camera. Did you get any footage from it? It's not a lot of street between the building and the corner. Maybe they got something on a feed?"

"It's been requested. Hopefully the bank manager won't be a douche, and their legal department will just hand it over. I've got a witness saying they saw a person—maybe a man—but he had on a hooded sweatshirt, so she didn't get a good look at his face. That's why I was hoping you'd spotted him. Maybe you remember him? She said he was walking with his shoulders hunched over—like he'd been scolded."

"Probably busy hiding his face." Connor didn't want to admit to Kiki he'd been more focused on Forest than paying attention to the surrounding area. Not yet. It was too *new*. He wanted to soak in his feelings first, and then there was the terror of Forest's injuries. He was worried too sick to focus. "No, I didn't see that guy. Could have been hidden by the van. Depending on the angle. That thing was huge and skewed at the right angle; it took up a lot of the open visual."

Talking to Donal was one thing. Sharing his intimacies with his siblings would have to wait. He had no idea when and how he was going to tell his family. Although, considering he'd spent a good amount of time exploring Forest's mouth after the wall collapse, he probably should give it some thought—like what the hell to say to his mother.

"How about someone from his past? Maybe someone he knew from the system?" Kiki tapped through her screens. "He was in eleven homes before Marshall petitioned to foster him. Mom's got a sheet longer than a California king, mostly soliciting but a few drug busts. Kid was on track as a repeat, but I guess Marshall put an end to that. Maybe she got into something and it's coming down on him?"

"I've not—" Connor stopped himself. "You opened his juvie?"

"Yeah, I opened his juvie, Con," Kiki sniped back. "It's my damned job. I do things like open files and dig into people's shit so I can figure out why someone's killed innocent bystanders, and here's a news flash, even if they *aren't* innocent bystanders, I dig around in the shit anyway, because no one deserves to be murdered, including your friend Forest."

"Look, I don't know what the fuck is going on, Kiki." He scraped his hands through his hair, suddenly realizing it'd grown out long enough to tug on. "Forest—he hasn't done anything to get this kind of shit left on his door. Anything he did as a kid? It's gone, water under the bridge."

"Really? What the fuck aren't you telling me, Con? Why the hell are you circling the wagons around this guy?" Height wasn't the only thing his sister'd inherited from their mother. No one in the family could shake Kiki off something once she'd gotten her teeth into it, and usually it was a quality Connor admired in her. At that exact moment, it wasn't her most appealing trait.

Stepping in closer to her brother, she whispered hotly, a low hiss only loud enough for the two of them to hear. "Give me one damned good reason why I shouldn't ask you what you're doing with a guy who by all accounts is a piece of trash more than a few guys fucked, balled up, then tossed away? Because it doesn't make sense to me, Con. Not one fucking bit of sense."

HE HURT everywhere.

Well, Forest amended, not in some places he'd normally hurt after waking up feeling like he'd been beaten half to death, but it was pretty close. No, he thought as he blinked away the sting of tears in his eyes, he felt more like the times he'd been shoved in a dryer and endured the tumble after his foster father turned it on.

But for the life of him, he couldn't remember which one had done it.

"Can you hear me, Mr. Ackerman?" A man spoke. Then a bright light flashed over his eyes, and Forest tried to shut them, only to find one of his lids was pressed up by someone's cold finger. "Pupils are responsive. Forest, can you—"

"Yeah, I hear you." He tried blinking again, wresting away the control of his eyelid from the man's finger. "Roger, Roger."

"Do you mind if I call you Forest?" The man continued his examination, probing at Forest's hips and side.

"Sure," he said through his chattering teeth. "It's too fucking cold."

It took Forest a moment to realize where he was. A hospital. One that didn't seem to mind also doubling as a meat locker. He didn't just hurt, it was also cold, and more than a little of the room's iciness crinkled pain through his bones. Shivering, he tried burying himself under the blankets but found he was lying pretty much bare to the breeze, draped only in a hospital gown that left his naked ass stuck to the sheets.

"I'm sorry. I promise I'll make this quick," the man said.

"Yeah, I've heard that before," Forest muttered to himself. "Usually they were the ones doing a dip and dash."

Forest could make out the man's face, and then the fuzziness around his vision cleared enough for him to see. A name tag pinned to the balding man's blue scrubs declared him to be Doctor Wyatt, and Forest nearly jumped out of his skin when the man's almost too warm hands pressed down into his abdomen. Someone stood to the side, just out of Forest's cloudy field of view. The grizzled older man flashed a smile at Forest when they made eye contact. Forest couldn't tell if he was a nurse or another doctor, but it didn't really matter. He needed to find his clothes and get the hell out before they charged him five hundred dollars for an aspirin he never swallowed.

If he could only get his legs to work.

"I can't move—" His knee jerked up, and Forest nearly nailed the doctor in the chin. The other man—an attendant according to his hospital badge—moved in to help Forest get his limbs under control. His leg muscles had another spasm, and the older man massaged Forest's shins, his fingers working to get Forest's blood flowing.

"I'm almost done. Just making sure nothing's making Rice Krispie noises," Wyatt murmured. "You've been out for a couple of hours, which is a bit of a concern since you arrived with a linear skull fracture. We're going to keep you overnight, and we've been running tests just to make sure you don't have internal bleeding. I need to ask you a couple of questions. Is that okay?"

"Sure." Unless the doctor had a sudden urge to calculate how many apples little Susie had after a hurricane came by at sixty miles an hour. He'd never been able to figure out the whole tossing words in a math problem.

"Do you know what day it is? Do you know where you are?"

"Sunday." Forest tried to find the date in his memory, but his head began to throb, and he gave up. "And I'm in a hospital freezing my nuts off."

"Who's the governor of the state, do you know?" Wyatt left off feeling Forest's ribs and went back to another pass of his flashlight over Forest's face.

"I gave up keeping track after John Pepys died in that tragic gardening accident," he drawled. "Unless the guy comes around and tells me I've won the lottery, it doesn't make much of a difference to me."

"So, current events, then?" Wyatt frowned. "How about—"

"What happened to Stumpy Joe Childs?" the attendant asked suddenly.

"Choked on vomit, allegedly, but not necessarily his own," Forest responded automatically. "Because you can't really dust for vomit."

"Kid's fine, doc." The attendant's sun-weathered face crinkled under his broad grin.

"Good. I'm done. Let's get some blankets on him now." Wyatt dodged the blow like a master, straightening his glasses. The two men helped spread a stack of warmed covers over Forest's shivering body, and then Wyatt pulled a chair up to sit next to the hospital bed.

Forest didn't care that the man was sitting too close to him for comfort or that the attendant turned the room lights up before he left. All that mattered in that moment was the blankets' heat spreading into his body and the sudden relief he got as his joints and muscles loosened.

"I'm going to want to do a couple more tests—just some blood work because your pressure's a bit low—but I wanted to talk to you about the man waiting for you." Wyatt had on a face Forest liked to call the tree hugger. He'd seen its sympathetic variations in social workers and new teachers who hadn't been dragged down by years spent working in the system. "He says his name is Connor—"

"Morgan. He's out there?" If he hadn't already been on his back, Forest would have fallen over in shock. "Shit. That's—kinda cool. Damn."

"I just need to reassure you that you're safe here," the doctor continued. "He says he's a close friend of yours, but—I have to be honest with you, Forest, your CAT scan results are… troubling. I don't want to let you go back into a situation where you're going to be hurt."

"Hurt?" Forest's head ached harder, and he struggled to get his hand out from under the heavy blankets. "I think a wall fell on me. Didn't it? Last thing I remember was Con showing up, and then all of a sudden—bricks."

"The injuries I'm concerned about aren't from the accident today, Forest. I'm talking about the ones you got earlier." Wyatt's face grew graver, and his eyebrows fought the wrinkles on his forehead for dominance. "You've had major trauma to many of your bones and joints. Those weren't from accidents. Someone deliberately hurt you, Forest. And from what I can make out, pretty badly. Do you want to tell me about that?"

"Not fucking really." The doctor didn't know what he was asking. It was like casually suggesting Forest strip naked and roll around in broken glass threads. Then for good fucking measure, taking a bath in the

Dead Sea. He didn't want to think about the fists that made those breaks, especially since, other than his mother, he didn't even remember a lot of their names. Shaking his head, he said, "Yeah, no. Look—"

"Part of my job is to make sure that once you walk out of here, you're not going back to a very dangerous home situation." The doctor leaned closer, and Forest smelled the mint on his breath. Placing his hand on Forest's arm, Wyatt said, "I can't let you go home with that man out there if he's the one who tore you up like this. It wouldn't be right."

"Dude, most of this shit is old," Forest grumbled. "Long before Connor came around. A lot of it's from… just shit that happened, you know? It's not Connor. Hell, can't you tell how old the crap is? Like, isn't it healed over or something?"

"I don't know how long you've been with your friend, Connor," Wyatt said softly. "You're very young, Forest, but I've seen men… take in younger boys and think they can do what they want with them. I don't want that for you."

"Okay, way off base," he protested from his prison of blankets. "Connor didn't do jack shit to me. Hell, I'm pretty sure if I even told him what some of my fosters did to me, he'd hunt them down and kill them."

"I've talked to him," the doctor admitted. "He's aggressive—"

"He's a cop!" He was too tired to fight off any more of the doctor's insinuations, but the idea of Connor doing to him what many of his foster parents did turned Forest's stomach. "No, really—"

"Forest, I'm saying these things because someone has to. Just because someone is a police officer, it doesn't mean they are going to treat people nicely. A lot of violent people seek out a career in law enforcement because it gives them a sense of power." Wyatt patted Forest's arm again.

"Yeah, I know."

He'd spent a good portion of his time on the street hiding from a couple of cops. Not because they'd take him in to CPS, but because those were the assholes who usually wanted something hot wrapped around their dicks and not pay for it. They were also good for a beating when Forest refused them, and he'd learned that lesson really quickly. Never say no to a cop unless he had a clear shot at running away.

Marshall had spent too many years fighting to break Forest of the habit of running. He'd run often, slinking into the underground and falling back into what he'd been doing before Frank found him. It was a familiar life. One he felt comfortable with. And every time someone knocked Forest's brain loose from his skull, Frank'd been there to pick up the pieces, dragging Forest back to the Sound until he finally just got tired of running.

"Really, not Connor. He's a white hat. Shit, his mom probably knitted it for him." Forest snorted, and that set his head off again. "Hell, the only reason I'm shocked he's out there is because I figured he must be sick of my shit by now. This is, like, the third time he's dragged my ass out of the fire. At some point the guy's just going to get up and walk away."

"I don't think so," Wyatt disagreed. "From my conversations with him, I get the feeling that he's not going anywhere, Forest. No matter how hard you push or how many brick walls fall on you. He doesn't seem the type of man who is going to just let you go."

CHAPTER NINE

Don't talk to me about your God
I don't need your broken bread
Not for my soul
Not for my heart
Not for my countless sins
You want to give me something?
Something to save my wicked soul?
Give me the same as you've got
Loving who I want, and leaving me alone.
—Freedom Torn

"SOME STUFF isn't any of your business, Kiki," Connor responded. "Do I want to find out who's fucking with Forest's life? Yeah. Do I think the shootings and this van are connected? How can they not be?"

"Random fuckery is never random," she agreed with a nod. "They've got to be connected. I just don't know how, and the only common denominator I've got between your raid and my cases is Forest Ackerman."

"The property?" Connor mused. "But it's not like anyone's going to try to drive him out. It's not like it's on the bay. It's Chinatown."

"Chinatown's stepping up its game there, Con," Kiki replied. "All of the old-world flavor but with Wi-Fi and boba shops. Your boy Forest is sitting on a big chunk of property, and most of it is a parking lot where someone left his father's shot-up body, then blew up the man's RV. You don't think that could be a big Get-The-Fuck-Out sticky note? It could be they didn't know Marshall had a son, or they figured Ackerman could be forced out easily enough."

"He hasn't gotten anyone offering to buy the place." He made a face, remembering they'd never really talked about the corner lot. "Shit, it'd be a way to drive the price down, but Keeks, it's Chinatown, not Rock Ridge. The drugs, yeah. I can see that, but who the hell would kill a guy for a half block of property?"

"That's why I get paid the big bucks—to dig this shit out while you break down doors and take names." She studied her brother for a moment, and Connor definitely saw a bit of their mother in her assessing stare. "I just feel like I'm not getting the whole story out of you, and that pisses me off, Con. If it's anything about the case—"

"It's not about the case," he promised. "And the biggest problem is that you're my little sister, the same brat who spent most of her life digging up shit on me so she could tattle to our parents. It's hard for you to break a lifetime habit of sticking your nose into my business."

"Promise me you'll tell me if you find out something about the case," Kiki pressed. "And that you're not going to go break someone's head in because they've messed with your friend."

"I can give you the first, Keeks," Connor rumbled. "But the second? I don't think that's a promise I can keep."

"I'll take what I can get," she conceded.

"Mr. Morgan?" The bespectacled, balding doctor barreled out through the ward doors, his coat flapping behind him. "Sorry, Lieutenant, isn't it? I'm Doctor Wyatt."

"Morgan's fine," Connor replied softly. "Forest? How is he?"

"He's awake and doing well. We're just going to do some blood work to rule out some things, and then he'll be set up in a room." The man flipped through a sheet of notes on his pad. "You'll need to have yourself named his domestic partner on his paperwork, but just so you know, we're keeping him overnight just as a precaution. He's got a linear skull fracture, nothing overly serious, but still, a fracture is a fracture. He's young and strong, so he'll heal up in a couple of days."

"Fracture? Skull fracture?" Connor chewed on his lower lip. He kept quiet about not being Forest's partner much less boyfriend, and he shot Kiki a telling look before she could butt in. "How bad?"

"Very slight. Nothing deep, but still, just something we want him to let heal up with rest. You'll have to watch him for any signs of dehydration. He might want to get out of bed and do laps around the block, but don't let him. A week of rest would do him good. One of the nurses will let you know when you can see him. For right now, sit tight and maybe get some coffee down at the cafeteria. It'll be about an hour and a half before you can see your partner."

"We're not—" The doctor was gone before Connor finished his sentence, and behind him, his younger sister suppressed a snorting giggle. Relief flooded through him, and a tightness he didn't know he'd built up in his chest suddenly deflated, unraveling with the doctor's prognosis, but his sister's chortle annoyed him. "Shush it, Kiki. You've got nothing to be laughing at."

"I can't see you in *any* kind of domestic partnership, man or woman. You're too much of a hardass." She gave in and barked out a short guffaw. Her phone chirruped from her pocket, and Kiki glanced at it, moaning when she recognized the number. "Shit, it's Mom."

"Better answer it. I left the dinner early. She probably wants you to swing by and take home part of that fatted calf she had slaughtered for Damien and Miki." Connor grinned at his sister's wrinkled nose.

"I'm just going to head there." Kiki pointed her finger at her brother. "Don't think this is over. I'll tell Mom you're okay. I bet the phone call wasn't so much about if I ate dinner as it was making sure you don't need anything."

"I think she already sent *that* cavalry," Connor murmured with a slight grin. A familiar Morgan-shaped man ambled out of the elevator and spotted Connor. Waving as best he could while holding two large cups of steaming coffee, he headed over to the siblings, his attention flicking from side to side as he took in his surroundings. Con punched his brother on the arm when Quinn got within reach, scoffing at the younger man's dramatic gasp of pain. "Look who the cat dragged in."

"Mom's cats wouldn't drag anything in without chewing it up first," Quinn murmured, leaning over to kiss their sister on the cheek. "Hello, Kiki."

"Hi, Qbert." She hugged Quinn, then tugged at the oddly striped long scarf wrapped several times around his neck. "Hate to tell you this, but this looks a little gay."

"Really? I was going for very gay. I wouldn't want anyone to think I'm wishy-washy about it." Their soft-voiced middle sibling looked at the knitted wrap trailing down his long body, its tassels brushing his thighs. "Next time I'll wear the celery brooch Ryan gave me."

"And on that note, you're on your own with the family freak, Con," Kiki said, slipping around their brother. "I'm going to go fight bad guys—right after I grab some dinner at the 'rents' house."

Connor caught the flicker of discomfort in Quinn's green eyes as she passed. It was gone before Kiki turned to wave at them, but he'd seen it just the same. Unlike the rest of the Morgan clan, Quinn strayed from civil service and went straight into academia, riding on the glory of his doctorates and steel-trap brain. Still, there was no question he was a Morgan. He shared their father's dark hair and bone structure, but his face and enormous emerald eyes leaned toward their mother's ethereal beauty. His lanky body was muscular under the loose clothing he liked to wear, but in a clan of giants, Quinn was their runt—a six-foot-tall, lean poet amid battle-scarred, thickly built warriors.

He was also one of Con's favorite siblings—and not just because he brought Con coffee.

Next to Kane, Quinn was the brother Connor simply *liked*. A curiosity of being an unobtrusive thinker in a strong-willed and loud family, Quinn watched and dissected, sometimes taking a well-honed word and using it to pierce through a family discussion. He was the cat among the wolves, and one that wasn't quite right in the head for most. Still, Connor was fond of his younger brother, amazed at the beat he marched to and the world only Quinn seemed to live in. He also knew the incredible darkness Quinn fought off at times and had been there during the steepest of his brother's malignant depressions.

Quinn was their most fragile Morgan—and yet the strongest, living life on a slant but refusing to slide down its hill.

Still, Kiki's careless words found their mark.

"She didn't mean to call you freak," Con said softly.

"Sure she did," Quinn refuted calmly. His voice didn't waver, a simple acceptance of the label plastered on him by another sibling. "It's one of the better F-words I've been called. Coffee?"

"God, I love you. Thank you. The swill downstairs is like drinking battery acid."

"It's so you don't get comfortable staying. This isn't a place someone should let become home. It makes leaving the dead harder." Quinn's attention was already wandering, taking in the people and conversations around him. "How is your friend doing?"

"Good. I'm waiting for them to let me go see him." Connor eyed his brother. "The question is, what are *you* doing here? Mum send you to shake me loose?"

"Nope, Da did." Quinn sipped his coffee. "Said you probably needed someone to talk you down off the walls."

"And he sent you, huh? Good choice."

"Kane probably wanted to go home and fuck Miki," he remarked. "Second string."

"You're never second string, Q," Connor replied softly. "I've got about an hour to kill. Want something to eat?"

"If I won't drink the coffee here, what makes you think I'll eat something? Coffee is just beans and water. They don't even touch it. Why would I risk them actually *making* my food?" He shuffled, running a hand down his thigh. The black corduroy squeaked slightly under his fingers, and Quinn looked up at Connor. "Remember when I tried to convince you ghosts lived in my corduroys because they moaned?"

"You had some odd ideas as a kid." He laughed.

"I have odd ideas as an adult." Quinn's sharp eyes were back on Connor's face. "Are you okay? You don't look okay."

His gaze pinned Connor in place, and he cocked his head, seemingly digging through his older brother's defenses with a flick of his eyelashes. Connor waited through Quinn's silence, wondering what scab his brother would find to pick loose from Con's psyche. A second passed, then another, and Connor looked away, unable to fight off the feeling Quinn was peeling him apart to unearth his secrets.

Connor wasn't ready to look at his own shit, much less letting Quinn in, but there his little brother stood, wielding a knife-sharp mind with soul-shattering eyes. After only a few seconds, he was ready to confess all his sins. If he gave Quinn a minute or so, he'd be begging to be forgiven for taking up air someone else could be breathing.

"Shite, your students probably hate your guts. Peering at them all sphinxlike and mysterious." Connor shoved his brother's shoulder, careful not to jostle his coffee loose. "Come walk with me. We can go talk someplace private."

"They should have a chapel here," Quinn supposed. "Sometimes those have antechambers. We can look there or just use the chapel."

"Someone might want to use it to pray in," Connor retorted.

"Ah, Con. Don't you know?" Quinn shot his brother a scalding look. "Nobody actually prays at the hospital. By the time they get here, they go straight to begging and negotiating. The chapel'll be empty as sure as God created the sky."

"HERE?" FOREST asked the nurse as he was wheeled into the room. "Oh man, this is a mistake. I didn't ask for this."

The room was nearly as large as his place above the Sound. It certainly had a better view. Heavy damask curtains were pulled back, showing off a foggy San Francisco skyline. The walls were painted a muted goldenrod, and a tapestry wing chair and its matching love seat were arranged near the picture window, a modern-looking coffee table set between the two for the sole purpose of holding up a bowl of green apples and oranges.

"Fuck the studio," Forest muttered under his breath and fought an IV cord to get his hair out of his eyes. He was still shaky on his feet, but the room was much warmer than the one he'd just been in, and his knees sang the Hallelujah Chorus in thanks. "This is like a damned hotel. Where's the fireplace?"

"Nope, just a private room—no fireplace. You do get your own bathroom, but that comes standard. It's taken care of. No worries." The fifth or sixth nurse he'd had that day—a cheery dreadlocked woman whose sugary smile made Forest's teeth hurt. She helped him into the bed and arranged a mound of blankets around his legs, patting his thigh as she reached for his hand. "Here, let me hook up the monitor to track your heart rate, and I'll be back in about fifteen minutes to take one last draw of blood. Do you want the remote for the television? Or maybe some water?"

"Um sure, either," he replied, then spotted the phone on the stand near the bed. "Actually, can I make a phone call? It's local."

"Hospital, sweetie." She grinned at him. "Call anyone you want."

"Oh, and um… there's this guy—"

"Lieutenant Morgan?" The nurse paused at the doorway, nodding. "As soon as I get your last draw done and some paperwork signed off, I'll tell him he can come in. There's a menu on the rolling table there if you want to pick something for dinner. The cheeseburger's pretty good, but stay away from the green beans. They cook them to death."

"Right, no green beans." He waited until she was gone and then another moment as he gathered up all his courage to grab at the phone to pull it into his lap.

The last number he'd been given was almost two weeks ago. It was done in passing, through someone who knew someone else's friend, but she'd at least made the attempt. Of course, he hadn't actually spoken to her, but there'd been an attempt to keep in touch.

It was more than she'd ever done in the past.

"Not like shit's gonna change, dude," he muttered. "Fucking hell, I don't want to do this."

The rational part of his brain was still scolding him even as his fingers flew over the number he'd committed to his memory a while ago. It'd been the most recent of a long string of numbers, each only lasting a few weeks, as if they were hothouse roses.

He was taking a chance dialing the number now. It was nearly past the expiration date of most of the numbers she'd given him before it, but Forest wanted something—still and forever something—even if his gut knew it would never be the reality he'd wanted.

Still—that chance. And even greater of a chance that she'd be sober enough to talk—if she picked up at all.

It rang, and before Forest's brain could pull the plug on his nonsense, a woman's husky voice tickled his ear, her tongue stumbling over her words as she spoke. He closed his eyes, willing the tremors in his bones to go away before he responded.

"Hey, Mom."

"Forest? That you, baby?"

"You got any more kids?" He snorted. "'Sides me, anyway?"

There was the sound of a lighter being scratched on, then a familiar suck of a cigarette. As if on cue, she coughed, a raspy boom into the phone, and his mother cleared her throat. "Always such a fucking smartass. Should have slapped that mouth off of you when you were still short enough for me to reach."

"Yeah. Probably," he agreed, despite sitting under a swaddle of blankets hoping to leech the cold out of his badly healed bones. "You got a little time? To talk, you know?"

"What time is it? Hold on. I've gotta go take a piss." More noises, a rattling, then she came back to the phone. "Shit, not even seven yet. Whatcha calling for? Frank's still dead, right? Fucker didn't come back like he's all Jesus or something?"

His mother laughed, and Forest once more felt the stab of her sour personality into his guts. Sighing, he ran his fingers through his kind-of-gritty hair as he tucked the phone under his chin. He didn't laugh.

He just waited for her to finish righting herself before speaking.

It was always the same. No, he corrected, sometimes it was worse. At least this time she knew who he was. There'd been a very uncomfortable call once when she thought he was someone she'd hooked up with before, and nothing said Merry Christmas like your own mother describing how she could suck a cock down into her throat. Of course, since it seemed to be a talent she'd passed onto him as well, Forest really couldn't complain.

"No, really, why're you calling?" she rasped.

"Things have kind of been shitty the past couple of weeks. Okay, maybe a bit longer than that," he confessed softly. "Guess I wanted to hear you. See how you were doing. Someone drove a van through the Amp's wall. Kinda got a bunch of it on my head. So, I'm in the hospital. And I was wondering—"

"Um, honey, don't take this wrong, but...," she hedged, grumbling a bit under her breath. "Don't think I'd be able to make it over there, you know? I mean, I get up early to get some stuff done, so there's money in my pocket, right?"

She didn't even know where he was, and his mother was making excuses. The hospital could have been right fucking next door to whoever's place she was crashing in, and she couldn't be bothered to poke her head out the window and spit in his general direction.

Forest blinked, hating she could drive him to tears without even being in the same room. Wiping at his face, he shuddered in a breath, for once thankful of the hospital's cold air. It helped freeze his lungs a bit and still his heart, deadening him enough to talk.

There were angry words he wanted to spit at her—hot, foul, leaden darts that might penetrate her skin and lodge into her already dead heart. Instead he said what he always said whenever she turned away from him. "Sure, no problem. I know you're busy."

"You're okay, though, right?" Another raspy drawl and she barked a laugh through the phone. "'Course if you'd died, I wouldn't have to be working anymore, would I? How much did old Frankie leave you? Everything, right? That coffee shop and shit."

"The coffee shop's a mess, Mom. That's where I was when the van came through the wall. It's going to cost a bit to get it fixed." The insurance would handle the repairs, but he didn't want her to know that. "But I'm doing okay."

Even if the insurance didn't cover the new damage, Frank's death left Forest decently off, and that made his mother dangerous. For all his hippie radical leanings, Frank's family liked making money, and he'd banked most of everything that came his way over the years, letting it build up under investments and properties. Giving his mother that kind of information would be like releasing a shark in a kiddie pool filled with bleeding minnows. Nothing would survive her rapacious appetite, including the pool keeping them alive.

"Tell you what, when you get out of there, drop me a line and we can go party." She sounded cheerful, as if recalling a better time. "'Member when we worked down off the Tenderloin that one time? God, that was a good week. We were like an all-you-can-eat buffet—something for everyone. One stop and we had everything you could want, remember that?"

They'd done a lot of things together during the times he'd run from Franklin—most of which he didn't remember. The Tenderloin crawl she began to rhapsodize on was a memory he couldn't shake if he wanted to. Whatever he'd been on during those few days seemed to have taken a chisel to his brain and then cold-flashed the whole time with thick cement, immortalizing every single moment he'd spent in his mother's company.

It'd been the last time he'd run from Frank. The very last time he'd had to crawl back to the man he knew was going to toss him away and beg for another chance.

If only Frank'd let him beg, but all the man did was pick Forest up and clean him up before rolling him into a clean bed—alone. They'd never spoken about anything without Forest bringing it up first, but after he'd spent two days throwing his stomach up against the bathroom walls, Frank finally spoke out.

"She's going to kill you, kiddo, like one of those animals who eat their own young," the man said, holding Forest's hair back from his face as he did his best to toss out the water he'd just gotten down. "Maybe not this time, but maybe the next. I'm always going to be here for you, kid, but I don't want the next time I hold you, it's to lie you down into a box. That'll kill me, dude, and you've got so much fucking talent in those hands of yours, it'll be a shame to waste it on a whore—even if it's the whore who gave birth to you."

He'd been right. Frank'd always been right.

"So, you up for it?" His mother broke through his memory of Frank's sad eyes and mournful voice. "It's been a while since we've done that. It'll be good."

"Nah, I think I'll pass," Forest choked around the lump in his throat.

"Your loss. Unless you've gotten uglier since the last time I saw you, you could still pull some in."

Another scrape of her lighter and she'd moved on to her next cigarette. "Not like when you were younger. Shittiest thing that happened to you was getting so tall. It fucking killed you."

"I've had shittier." He wanted her off the phone. He'd taken in as much as he could handle, and calling his mother turned out to be a trip down a rusty-tack-strewn memory lane. It was never going to change—she was never going to change. It all came down to how much she could get out of people and how much of his ass she could sell—because selling her own tail wasn't enough. "They're coming to do more tests on me in a bit. You going to be around later?"

"I dunno. I might change this phone. This one's crackly." It sounded fine to him, but reception and hearing was on her list of complaints before she ditched a phone she more than likely stole. "Hey, you got something you can spare? To tide me over. I've got a party I'm going to this weekend. Guy's paying me some bucks to be there. If you can front me, I'll shoot it back to you."

Another small part of him died. Not because his mother hit him up for money. He'd expected that. What hurt was that she saw him as another mark to lie to, as if he hadn't grown up suckling on her lies for sustenance. Hell, her breast milk had been a lethal mix of coke and delusions, and he'd been weaned off that into working the system. To have her pull one on him—a tired old lie at that—angered Forest as much as it saddened him.

He wouldn't give her anything—he couldn't—not unless Forest was willing to contribute to her cooking herself to death.

"I don't have any extra." It wasn't quite a lie, mainly because he didn't know where his wallet was, but she'd suck him dry if he let her. "I would if I could, you know?"

"Maybe they'll figure out a way you can get some cash off of Frank's shit." She laughed right through his lie. "Then we won't have to worry about anything."

He almost offered her a place to crash. They'd spent so much time looking out for one another, it was ingrained. He had someplace safe. He was supposed to bring her into it. It was a habit or just how they'd run together, but Frank'd been right then, and he was right now, even in death. She'd kill him if she got the chance—even if it was by accident, his mother would be the end of him if he opened the door to her poison.

"Keep me in mind, okay?" His mother coughed, and someone said something indistinct next to her. "Look, I've got to go. Seriously, when Frank's stuff comes in, hook me up. I did you more than a few solids before, right? I'll let you know what my new number's going to be."

She was gone before he could say good-bye or even deny any solid she might have done. The cold was back, but this time it burbled up from inside him, streaking out of his damaged heart and into his fingers. His hands grew numb, and Forest flung the receiver, tossing it onto the floor with a clatter. He let the tears hit, feeling the sobbing break out of him in an uncontrollable wave.

Forest swallowed, unwilling to let her have the last good bit of him, but it was already gone, marred by her greasy touch even as he tried to wrestle back what little hope he had of being loved. Rolling over, he curled up on his side and drew his knees in, making himself as small as he could. Even as the IV needle tugged at its taped-down perch in his arm, he pulled in even tighter, anything to keep himself from shattering apart.

"God, I fucking hate you." He bit down into the pillow, tasting the cotton and fiber on his tongue. His sobs shook him, and they grew guttural, animalistic as he fought down his pain. "And why the fuck do I even want you to care?"

CHAPTER TEN

Death kissed me low
Left me on the road so black
Took my brothers up with him
They ain't never coming back
Heaven saw me cryin'
Tearing up my soul inside
Reached down into its golden grace
To bring a Sinner to my side
—Saving a Sinner

THEY FOUND the chapel.

It was as empty as Quinn said it would be, but there were small meditation niches nearby Connor steered his brother to. The brothers found a space with a raised platform filled with large cushions upholstered in what someone decided were peaceful colors. Connor thought they looked more like a game of guess-what-candy-Bobby-puked, but then he'd also nearly coated the walls of his house in a shade of sad brown-cream before his mother stepped in with a shake of her head and paint swatches.

It took Quinn about a second to shed his shoes and plop down into a boneless heap. Connor was much more cautious, easing into the pod-like area, briefly wondering if anyone'd used the space for sex and if he was sitting where he shouldn't be. Then his brother nudged his shin with a sock-covered foot, and Connor lost control of his mouth in a silly grin at Quinn's crossed eyes and wiggling brows.

"Your face is going to get stuck that way," Connor remarked, pushing his brother's foot away.

"You should know. Yours did."

"Oh, so funny," Con snorted, moving a pillow out from behind his back. "Thanks for the coffee. And the company. I meant what I said, Q. You're never the second string. Riley might be, or Brae and Ian, but that's because they still laugh at fart jokes."

"Con, even Da laughs at fart jokes. You've gotten old," he teased, settling farther down into the cushions.

"Aren't you supposed to be the mature one? College professor and all that?"

"Nope, where do you think I learn all those fart jokes?" Quinn winked and sipped his coffee. "So tell me, why are we down here in the hospital? Who are we waiting for?"

"A… friend of mine." Connor picked at the plastic lid on his cup. "Shit's been going down around him and, well, Kiki's pulled his case. Long story short, looks like someone's fucking with him. Or maybe even trying to kill him. I don't know—someone sent a fucking van through his coffee shop. I don't know if they meant to hurt him, or it was just stupid luck he was inside *right* then."

The realization about the danger Forest was in punched Connor in the gut. Suddenly the coffee turned sour in his stomach, and his mind raced for any bit of information he could share with Kiki. Nothing emerged from the confusion in his thoughts other than wishing he could wrap Forest up someplace and keep him safe—a thought more terrifying than a murderer stalking Forest.

And sitting next to him was his oddly construct-ed brother with a mind more complicated than a twen-ty-sided Rubik's puzzle but with a mouth seemingly sealed shut against leaking any secrets.

It was an opportunity for Connor to shake loose some of the troubles he'd come up with, and more importantly, what he said wouldn't work through the Morgan grapevine. He wasn't ready to deal with his mother—no sane man would be—but as he stumbled through his growing awareness, Connor needed a sounding board, not advice, and Quinn was like a gift come down from the heavens.

Or at least from the Morgan living room, sent by a father who always seemed to know what his children needed—even when they couldn't find their way out of an open paper bag.

"How did you know you were gay?" It wasn't where he'd planned to start, but his brain obviously had other ideas, picking up the ball and running off in a wild stumble. "I mean… shit…."

In true Quinn fashion, his brother didn't blink at the curveball he'd been thrown. Instead, he chewed on his lower lip for a second and replied, "Guess I never thought about it. It just always was there. The first time

I acted on it was when I kissed Chance Delany when we were seven."

"You kissed one of the Delany boys?" He sat up and stared at his brother. "Dude, we spent years warring with them as kids."

"How do you think it all got started?" Quinn saluted Con with his coffee cup. "The one and only time my preinstalled gaydar worked. He's a go-go dancer or something down in San Diego now. He came by last summer to apologize for siccing his brothers on me."

"Well, fuck. Those assholes screwed with you every time Kane and I weren't around."

"They thought I was going to make their brother a faggot." Quinn dropped the word as if it meant nothing, but Connor winced at hearing it ring out between them. "He was that way when I found him. I just wanted to see what it felt like to kiss a boy."

"They made your life miserable, Q."

"They didn't." His brother shrugged off the years of sporadic bullying. "Instead, they made their brother feel like shit for being different. Now his whole family pretends he's dead, while mine just makes fun of how I think sometimes. Who's the one with the miserable life?

"Until they started in on Chance, I didn't even know I was different—not, like, really different. I just thought my wife would be a husband when I grew up," Quinn continued. "I saw what they were doing to Chance, and I thought that's how the family would be to me too. It's why it took me so long to just say it out loud—that I liked other guys."

"You never should have been made to feel that way," Con replied softly as he drew his brother into a fierce one-armed hug. "You're a fucking Morgan. We don't do family like that, Qbert. You have nothing to be ashamed of. Then or now. Da had to remind me of that today. I seemed to have forgot."

"I wasn't ashamed of being gay until the world told me I should be. I'm over it now." He shrugged at Connor's disgusted snort. "So then, big brother, if I'm not something to be ashamed of, why are you having trouble admitting you like this Forest?"

Once again, Quinn laid him out, and Connor fought to breathe. Quinn studied him—as if Connor were a brightly colored bird having just flown out of a gray-fogged San Francisco morning, a splash of movement in the still, dead quiet. Connor had to look away from his brother's nearly emotionless face. Everything he'd been wrestling with—from his attraction to Forest to the panic he'd lose the blond to a pile of falling bricks—overwhelmed Connor, and he couldn't fight off the swaddle of fear choking him.

He stumbled over his tongue, caught in a spiderweb trap laid out by the family's master spinner, and Connor nearly congratulated his brother on his successful capture. But then, perhaps all the accolades belonged to their father, the man who'd sent Quinn on his path.

"Don't look surprised, Con." Quinn made a face at him. "This gaydar thing is like a broken clock, only right twice a lifetime. If it worked better, I wouldn't have such a shitty social life."

"How'd you know?"

"Does it matter? Are you thinking of hiding it?"

He thought about it for a second, then said, "I don't know what I'm thinking. Things are moving way too fast for me, Q."

Quinn might not have chosen to be a cop like the rest of them, but it didn't mean he hadn't picked up their father's tricks along the way. He stayed silent and merely waited, letting Connor fill the empty space between them.

Connor spilled, uneasy with the role reversal, but he had to admit, between the two of them, Quinn would be the one who could help him sift through what he was feeling. Even if his baby brother sometimes had an odd way of scraping tender parts of a person's psyche until everything felt bleeding and raw.

"I met Forest right after he found out his da was murdered. I didn't even talk to him. I just held him when he cried. God, he cried. So fucking much." Connor shoved his welling emotions down, but they rose up anyway, cracking through his stoicism. "He was so damned alone, and something in me—reached out, and I just… *liked* what I saw. So I kept going to him, to see if he was okay, or even just to watch him wake up in the morning and stumble out for coffee. I'm surprised he didn't get me arrested for stalking him."

"You're good-looking and huge," Quinn snorted. "And he's gay?"

"Yeah, that was pretty obvious after the first couple of times I saw him at the Amp. Some of his customers are… very expressive. He flirts right back with them, but shy. Quiet."

"Then yeah, he wouldn't arrest you for stalking him. You're hot. Hell, I'm surprised you didn't admit you were bi before now so you could get laid twice as much."

"It's not like that, Q. He makes me feel… something inside. I don't know what. Like I can't shake the thought of him," Connor confessed. "I don't even know him. It was just one night… one fucking moment and I was lost. It scares the shit out of me. I'm man enough to tell you that. Scares me down to my balls."

"Sounds like the flu." Quinn chuckled. "Or a really scary roller coaster. But is it bad? This thing of yours?"

"I don't know what to do with him—well, yeah, that part," Con amended when Quinn rolled his eyes at him. "That part's not important, and see, that's where the scary fucking shit comes in, because how does *that* part stop being important?"

"Have you ever felt like this before? About anyone else?" His brother was a soft presence next to him, but even a feather became torture when applied properly—and Quinn Morgan certainly knew how to apply himself properly. "Or are you just scared to say you want him *because* he's a guy? Because you think that makes you less than a man? Less than who you thought you'd be?"

"Oh, brother, serpents envy your fangs," Con murmured.

"I do not inject a poison into you, brother, but rather I seek to free you from it," Quinn replied.

"Who said that?" He glanced over at his brother.

"I did. Just now." Quinn waved away Connor's snort. "But isn't that what they do? Use snake venom to cure someone who's been bitten? It's the same thing."

"I'm not sure exactly how it applies here, Q."

"You're not asking yourself these questions, not out loud. So it's me. I'll ask. What the hell are you afraid of, Con?"

"I don't know, and yeah, I haven't… scraped at it, Quinn. It's been looming up around me, and then today—oh, fucking God in heaven—*today*. I thought he was dead, and in that moment, I was gone." Connor set his now empty cup down and stretched out his legs. A quick look at his watch said he had another forty-five minutes to go before the doctors would let him in to see Forest, and the wait itched at his insides, imaginary nettles prickling away at his nerves. "Really, how did you know? And not because I'm ashamed I'm… feeling this way. I've been trying to get my arms around this whole mess from the start."

"First, you've got to stop thinking about it as a mess." His brother smacked Con's thigh with his open hand. The sound echoed through the alcoves. "Second, if you're going to sit here and tell me you don't know what you want, then I call bullshit, because you either want him or you don't want him."

"He's not like a piece of cake, Q. I can't just take a taste and say 'No thank you. Not for me. Don't like this flavor.'"

"He's exactly like a piece of cake," Quinn retorted. "The question is, does it really fucking matter if it's a flavor you're used to or something you really badly want to try? The only person in this that's arguing about who and why is you. It's not going to be easy if you love him. People are assholes, Con. Some people hate when the world doesn't look like they want it to, and they hurt other people."

"This is different," Connor protested, trying to find the words to explain his unease, but he kept coming back to the consuming terror he'd experienced as he dug Forest out of the rubble. "I barely know him, and it's… so fucking huge… this thing. Him. Me. Everything."

"You're not a chickenshit, Connor. You face death and crap every day. You're going to let people you don't even give a shit about tell you who to love." His brother scoffed, drawing his knees up and reaching for his shoes. "You should never play safe with your heart.

It doesn't get to grow if you don't take it out. You break it. You give it away. And sometimes, you kind of hope someone gives it back to you—maybe wrapped up and taped, but better because they held it for a little while."

"Says the man who's never been in love," Connor pointed out.

"No, I have. And you know what? It hurt like fucking hell because I wasn't what he wanted. But I tried. Sometimes, Con, you've got to just try." Quinn sighed, fighting with a knot in his laces. Connor took the shoe from him, then worked the tangle free.

"I don't want to spend my life fighting, Q. I'll admit it." He shrugged. "And I don't even know if this thing I feel for him is solid. Yeah, I've had these kinds of… hits happen to me before. He's not the first guy I've thought about. He's just the one that seems to be digging into me."

"Then isn't he worth fighting for? Aren't you worth fighting for?" Quinn cocked his head at his older brother, unerringly echoing their father. "What you're saying here is, you don't want to go through what I went through—still go through sometimes. You don't want to be called faggot by people you work with or maybe even find 'cocksucker' scratched into your car's paint. Is that it?"

"People still call you names?" Connor's head came up, his temper sharpened by Quinn's words. "At work? You're a goddamn professor! At a damned university. Shit like that isn't supposed to happen to you anymore, Q. Not—"

"And you're a cop. You've got a gun. Someone calls you a name, and you could shoot them," his brother snarked. "The most I could do is possibly call their mother something nasty and hope they don't speak Wu."

"I've been on the wrong side of that tongue of yours. And yeah, I could shoot them, or I could just walk away."

"Yeah, you can walk away and not have to worry about someone picking a fight with you because you leaned over to kiss another guy in public. Because it'll be safe. Because you're *so* safe now—like going on drug raids in places God's scared to look at with only a prayer and a gun. That kind of safe. You already spend your life fighting. You're stupid if you can't see that no one is *safe* in this world, Con. You're naïve if you think I am—or anyone else. There's always going to be someone hurting someone else.

"Thing is, you're not a coward. Don't start being one now. You're stronger than that, Con—better than that. Be the brother I know I have. The one who did battle with the Delanys. The one who pulled me off the roof. Even the one who sometimes pushed me onto the dodgeball court in school because he knew I'd enjoy the game even when it scared the crap out of me. Be *that* brother, Con—the brother that won't be ashamed to love another man, even if the world might hate him for it."

"Da told me it doesn't matter who I love so long as I love," Connor whispered.

"Then you're a fucking *idjit* more if you don't take a chance," Quinn declared, taking his unlaced shoe from his brother's hands. "Because no one's more right than Da—and I don't know anyone who loves more than him. No one."

"Ever thought about being a priest, Q? You're damned good at it." Connor grabbed his brother's foot, then tied his sneaker as if Quinn was once again three and looking to his older sibling for help. "And you kind of already dress like one."

"Yeah, but I didn't think I'd like celibacy." Quinn's eyes snapped with humor. "Besides, Quinn Éanna Morgan, gay Irish priest, way too much of a cliché."

FOREST HEARD the door open behind him, but the cold was back, and he hurt in places he didn't even know *could* hurt. The nurse promised pain medications, but he wasn't sure. Especially after swimming in the slurry ocean of his mother's conversation, Forest felt dragged down enough. He didn't want to add a morphine drip to the mix—even if he sorely wanted to drug himself to oblivion so he didn't have to *feel* anymore.

And despite his best efforts, he couldn't get the clammy feel of his mother's proposition out of his mind. It nested there, curling its sticky talons around his thoughts, reminding him of the times he'd been—if not eager, then at least willing—to do anything she'd wanted him to do.

She'd told him more than once she'd been glad she hadn't dug him out like she'd done the other babies she'd almost had. It was her way of saying she loved him—or at least her way of saying she was happy he could provide some kind of income on those days she didn't feel like lying back for sloppy, drunk johns. Forest was never really sure. Or even if he cared one way or the other.

Until he'd called and found he really hoped she would come by. At least for a moment. Anything at all to show he meant something to her. There'd been too many times when he'd hauled her ass out of an unpaid-for motel room when she was too stoned to walk, or the times he'd found her with a needle sticking out of her arm and the cops were banging on their door. He'd grown up knowing how to jiggle loose a soda from a vending machine and how to pull a short-change con. Frank put an end to all that, and he'd been okay for years. He'd even fucking thought about having a cop for a friend—a man who seemed to be there every time he turned around—and probably would turn around and walk away as soon as he understood how filthy Forest really was.

"'Cause that's just how shit is," he mumbled to himself, expecting a nurse to plunge more needles in him and take what little blood he had left in his veins. "Don't get too used to normal, dude. It all just eventually goes to shit anyway."

A large hand on the small of his back startled him, and Forest curled in tighter, instinct driving him in. Then a warm Irish voice poured over him, and the whole drug lust slipped away, replaced with a much more carnal desire.

"Are you asleep there, Forest?" Connor murmured.

"No, I'm… just cold." He couldn't stop shivering. It came in waves, but the cold was insistent, crackling through any heat Forest stored up.

"Hold on, I'll get you a blanket. Be right back," Connor promised.

Forest blinked and turned over to watch Connor digging through the room's closet for more blankets. He came back laden with a thick cover, then neatly tucked it around Forest's prone body. His hands brushed over Forest's thighs and stomach. Connor's touch warmed him more than the blankets, and Forest groaned softly, wishing he could bury his face in a pillow because it felt like his cheeks were on fire—a licking heat thankfully spreading through the rest of him as well.

"Hey, you." Connor patted again. Moving his hand to Forest's hair, he gently pushed a fall of blond out of his eyes. "How are you doing?"

Forest lay there, mute—shocked, really, that the man not only stayed to see how he was but was in his room, probably past visiting hours, and tucking him in as if he'd done it a thousand times before. The man had more siblings than Perdita had puppies. Frank'd loved that damned movie, and he'd seen it more times than he could count. At least he thought it was Perdita. It could have been Ping because the other one was Pongo.

Not remembering a damned cartoon dog's name was suddenly the most important thing in the world, and Forest sniffled, fighting back tears he thought he didn't have in him. He'd just soaked through the sheets before the nurse came back. There shouldn't have been any more sorrow left in him, but there it was, pouring out and sliding between him and a man who shouldn't have been there.

"Okay. A building fell on me, but I'm better now." He was lying. His head hurt. He wanted to whine, and most of all, stop crying. "Thanks for... fuck, everything. You don't have to stay—"

"Look, let's not go there." Connor cut him off, and the man's hands moved again, creating delicious circles over Forest's cocooned body. "I'm here, and they've even got a love seat I can crash on if I need it."

"You've got a life, remember? House and um... wife? Kids?" His head ached too much, and he couldn't recall if there was even a girlfriend on Connor's horizon. "Dog?"

"No dog." Connor shook his head, and his fingers once again found Forest's hair. "They should have cleaned you up a bit more. Feels like you've got grit on your scalp."

"They probably didn't want to shake out my brains. There's very little in there to begin with. Now that I've cracked the case open, they can't get full price anymore. Can't ever open the original packaging." He knew he was babbling, but Forest didn't care. "Hell, you weren't even supposed to be there today."

"I told you I was coming." Connor looked confused for a second. "Wait, I've heard that before. Where?"

"Movie quote. I'll make you watch it someday. You'll either love it or hate me forever."

"You sound like my idiot brother, Quinn. His mouth bubbles out the oddest things." He laughed, rumbling noises as softly comforting as his slowly roaming hands. "He was here, actually. Along with my terrier sister, Kiki."

"God, she's like the fucking Spanish Inquisition," he blurted without thinking. "Fuck, maybe I should have them drug me so I can't talk. Sorry, dude. I know she's your sister—"

"She's a menace," Connor agreed. "But she'll do the job. Kiki'll find who did this."

They sat together in silence, and for a moment Forest could pretend Connor was there for more than just an oddly constructed, misplaced friendship. He promised himself he wouldn't relax, wouldn't depend on the man, but when he dug his hands out of the now toasty covers, Connor's fingers found his, and Forest's heart skipped into a rattle a hyped-up electro drum would envy.

It was stupid that Connor's skin on his made his cock thick and hard.

It was damned fucking lucky the blankets hid it, because from what Forest could feel, the hospital gown they'd given him to wear wasn't good for hiding anything other than maybe his belly button, and even that was suspect.

"Thanks, really. For everything," Forest ventured softly. "You've done so damned much. You really don't have to stay. I mean—"

"I want to stay, Forest," Connor murmured, and his fingers moved, tightening over Forest's in a slow, seductive dance of sliding skin and rasping glides. "I'm going to stay. Maybe even after you tell me to get the fuck out, I'll be here."

"And here you told me I couldn't have you." He laughed it off—that feeling of dreadful hope he'd buried every time it stuck its head out of his soul. Forest couldn't risk it spreading, not if he wanted his heart to survive Connor walking away.

"Yeah, I was wrong about that," Con whispered, shattering Forest's mind as he leaned forward and kissed the corner of Forest's mouth before murmuring, "You'll have me, *a ghra*, for as long as you need me and maybe even long beyond that."

CHAPTER ELEVEN

*Hey D, you ever notice we don't write any
    songs about God?*
*I don't think God's been paying us much
    attention there, dude.*
*Really, maybe. But for all the shit things
    that hit us, life's been okay. Good
    even. Sionn. Kane. Hell, even Brig-
    id when she's not too fucking crazy.
    Kane says he thanks God for me all
    the time. Kinda nice to be in there,
    you know?*
*Oh, is that what I'm hearing when he's
    screaming in the middle of the night,
    Oh fucking God? A prayer? Shit, and
    here I've been thinking you've been
    getting some.*
—Rooftop Writing Session

IT'D BEEN definitely a kiss. Forest was damned sure of it. It didn't last long. And when the damned cheerful smiling woman with her white buck teeth burst in just as Forest was about to take a breath to ask for another, Connor was shoved aside and a long needle was plunged into Forest's unsuspecting IV, sending him off into la-la land before he could tell her to get the fuck out.

If anything, he was more pissed off he hadn't gotten a good taste of the man before the drugs took him under, and when morning hit, as bright and sunny as that damned nurse, he didn't have it in him to ask Connor what the hell happened.

Because Forest suspected he'd been crazy from the pain, and he'd hallucinated the whole thing.

He'd been released into Connor's care, and there'd been a quick chat about getting Forest's things. Problem was, Forest didn't know where exactly he and his things were supposed to be going. Hazy from the mild confusion he'd woken up with, he'd been lost in his thoughts for what seemed like an instant, but suddenly the Hummer was pulling up in front of the Amp.

Now, instead of being able to grill Connor like he'd hoped, the world seemed to be crawling with Morgans, and he couldn't really open up to the one he actually wanted to talk to. Two redheads and a couple of tall black-haired men. He counted four people, and then another man popped out of the back of the building. From a distance he looked to be the other detective Forest met earlier, a supposition kind of confirmed when Kiki, the younger of the two redheads, ambled over to talk to him about something.

The building was a mess. Someone'd covered the front with plywood, but the whole building seemed to be wreathed in crime-scene tape. The two detectives he knew were stomping around the perimeter, debating something, from what Forest could see. The others milled about, and the taller of the two men spotted Connor's Hummer, saying something unintelligible, but it caught everyone's interest and they turned, en masse, to stare at the vehicle.

Then they began to move toward it like a zombie herd drawn to an all-you-can-eat brain buffet.

It was like watching a scene from the *Ten Commandments* or a live-action D&D game with a cleric turning the undead. Connor held up his hand and shook his head. As one, the shambling horde stopped, then slowly backed away. Forest wondered if he could get Con to show up for studio sessions, because if it was one thing he hated, it was gathering up musicians when it was time to play. They were like the mindless dead. Or close enough.

"Dude, you parted them like the Red Sea. I'm impressed." Forest whistled under his breath. "You do the whole salt pillar thing too?"

Connor ignored him for long enough Forest was beginning to wonder if he'd somehow offended him. Sighing, Con gripped the steering wheel tight enough to turn his knuckles white and then let go, sliding his hands down to rest in his lap.

"I've got to talk to you. Before we go out there. Before—shit—before everything." *Dire* wasn't a word Forest thought of often, but a tint of it was in Connor's voice as he spoke. "We need to talk. Well, I need to talk and then see how you're feeling. I hadn't planned on everyone being here, so I'm sorry we're not going to have the privacy I'd wanted."

"And not like you can drive away. We've been seen." Forest eyed the milling small crowd. "They could break out the pitchforks at any time. I guess that's your family."

"Not even half of them," Con drawled. "That's my mum. She's going to take over your life. Whether you want her to or not. She scares the fuck out of Miki, and that's no mean feat. He's not someone easily shaken. The other two are my brothers, Kane and Riley. Kiki, you know."

"And they're here, why?" He cocked his head, taking a quick glance out of the window.

"Because you're not going to stay here. The place is unstable, and I think someone's trying to kill you." Connor's words shocked him, driving Forest into a stunned silence, and what followed did nothing to help his nerves. "And we need to talk about you and… me."

"Yeah, I'm getting a bit confused—"

"You and me both," Connor muttered.

"You're straight—"

"I'm… exploring that." The man shrugged, then turned to face him. "Forest, I need you to listen. Because what I'm going to tell you… what I'm going to ask you is going to be hard. Can you do that? Just hear me out?"

"Yeah, sure." He nodded and tried to dismiss the fact Connor's family hovered outside, their eyes glancing curiously toward the Hummer with every passing moment. "But you kissed me, right? I didn't read that wrong."

"No, you got that part right. Hell, probably the only part of this that's right." Con rubbed at his face for a moment, then reached for Forest's hands.

Con's hands were warm, warmer than his own, and practically engulfed Forest's long fingers. Still, they felt good, and Forest bit his lip before saying, "Okay. Shoot. What's up?"

"I've never dated a man. Hell, I've never even really accepted I've looked at men. These past couple of weeks—with what's happened to you—it's changed…." He exhaled, and his grip tightened. "I got scared when the wall fell in. Like I've never been scared before. All of a sudden, me being—loving another man—didn't seem like such a big fucking deal. It didn't scare me as much as me finding you dead. Because that's what terrified me. That I'd find you under all of those bricks, and I wouldn't have the chance to tell you—I wanted you. I want you. In my life. However I can get that. I don't know."

"But you're *straight*." Forest blinked, unable to process what Connor was telling him. "You—fuck. Dude, you said—Con…."

"I know what I said. And that's why I wanted to talk to you. Because things haven't really changed as much as I've got to man up and accept who I am. Who I want to love. Shit, it changes how the world sees me, but I've got to be honest and say, it shouldn't change who I am." Connor's blue eyes were bright, shimmering in the pale, watery light. "I don't know you as well as I should. Hell, you don't know me as well as I'd like. But there's something about you that sticks with me. You make me want to be brave enough to cross this line and say I want to love a man. The question here is, will you let me have that chance?"

"So you're gay now? Shit, that sounds… I sound stupid." He wasn't going to let go of Connor's hands, but Forest didn't know what to think. In the middle of a shitstorm, he'd somehow found someplace—some-one—to shelter him. But the man needed as much shel-tering as Forest did, and Connor was asking Forest to be the someone to walk with him through his storms. "But you're asking *me* to… *dude*."

"I'm not saying I'm anything other than… well, who I should have been before. Do I like women? Yeah, some of them do it for me. It's just that I was too fucking much of a coward to admit, some guys—you, in particular—drive me crazy too," Connor said rue-fully. "All I'm asking here is for you to just to give me a chance… that's it. While I explore who I am. Hell, while I explore you."

Connor's grin was lopsided, and Forest spotted a tiny chip in one of his front teeth. It made the large man human. More human. Because up until then, Connor only needed a giant *S* on his chest, and Forest wouldn't have taken much convincing to believe Con was a su-perhero. Not that he needed any convincing at all.

"Have you seen you?" Forest whispered. If he'd thought the Amp's walls falling on him nearly killed him, he hadn't even contemplated the danger of Con-nor Morgan coming out to him in a Hummer while his family looked on. "You're like… sex and muscles and hot. And Irish. God, the accent. Kills me. And you dug me out of a fucking building! I'm having a hard time believing you'd want *me*."

"Have you seen you?" Connor parroted, laughing at Forest's wrinkled nose and snorted disgust. "You're funny and a little bit too quiet, but I like making you laugh. It's like a small gift—honeycomb for my heart. I'm finding I've got a preference for rough-around-the-edges, handsome blonds. I like that it doesn't feel like I'm going to break you. Hell, you've survived a wall, so I'm hoping you'd be willing to try surviving my bad attempts at sex. Because I won't know what I'm doing. It'll all be new for me."

"You're a virgin?" Forest eyed him. "Yeah, pull the one between my legs. Like you've never worked that dick into someone."

"Heh, no." Connor barked a laugh. "Okay, yeah. Not a virgin, and yeah, the mechanics of sex is the same. Guess I'd also know how to work a cock—yours if I need to—if you want me to. I've worked my own for years."

"I cannot believe I'm having this conversation." Forest finally pulled a hand free so he could rub at his temple. "I'm in a coma, right? My head hurts, and my brain's just walking me through a life simulation so I don't get bored while everyone decides to pull the plug or not."

"No coma," Connor promised. "But if you *are* asleep, maybe this will wake you up."

It was stupid. Probably the worst pickup line Forest'd ever heard. And he'd heard plenty. Mostly involving his ass and money with promises of a cock inside the first to get the second. When he'd gotten older—and just a little bit wiser—his hookups were casual, sometimes little more than a couple of shots of tequila and a head nod toward a back room.

Most of his "dates" included talking. Most had some kind of kissing involved. None—until now—included the possibility of forever.

A forever he wanted to pull over himself the exact moment Connor Morgan's mouth touched his and took Forest's breath when Con inhaled.

So many things were happening at once—too many for Forest to slide into his memory, even if his cracked head was willing to gather it all up anyway. The hands that'd held his a few seconds ago were cupping his face, Con's rough calluses strangely soothing on the tender skin of his neck and jaw. The man's mouth was wicked enough to be illegal, because whomever taught him to kiss had fallen from the heavens to hell. It was a descent from angelic bliss to deliciously sinful, with a stop in between.

He relaxed into the seat, letting Connor push him back into the upholstery. Forest opened his mouth, silently begging Connor to slide in. The man took the invitation and stole more of Forest's lips, nipping at the tip of Forest's tongue before plundering deeper. Forest couldn't breathe—didn't really want to. Connor's mouth was a smooth, powerful glide over his lips, and when their tongues met, it turned into a delicate, sweet dance—a ballet amid the battle.

Those glorious hands were everywhere. Down the sides of Forest's body, then across his hips, holding him down for a moment. Then he shifted so Forest could get his arms around Connor's shoulders. He felt safe and wanton, a curious blend of sweet innocence and hot desire. There was more to sex in Connor's kiss. Odd from a man who up until that moment hadn't really owned up to wanting another man, yet Forest couldn't imagine being anywhere else.

The kiss ended as it began, an explosive pop of Connor sliding around him, and then Forest was left gasping, his body aching more for the man who'd kissed him than for the oxygen his lungs seemed to be demanding. His mouth felt swollen, and more than his head ached. His cock was climbing up his thigh, trapped by his underwear, and his tongue longed for more, missing the feel of Connor's lips and teeth.

Forest was startlingly and suddenly empty, as if Connor'd pulled free of the clench of Forest's body— even if it was only a kiss.

And outside the world continued to spin, although the only sound Forest heard was the crumbling smack of a brick falling clear of the wall and hitting the sidewalk below. He didn't want to look out the window. There was an eerie silence there, and he wasn't sure if he was ready to face it. Not yet. Not when he could pretend his entire life existed in the confines of a giant black square car and the man nearly lounging on top of him.

"So, yeah. That chance? It's yours." Forest swallowed and asked, "Does the family know about the not-quite-straight? The ones probably staring at us right now?"

"A couple of them do," Connor confessed. "None of whom are here. But shite, I guess they know now, don't they?"

"SO...." KANE started off, falling into step with Connor. "A guy."

Just beyond the circle of crime tape, Forest stood with his hands shoved into his jeans. Connor'd begged one of the orderlies to toss Forest's clothes in the wash so he'd have something clean to wear. Most of the bloodstains came out of his T-shirt, but a few spots remained, mottling the already dingy white fabric. His jeans survived pretty much intact, as did his underwear, and Connor'd spent an uncomfortable night knowing the man he lusted for lay practically naked on the bed with only a few blankets keeping his modesty.

The world felt lighter. A bit warier, but definitely lighter. Until he spotted his mother coming toward him, and then the already shy sun took the cowardly way out and hid behind a cloud, taking what little heat it'd been willing to share with it.

"A word with you, Connor Donal Morgan. Kane, you go off and make sure that boy's safe from your sister. I'm going to have a few moments with your brother." Brigid Morgan, scourge of Catholic school nuns and school boards alike, descended on them like a fully armed galleon cutting through pirate-infested waters. For a short woman, she always seemed larger in Connor's mind, probably because he'd grown up with her fierce temper and even fiercer spirit.

There'd be no question of her loving him—he'd never even imagined his mother turning away from him—but oh, he'd get the hide stripped off his ass for not telling her beforehand.

Brigid Morgan hated surprises. Especially when they were about her children.

"You can take her. She's short," Kane whispered into Connor's ear. "I'll feint a block if you need it."

"She'd hand you your ass," Con muttered back. "Run away now, brother. I'll hold her back so you can live. Tell your children of my bravery."

"You brought this down on yourself, Connor. Your bravery's not going to be what I'll be telling my children." Kane slapped his back. "Good luck. I've always wanted to be the eldest. Pity I don't get your room."

"You've already had my room." But Connor was talking to the air. Kane deserted him in a few quick strides, his powerful long legs taking him over to Forest's side. Brigid made it over a stack of bricks, her vibrant red curls practically crackling with energy as she reached Con's side. "Hello, Mum."

He didn't know what he'd expected.

Tears certainly wasn't it.

"Oh, don't cry, Mum," Connor murmured, folding his mother into his arms. "God, please. Don't. Shite."

She clung to him, a tiny tempest stilled by emotions Connor couldn't begin to understand. He held her for a minute, maybe longer. Then she sniffed and mumbled into his chest.

"I can't breathe, you git. Let me go." He didn't, and her arms remained tight around his waist as Brigid looked up at him. "Why didn't you tell me?"

"I just told Da yesterday," Con replied softly. She always smelled the same, a brisk lemon verbena he'd come to associate with mothers in general. "I figured he'd have told you."

"Your da would sooner cut off his own balls than share a secret that's not his to tell." Brigid lapsed into Gaelic. "Tell me what's going on in that thick head of yours, or I'll crack it open to find out."

He laughed, despite the tears and the lump in his throat. "I didn't… know. Well some part of me knew, but I wasn't willing to look at that. Here, come sit down."

They found the stairs, a quiet spot on the side of the building. Sitting beside him, Brigid took his hands, rubbing at them as she spoke, "Talk to me, Con. I don't know where to start."

"I don't know what to tell you. Well, I do. Some," Connor explained. "I went to Da because I felt like I was letting him down—you down. I wanted to be like him—maybe even in some ways, be him. I wanted to be a cop, have a wife and children. Build a good life, but when it came time for the wife bit, I guess it didn't fit as well as I thought it would. I couldn't find a woman I liked as much to be around. Then Forest—God, Mum, Forest. He's a bit like Miki, but gentle, fragile in some ways, but he keeps going. All of the shite that's rained down on him and he keeps going."

"He's stronger than you gave him credit for, then." His mother laughed, a tender sound he loved. "Your da used to coddle me. Treated me like I was breakable."

"When did he stop?"

"Who says he has?" Brigid flashed him a smile. "The question I have for you, son, is why did you think you had to be your da? Where did I go wrong in raising you there? That you'd think—even after you've seen us love your brothers, that you'd hide this?"

"Ach, you raised me fine. I just took a wrong turn in my own head. Maybe Quinn's right, and I was too much of a coward to face the truth until I had something—someone—to lose."

"So Quinn too?" She snorted. "That one's worse than your da. I'm pretty sure he knows why Stonehenge was built, and someone asked him not to tell."

"Mad at me?" Con asked softly. "For not… shite, that's not what I want to say. I know you want me to be happy. I *know* that in my bones, Mum. I guess I should apologize for not listening to what you were telling me all these years. To do the right thing, even if it's difficult. Because that's what this is going to be—hard. For me. For people I work with. I've been a lie, Mum. Pretty much."

"Your life's not been a lie, Connor Donal Morgan," Brigid scolded tartly. "You're the same man you always were. You've just expanded your horizons, as it were. And if anyone should apologize, it's me. I failed you. In some way I failed to teach you how to know yourself. I'm sorry for that. I can't even begin to tell you how sorry."

"Well, now we'll both be wearing matching hair shirts," Con teased his mother, who slapped his knee.

"Your Forest—his family? Are they nice to him?"

"He was adopted by a man—the man in the RV. I told you about him."

"Oh God, then he lost his da." Her face softened, and Connor briefly sent a prayer to the heavens for Brigid to go easy on Forest once she got her hands on him.

"His mother's… I get the feeling she's a shitty piece of work. He's reclusive a bit, Mum. Quiet, then you get him going and he shines up, like the sun out of the clouds. I live for that smile of his. And when he laughs at something I've said, it makes me warm inside," Connor admitted. "I just was too stupid to see it. Not until it was almost too late."

She grabbed him into a fierce hug, and Connor choked on his mother's curls until he could get her red hair out of his mouth. Turning his head, he held her tightly, rocking the woman who'd given birth to him and sent him on his way, always shadowing his footsteps but holding back when he fell. She'd waited for him to stand up, reaching to give him a hand when he'd needed one. He fell less as he got older, and somewhere along the way he'd forgotten she'd always be there, following his path and watching, looking for the times when Connor needed her—even if he wasn't man enough to admit it.

"I want to fix him, Mum," Connor admitted. "And I know I can't, but damned if it's not what I want to be doing."

"Aye, I want to fix all of the ones you boys seem to be bringing home," Brigid replied.

"Well, maybe with this one, you'll get the chance. He needs love, Mum. Like no one I've ever seen. Frank

Marshall tried, I can see that, but it wasn't what Forest needed. Not all of it. He *needs* to know the world's not going to be yanked out from under him. Because he keeps waiting for it. That feeling of it… it fills him."

"Then you and I, we'll have to change that." Brigid let him go and craned her neck, looking up and past Connor's shoulder. "Is that door supposed to be open? The one at the top of the stairs?"

Connor turned, nearly twisting in half to look. The door to Forest's tiny apartment was ajar, enough of a crack for Con to see the bilious green paint someone'd painted the frame. He reached for his gun, dislodging it from its holster, and slowly stood up.

"Go get Kane and Keeks, Mum. Tell them to call it in, and one of them needs to get their ass over here to back me up." Connor took a step up and motioned his mother back when she opened her mouth. "Go. Please. No arguing. And if you could please keep Forest to the front. If someone's broken into his place, I want to see how bad they left it."

He climbed the rest of the way, taking the stairs carefully. Keeping his Glock down, Connor eased into the apartment, using his shoulder to push the door open. It gave him just enough light to see the former storeroom, and Connor didn't like what he saw inside.

The place was trashed. Anything edible in the fridge was lost. Its contents had been emptied out onto the floor and smeared over the walls and counters. The air was ripe with sour and something else—a metallic taint Connor knew all too well.

No shadows jumped out at him. No one came out of the corner of the room in a rage, holding one of the dull kitchen knives Connor'd used to make them break-fast. If anything, the place was too still—too quiet. The futon littered the carpet, pulled off its frame and ripped to shreds. The drum kit dominating the room didn't go unscathed, and Connor's heart twisted at the sight of its stabbed skins and buckled rims.

While the equipment could be replaced, it was a violation of who Forest was—the one thing Connor knew gave him some peace. He'd spoken of it—of the Zen he achieved when finding the beat of a song—and to see Forest's center twisted apart ached.

Then Connor spotted the slack hand poking out from behind the torn-down drum kit, and his senses went on wide alert. Drawing up his weapon, he stepped in closer, cautiously moving over the debris of Forest's belongings. The hand didn't move, and a faint wet sound reached Con's ears as he drew around the kit and found himself staring down at a long-legged young man, his blond hair sticky with dried blood and his chest jerking up and down as a large rat ate away at the deep, long slice on his throat.

At first glance, Connor's eyes saw another man—blonder and prettier, with a fuller mouth and melancholy brown eyes. Then he blinked, and the image whispered away, leaving only the rat and a dead man at his feet.

Kane came through the door, his weapon drawn, and he glanced first at the kitchen before joining his brother. He must have seen the body as well, because Connor heard him give a slight gasp of shock. Then the room steadied again when Kane's hand clamped down on his shoulder.

"It looks like your boy down there, Con," Kane murmured. "He must have surprised them while they were ripping the place off—"

"Someone came to kill him—Forest, K. I don't know who this is, but I'm guessing whoever slit his throat thought he was Forest. No such thing as coincidence, Kane. Not like this." Connor cut his brother off. "He's not coming back here. Not ever if I have my say in it. We're going to catch the bastard who's doing this. Even if I've got to call in every damned favor owed to me. I'm going to find who did this—who wanted to do this to him—and I'm going to make them pay. With every damned drop of blood in their bodies."

CHAPTER TWELVE

Don't care what you look like
Don't care who you know
Don't want to see you 'round
Don't come down to my show
You're always bringing Trouble
Trouble knocking at my door
Don't fuck with the guys I play with
I don't want you here no more.
—Trouble in Spades

"SOMETHING HAPPENED up there, didn't it?" Forest asked when Brigid came back from her talk with Connor. She'd sent Kane upstairs, a worried frown ushering her son on his way. A brief whisper to Kiki, and then she'd approached Forest. The woman grabbed him, giving him a deep hug, hard enough to rattle his spine.

"I don't know about that, love," Brigid said as she let him go. She sounded even more Irish than her eldest son, a gentle burr roughening her words when she spoke. "But they'll keep you safe. My boy's good at that. In the meantime we'll find you someplace to rest up. Connor's said you've cracked that head of yours open."

She was teeny, and her face was haloed with long red curls. There was a faint scatter of freckles over her pale skin, and her enormous green eyes tilted up, giving her an elfin look. If she'd actually given birth to eight children, no one told her body or her face. If anything, she looked more ready to take on a hoard of Saxons or Vikings, just as soon as she found her sword.

And oh, she could hug.

He was going to cry. Forest knew it. Her hug shook more than his body. It was as if she reached down into the darkest, dankest bits of his soul and touched them with light. He recoiled at first, then sank into her warmth when her arms came at him again, swaddling him tight. Another hug, then a kiss on his cheek when he buried his face in her fragrant hair, and Forest knew he had to pull away or he'd lose any sense of control he had over his tears.

"I can get a hotel room to stay in," he protested softly, wiping his face with the back of his hand. He refused to cry. Hell, he refused to even look at the older woman because he knew he'd cry. "Fuck."

"*No.*" The remaining Morgans spoke as one, a hallelujah chorus mixed with Irish and stubborn. Forest noted the older Hispanic man kept his mouth shut and ducked under the crime-scene tape to take a look at the dining area.

"You can stay with the family. Con's house is barely habitable for a roach," Brigid pronounced. "Have you met the others? Or has Connor kept you squirreled away like a cookie?"

"Brae's the one that squirrels, Mum." The remaining Morgan male held out his hand. When he leaned forward over a pile of debris to shake Forest's hand, his police badge flashed from its spot on his belt. "I'm Riley. Fifth in the Morgan dynasty—too many to kill to take over the kingdom—"

"Too fucking lazy too," Kiki said before continuing her call.

"The virago talking on the phone's my twin, Kiki. Pretty sure we had an older triplet, but he got in her way, and she ate him in the womb. Me, she finds beneath her notice." Riley scoffed at her uplifted middle finger, then dropped his voice to a loud whisper that was practically impossible to ignore. "I think you've met her already. I can see you wincing when she comes near you."

"Yeah. Kind of met her. A little bit," Forest replied, taking a deep breath. Riley was handsome, a clean-cut pirate of sorts compared to his larger, craggier brother. He had the same freckle spray as his mother, but the rest of his face was a more-defined echo of Connor's. He'd spoken to Kane for a moment before going to poke around the remains of his shop, trying to avoid the whole meeting-the-family thing until Connor was around to run interference.

Kiki swore softly and came up to nudge her brother. The affable charmer turned hard, and Forest saw the cop in Riley Morgan emerge. The twins huddled and held a private conference, with Riley motioning to Kiki's phone. Nodding, she pulled back and called out to her partner, who'd somehow found his way through the maze of damage without a speck of dirt on his tailored tweed jacket.

"What's up? Everything okay up there, Keeks?" Duarte approached the twins, and they immediately walled Forest off from their conversation, standing as close to shoulder to shoulder as their disparate heights would allow. They muttered among themselves, a cardinal and two crows chattering about something obviously involving Forest, if the glances over their shoulders were any indication. When Duarte glanced at Kiki's phone, he uttered a succinct, hot curse. "Fucking mother of God."

"Yeah," Kiki agreed. "Let me see if Ackerman can ID the body. That'll give us a jump start on things. If not, we're going to have to wait for the lab to process him out."

"Body?" Forest stumbled back, and Brigid was there, her hands on his sides to hold him up. "What body?"

Kiki closed the small distance between them. "Is there any reason someone else would have been up in your apartment? Did you send anyone to get you something?"

"No, shit. Jules was the only one who knew I'd gone into the hospital, and she went home. They looked her over, and her mom took her home after they re-did her cast. Con got them to wash my clothes, and he picked me up a toothbrush and stuff from the market. No one should have been up there. Shit, I'm barely up there," he replied. "Why? Did they find someone? Shit, *you* said *body*. Is there someone dead up there? Jesus fucking Christ."

He knew his voice was going hysterical. Either the fracture in his skull was deeper than they'd told him, and his brains were leaking out, or Forest was just getting tired of being dragged through life's sudden dramas. Soft hands patted him, and a pair of strong arms wrapped around his waist.

"Listen to what Kiki's got to say, honey." Brigid rolled her comfort over his panic. "She'll tell you what she can, all right? And then we'll go from there. Keeks darling, do you need something from him?"

"I've got a picture, Mum, but if you're not up to it, Forest, then I don't want you to be looking. We can have the lab people try to track him down through fingerprints and the like." Kiki kept her phone down, out of Forest's view.

"If it's someone I know… fuck," he groaned, suddenly sick to his stomach. "Goddamn it."

The woman holding him—Connor's mother, for God's sake—stroked at his hair, refusing to let him be alone in his drowning. He couldn't remember a time when his own mother'd held him like that. Even after some of her guests were done with him, and he'd sobbed from the pain, she'd patted his head and told him he'd better learn to like it because that's pretty much all he was good for. If anything, Forest wanted to yank himself clear of Brigid's arms, feeling like he'd somehow stain her, but it just felt too damned good to be held. Another moment more, then he'd pull away. But that moment never came, and when she gave him a tight squeeze and another pat, the tears he'd banished from his eyes swept back down to wet his lashes.

"You're not a suspect, Forest." Duarte raised his eyebrows at Kiki, and she filled in, "DB is too new. Maybe even right before we got here."

"Do you feel up to it, Forest dear?" Brigid asked softly. "Because you don't *need* to—if you don't want to."

"If I don't—I can do this. Fucking hell. Shit, sorry. I keep swearing—"

"If you're calling that swearing, Mum will teach you to do it proper," Riley drawled. "You're not even close to what she taught me in kindergarten so I could shock the nuns."

"Hush, they deserve to be shocked. Tight asses, all of them." Brigid waved away her son. "Are you sure?"

"Only if you're certain, Forest," Kiki murmured. "You've already taken a couple of shots to the head. You keel over, and Con'll have my ass carved up for Christmas dinner."

"Like your skinny ass could feed anyone but one of Mum's cats," her brother snorted. Duarte chuckled along, and Kiki shot them both a stern look.

"Show him the picture, Morgan. See if a name pops," Duarte said, cutting Kiki off before she could reply to her twin. "They're sending out the wagons in a bit. Con will want him out of the way and safe before they start tearing this place apart."

Forest nodded, and Kiki brought her phone out, showing him the picture Connor or Kane sent to her. Shock grabbed his throat, and he couldn't breathe. It took a second for him to choke in some air, and he coughed, unable to get out the surprise of seeing someone he knew—a familiar someone—lying still and motionless. They'd taken care to only show him the guy's face, but the speckled blood across his mouth and his graying skin told Forest the man was very dead.

It was too close to home. Death seemed to be circling him, and he couldn't seem to run away fast enough—far enough for it not to touch him with its steely cold hands. Numbly, Forest opened his mouth to tell Kiki he knew the man, but his stomach rebelled and he doubled over, puking out the oatmeal and sweet black tea Connor'd forced on him before they left the hospital.

"Take that away, Kiki," Brigid admonished softly.

"Do you know who it is, son? Does he look familiar?" Duarte cut in, crouching next to him. Forest nodded and swallowed the thick saliva coating his tongue.

"Darcy. Darcy... Martin. We use him sometimes—at the Sound. Used to. He started using too much and missing gigs." Forest took the open water bottle Riley shoved at him, then drank. "Tried to give him another chance, but he ripped a few of the guys off. Emptied their wallets when we were having a session, so I banned him."

"When was this? The theft?" Kiki asked softly, scribbling down notes in a tablet. "Recent?"

"Four... five days ago? One of the guys—shit, Marcus... um, he's a singer for Tweaked Possum... he wanted Darcy to sit in on the session. He was bringing in his own musicians, so it wasn't like Darcy was on my rolls. Marcus was the one who caught him going through the band's stuff. I told Darcy not to come back and struck him off the list. Wasn't going to use him even if the band brought him in." Forest tried standing up, but the world went wonky on him, and he staggered back. Riley caught him, then handed him over to Brigid. "I don't know why he'd come back here. He pissed a hell of a lot of people off."

"Did he have a key to your place?" Duarte asked. "Is there any reason he'd have come here to get back at you?"

"The shooting took place before or after you kicked him out the first time?" Kiki interrupted.

"Before," Forest replied. "And no, he didn't have a key. We weren't even friends. He's an… was an asshole. Abusive. I had to tell him to not swear at the coffee shop staff when he went in to get something to drink. The Amp gives anyone working the Sound free coffee and shit on the days they're needed. I don't know why Frank even let him sit in on anything. He'd come by and beg for work but then fuck it up or wouldn't learn the tracks."

"How many people use stand-ins?" Kiki filled a page and flipped over to a new one. "Was this Marcus guy the only one? Could Darcy have been trying to get back at you somehow?"

"I don't think he'd want to get back at me. He's lazy, barely did the minimum, you know? Hell, it's not like we were a huge source of cash for him. I don't think we used him a lot to begin with," he said, sighing. "Lots of people use studio guys, especially if they're doing their own stuff. I drum for a shit-ton of people. It's cheaper to use studio musicians than it is to hire your own crew. The Sound's got packages set up—for stuff like that. It's how I pay the bills."

Kiki's pen flew across the page. "What sessions do you have planned? Could Darcy have wanted to talk you into letting him play?"

He shook his head, instantly regretting it when a storm of sick threw lightning-flash warnings across his eyes. "Shit, I've got to get the calendar. Check what I've got going on."

"Do you have an assistant?" Duarte cocked his head.

"Dude I *am* the assistant." He snorted. "Frank ran everything. I just had to learn my parts and show up, or I'd rearrange their bass lines or percussion, depends if

I liked them. I'd schedule sessions, but pulling in the talent, that was all him. It's like trial by fire for me. I just want to drum. I hadn't planned on running the damned place."

Sirens cut through their conversation, and in a few seconds it seemed like the world exploded into a snowstorm of sound and uniforms. It took Brigid only a moment to disconnect Forest from the fray, dragging him away from the center of activity with a gentle pull on his hands. He was lost, more lost than he'd ever been, and other cops came by, some to take his fingerprints and DNA so he'd be excluded from the scene's results and another with hot sweet and sour soup, bought from one of the many restaurants in the area. He was bundled up into Connor's jacket and put into the Hummer, sharing the back seat with Con's mother so they could watch from their fishbowl existence as what seemed like the entire SFPD descended upon the building.

The soup warmed him, as did the comforting touch of the woman sitting next to him. Forest finally spotted Connor among the other Morgans, popping up a few inches taller than Riley and Kane. The man's attention was definitely on the case, but he'd caught Forest's eye once and smiled.

It was a damned sight better and warmer than the soup, and Forest huddled back into the seat, drawing the jacket even tighter around him.

"He loves you," Brigid said softly. "Ah God, does my boy love you."

"He doesn't even know me," Forest countered, but his eyes continued to search through the crowd, his attention firmly on the man who seemed intent on being his white knight. "How can he love me? Shit, I don't even love me."

A large vehicle pulled up, a black-and-white SUV emblazoned with yet another SFPD shield. A man got out, older than the Morgans, but the stamp of their bloodline shone in his features. Nearly as wide shouldered as Connor, the man approached with authority, a solemn cast to his face. The sun peeked out of the clouds, picking at the silver strands in his hair, and the wind caught up the edge of his long coat, flapping it away from his pants leg. He stopped in front of the siblings, listening as they went round-robin on the goings-on. Forest could see them talking, and even from a distance, he could see their deference to the man as they worked through whatever it was they needed to tell him.

When the man glanced at the Hummer, drawn there by a point of Kiki's finger, his eyes narrowed slightly and sought out the faces of the car's occupants. He caught Forest's gaze and then shifted, moving to the titian-haired woman next to him.

The man's face softened, and Forest saw Connor in the man's expression. He *knew* that face. He'd just been given that face by Connor right before he turned away to talk to his siblings. Brigid smiled and brought up her hand so the man could see it and waved her fingers at him, a delightfully whimsical gesture that made the man smile. He returned the wave with a firm salute and a definite wink before turning back to the Morgan siblings to ask them something.

"*That* man there, Forest? That is my husband and Connor's da." She sighed, sounding as if she were still in the first blush of youth. "That's the exact same expression Connor has when he looks at you, and I've cherished it since before you were born, son. *That* is how I know he's in love with you—just as I know Donal is in love with me."

IT'D BEEN a short skirmish, and to be fair, Forest was outclassed. The only person other than himself who could have possibly come close to winning it was Brigid, and his mother backed down once Donal put his hand on her shoulder. It was a quiet, silent reminder of their marriage. Not a remonstration but rather more of an urge to let Connor win. He'd seen that gesture used right at the point Mrs. Delany'd come up the walk to tear into the Morgan boys.

It was a reminder to, sometimes, pick your battles.

Kind of like letting Forest sleep off his exhaustion for two days but still not arguing when the man wanted to check his email, get a new phone to replace his damaged one, and coordinate studio sessions. Jules—thankfully—took over the coffee shop repairs, and it was one more burden off Forest's shoulders.

He'd winced over the damaged drum kit, but then he'd wept over Darcy's body, silently weeping silvery tears when they'd brought the dead man down the stairs and pushed him up into the coroner's van. He'd come out to pay respects to Darcy, because as much of an asshole the man'd been to everyone around him, Forest wanted to see him off. Connor'd been there then, pulling Forest into a loose embrace, then patting his back, asking him if he wanted to go home.

"Home's upstairs," Forest snorted through his sniffles. "Fucking hell, when is it all going to stop?"

"Home's up the hill, *a ghra*. You'll be staying with me." And with that, Connor fired the first volley, and the battle ended soon after, fought silently through mumbled objections and then Donal's tacit agreement.

That'd been a week or so ago, and Connor'd spent as much time coddling a sleepy Forest as he'd been down at the station, working his shift. The drummer insisted he'd be okay, and from what Connor could see, he'd been right. Still, it hadn't hurt to have Jules sit with him, although she'd informed him Forest mostly slept, and Connor needed new furniture for the family room because it was fucking shit on their backs.

He'd arranged for something to be delivered that next day, a wide, comfortable L-shaped sectional with recliners built into it. The couch was a damned sight better to sleep on than the old one, and Connor had to admit, Jules'd been right. His back and shoulders felt much better after spending the night on it.

His dick would have preferred to be lying in bed with Forest, but Connor knew the man'd needed time to heal. At least his brain had some common sense— even if it probably more than partially agreed with his cock—he fell asleep after only lying awake on the very comfortable couch for an hour or so, listening to the house rise and fall around him.

They'd spent a lot of time on the new couch, watching movies or just talking. He'd licked butter from Forest's fingers after they'd eaten more than enough popcorn to make them sick, and he'd been fed mint chocolate chip ice cream from a spoon that tasted of the man's mouth. They'd explored each other's lips and gently spooned during flashes of storms moving over the neighborhood.

No, Connor was quite fond of the new couch.

It was also where he found a sleeping Forest when Con came home from his last three-day shift, the blond man curled up into a corner of the brown sofa, an old knitted afghan wrapped around his long legs.

Jules was already gone, having been picked up by her boyfriend, Randy, and Connor set down the *banh mi* sandwiches he'd picked up for their dinner. The couch let off the smell of new fabric, where the man smelled of Connor's soap and fabric softener. Most of Forest's clothes were ruined, but a few sweats and jeans survived, and Con supplemented the wardrobe with an offer of his own shirts.

Still, seeing Forest curled up on his couch wearing one of his old police academy shirts did funny things to Connor's insides.

Forest's enormous brown eyes flickered open when Connor sat down. They were unfocused, his lids heavy with sleep. Connor'd been so good—doing nothing other than touching the man and spending his nights on the new couch, sacrificing his bed and biting his lip as he palmed his own cock to climax. His world became steeped in Forest's scent, and even his quirky habit of scooping out a spoonful of peanut butter, then slathering it with jam so he could eat it while watching television, made Connor smile.

The blond fought to stay awake when Connor came home, but healing took a lot out of him, and he often nodded off before Connor could shower off the day's dirt from his body. What little time they'd had was spent together, Forest leaning against him, often falling asleep on Con as he caught up on games he'd missed while working.

The man's hands were never still, always tapping out a rhythm, sometimes even as he slept, slack-jawed, loose-limbed, and sprawled over Connor's lap. It was like owning a cat in some ways, Connor thought once as he petted Forest's soft blond hair. Someone to come home to who was happy to see him but then immediately curled up into a ball and snored whenever Connor offered his lap.

Except for this time—this now—because Forest sat up and pushed the hair from his eyes, smiling sweetly as he rubbed the sleep from his face.

"Hey." He yawned, catching himself with a hand over his mouth. "Sorry. Shit, it's late."

"How's the head?" Con asked, feeling the top of Forest's skull.

The man laughed, pushing Con's fingers away. "That's not even where it was cracked."

"Yeah?" he retorted, twisting over Forest's long body and sliding his still chilled hands up under the man's borrowed shirt.

Forest yelped and laughed, a hearty, sweet near-giggle. Then he pulled away, burrowing deeper into the couch cushions.

"I brought Vietnamese. Sandwiches, you said you like those."

"Yeah, I do." Forest stared up at him—those damnable all-seeing eyes drinking in Connor's every expression. He bit his lip and then reached for Con's hand. He pulled it against his stomach, cradling its warmth. "We okay? I mean, you and I? We haven't talked about anything since—haven't had time, and I've just been fucking sleeping my life away."

"We're more than okay," Connor promised, leaning in to give Forest a gentle, brief kiss. Those were the only kind of caresses he was allowing himself, and he lived for each one, keeping them tallied up in his mind so he could remember them when his day lagged.

"Kiki have any leads? On *anything*?" Forest rubbed at his nose, scratching an itch.

"No, not yet," Connor admitted. "No one's seen anything. Biggest problem is that your places there have so many different people coming in and out of them, people don't know who belongs there or no. And we can't find a nosy old lady who watches the street with binoculars. Those are mighty handy a lot of times, I tell you. They're a dying breed. Now they're all out doing spin classes and the such."

"Then we're shit out of luck?"

"No, they're going through the footage from the bank, and they've tapped another feed from down the street. The Canadian couple didn't see who ripped off their van, but we're hoping someone else did. Kiki's arranging for interviews around the motel they were staying at. A lot of it is leg work."

"I feel like a sitting duck or something." He was bitter, and Connor didn't blame him. "Fucking hell."

"Hey, we'll find him." He kissed Forest, gently but insistent. "The bastard's leaving a trail of dead bodies, and I'm not scared to admit it, but I'd rather you not be one of them. We're all after this guy. Boys in blue are going to nail his ass. Pissed us off something fierce."

Forest stared into his eyes, searching for something. Connor was content to let him, enjoying the feel of the man's hard body against his. His own cock was debating going to a full-blown salute, and from the press of heat he felt on his thigh, it appeared Forest's dick was of the same opinion.

They kissed again. Deeper, longer, and their bodies rubbed together, creating a lingering friction between them. Connor sighed after a few minutes, wondering if he had the strength to get up off the couch and take a cold shower.

He should have been the reluctant one, the untried man in a game he'd only just joined, but his body seemed to know *exactly* what his heart wanted—what his soul thirsted for. There were times he'd imagined he'd go mad with the *wanting* of Forest, and then there were times when he was certain he already had.

"What are you thinking about?" Forest's voice was soft, but there was a heat to it, a lingering promise to go with the seductive thrust of his hips as he shifted beneath Connor's weight.

"I was thinking I should feed you." Damn if he didn't want the man. As terrifying as it'd seemed not more than a month ago, Connor *needed* Forest in a way he couldn't begin to describe. "Are you hungry?"

"Sorta. I don't want a sandwich," the blond murmured, reaching up and tangling his fingers into Connor's hair.

"Sandwiches are what I brought there, boyo," Connor teased.

"Yeah, they'll hold. It's kind of not what I'm hungry for right now."

"What are you hungry for, then, *a ghra*?" His heart was trying to break its way out of his rib cage, and Con scolded its silliness. He wasn't some fumbling teenager in the back of his father's car. He'd *had* sex before. Hell, wet, sloppy sex in places he'd be kicked off the force if someone'd caught him, but bending over Forest, being held in close by a tug of the man's fingers and having their breath mingle together touched off a chain reaction in Connor's body he'd never dreamed could happen. "What do you want, then, Forest love?"

Forest dragged him down, forcefully pulling Connor in until their mouths touched, and whispered, "You, Connor. I want you so fucking bad."

CHAPTER THIRTEEN

You ever miss living at home, Con?
Fuck no, a ghrá. You know what it's like living in a
*   madhouse? I'm fine here with you.*
Kinda be cool. You're never alone, you know?
The shouting. Having to find a free bathroom.
*   Worst part about it? I don't think I could have*
*   sex in my parents' house. Too odd.*
Okay, here it is.
—Conversations in the Family Room

"YOU SURE?" Connor had to whisper, because if
he spoke any louder, he'd shatter the crème brûlée sugar sweetness of their kiss. His cock was ready, heavy
and ponderous between his legs. The department-is-
sued uniform was made of thick, durable black fabric,
but his dick seemed to have plans on breaking right
through the weave.

If he'd had any question about being attracted to Forest Ackerman, it was certainly gone now.

Connor tried not to think of all the times he'd had a woman beneath him. Forest deserved better than that, but the comparison was still there—maybe it would always be there, but then, he thought, it didn't really matter. Not so long as he found pleasure and gave it back tenfold.

And pleasuring Forest was the only thing on Connor's mind at the moment.

The differences were startling. For some reason he'd imagined Forest's skin to be rougher or coarser to the touch. Instead, what he could feel under his shirt was soft, a silken landscape his hands glided across as he reached beneath the cotton fabric.

"Have you seen you?" Forest teased, and Connor groaned in mock anguish. "Shut up. And yeah, like since the first time you walked into the Amp. Maybe even before then."

"Not here," Connor muttered. "Not on a damned couch. I want to take you to bed. I want to stretch you out and take my time. If I'm going to do this, I want all of you. Not some fumbling around like we're waiting for my parents to get home—"

"You were doing pretty good until the parents thing there," Forest grumbled, but he let himself get pulled up off the sofa. "Good thing you're sexy, or I'd walk right out. If I had someplace to walk out to."

"Anyone tell you that you talk too much sometimes? Normally can't get a damned peep out of you, and now—"

"*Now* I'm nervous," Forest replied softly. "'Cause this is your first time with a guy, and what if I fuck it up?"

"What if I fuck it up?" Connor turned around, walking down the hall backward and pulling Forest behind him.

They both stumbled on the runner Con bought to keep the dust out of the one downstairs bedroom he'd refinished. He'd told himself he didn't need to get the master suite done. There'd been no plan on getting someone in bed—not anyone he'd wanted to impress—and now he regretted spending all his damned time on restoring the dining room.

Who the fuck really needed the dining *room?* he thought. He should have spent those hours on turning one of the upstairs bedroom suites into someplace Forest could enjoy.

On second thought, the guy probably would have preferred if the small carriage house on the side lawn was soundproofed and had power so he could hook equipment up—and Connor stopped his mind from wandering into a very dangerous space.

For right now, Connor was intent on stripping Forest bare and finding out exactly what the man looked like under all his clothes.

They made it as far as the bedroom door before Con tore the shirt from Forest's body. The other man gleamed ivory, with a faint brush of gold under his skin. His nipples were pink, a bright blush of color on his pale chest, but the surprise was the man's sculpted, lean body and the seemingly endless curves of muscles and flat planes Connor's mouth itched to taste.

"God, you are so beautiful," Connor whispered as he gathered Forest up in his arms. "Shit, I just thought—we can't—your head—"

"Swear to God, if you don't fuck me tonight, I'm going to break. My head's fine. You're going to *kill* me here." Forest slid a hand down Connor's front and grabbed at his cock, squeezing lightly. "See this? I want this. My head is fine."

Fisting his hands into Forest's gold-streaked hair, Connor pulled the man's head back, a gentle-rough tug to expose his throat. He bit, sinking his teeth into Forest's long neck, pulling at the mouthful until the other man squirmed against him.

"Jesus—Con, thank God...." Forest groaned, a hoarse erotic clench in his voice. "Fucking hell—"

"Get on the bed," Connor ordered, letting go of Forest's hair, then lightly pushing Forest to the enormous bed dominating the small room. "Because damn, if you're sure, then I can tell you I'm ready. I've been ready for a damned long time."

There wasn't much space to move about, and at the time he'd chosen the bedroom to sleep in, Con'd not given much thought to it. The downstairs bedroom was supposed to be temporary, but he could have used more floor to kneel on. There were things he wanted to do— hold on to Forest's hips and suck him down, tasting the man's cock for the first time.

Hell, just tasting any cock for the first time—but mostly because it was Forest's.

Con stood, staring down at the wide-eyed, sprawled-out blond—half-naked, fully aroused.

Forest wasn't much of a make-the-bed-after-waking-up kind of guy. The bed's faded blue-striped sheets were more for comfort than for looks, and they provided a crumpled frame for his sculpted torso. A thick quilt was somewhere, probably on the floor. From what Connor discovered during his nights of checking on Forest's slumber, the man roamed as he slept, leaving

Con to wonder how he'd managed to get any rest on his futon.

Not like Forest was going to get any rest that night either.

Connor debated seduction, or rather how to seduce the obviously aroused man. Forest's cock jutted up against his sweats, tenting the cotton in a straining line. The man's stomach jumped in and out, partially from nerves but mostly from his staggered breathing. A downy line of light brown hair trailed down from Forest's belly button, a shallow dip tucked between the ridges of his hard, muscled stomach.

He would start there, Connor decided. Or maybe Forest's throat, where a dark purple bruise was already blooming down the cords of his neck. No, he focused on the man's pink-flushed mouth—*that* was where he'd begin his exploration and then work his way around until Forest begged him for release.

Connor liked the sound of that. He also enjoyed the growling mew Forest gave when Con hooked his thumbs into Forest's waistband and tugged his sweats and underwear off in a single fluid pull.

"I don't want to have to stop and do that later," Connor rumbled. Then he eased onto the bed and covered Forest's lanky body with his own heavy frame.

The room grew hot. Even stripped bare with nothing on the walls but flecks of old wallpaper glue and exposed woodwork, the house's thick plaster walls normally kept the place relatively cool, holding in the city's chill and keeping out the worst of its heated tantrums.

Connor shifted, moving to find the places he fit into Forest's body while exploring the man's unfamiliar planes with his hands. Their mouths were close, and Connor resisted savaging Forest's lips. Their eyes held, and when Connor's fingers dusted down Forest's ribs, he gasped, puffing a breath over Con's parted lips, and Connor knew he was lost.

He took what was his, sliding his knees between Forest's legs to support his weight, and captured the man's mouth, forcing Forest's lips open so he could plunge his tongue past Forest's sharp teeth and into the hot depths beyond. Connor suckled and pulled, drawing gasp after gasp out of the man underneath him. Unused to the sleek feel of another man's skin, Con reveled in the newly discovered delight, his fingers roaming over his lover's body, finding defined muscles. Then the nip of a nipple on Connor's palm drew him in, and he played with the nub, rolling it between his thumb and finger until Forest gasped and thrust his hips up into a grinding dance along Connor's belly.

Everything tasted different, tasted right, and felt even more glorious than Connor imagined. He didn't know if it was the culmination of his surrender to desires he'd long held back or the sheer erotic pleasure of exploring Forest's pale flesh. Either way, Connor knew in that moment he'd never let the man go. He'd never get enough of him—never feel or swallow enough of Forest to be satiated.

And he'd not even begun to sample the delectable flavors awaiting him beyond Forest's mouth.

Connor moved onward—traveling down the man's throat, then coaxing first one nipple, then the other into a hard peak he could have cut glass on if he so desired. Even there, the masculine hint of sweat and earthy skin was an explosion of sensations in Con's mouth.

He dared his hands to go lower—to find the hard press of the man's shaft and palm over Forest's cockhead and smear the leak he knew would be pearling at his lover's slit. Connor wasn't disappointed. Forest's cock was wet and hard. Steel-firm and velvet soft at the tip, it bobbed before Con grasped it, sliding about on Connor's palm until it too gave in—as Forest writhed and clutched at Con's shoulders.

"Con—" Forest's voice was tight, urgent, and begging. "I can't—fuck, it's been too long. I'm going to lose it on you."

"Hold on, baby," Con urged. "I want to taste you. My first—hell, my *only*. I want to take you in. Feel you there, okay? Can you hold on just for that? So I can feel you there? Pressed against the roof of my mouth?"

"Maybe," came Forest's husky whisper. "Yeah."

His balls rolled in Connor's palm, a curious, unique male thing only another man could understand. Connor *knew* the feelings Forest was having. Connor's pants squeaked on the sheets, making him aware he'd wasted precious moments wearing clothes when he could have been lying naked on Forest's hot body.

Con stripped quickly, tearing off his shirt and unzipping his pants before tossing both aside to land in a pile on the bedroom floor. The air cooled his skin, a brief, wistful chilly kiss over his skin, prickling his flesh with goose bumps, but his dick throbbed with its own coursing heat.

"Jesus, you're fucking huge," Forest muttered. "Lube. Better have a shit-ton of lube."

"There's some in the nightstand." Connor fumbled at the squat piece of furniture, digging out a couple of condoms and lubricant. "I'm not exactly sure how much a shit-ton is, but there's probably more than enough here."

His dick left a salty trail on Forest's arm and leg, his shaft tightening with excitement when the man grazed his fingertips over Connor's uncircumcised head. He twitched, hissing at the touch to his sensitive tip, and Forest grinned up at him.

"Not what I expected," Forest said, sliding his thumb around the base of Connor's head. "You're not cut."

"No. Born in Ireland. They tend to leave the boys as they find them." Connor hissed again, drawing back. "And stop that, *a ghra*. You're not the only one close to the edge."

Con tossed the lubricant on the bed. It rolled, then rested near Forest's hip, trapped in the folds of Con's rumpled sheets. He shot a grin at Forest, then lowered his head, licking down the man's stomach and tickling the down under Forest's navel with the tip of his tongue. Shifting his knees, Connor guided Forest's legs apart and skimmed his hands down the man's lean thighs, marveling at the feel of wiry hair on his palms.

He was blown away by the exquisite sensations of Forest's body on his hands and in his mouth. The scents of the man were so very unique, even as Con recognized the aroma of his own soaps on his lover's skin. The familiar lemon chiffon scrub, an indulgence Connor allowed himself, perfumed Forest's stomach and groin. While the sweet citrus hint was pleasant, it was the powdery musk undernote that drew Connor's cock to a raging stiffness.

Everywhere he touched felt different—unique to the man he longed to delve into. Connor studied the other man's cock, taking in its pink tip, shorn of its foreskin. The texture of it was so foreign to him, more like velvet than the sleek felt of his own cock, and Connor played with its tip, reveling in the gasping mewls he could draw from Forest's panting mouth when he flicked his thumb over Forest's slit.

"Con…," Forest begged, husky and dark with promise. "Please."

"Yeah, baby," Connor replied. "Anything you want. Just—let me do this. Once."

He then leaned in and took Forest's cock into his mouth, pressing his tongue under its bulb, and sucked, drawing Forest's hips off the bed as pleasure flooded through the blond's body.

The hint of salt, lemon, and man flowed over Connor's tongue in a rush, and Forest's body bucked under Con's hands. He spread his fingers out, digging into the man's hip bones to hold him. He was going to take however long he had and explore Forest in depth, but the blond wasn't having it. Forest's hands scrambled at his shoulders, searching for purchase with frantic fingers.

It was a magical taste—that first savoring of a man—of Forest—in Connor's mouth. It filled him, completed him, and Connor wondered how the hell he'd gone on for so long without that burst of Forest in his memory.

The lubricant nudged at Con's fingers, rolling about with Forest's gyrations. Connor let go of Forest's side and popped open the bottle. He liked to slick up his own cock while getting himself off, and the condoms were probably only a year old, but he couldn't remember the last time he'd had sex. Sending a brief apology to his faceless and forgotten lover, Connor lubed his fingertips and slid his hand down between Forest's legs, searching for the hot muscled swirl he needed to prime.

Connor knew he'd hit the right spot when Forest gasped and his knees parted. Cock leaking hot pre-come down Connor's throat, his ass clenched and gave, guiding Connor's oiled fingers in. His body tightened, molten and sweet over Con's fingertips. He worked two in, coating the rim as thickly as he could. Forest was tight—so tight Con wondered if he would fit, but when he drew his hand back, Forest's hands tightened painfully on Con's shoulders.

"Swear to fucking God, I'm going to kill you if I don't get you in me," Forest muttered darkly.

"Almost done," Connor replied, kissing Forest's cheek. "And I'll be right there."

Strangely enough, his hands shook as Connor tore open the foil packet, and trembled even more when he worked the sheath down over his own cock. The tight ring at its base caught on his shaft, and he struggled for a second, then unfurled it the rest of the way. With his dick covered in more lube, Con gripped his base and guided the tip of his cock down between Forest's trim asscheeks. The blond lifted his legs, hooking them up onto Connor's hips, and Con grabbed a pillow to shove it beneath the small of Forest's back.

Connor savored the moment, taking in the sight of Forest's wanton splay. Forest's mouth was roughened to plum from Connor's kisses, and small bruises marked his throat and chest where Con's teeth had nipped. Forest was ivory and golden, hot with lust and run wild with need. His eyes were nearly black with desire, their mocha depths swallowed in a stygian pool. With his hips canted up and legs spread, Forest was open to him, surrendering every inch of his body to Connor's cock—to Connor's desire—and Connor could not wait to enjoy what the man was offering.

"All of it," Forest whispered. "No teasing me. Just… all of you, Con."

Leaning forward, balancing his weight on one hand and his knees, Connor gently kissed Forest's lips, inhaling the puffs of strained breath and little kitten cries coming from Forest's mouth. Whispering softly, Connor said, "Thank you for this, *a ghra*. Thank you for giving me this—for giving me you. You are a treasure to me, and one I will cherish my entire life."

With that, Connor pushed, and his mouth clamped down, swallowing Forest's scream as he slid the length of his heavy cock into the tight of Forest's body.

THE MAN was enormous. From his broad shoulders to his trim hips, Connor Morgan was a rippling mass of muscle and sinew, and Forest tried to touch every single inch of him that he could reach. There was *so* much to reach for.

So much so Forest wondered if he could even take the man in.

When he'd first felt the prickling of want, Forest had been horrified to discover he liked men. Unable to comprehend *why* his mind drifted into sexually charged thoughts at the idea of a man's hands on him—a man's cock inside him—he'd driven himself down into his drumming, needing to pound out his fears and aggressions. Men were— they hurt. Even as his mother dragged him through her partying—even as she handed him over to rough-mouthed, drunken men who seemed to crawl out of the woodwork whenever she needed money—he'd done it because his mother needed him to—wanted him to.

There'd been too many times when he'd woken up sore, his voice hoarse from taking a man's cock down his throat and his lips cracked from being stretched too wide—stretched too hard—and all the while, as Franklin waited for Forest to come to his senses and not trail after his mother like an oblivious duckling—Forest'd wished Frank would have just told him to stop.

Because his mother was the only person who'd ever told him he was needed, wanted, and the brutal fucking he got every time her friends passed him around was merely the price to pay to hear her say *You did good, Forest. Real good.*

By the time he'd thrown off her influence, Forest told himself he wanted something normal; a sweet-faced girl who'd giggle when he told a bad joke or even sit to listen in on a session. Quite a few of the musicians he played for had those kinds of girlfriends, smiling bits of sugar and candy who'd clap when they were finished playing and give fierce hugs of appreciation when the set was done.

Then he'd found himself looking more at the musicians than their girlfriends and wondered how truly fucked up he was, longing for something that'd only brought him pain.

Frank—God love Frank—for noticing and talking to him. They'd worked it out, small tidbits of conversations and reassurances of Forest's sexuality, until Forest understood—realized—the men he'd gone with before weren't partners, weren't lovers; they were men interested in satiating their need for power or maybe even trying to exorcise their own demons. None of the pain, none of the trauma, had to do with love or want. If Forest wanted a man in his bed, it wasn't because of something his mother or any of the countless, faceless nobodies who'd used him before had done. It was because that's what his heart wanted.

And God, did his heart want Connor Morgan.

Especially now, because even as the man tenderly stroked and played with Forest's body, he ached to have Connor in him.

He *wanted* Connor to erase every touch that'd come before him. He needed to believe the man when he whispered how much he wanted Forest. Most of all, he wanted to be held, to know Connor wasn't going to let him go, wasn't going to toss him out like he'd been tossed away so many damned times before. Forest needed *that* most of all, and in the murmuring Irish he heard those things.

His heart beat rapidly, urging his mind to fall into the man's promises, but the slithering doubts—the evil, dark shadows lurking in the recesses of his mind—whispered of Connor's disinterest once he'd gotten his fill of Forest's body.

No, he told himself. He'd seen the look on Con's face—that precious moment when he'd spied Forest through the glass and turned Forest's world on its side. There'd been something tangibly magical in that glance—that smile—and it'd burned away every cobweb and flick of ice on Forest's soul, baring him to the sun and stars. He'd die happy knowing he'd gotten that look just once.

He'd do anything Connor wanted of him just to have the man look at him like that for the rest of his life.

"God, I love you," Forest muttered softly, too low for Connor to hear, and hot tears stung Forest's eyes. "When the fuck did *that* happen?"

His mind burned and roiled with the knowledge, tearing at his thoughts and flinging back sharp darts of denial. They didn't get very far. His heart caught every whisper of doubt and crushed them into a silvery ashen nothing, leaving only a smear of awareness behind.

Enraptured by the large man on his knees in front of him, Forest lifted his legs up, hooking his ankles at the small of Connor's back. Slick fingers played with him, coating his hole with lubricant. It smelled familiar, then turned erotic when a simmering warmth kicked in, making Forest gasp in surprise. The sounds of a condom wrapper tearing sent tingles of fear and need through him—would he be able to take all of Connor's girth—would he be able to be what Connor needed—and would Connor find pleasure in his already ill-used body?

He said something. For all he knew, he was complimenting Connor on the ink covering one of his upper arms. Forest couldn't even remember the words as soon as they left his mouth, but whatever he'd mumbled made Connor smile. God, he *lived* for that man's crooked, chipped-tooth smile. A thrust of Connor's hips, and suddenly Forest's skin was singing, tightening over his flesh and bones as Connor filled him, a rush of hot silken steel driving deep into the depths of Forest's body.

And if there were a God, Forest thought, he'd die right then and there because he couldn't imagine anything more perfect than Connor Morgan splitting him open and whispering hot whiskey Irish into his ear.

Then Connor began to move, and Forest simply gave up thinking.

Forest rode the waves of Connor's thrusts. He could only hold on, tightly gripping the man's powerful arms as they supported Con's weight. His lover—because Connor was *his lover*—worked his hips in and out, angling up in a rolling snap slow enough to drive every single inch of Connor's cock along the ridge of Forest's hole and push the man's shaft in deep. Forest's hips rose with every thrust, his ass driven up on every motion.

Sweat glistened on their bodies, and Forest caught a drop of Connor's when it fell from his throat. The salt of the man would echo the rush of come from Connor's release, and as pale of a comparison as it would be, Forest was glad for the taste. He'd have the man's taste in his mouth as he filled Forest's depths, but that too became nothing but a rush of burned thought as Con found Forest's sweet spot and the universe went black around them.

They slapped together, skin hitting wetly and teasingly. Forest ached for more, and Connor gave him his all, resting on his knees so he could slide his hands under Forest's hips to get a better grip on the meat of Forest's ass. Connor's fingers dug in, a punishing grip, but Forest gloried in the man's grasp. Connor wasn't going to let him fall over the edge of his release alone. With every massive stroke, Con drove Forest further along until the tingle of his climax began to boil in his balls.

"Touch yerself, *a ghra*," Connor growled, his accent thickening to emerald and gravel. "I want to see ye pull at yer dick and come for me. Can ye do that?"

Forest couldn't find his hands; then his dick seemed to be as reluctant to be located. His nerves were shot, his mind blown beyond where it was supposed to be. Fumbling, Forest covered his cock with his hand, his fingers numb from the cascading pleasure rising up from his ass and balls. He couldn't think straight enough to pull on himself, not in any sense of rhythm.

For once in his life, he couldn't find the pattern of his own body. His heart'd fallen into time with Connor's pulse, and the beat of it drove their sex, a shattering plunge on every downstroke.

It was too much for him when Connor's hand rose up to cover his fingers and the man began to work Forest's cock, sliding up and down in a single shuck before rubbing the rough of his palm over Forest's head.

Something caught on his slit—either the edge of a fingernail or a callus—either way, the rough scrape was the limit of Forest's body, because the storm building up in his balls broke, and he screamed his release, arching his body up and clenching down hard on Connor's wickedly hard cock.

Something hot came up into his ass, but it was held back, simmered by the sheath around it. In some part of his mind, Forest knew it was Connor's spill, and he sighed, riding the tiny shivers of his climax while Connor continued to stroke at him, both inside and out.

Connor's dick was still buried in him, Forest realized. Even softening from release, the man was firm enough to remain inside, and every shift of Connor's weight reminded Forest of the ride they'd just taken together. The faint light coming from the bedroom's overhead lamp dimmed when Connor bent over Forest, his dark hair catching up most of the bulb's glow. Forest could still make out Con's features and certainly the man's sinfully delicious mouth before he tenderly kissed Forest's lips.

"I love you too, *a ghra*," Connor whispered against Forest's kiss-swollen mouth. "And yeah, I'm never letting you go."

CHAPTER FOURTEEN

Hey there pretty boy
Whatcha doing over there
Come on over now
Don't just sit and stare
Show you a right good time
Show you everything I got
Blowing town in an hour
But I've got time to hit the spot
—Talk is Cheap

"WHO THE fuck is Forest Ackerman, and why the hell are we letting him use Dave's kit?"

Damien'd known the firestorm would hit. Miki was, if nothing else, predictable—at least to someone who knew him. It wasn't that the singer was selfish. If anything, Miki would give the shirt off his back to anyone who even remotely shivered within five hundred feet of him. No, this was about the guys—the band—and Miki was extremely protective of the members of Sinner's Gin, even in death.

Especially in death.

"It was never Dave's kit, dude," Damien reminded softly. "The drum company sent it to him to try out. Dave never touched it. Hell, he never even saw it."

He steeled himself against his brother's hard hazel glare, focusing on the tiny gold dollops in Miki's right eye. The pattern was a constellation, Damie was sure of it, and he'd been trying to figure out which one for years. It also helped him shift his focus away from Miki's fierce glower, and he'd seen a pack of Morgans back down from *that* stare.

So Damie played his trump card. "Brigid asked."

Miki's response was swift and hard. "Fuck."

The argument, if it could be called that, was over before it could really get started, but Damie didn't gloat. Although he did allow himself a tiny smile.

"'Sides, you know him. Remember the blond kid at Frank Marshall's?" He slung down onto the couch next to his brother. "At the Sound."

"Yeah?" Miki scratched at his cheek with the eraser end of his pencil. "Shit, I'm trying to remember—"

"He was a drummer—"

"Figured that since you're willing to toss him at Dave's kit."

"Not Dave's kit," Damie began to argue, then caught the wicked gleam in Miki's tawny eyes. "Fuck you. You gonna listen to me?"

"If ever you stop talking about shit, maybe," Miki replied. "Oh wait, I remember him. Hell, he was, like, a little kid. And his mom—Frank went off about his mom when we were there. Said she kept whoring him out or something."

"Yeah," Damie growled. "Fucking bitch. Getting slow cooked on lava would be too good for her."

He'd recalled the broken, wide-eyed boy when Brigid first called to ask if Damie knew of a place Forest could practice. Pretty as a Keane painting, the blond teen'd hovered mostly near Frank, helping set up equipment, then scurrying out of the way when the band came in. Dave'd liked the kid, spending his down-time with Frank's adopted son and teaching him what he could in between their sessions. The Sound was where Sinner's Gin cut their first CD, an eight-track demo they'd sold at their early shows.

Frank Marshall taught Damie a lot about mixing and melody, even so far as to cut the band a deal on the session cost because he'd seen something in their ragtag group of fuck-ups.

Damie sent Frank a thank-you, along with a bottle of twenty-five-year-old whiskey, when Sinner's Gin signed their contract, then lost touch, but Frank's name was in their first real album's liner notes, and Damie felt he *owed* the man something. It was time for him to pay the bill—and he was going to get Sinjun on board if it was the last thing he did.

"Think he's any good?" Sinjun asked suddenly, jarring Damie from his trip down Memory Lane.

"Who? The kid? Forest?" He flipped Miki off when the man rolled his eyes. "Dave liked him. Said he had talent. Just needed to get his shit together."

"Who *doesn't* need to get their shit together when you're that age?" Miki snorted, then gave Damie another skeptical glance. "You didn't fuck him, did you?"

"Frank's kid? Fuck no. He was a *kid*!" Damien protested. "Dude, besides—don't shit where you eat."

"*That* took you a little bit to learn," his brother reminded him. "It's how we lost our first drummer… and second one too. And that bassist. It was like a fucking Wonka factory tour—but without the chocolate river."

"Didn't touch him," he swore, holding his hand up.

"Yeah, like you were ever a Boy Scout," Miki muttered, then paused in his scribbling. "Hey, think he's any good? At drumming. Not sex."

"Dunno." Damie shrugged. "Why?"

"'Cause I'm sick of tapping things out on a drum machine, and I want to try out a few bass lines." Miki pondered what he wrote, then reached for a blank music sheet. "I mean, if he's going to be here anyway, might as well get some fucking use out of him."

"And if we're in the studio, Brigid will leave you the fuck alone," Damie mused.

Miki nodded and grunted. "You got that fucking right. Woman rattles my brain."

FOREST SAT in Brigid's SUV and stared at the warehouse's front door. He'd remembered Damien and Miki from their time at the Sound, but he'd been younger then—stupider too. Instead of taking advantage of listening in on a band that would make it big, he'd skipped out a few times when his mother'd tugged on his leash. Their quiet Southern-born drummer spent a lot of his spare time with Forest, working through some of the harder rolls and laughing softly when Forest finally got something right.

And now he sat outside of the surviving members' home to come beg to play on their equipment.

"It'll be fine," Brigid said again. "The boys are nice. Sweet even."

"I've met them. Miki St. John is about the furthest thing from sweet as it gets." He made no move to get out of the car, and Brigid seemed to be fine with his waiting. "I have no idea why I'm scared to go in. Fuck, it's not like I haven't heard them play. Or sat in on one of their sessions. I've even learned their damned songs so I can do covers when someone wants to. I should just go in."

But Forest just sat there, still staring.

"What's the real reason, love?" Brigid pried gently. "I know them well enough to say they'd not mock someone's musical skill. And Miki's probably mellowed a bit since you'd met him." When Forest side-eyed her, she amended, "*A bit*. The words I used were 'a bit.'"

"Dunno," Forest said, then made a face. "No, I kinda know. I think it's 'cause they *knew* me, back then. When I'd just gotten to Frank's. Things were so—fucked up. *I* was so fucked up. I don't know if I'm ready to deal with that."

"What do you think they know?" she asked. "If you'd want to be sharing. And why would you think either one of them would say something about it?"

Forest took a deep breath. There was so much riding on him blending in with Connor's life. Hell, he was still fucking scared down to his spine that the cop would catch shit for hooking up with a former whore, and when he'd mentioned it to Con, the man lifted one eyebrow and said *I'd fucking welcome the chance to put my fist into any asshole who says jack shit about you.*

It'd been pretty much the end of that conversation. Connor ended a lot of conversations that way. A declaration in his rumbling, deep voice, and then the matter was done. He seemed to reserve it for certain instances—defending his passed-around lover or deciding Forest needed new clothes, even if Connor said he loved seeing Forest in his shirts. Forest just didn't know if he wanted to shatter his tentative relationship with Connor's firebrand mother, even if she seemed to be where Con got his engraved-in-stone stubbornness.

No matter how quickly and terrifyingly things were moving, it was one thing to talk about his past with the man he shared a bed with—a life, even—he wasn't so sure Brigid would be as sanguine as her granite-willed son.

Another deep breath, and Forest spilled his guts, staring out of the window as he did it. He kept it short, the barest of details, but the warehouse swam when his eyes watered up. He was sick of crying—sick of whining about his life and his past. If there was some way he could just make it all—

"Come here, love," Brigid cut him off, wrapping her arms around his body, and pulled him close. "Don't you ever apologize for what someone did to you as a child. You're strong—stronger than anyone who'd speak against you for it. I'll be telling you, if ever someone spits on you in the earshot of *any* Morgan, they'll be gumming their ass bits. And that would include those boys in there if I'd thought they would be that ignorant. They're not, sweetie. They've had their share of horror and have come out the other side. So don't you be worrying about them."

"I'm tired of—crying." Forest sniffed, and his face was lost in the riotous mass of Brigid's hair. "God, I'm so fucking sick of crying about this shit."

"I'm guessing you've not really done any of the real crying you've needed to do," she consoled. "A body can't work out their grief unless they're someplace safe. We're like every animal God has created. We need to feel protected before we can let ourselves be vulnerable. You can be that now—with us, with me. That woman who carried you? She did it for me. It just took me a bit to find you, but I've got you now. I'm sorry for not being here sooner."

He laughed, amused at the woman's fierce growl. "How the hell would you have known I was going to have a shit life when I was born? And wouldn't that kind of be icky with me and Con?"

"Shush, it sounded good," she admonished with a light laugh. "There's no saying I can't have a hand in raising my sons' lovers—no matter how old they are when I finally get my hands on them. At least you don't rear back like an alley cat when I hug you. Miki nearly quivers when I grab at him."

"Okay, that I can't—" Forest chuckled, pulling away to wipe his face. "Why?"

"Because unlike you, Kane's Sinjun is wary of being loved. Affection—real affection—came to him too late in life, and only then in the form of a very screwed-up Damie. So I hug him every chance I get. One day he'll get used to it, maybe even like it, but for right now, he's just suffering through it until I let him go." Brigid leaned in and whispered, even though only she and Forest were around. "And sometimes I just hug him because I know it pisses him off, and he can't say *shite* about it."

THEY CIRCLED each other like tomcats, feeling one another out, and Brigid wondered aloud if it was even safe to leave Forest with the two musicians. Damien waved her out and promised they'd be good. She was reluctant to leave. Something very maternal hovered in her expression, much more so than normal. It gave Miki the twitches. Even Forest could see the tightness in his shoulders whenever she got within arm's length of the singer.

Feeling sorry for him, Forest said, "I'm fine. It's like a play date. Kids have that now, right?"

"Huh." Brigid sounded unconvinced, but she went anyway, leaving them alone in the vast, echoing warehouse.

A small golden scruff of a dog snored from his spot on the couch, and his tail set up a short, sleepy tempo when Forest rubbed his belly. Forest tried to ignore the stacks of music sheets and worn notebooks lying on a shipping trunk in front of the sectional, but it was hard. He caught a glimpse of a rapid-fire drum line, and his mind caught at the beat, working it down to his fingers. Turning away from the crate, he left the dog lolling in pleasure and looked up, surprised to find Miki studying him.

"Hey," he said. "Nice dog. What's his name?"

"Dude," Miki offered back with a shrug. "We going to do this or what?"

"Come on. Studio's down here," Damie said with a grin.

He trotted off through a door, and Miki followed. After a second, Forest fell into step and found himself in a garage. Two heavy-bodied cars sat side by side. From what he could see, they were older, steel muscle, and brash. They were both black, gleaming and aggressive even as they sat in silence. Miki glanced over his shoulder at Forest as if to see if the other man was following.

Nodding at the cars, Forest said, "So, you keep your balls in the garage? Nice."

"Yeah, you'll be okay." Damien laughed, and a beat later, Miki joined in with a soft musical chuckle. Slapping Forest's shoulder, Damien guided him around the cars and toward a door on the other side of the garage.

His nerves were eating him alive. Forest *knew* he'd already met the pair, but something was different this time. They were definitely road worn—a far cry from the slightly naïve-about-the-industry musicians he'd met before. If anything, Miki St. John was even more feral, taking in everything Forest did and said as Damien chattered on about life in general.

Damien Mitchell was definitely the social one of the two. His softly British-stained lilt rolled over a variety of subjects until he found something that made Forest's eyes light up. Unsurprisingly, it was music, and even Miki'd chimed in a grunt when Forest started talking about who influenced him.

The door opened and Forest stepped in, his heart caught in his throat at the sight of the tiny studio. It was set up for practice, nothing as elaborate as the Sound, but the sound board was fairly new—so new it still had plastic on it. A glass wall separated the mixing room from the actual studio, and while the equipment space was functional at best, someone'd gone to some trouble to make the playing space something of a home. Old carpets covered the floor, warming the area up with color, and a suede love seat took up residence against the space's long wall.

Instruments were everywhere, mostly on stands, but some lined the walls, signed pieces or elaborately painted. They were obviously art or memories, silent icons more precious to their owners than solely something to play. Prominent in the room was a gleaming oak drum kit, a powerful beast of a set. He approached it slowly. Tapping at the skins, Forest was pleasantly surprised to find they'd been tightened for use.

Yet even as comfortable as the space tried to appear, it seemed… lonely, as if the room was holding its breath, waiting for something, maybe even someone, to fill it with life.

"You know what you wanted to work on? Or you're just up for some practice?" Miki said, appearing at Forest's elbow with a set of sticks.

"Practice mostly. I just… I can't *not* play. It's fucking killing me," he admitted.

"You know any of ours?" Damien's voice had a slight challenge to it, and Forest squared his shoulders, rising to the bait.

"Sure," Forest said, taking the sticks from Miki's grip. "Anything you've written, I can play."

"Good." Miki reached down to pick up a bass guitar from a stand by the drums and slung it over his neck. "Let's see what you've got."

CONNOR PARKED his Hummer on the curb, turning the vehicle off before swinging out of it and locking the door behind him. In the early-afternoon light, Marshall's Amp coffee shop and its nearly windowless partner, the Sound, looked abandoned. To be fair, the entire block looked like it'd taken a beating. The older Chinese woman's flower stall had been broken down and stood empty, shuttered tight with locking steel doors. A black ribbon taped to the stall's wall flapped in the faint breeze working down the street, its painted gold *hanzi* cracked and faded from San Francisco's brutal weather.

Someone'd set up a small altar of burned-down candles and rain-soaked notes against the plywood and beam patches across the Amp's front. Rotting flowers scattered throughout the tribute kicked up a stink, mimicking the decay of the dead. If anything, the collection was more funereal than Connor was ready to deal with, especially since he still had flashes of digging through heavy bricks to find a seemingly lifeless Forest beneath the stone and grit.

He'd come by to get his own idea of how damaged the building was and if the Sound was affected structurally. Forest's nerves were beyond razor thin, and they'd built up some tension between them when Connor forbade the man from going into the building.

"There's too much risk," Connor'd argued. "Someone's trying to *kill* you, Forest, so *no*."

Forest's chin came up, but he didn't argue. Thank God Brigid stepped in with an alternative plan, because Con was pretty certain Forest was about to draw a line in the sand and come out swinging. Verbally. Although from their time spent under the covers, Connor'd gained a deep respect for Forest's sinewy strength.

The Amp was still cordoned off with crime-scene tape, but someone'd been at it, taking a chunk off the plywood. Shaking his head, Connor went to undo the padlock on the Amp's remaining intact front door and muttered, "Fucking ghouls."

Problem was, the padlock was already open, and Connor pushed open the door—only to find he'd stepped into another nightmare.

Death'd come again to the Amp and left evidence of its sharp scythe.

A middle-aged, slightly portly man was flung over the shop's shot-up counter. Even from the door, Connor could see he was gone. There was no mistaking that. Even more alarming, he appeared to be freshly slaughtered, blood still seeping from his torn-apart belly to form a pool beneath him. His arms were sticky and red, causeways for his blood to travel down, and his fingers looked like talons from the long, heavy drags of red dripping from them.

Intestines trailed out of his belly wound, and his face was slack, a gray mass of skin and wrinkles. His work boots were gone, and one of his socks had a hole in it, his big toe sticking out of the gap. A wedding ring cut deep into his now swollen finger, the burnished gold nearly lost under the gore of its owner's death.

Drawing his weapon, Connor stepped up against the wall, ducking behind the semisafety of a bank of espresso machines. His gaze flicked over the graffiti spray-painted on the back of the plywood patches, taking in the violent neon-green letters. He swore to ignore the gurgle of nerves coming up in his belly. He was used to fear. He dealt with it every day in his line of work.

Whoever was doing this needed to be stopped. For Connor, it'd become long past personal—someone was moving against his own.

It took him a second, but he then recognized the man, the main contractor Forest'd hired to fix the store. The man shouldn't have been in there. Not dead—not like a piece of garbage left for someone to pick up. He'd obviously come to do some work, because a briefcase lay on the floor at Connor's feet, and there were rolls of blueprints bound with rubber bands a few feet away. *Someone'd* followed the man in, surprised him, and killed him.

The problem was, Connor and the rest of SFPD were no closer to finding out who was murdering the people in Forest's life, and if he wasn't stopped soon, there was a good chance he'd be moving on to someone in the Morgan clan itself.

Connor stopped short, catching a hint of a sound coming from inside the Amp. Turning his head, he heard the whimpering cry of a woman. Stepping carefully around the counter so as not to disturb the body, he hefted his weapon up and entered the kitchen, waiting to hear it again. Another mewl, loud and coming from under a counter in the kitchen, drew him farther into the room. His foot came down on a piece of Styrofoam and it snapped, a loud cracking sound, and the cry came again, louder and fraught with terror.

"Jules?" he called out. "It's me, Connor. Is that you? Come out, honey. It's okay. I'm here."

Nothing. Not even another whimper to draw Connor in.

"It's all right, love. Come out. I won't hurt you. I'm here to help," Con reassured and spun about on his heel when a stack of boxes near the wall exploded with motion.

A woman, skinnier than Jules, darted from her hiding place, arms and legs flailing as she tried to make it to the Amp's back door. Connor lowered his gun and sprinted after her, snagging her shoulder before she could get a grip on the heavy industrial pull built into the safety door leading out to the parking lot. Whoever the woman was, she fought hard, and her nails dug into Connor's face and arms, scooping out small divots of flesh wherever she could get a hold.

It was like fighting a rabid dog. Her straggly hair was everywhere, a brittle blonde kraken snapping across his face as Con bent over to get a good grip on her. He tucked his gun away, then reached into the fury of fists, nails, and suddenly teeth—a shock he should have planned for but didn't.

He hated hitting women. Years of being told he was bigger and stronger than many of his playmates hammered in the need for delicacy, especially where someone much smaller was concerned. Her clawed hands came at his face, and Connor almost gave in to his instinct to slap her away. Instead, he grabbed her wrists and hauled her up, lifting the woman clear off the ground and away from his body.

Enraged, she screamed, and he heard the sounds of spit being gathered in her throat. She hawked out her saliva into his face, as quick as a cobra, and he nearly didn't duck in time. It caught his cheek, trailing down his neck, but he'd avoided getting her fluids in his eyes or mouth.

Snarling, Connor shook her and said, "Cut it the fuck out. I'm a cop."

She fought on for a moment, then surrendered, her feet kicking for purchase even though the floor was nearly a foot and half beneath her. He nearly let her down when he heard the telltale scratch of another spit bomb coming his way, and Connor hoisted her even higher, slamming the captured woman up against the kitchen's brick wall.

"Cut. It. Out," he growled, then nearly dropped his assailant. Staring into her time-leathered face, his stomach careened down into the abyss and his heart skipped, because she glared right back, looking at him with his lover's eyes.

CHAPTER FIFTEEN

Wrap me in leather
Buckle me down in hard lace
Drape me in white
Slap a mask on my face
Tie me down to your cross
Thorn ribbons in my hair
Blood down on my face
Kill me if you dare
—Skywood

"WELL, SHIT," Duarte drawled as he walked past Connor. "You find any more dead bodies, someone would think you owned a mystery bookstore in Pasadena."

Kiki came up behind her brother, sniffling into a wad of tissue. She waved at Connor with her free hand, then gestured toward her partner. "Fucking asshole gave me his cold."

Connor frowned, thinking back to how healthy Duarte seemed over the past week. "He didn't have a cold."

"Yeah, I know," she snuffled. "He sidestepped the damned thing. It was his. I know it."

"And if there was any wonder if Mum's crazy got to one of us, it's you, Keeks," Con replied.

"Morgan! Get your asses over here," Duarte shouted from the Amp's open front door. "Both of you!"

Connor kept his stride shallow so his sister could keep up. Kiki shot him an evil look and hastened her step, forcing him to fall in beside her.

"Save me your chivalry, Lieutenant," she muttered under her breath.

"If you save me from your macho bullshit, Inspector," Connor shot back and stalled at the door, sweeping into a mocking bow. "After you, sis."

"I don't know why I look up to you," Kiki grumbled but went in first.

"Because you're really fucking short, Keeks." He was stopped by Duarte clearing his throat.

"Children," the man greeted them.

"You need me to walk through what happened, Henry?"

"In a bit," Duarte said. "Come over here and tell me what you think about the asshole who did this. I want your thoughts. You've been knee-deep in this since the beginning."

"So what, now he's homicide?" Kiki teased lightly, jabbing at her brother's ribs. "I thought we just paid his kind to bust heads for us. Now you want him to think? Might catch the building on fire if he sparks that thick skull of his."

"At some point he's going to be too old to be rolling through doors," her partner replied. "Actually, I'm hoping we brainstorm this. Captain's getting kind of pissed off about this case dragging."

"Well, it's connected to Marshall's murder." Kiki paced around the edges of the coffee shop. "I think we can safely assume that. The guy's after Ackerman, but there's no demands for anything. Does he just have bad luck and keeps missing, or is he just toying with the kid?"

"Forest's not a kid," Connor asserted. "Trust me on that one."

A few feet away, Horan from the coroner's office was making her initial inspection. The blonde woman spared the Morgans and Duarte a glance. Connor smiled a hello and felt her eyes drop down the length of his body.

"You okay there, Morgan?" She nodded at his thigh.

He looked down at the tear in his jeans, dried blood sticking the ends of torn fabric to his skin. "Nah, I'm okay. Thanks, though, Doc."

"Well, if you need to get stitched up—" She grinned back at him, winking. "—any time."

Connor looked around, examining the shop's remains. Amid the organized chaos of forensics and the occasional uniform, he took in the scene, then studied the graffiti painted over the wall. The letters were tall and thick, uneven at the edges and splotchy. The neon paint was a lurid slap of bright against the dull beige plywood, and Connor noticed a tech carefully handling, then bagging, a green-splattered spray can.

The message was ugly, a warning to Forest or maybe just to the world in general. *One Down, More To*

Go definitely wasn't a love letter, but it didn't shed any light on who'd slaughtered the contractor.

"He's tall. Probably a guy." Connor stretched his hand up, measuring the length of his arm against the height of the letters. "Keeks, come over here so we can compare."

"We have the lab for that, but sure," Kiki agreed.

"Wouldn't hurt to know who we're looking at." Duarte gauged the differences between the two siblings' reaches. "Definitely shorter than Connor—"

"A fucking Balrog is shorter than Connor," Kiki sniped. "From the looks of things, based on average arm length and all of that shit, this guy's about six feet tall. About there."

"Educated. Or at least schooled," the older man commented, inspecting the letters closer. "Everything's spelled right. We've eliminated Forest, by the way. His financials don't show a cash layout for insurance, and motivation wasn't there for the father's death."

"Really can't be Forest. His handwriting's not this neat." Connor studied the wall intently. "Guy took his time, like it was really important."

"Even. Too even." Connor's sister lowered her hand. "The lettering, anyway. Nothing street about them. More like a font than actual handwriting."

"But the guy didn't know how to work a spray can. Look at the runs and splotches. A tagger would know better, even a newbie." Connor shoved his hands in his pockets. "Chances are he got paint all over his hands. Or gloves. Left the cans behind. Maybe prints?"

"If we're lucky," Duarte murmured. "Wouldn't that be great?"

The urge to step in and pick up evidence was overwhelming. He knew better. Hell, he'd walked past mountains of evidence on raids and never felt the urge to investigate further than he'd had to, leaving the sifting to the clean-up crew. He broke down scenes all the time, working with on-call detectives to close out a case, but this time it was different. This time it was Forest's life on the line.

"So we're looking for a tall guy with neon-green hands." Kiki snorted. "That eliminates the huffers. They go for gold and silver mostly, right?"

"Yeah, those have more toluene," Connor remarked absently. "So Henry, think we can get hardware stores to tell us who bought two green neon paint cans if we don't get prints?"

"This ain't no fucking TV show, Morgan." Duarte gave him a sarcastic low laugh. "What the hell does this guy have to connect him to Ackerman and Marshall?"

"Think it's got to be both of them?" Kiki took pictures of the wall with her phone. "Following the money isn't taking us anywhere. Ackerman's the sole beneficiary—"

"Yeah, but he doesn't have a will," Connor cut in. "His mother—the blonde you've got cooling her heels in lockup's going to get anything Forest has if he dies suddenly. She's got motive. And she was here."

"Something doesn't fit right. Didn't see any paint on her. Not that we won't look at her." Duarte turned to look at the counter where Horan and her crew were delicately removing any evidence connected to the crime scene. "Marshall's death was pretty clean, but the rest of it—it's dirty."

"He might have had time with Marshall. He's scrambling around here. Marshall's death wasn't meant to be the main event," Connor said softly. "If we shift the focus away from money and onto Forest, it makes more sense. Whoever's pulling all this shit is doing it to terrorize—specifically Forest."

"Then—what's her name? Ackerman's mother?" The senior inspector frowned and looked at his notes. "Ginger? That her legal name?"

"Yeah," Kiki replied. "Looks like. They ran her prelim sheet. Ginger's very well known for being in some pretty wrong places at the wrong times. And she dragged her little boy with her."

Connor knew what Kiki was saying. From the tone in her voice, it was a subtle way—in true Kiki fashion—of calling out Forest's own record. He smiled softly at her and said, "I know what's on his record. We've talked about it."

"And you're okay with—"

"What I'm not okay with is the fact his mum was out hawking his ass to guys when he should have been doing homework or playing soccer. When's the first time he got popped? Twelve? Thirteen?" Con rumbled. "And what kind of society is it when we're arresting kids for hooking? Something—or someone—puts them out there. They're fucking kids, love. Where the hell where you at twelve, Keeks? 'Cause I can tell you it sure as hell wasn't out on the streets hoping you'd make enough money to get food."

"Mum would have had my fucking ass," she agreed. "Only hooker I knew about was playing Pygmalion with a rich guy who couldn't drive a Lotus. God, she had great boots."

"I worry about the education your parents gave you both," Duarte muttered with a shake of his head. "So let's do the money thing first, but yeah, this is something about Ackerman. Say his mom is driving the crazy train. She'd have to eliminate Marshall, then knock her own kid off."

"She'd want to wait so he was declared Marshall's sole beneficiary." Kiki chewed on her pen. "But why'd she do all of this shit? She's his mother. It wouldn't be hard for her to get him alone. Would it, Con?"

"I don't know," Connor admitted. "I didn't get the feeling they had a lot of contact other than a couple of phone calls. I don't know if he'd come running if she crooked her finger. He might."

There'd been a longing in Forest's face when Con spotted Brigid embracing the drummer. And Brigid hugged Forest as often as she could. She'd taken a deep fondness to him—a quick, fierce affection rivaling even how she felt about her own children. Unlike Miki and Damie, Forest appeared to welcome the attention— warily, as if Brigid might change her mind—but that was something Connor would have expected from him. *A kitten bitten by a snake would be afraid of a rope*, Connor thought, *or even a soft blanket used to keep him warm*.

"Seems like we should start off with Ginger." Duarte began to pick his way out of the coffee shop, carefully stepping around any debris. "I agree with you, Keira. The mother would be able to have gotten this done quicker, so to Con's point, it's got to be about rattling Ackerman up. Let's head back in and see what Ms. Ackerman's got to say."

Connor held his hand out to Kiki to help her over a stack of plywood. She slapped his fingers away and stomped over the pile, pushing at him when she made it over. Rolling his eyes, he asked Duarte, "Mind if I sit in to listen?"

"Mind?" Duarte turned to raise a bushy eyebrow at Connor. "I didn't think I even had a say in the matter."

FOREST WAS fucking flying. Hell, they all were. There'd been no stumbling about or fighting to find the beat between them. Within a few seconds of playing, Damien and Miki stopped being rock stars in his head and turned into just another couple of musicians.

And at some point after that—he couldn't tell when—he felt like he'd been playing with them for years and couldn't imagine ever *not* sharing the thread of music with them.

It was a scary thing.

And at the same time, almost better than sex.

Almost, Forest thought. Because sex with Connor was pretty fucking incredible.

Miki acquitted himself well enough on the bass. While Damien was the better overall player, they'd all agreed Miki's bass skills could hold up—strong enough to let Damie's fingers fly through complicated lead pieces, leaving Miki to his singing.

And God, Forest had forgotten how damned good Miki St. John sounded. Stripped down to just the three of them, the man still shone, and Forest realized so much of Sinner's Gin's success had been just that—a stripped-down rock band with powerful vocals, ripping guitar, and lyrics torn out from the pair's souls.

When they finally stopped, Forest found his arms were hurting, and he was in sorry need of a shower. Hair plastered down to his face and neck, he dripped and shook from overusing his muscles. He'd tossed his shirt to the floor at some point during the set. It'd gotten damp and stuck to his back as he played, itching in places where it dried against his skin.

Ears ringing but smiling broadly, he bent forward, clenching the drumsticks in his fists, and leaned on his knees.

"Fuck, you're good," Miki finally said, shaking his fingers.

If Forest thought he'd been flying before, those three words from Miki's mouth sent him soaring up into the clouds.

"Thanks," he replied softly. "And thanks for letting me play. It feels good."

Damie studied him, a careful assessment of something Forest couldn't name. The guitarist shook out his own hands, then sucked on one of his fingers. Talking around his hand, he laughed. "Been a long time since I've played to blood."

"Dude," Forest exhaled the word, catching his breath. "You okay?"

"Yeah, just—been a long time," Damie replied softly. "And yeah, it feels good. Really fucking good."

They'd played everything—old blues standards, Sinner's Gin songs, and even a few things Miki'd written since the accident. A few times, Forest slid in an opinion, replacing a beat or quickening a spot. Miki listened, free of anything even remotely resembling an ego, and changed the music to reflect Forest's suggestions. At one point they'd agreed the change didn't work, but Miki shook his head, insisting it worked—they'd just not found the place for it.

As if something Forest wrote would be used in something Miki hadn't come up with yet.

"God, I reek." Forest looked around for his shirt. He needed something to wipe the kit down with.

"Want to grab a shower?" Damie tossed him a shop rag from a bundle he'd opened to use on his guitar. "I can loan you some stuff to change into. We're about the same size."

"That'll be great. Thanks. I—um—should probably call Brigid to see if she can come grab me." There wasn't a clock in the studio, and he'd left his phone back in the warehouse. "Do you know what time it is?"

"No fucking clue." Damie nudged Miki's shoulder. "And I'm hungry. You guys wanna order something in to eat?"

"Damie dials a mean Thai," Miki said to Forest. "You like Thai?"

"Yeah." He made a face. "Actually, I pretty much will eat anything that doesn't move. I'm not picky."

"How about if we all go grab showers, and I'll call some food in." Damie stretched his arms over his head, and Forest heard his spine crack. "You know what this band needs? Someone who can fucking cook."

"You know what this band needs?" Miki tossed Forest his shirt from the floor. "A fucking name."

"I DON'T know what you're asking about." Ginger Ackerman simpered when Senior Inspector Duarte set a cold soda down in front of her. "I went to go see my kid. He owns that place now."

"What I'm asking you, Ginger," Kiki replied softly, waiting for the woman to open her diet Sprite and take a sip before continuing, "is whether or not you'd seen who killed Brian Collerton, the man we found in the coffee shop, and more importantly, what the hell were you doing there?"

"We *did* find boxes of the Amp's supplies in your truck, as well as a couple of the higher-end appliances." Duarte pulled out a chair, positioning it at an angle near the table before sitting down. "Did you come with someone? Did Collerton see you guys, and the person you were with jumped him?"

"I didn't *come* with anyone. My kid asked me to help move some of his stuff out because it was expensive." Ginger smacked her lips after she drank, nervously plucking at her lower lip. "He didn't want anyone to steal it. I was moving it to a storage place for him."

"That's bullshit," Connor said aloud from his spot behind the one-way glass of the interrogation room's antechamber. "We even talked about moving it, but the place was locked up tight. The renovation crew was going to move it over to the studio space in a week. Why the hell would he *pay* for that stuff to be in storage?"

"That, my brother, is what we inspectors like to call a lie," Kane informed him, crossing his arms over his chest as he listened in on the discussion. "Kind of like what Mum does when she says you're pretty."

Reflected in the glass, Connor was struck by how similar he and his younger brother looked. Only a couple of years separated them, but while they'd been growing up, those few years seemed like such a chasm. Now he had to double take when he saw Kane—always a little bit surprised to find the scrawny, clumsy young boy'd become a wide-shouldered, tall man.

Glancing at Kane, Connor noted he was *still* taller—if only by a couple of inches.

Straightening up, Connor squared his shoulders. "I know what a lie is. I grew up hearing you do it."

"I learned it from you, brother," Kane shot back. "I learned it all by watching you."

"You'd think you'd be better at it," Con muttered, but his attention was on the woman Kiki was questioning.

It was odd to see a woman—an older, dried-out woman—having the same gestures as his lover. Forest played with his lower lip when thinking, and sometimes when he needed time to gather his words, his fingers tapped along the table, much like Ginger was doing at that moment. And while the brittleness in her son was evident in Ginger, there was also a cloying, manipulative air about her, as if she were waiting for the chance to gut the person next to her because she knew the going rate for a black-market kidney.

He couldn't imagine having the reaching, grasping woman as a mother, and Connor made a mental note to send Brigid flowers or chocolates as soon as he could. Still, she was fascinating to watch, her behavior going from outraged to submissive, oftentimes within the space of a second. One thing was for certain, Ginger had a loose grasp on reality and an even looser grasp on the truth, because Kiki and Duarte kept having to circle around her and hammer at her story, breaking apart every supposed fact she trotted out.

They were taking a break in the actual questioning. Instead, Duarte was pulling out photo after photo of the crime scene, asking Ginger to take a good look at what was going on in the main room when she supposedly was helping her son move his shop's equipment. Ginger looked at the pictures with an impassive stare, nothing registering on her face as photo after photo was placed on the table.

She asked to go to the bathroom, and the partners conversed a bit. It was an old trick used by people familiar with being dragged in by the cops. Still, Kiki motioned for Ginger to stand up, and there was a mild grumbling about being shackled up again, but the woman acquiesced. Duarte was left cooling his heels, and the brothers returned to their conversation.

"Your guy came out surprisingly well, considering he crawled out of that," Kane said softly. "And that's not something I thought I'd ever say in my lifetime. How're you doing with that? The gay thing."

"We're going to do this here?" Con asked, sliding a look at his brother.

"Might as well. They're sitting down for a game of 'let's play shake the lying witness' right now," Kane remarked. "Really, just quick. Tell me how you're doing, and I'll leave it be for a bit."

"I'm doing—okay," he admitted slowly. "It's kind of a punch to the teeth sometimes, but honestly, I fucking can't imagine him not being there. He feels good—feels right, even. I love him. It isn't even a question—between us, it just *is*. I don't know if I can explain it."

"You don't have to. I know exactly what you mean."

"Yeah," Connor murmured, thinking of how Kane's eyes lit up when Miki walked into the room. "You do."

"People giving you shit at work?" Kane studied his brother. "You giving yourself shit too?"

"Little of both." It was hard to admit, but Connor owned up to the qualms eating at the edges of his belly. "Some asshole put a pair of panties in my locker. Shoved them through the slats but wasn't man enough to come confront me."

"Asshole is right."

"Gotta tell you, brother." Connor turned and leaned his shoulder against the glass, crossing his arms over his chest. "It hurt a bit. I don't know who did it. I told my team directly. They're all fine with it, but someone on the squad's got some shit. I don't want to have to worry about who's got my back when I'm going in under fire."

"And you can't say shit without looking like some whiny bitch," Kane snorted, then grew serious. "How are *you* doing with it?"

"I talk a lot to God," he admitted. "I make deals, mostly. Begging him to let me have patience. To help me convince Forest we're good together. We've gotten to be good friends, me and God. It feels like it happened so fast, and Forest—God, he needs to be loved. I worry I've forced him into this, but when he looks at me, I can see he cares—shit, I make him smile. I don't think he's smiled a lot before. He's under my skin, K, and I'm just going to run with it. Put my arms around him and never let go."

"You've known him for months now. Not that quick, really. Gotta admit, you seemed to have gotten the easier one," Kane teased. "Less wild than mine."

"Miki'd chew your face off if you piss him off," he grunted. "Forest's more… mellow. He's not a pushover, but more like he'd rather flow around things. Honestly, that woman in there didn't do him any fucking favors, but he's—strong. In his own way. He's more like water—most of the time like a gentle rain, but then when pushed, it's like drinking from a fire hose. Tear your lips off if you get too close."

"Mum adores him." Kane laughed. "Said she was finally glad she got a son-in-law in her corner instead of Da's. You'd think it was a competition or something."

"Hard to live up to a man like Da," Con replied gently. "Trust me. I know."

Kiki returned with their prisoner and sat Ginger down. While they were gone, the senior inspector'd laid out all the photos he had of Collerton's murder as well as the other victims. The table was washed in death and blood. Ginger visibly recoiled when seated in front of the collage. Duarte cleared his throat, and the Morgans' attention snapped back to the room as Ginger's agitation rose.

"I don't know what happened to the guy!" Ginger growled out. "I was in the back. Okay? I just got there, and then I heard some screaming, so I hid."

"It would have taken you at least half an hour to get this stuff into the truck," he pointed out. Duarte tapped at a photo of a truck, its bed partially full with sloppily boxed supplies. "Now, either you had help and someone cut fifteen minutes of that, or you were there a hell of a lot longer than a few minutes. That tells me if you heard screaming, it had to have started while you were ripping your own son off. Let me tell you what I think happened, and I'm cutting you slack on this, Ginger, because I'm going to assume you are telling me the truth and *were* alone, got it?

"You knew Forest wasn't going to be around. He's been staying with a friend while he recovers, so you thought maybe now was a good time to help yourself to a few things in the shop. Maybe you thought he owed you—hell, Marshall probably owed you because you let him have the kid when he asked to adopt Forest. You had it coming to you," Duarte said.

"Reasonable," Kiki interjected. "But see, I'd say she heard Collerton come in and hid then, because she didn't want him to catch her shaking the place down. Am I right? Did you hide when you heard him come in?"

"I thought someone was going to rip the place off—"

"Someone was already ripping the place off, Ginger. That was *you*," Duarte pointed out. "But you came in the back door—probably because you got a key from someplace and you *guessed* the alarm would be off. No one turns on an alarm when the building's been beat up. Stuff falling, plywood instead of windows—none of the glass connections were working anyway, so the alarm would have kept bumping up with alerts. You *knew* they'd be off."

"Marshall *gave* me a key." The woman shifted. "I—"

"Let's say Marshall gave you a key. For whatever reason he'd give you a key," Kiki said. "And even if Forest *did* say, 'hey, Mom, come help me move some stuff,' why didn't you call the police when you heard a man screaming in the front of the shop? You had your phone on you."

"I didn't think—" Ginger's eyes shifted, bouncing between the detectives. "You're confusing me."

"Why didn't you leave out the back? You've seen Collerton. He didn't die easy. You were sitting there and listening to it. Unless you were helping. Maybe it was you who'd spotted Collerton and knew he'd IDed you." Kiki leaned in. "Is that why you're covering up for who helped you out? Because the guy who came with you killed for you; then he split? Is all of this on the walls just to cover it up? And then you hid when you heard the door opening again? Or maybe you were scared your friend was coming back for you?"

"I didn't kill anyone! Fuck, the guy was already there when I showed up. The fucking back door key wasn't working, and I went to the front. It was already open!" Her lips peeled back from her teeth, and Ginger snarled at Kiki from across the table. "He was *already* there."

"So no screaming, then. No opening doors. No one else coming in. Just the cop who caught you red-handed." Duarte stood up from the table, letting out an exasperated breath. "You walked past a dead man and thought, what? Time to go rip my son off? Nothing else? No worries about the man's life? His family?"

"He was already dead," she sneered. "Who the fuck cares about that? Not like he was going to get any deader while I was in the back. I was going to call the cops when I was done."

"See, that's how I know you weren't there to help your kid, Ginger." Kiki's snarl shoved Ginger back in her chair. "A decent person would have stopped worrying about storing equipment and called for help. A *thief* would just continue stealing. *That's* why you're being arrested, you piece of shit. For whatever we can pin on you."

"I want my fucking lawyer," Ginger screamed at Duarte. "I want my fucking lawyer, and I want someone to call my damned kid. He'll bail me out. You'll fucking see, and he won't press any goddamned charges—"

"See, I don't need your son to press charges, Ginger," Duarte said, calmly flicking a bit of lint from his jacket. "You were caught breaking and entering by an SFPD officer, in addition to having already discovered a murder victim and doing nothing. If we can show there was a speck of life in Brian Collerton at any time you were in that shop, I'm going to nail you for accessory to murder. Because you did *nothing*."

"You can't—" Ginger sputtered. "Look, my kid—"

"Might as well start hoping he'll even pick up the phone when you call, Ginger," Kiki said as she gathered up the crime scene photos. "Because really, what kind of mother walks past a dying man just to fuck over her own son?"

CHAPTER SIXTEEN

*Pick up the beat, Sinjun. You're falling
    behind.*
*Fuck you, I'm the goddamned singer. Not
    the bassist, man.*
*I already got you a drummer, what the
    fuck else you want?*
*Brigid got me the drummer. What? You
    wanna add something, Fore?*
*Nah, I'm just trying not to geek out and
    say Damn it, D, I'm a singer, not a
    bassist, but you two go on and work
    that shit out.*
—Home Studio Session #1

"I CAN'T believe you arrested my mother," Forest grumbled under his breath while he paced around the Victorian's family room. He ran his long fingers through his blond hair and rubbed at his skull. "No, forget that. I can believe it. She's my mother. Of course I fucking believe it."

"I can't fucking believe she expected you to bail her out." Connor came in from the kitchen and handed his lover an opened bottle of strawberry lemonade. "Hey, don't glare at me. I keep telling you, my mum's already decided you're her son. I've got to watch my step or I'm out of the family."

"Right." Forest rolled his eyes as he took the lemonade. The couch looked really good, especially since his thighs hurt like a son of a bitch and his arms felt like Jell-O. Flopping into the curve of the sectional, he moaned when the cushions cradled his aching body. "God, what the hell were we thinking, playing that long?"

The house was warm, helping his clenched muscles. Another hot shower helped, and he'd pulled on a pair of black sweats but hadn't bothered with a shirt, since Forest hadn't been too sure he'd be able to lift his arms up high enough to get one over his head. He hesitated to lean into the couch, but Connor gently pushed him back.

"Your shit's too nice for—"

"Only thing of mine I worry about is you," Connor growled at him while setting his beer down on the coffee table. "You were there all day. How much of it was spent playing?"

"Nine hours." Forest made a face when his spine disagreed with his shifting about. Something popped in his lower back, and the rush of relief sent sparkles along his vision. "Oh yeah, I needed that to give. Damn, D's hands must be bleeding. Fucking Miki—not even hoarse. His throat's got to be made of adamantium

or something. Con, really—what was I thinking? Nine
hours!"

"You were thinking it was nice," Connor replied.
The man tapped Forest's thighs. "Lift up. I'll massage
your legs."

"Nice?" Forest contemplated the word. *Nice* didn't
seem to fit. Brutal. Heartbreaking—especially when
he joined in on the chorus of "Whiskey and Rye." The
shock on Miki's face was palpable, but a breath later
he'd recovered, his raspy, hot vocals returning as strong
as ever. They'd found their sync right then, and Damie
nodded once at Forest, a silent encouragement to continue on.

That's when he'd found his wings and he'd fall-
en into the music, rising up to the challenge of dou-
ble-timing "Gin and Demonic." Miki's laughter was
as sweet as the riffs coming off Damien's guitar, and
they'd pounded through another set, teasing one another with long, drawn-out battles of chords, beats, and
vocal acrobatics.

It all felt so right, but still, Forest was taken aback
when Miki—damnable, street-suckled Miki—told
Forest to show up for practice the day after next. He
couldn't breathe then. He didn't even start breathing
until Damie came and slapped him on the back.

Shoving some clothes into Forest's arms, the guitarist had said, "Welcome to the Madhouse."

He was paying for that contentment. Forest's mind
buzzed from stimulation, and his thoughts kept going
back to song bits, hammering out rough burrs in spots
they'd hung up on. He'd need to get some music sheets
and notebooks, maybe even work out a vocal harmony
to support Miki's melody on the last song they'd done
before collapsing from exhaustion.

Connor picked up Forest's bare foot and rubbed at a knot in his arch. Forest moaned at the tingle of pain and pleasure of his tense muscle being dug into.

"Did you get a hold of that guy's family?" Forest asked softly. "Shit, I should probably call them—"

"Maybe in a bit, love," Con suggested. "Right now, they'll need time. You did, remember?"

"Yeah." He nodded, his expression going soft. "Except I had this cop stalking me, so I don't know exactly how much time I had."

"Yeah, well, that turned out okay. Hold on, there's a bad knot here."

Leaning his head back against the couch cushion, Forest gritted his teeth against the groans crawling up from his throat, but one escaped anyway, drawn out when Con's thumb found a particularly hard spot.

"Con... Jesus!" Forest bit his lip, hard enough to almost taste blood. "God, I don't know if that feels good or not, but fuck, don't stop. I hurt fucking everywhere."

It was late. Late enough for Forest to have eaten twice at Miki's and worry about Connor's late appearance at the warehouse. The cop in Connor filled Forest in with brief bursts of information, a staccato report of words and gestures, but the delivery'd been sweet, a rocking of embraces and kisses hot enough to make Forest blush even as Damie and Miki wolf-whistled and catcalled their drummer. They'd come home, and Connor'd lit a fire in the family room's massive fireplace while Forest went to climb into a hot shower, his body finally acknowledging the shock of having played steadily for too long.

"I'd figure your arms, but your feet?" Connor's fingers ghosted over the spot again, and Forest twitched in anticipation. "Take some of that ibuprofen I gave you, because, babe, it hurts to watch you move."

"Feet. Legs." He tried to lift his arms, but they wobbled a bit before he let them drop. Connor shook out the requisite number of tablets into his hand, then gave them to Forest. He swallowed them with a mouthful of sweet-tart lemonade, gagging slightly at the powdery drag of the pills in his throat. "Drumming beats down your ass. You've got kicks to worry about and twisting around to get the upper part of the kit. I haven't done a long session in fucking forever. Usually it's just a couple of hours, then a break. This was… intense."

"But you had fun?"

"Fun?" Forest had to think about it, then nodded. "Yeah, it felt—good. Like it was easy but at the same time hard. Damie writes some hard licks to keep up with, but Miki's got some stones. The shit he writes, it blows my mind. I just sat there thinking fuck, I want to play this. Hell, then he asked me what I thought about something, and suddenly they weren't rock stars, you know? Just… really fucking good musicians… guys I'd want to play with—for, like, forever."

Connor's crooked smile warmed him, nearly as much as the man's hands roaming over his calves. "So yeah, you had fun."

They sat in companionable silence as Connor kneaded the hard muscles in Forest's calves. Forest's sweats rolled down over Connor's hands, and he hissed in frustration.

"Here, lift your hips," Connor said as he reached up to grab Forest's waistband. "These need to come off."

"If those come off, am I still going to get my massage?" He tried for a leer but must have been so off the mark, because Connor let out a rolling chuckle. "Fine."

He lifted his hips, and a burning ache shot through his thighs. Wincing, Forest held still for a few seconds while Connor tugged his sweatpants down, then let his bare ass hit the couch.

"You're not wearing underwear under these," Connor said flatly. "And you expect me to ignore you long enough to give you a massage?"

"You took my underwear with you," he protested. "Give them back."

"No, I don't think so," Con refused with a shake of his head. Tossing the pants over Forest's crotch, he said, "Here. Keep the bits part covered. I'm strong. I can do this. Talk to me about something. Take my mind off the fact you're lying across of me naked and pretty."

"If a pizza delivery guy shows up, you're going to be doing this porn shoot by yourself," he grumbled under his breath.

"Hey, I picked up a lot of good tips from that pizza delivery guy," Connor shot back. "Don't hear you complaining."

"I'll start complaining when you're done."

Connor's hands began moving again, and Forest gripped the couch, whimpering.

"Hold on, I'm going to get some Tiger Balm." The man lifted Forest's legs and slid out from under him. Connor returned to the couch with a small glass jar and maneuvered back under Forest's lower limbs. The smell of cinnamon and cloves hit the air when Con unscrewed the jar, and Forest hissed at his lover when Connor smeared a large dollop of the salve over his palms.

"You are *definitely* not fucking me with that on your hands," he warned. "I don't care *what* the pizza guy taught you."

"No sex. Not now." Connor chuckled. He picked up where he left off, soothing the ointment's heat into Forest's aching legs. "I'm not even sure you could bend in the right direction. Now, talk to me. Remember? You're supposed to distract me."

"What am I going to do about my mom?" Forest said suddenly. Connor's eyes found his, and the man's mouth tightened under Forest's stare. "About bail. When she called me—well, her court-appointed lawyer did—he thinks he can get her bail tomorrow morning. She can't even get her shit together to see me in the hospital, but—*fuck*."

Connor didn't say anything for a long while. He continued to rub and dig into the knots along Forest's calves, then shifted up to reach the ache in Forest's thighs. Finally he said, "What do you want to do? And whatever that is, I'll stand by you in it. You just need to tell me what you want."

Sitting in the quiet comfort of a peace Forest never thought he'd ever experience, he whispered, "Would it be bad if I just wanted her to go away?"

"No," Connor replied softly. "No one would blame you for that."

"I feel like I'm—dirty." Forest leaned forward and put his hands on Connor's, stilling them. "What I did with her—what she—shit, just everything—like I can't ever get clean. And then, it's like you're here, and I'm thinking—shit, I don't want to get this on you.

"I feel like every time you touch me, I smear it on you—this stinky, oily me I can't ever wash off. You're so fucking good, Con. Sometimes it hurts to touch you, because it's like I'm holding on to the sun. And I hate feeling like that—hating myself because I'm scared to

touch you—scared to—love you. And I hate her for it.
I really just—"

He had to look away. In all the time since he began
living with Frank, he'd ignored the whispering of disgust coming from the back of his mind. But being with
Connor changed things, and the walls he'd built to hold
back the grime broke, flooding his awareness with just
how deeply he'd bathed in the gutter's filth.

"*A ghra*." Connor sighed. Then his hands came up
to cup Forest's face. The strong sting of balm on his jaw
made his eyes water, but Forest didn't mind. Not when
the cupping was accompanied by a slow, lingering kiss
turned to a deeper ache when Connor growled at the
stretch of their tangled bodies. "Shit, that stuff burns."

Connor dropped his hands to Forest's shoulders,
kneading them lightly. He stole another kiss, this time a
delicate whisper of lips and their breaths, scented berry
and citrus, drifting together in a swirling warm current.

"I look at you, and all I think is—God, thank you
for his strength," Connor murmured into their kiss. "I
can't imagine how you put one foot in front of the other every single day of your life. That woman—the one
whose only thought should have been for you—she
may have given birth to you in that filth, but that's a
stew of her own making. *You* were the one to walk out
of it—that foul, depraved mire she wallows in. It's her
soul that's wrong—so fucked up she's happy in that
kind of life—but *you*, *a ghra*, you survived her trying
to drown you in it.

"Then you picked yourself up and fought her when
she tried to drag you back into it." He paused, stopping
long enough to curl Forest's toes with a sensual, fierce
kiss, then continued. "I'd be happy to have any of your
power, any of that strength, smeared on me. Touching

you—is incredible, but loving you, Forest mine, makes me feel invincible."

CONNOR SCRUBBED his hands before locking the house up for the night. Swaddled in the sheets, Forest sniffed at Con's fingers and eyed him suspiciously.

"I can still smell it," he grumbled.

"Then I guess you're going to have to be the one to spread lube over yourself," Con replied smoothly. His cock liked the idea, because it steeled itself immediately, tightening up his already hard length. Tossing the lube toward Forest, he chuckled, "Actually, I really like that idea, but can you bend that much? 'Cause if not…."

"Oh, I'll bend," Forest muttered. "Help me find the damned tube."

They had a Benny Hill chase with the lube, especially since Connor decided he'd spend more time with his hands on Forest's hard abdomen and ass than locating the small plastic vial. While swearing at Con's interference, Forest burst into laughter when Connor half rolled him over under the pretense of looking for the lubricant. Instead, he bent down and sank his teeth into the meat of Forest's ass, getting a playful yelp from his lover.

Connor let Forest roll back over. He straddled the lanky drummer, then placed his hands on either side of Forest's shoulders, resting his weight on his palms and knees.

"God, it is good to hear you laugh," he said.

It was good. He'd never really thought about how little he'd heard laughter in Forest's voice until a few days before when the blond chuckled while they watched a movie, and his smile shyly stretched over his face.

Connor felt like he'd taken a shot of whiskey when he saw that smile—or maybe even swallowed a mouthful of sunshine. Either way, he'd sworn there and then to keep Forest laughing, every day and for as often as he could, selfishly wanting to bask in that warm glow.

"Shit, I hope I can do this." Forest slathered lube onto his fingers. He pushed Connor's hand away before he could help.

"Hey, I scrubbed them!" Connor protested lightly.

"Yeah, like I'd gotten all of the rooster sauce out from under my fingernails before I got that eyelash out of your eye."

Connor winced, remembering the half hour burning sear he'd endured, and dropped his hands back down to his sides.

If there was anything hotter than seeing Forest kneel on the bed and dip his oiled fingers down his own crack, Connor didn't know what it was. Resting on his shins and his feet angled out into a V, Forest's pale body arched forward and his shoulders twisted about, his arm down along his hips. His hands were graceful, artistic, and fluid, and Forest's long fingers slid farther down, smearing the fragrant oil on the cheeks of his ass.

Hooking his fingers down between his cleft, Forest looked up through a tangle of gold-streaked hair, his enormous brown eyes hooded with lust. Connor saw the shift in the man's awareness when Forest realized his pose—his movements—enflamed Connor's lust. Forest finally realized how much power he had over his lover, and he licked his mouth, a long sweep of pink tongue over plump lips. He arched his body farther, the tilt of his hips splaying his asscheeks apart and giving Connor a clear view of what lay between them.

Connor swallowed, clenching his fingers into the sheets. Then Forest's long, elegant fingers stroked at his hole, plunging the tip of one past his dusky rim, and Connor lost his mind.

The faint golden light from the overhead lamp threw every rise of muscle on Forest's body into a study of bright and dark. The ropy cords on Forest's arms stood out as he slid his fingers in deeper, coating his hole with a thick slather of fragrant oil. Heated by Forest's warm skin, the lubricant's faint vanilla scent turned musky thick.

"God, baby," Connor growled. "You have no idea what you do to me."

He couldn't wait. Didn't want to wait. Connor snapped a condom over his eager cock. Gripping Forest's wrist, Connor guided his lover's fingers out of his suckling hole. The blond surrendered to Connor, allowing himself to be placed on a rise of thick accent pillows, his back resting against the headboard.

Forest's hands came up to skim over Connor's shoulders, tracing out every bulge and dip of his broad chest and arms. They kissed, and Connor moaned into his lover's mouth, his cock dancing up against Forest's length, a quick bow of hello, then a rub for good measure.

"I like this," Forest rasped. "I like being able to see you."

"I like being able to see you too." Connor slid his hands under Forest's thighs, spreading him open. "Hold on to me, *a ghra*. I'm planning on giving you the ride of your life."

He slid in, hot and hard. Forest took him, grunting from the intrusion, but Con's legs came up, and Connor slipped his bended legs under his lover, cradling

Forest's hips with his hands. He shoved up again, thrusting deeper, and bent his head down to kiss the length of Forest's neck. The man moaned and writhed, twisting around Connor's dick as it throbbed in Forest's depths.

"Fuck," Forest stammered. "Shit, you're so— fucking huge."

If there was a heaven, Connor was sure he'd found its gates or at least an angel guarding it, because Forest's face shone with deep pleasure, and the shadows of Connor's day burned away under the sheer delight he felt at hearing Forest begging for more.

"Grab my shoulders, *a ghra*," Connor ordered brusquely. "And hold on."

Forest did as he was told, gripping Con's shoulders tightly. Anchored on Connor's dick, he leaned back, resting against the headboard. Grabbing the high wooden slat board on either side of Forest's shoulders, Connor slammed up, rocking into his lover's clench. The bed held—as did Forest, and Connor grinned wickedly, poised to fuck Forest until the man went boneless and sleepy.

It took him a few seconds to find the right beat, but after a couple of tentative thrusts, Connor hit the mark of Forest's body. He felt the shiver work through Forest's thighs when he hit the man's sweet spot, and Forest's balls tightened up, rolling in the curve of Connor's body.

Connor caught himself and fell into a steady rhythm, shifting and rolling his hips to angle his cock into Forest's tight channel. His body grew slick with a dewy sweat, and Forest licked at his nipple, catching the nub with a nip of his teeth.

The slight pain drove needling sensations down his belly and straight into Connor's balls. Hitching his lover up with a thrust of his thighs, Connor worked in hard, stretching Forest's legs farther apart. The man's hands slipped down to Con's arms, and Forest grunted again, bending toward Connor. Panting, Forest dove a hand down between their pressed-together bodies, finding the length of his dick plastered against Con's stomach.

Forest's moving fingers tickled, and Connor laughed, the tiny jerking movements from his chuckles jostling Forest's ass as he bounced up and down on Con's dick. Supported by the curl in Connor's form and the high headboard, Forest began to stroke himself off, the squick of his hand moving over his cock an erotic counterpoint to the steady slap of their bodies meeting.

Their existence stretched only as far as their bodies, and Connor felt *everything* else disappear. The only thing—the only person—to matter in that space and time was Forest. His heartbeat skipped along, matching Forest's erratic panting and groans.

"Love you," Forest murmured softly. "God, I'm sorry…."

It broke Connor's heart to hear the tender plea in Forest's voice. Even after meeting the man's mother, Con couldn't wrap his mind around Forest's life and what he'd survived—endured—just to be with Connor in that moment.

He slowed his beating thrusts and used one hand to cup his lover's jaw, turning Forest's tearstained face toward him. Kissing at the silvery trails, Connor pressed his lips against Forest's damp lashes, shushing him with low, cooing murmurs.

"So fast—us," Forest mumbled. "Not. Even. Real."

"Yeah, baby, it's real," Connor reassured him, stroking Forest's face with his thumb. Rolling his hips, he worked in and out of Forest's body, his dick pulling at the tight ring. "This. You. Me. Fuck, us. How can this not be real? You feel so fucking good. On my body. In my soul. In my fucking heart. So yeah, *a ghra*, so fucking real."

Forest clung to him, weathering the storm of Connor's lovemaking. Then he arched back, reveling in the long strokes. Forest reached again for his cock. Running his fingers down his shaft, his knuckles caught on the ridges of Connor's abdomen.

"Come for me, baby," Connor urged softly. "Show me how much you like this. Show me how much you love me."

Forest's spill hit them hard and fast, a torrent of hot, milky seed over the ridge of his cock. It flowed down his fingers and worked through the hair trailing from Con's navel. Bending over, Connor kissed his lover and rocked, matching his strokes to the shuddering tremors of Forest's release. Forest tasted sweet and dark, a thread of sensual honey woven through the dim shadows of their bedroom. When Forest's tongue flicked over the roof of Connor's mouth, he flung himself into the rising swell of pleasure coming up from his balls and plunged as far as he could into his lover's body, his balls sliding through the part of Forest's cleft.

The slight squeeze of Forest's ass on his balls drove Connor the rest of the way, and he emptied his load, his come shooting up hot and strong into the hollow of Forest's body. His cock sang and spilled, enrobed in his release. Forest gave one last shuddering mewl and went limp, panting hard as Connor's cock spat out its last few curls, his balls twined up to cuddle Forest's body.

Gently, he rolled Forest over, sliding free of his lover's limp form. Connor tossed the knotted condom in the general direction of the room's trash can, then tugged a sheet over them, not caring if they woke up stuck to the fabric and probably each other.

"Fuck, I'm going to pay for that in the morning," Forest laughed. "Like drumming wasn't enough."

"Want me to take it back?" Connor teased. "Because I'm pretty sure I can do it in reverse. Maybe not all of it, but the important bits."

"Wouldn't live through it." Forest yawned, his eyes heavy from fatigue. "Thank you."

"For?"

"Loving me. Fuck, even thinking about wanting me." Forest sighed, snuggling his shoulder against Connor's chest. "It's like a dream. Except with some of the world still pushing in. Like… whoever killed those people at the Amp."

"And your mother," Connor reminded him, kissing the tip of Forest's nose.

He made a face and said, "Yeah, her."

"How about if we worry about all of that in the morning?"

"Yeah, if I can move," Forest said through a yawn, "I think I'm going to bail her out."

"Okay." He stayed quiet after that. Connor could almost hear Forest thinking, the wheels turning carefully. "If that's what you want."

"I need to see her," he confessed in a low voice. "I need to tell her we're done. I can't have her shit on me anymore. She can't keep—I won't let her fuck me up any more. And it fucking hurts, but she's—my mother poisons me—my life. Is that wrong? Asking her to just… walk away."

"No, babe, it's not," he replied, kissing the damp blond strands at Forest's temple. "Sometimes, even if you want to love someone, they're so bad for you—they'll kill off parts of you even as you try to love them more. I can't say I'll be sad if you never have anything to do with her, but if ever you change your mind, I'll support that too. Whatever you need, so long as she doesn't get to hurt you anymore."

"Because you love me." Forest's whisper could barely be heard over their breathing, but Connor caught it anyway.

"Yeah, baby." Connor tucked his fingers under Forest's chin and gently pushed up so he could look down into his lover's face. "Because I love you."

CHAPTER SEVENTEEN

Restless itch
Need to scratch my sin
Fingers in deep
Don't let it end
Confused and alone
Someone's puppet again
—Scratch My Sin

"DID YOU have to bring all of Sinner's Gin with you to look at these?" Kiki grumbled, passing a stack of booking photo slips over to Forest.

"No, just the ones that are alive," he muttered under his breath. "They wanted to come. It's for support."

"They're signing autographs." She rolled a chair over to the desk where he sat, staring at the musicians standing at the edge of the bull pen. "Shit, now Damie's autographing some chick's boobs. They're going to get my ass kicked."

Forest glanced over his shoulder at the guys who'd brought him in. Damie looked like he was eating up the attention, and Miki had what Forest now knew was his "public" face on, an inscrutable, polite mask he donned to work through a crowd of grasping people. He met the singer's eyes and winked, getting Miki to crack a wry smile at him.

It'd been almost three weeks since the stolen van crashed through the Amp, and in that time, the shift in his life was nearly too much for Forest to wrap his mind around. The band—*the band*—was his lifeblood. Spending hours with Miki and Damie playing made him almost forget someone was trying to kill him. At first he'd wondered if the two guys were merely humoring his presence so Connor didn't worry about him being alone, but they'd clicked. He endured Damie's boisterous ego and laughed with Miki when the guitarist went off about music in general.

And the playing—God, the music they made—it flowed through his soul and filled him. Then there was Connor.

He tugged at his jeans, silently scolding his quickly hardening dick. Shit, even thinking about the man gave him a hard-on. Not something he wanted to deal with in the middle of the day without Connor around to help him get rid of it.

"Perv," Forest scolded his cock. "You're at a god-damned police station."

His cock ignored him, continuing its merry little happy dance as if to remind him *cop* was now on the list of erotic words that got Forest horny.

"Fucker," he muttered halfheartedly.

"Hey." Miki pulled up a chair and sat by Forest's elbow, peering over his arm to look at the photos. "These the guys Frank had a beef with?"

"Some," Kiki replied. "Mostly people he knew back in the day—when he was more of a druggie. Or at least getting popped more for possession."

"He was a stoner, sure," Forest murmured, staring at the photos. "But nothing hard. Nobody gets killed over pot."

"Ackerman, people get killed for stealing someone's pen," she replied caustically. "Take your time and just look through the photos. See if you recognize anyone who'd come by the Amp recently. It's a long shot, but something might hit you. You wait here. I'm going to get Mr. Rockstar out of sight before my captain spots him and I get chewed out."

He sat, listening to Miki hum and sing next to him. The man was never quiet, not really. He vibrated with sound, a thrumming soul only silent when he was asleep. And, as Forest discovered one day when Miki'd passed out on the couch, he sang then too.

"I like that," Miki said softly. "What you just tapped out. Here, write it down."

"You write it down," Forest said, ruefully discovering he'd started drumming on the tabletop in time with Miki's humming. Passing over a pen and notepad from a stack on Kiki's desk, he waved the photos in the air. "I've got homework. Jesus, Frank knew a lot of lowlifes. This is going to take forever."

They worked in silence, Miki scribbling down music while Forest stared at faces he didn't know. He pulled out five shots of maybes, then glanced over to where Damie still stood, talking and smiling at the small cluster of people around him.

"He really likes that, huh?" Forest murmured to Miki.

"Yeah, D's always been the rock star. Even before he was one." Miki's mouth tugged into a smirk. "He used to pour on the charm to get laid. Now he's getting laid, and there's nowhere for it to go. Going to explode if we don't do something about it soon."

"Eh?" Forest cocked his head, not following what Miki was saying. "I don't get it."

"We're going to have to get up on stage soon." Miki stopped writing long enough to look toward Damien. "He kind of needs that. Always has. So, there it is. Got you now on drums. All we're missing is a bassist. 'Cause yeah, I can play one, but I'm fucking mediocre. I don't want to sing in front of crappy music."

Forest let the man's words sink in, and he swallowed. "Wait, *I'm* your new drummer? For a band?"

"What the fuck do you think we've been doing these past few weeks?" he growled under his breath. "Knitting? Yeah, you're our fucking drummer. Shit, Forest. Dude, what the fuck?"

"I didn't really…." He trailed off. Leaning back in his chair, Forest let out a long whistle. "Fucking hell. I'm your *drummer*."

"Nice of you to catch up," Miki grumbled. "I don't think it's going to be a huge long touring shit. It's like we're starting at square one again, and I… can't deal with that crap again. Hell, I'd be fine if I never crawled back up on stage, but it's kind of fun once you get there. I'm okay with hitting a few big cities. And studio shit— *that* I love. You up for that?"

"Yeah, I um… yeah," Forest babbled quickly. "What about if Con and I… you know. I mean, he's Kane's brother, and if we go south and…."

"If you say we'd dump you or you guys might break up, I'm going to punch you in the face." Another pause in Miki's writing and then a furious scribble as he crossed out something he wrote. "The band's the band. Nothing touches that. 'Sides, you and he are probably going to have the whole kids, minivan, and one-point-five dogs thing. Now shut the fuck up, keep looking at the photos, and give me a damned pencil. This pen's for shit."

"Yeah, I'm good with that," Forest replied softly, passing Miki a pencil. "But I'm *not* driving a minivan."

HE WAS sick of looking at photos. He was tired of trying to stare at men's faces and find some feature to trigger his memory. Even worse, Forest was beginning to think he was looking at the same five guys, just from different angles or maybe even with fake mustaches. Covering one man's upper lip with his finger, Forest chuckled at the heavy walrus whiskers he'd given a bony criminal's face.

"Hey, baby." Connor slid up behind Forest, leaning over the chair. "How're you doing?"

The man's Irish was as hot as his kiss.

And the station's noise dropped to a stony quiet— becoming so still he could hear Con's heartbeat.

Forest's heart, however, came to a dead stop.

He was so shocked he couldn't even enjoy the kiss.

And it'd been a *hot* kiss.

Hot enough to start Forest's heart up again despite the shocked still hum reverberating through the station.

He drowned in Connor's deep blue eyes, unable to look away, and whispered, "Dude, you just came *out* to the cops."

"Yeah, well—I'm not going to hide you, Forest," Connor murmured, pressing his mouth against Forest's lips. The man was big, made bigger by his SWAT uniform, unrelieved black and form-fitting body armor. "I'm my father's son—my mother's son. I back down to no one, especially if they come after someone I love. That's the way of it, *a ghra*. I'm a *Morgan*."

Halfway through their next kiss, the station began to thrum again, a cacophony of voices, clinking cups, and mumbled profanities about shitty technology and wayward criminals. Forest savored the affection, flicking his tongue briefly past the part of his lover's lips to tickle at Con's teeth. Laughing, the man pulled back—just in time to get smacked on the shoulder by his younger sister.

"Lieutenant, keep your hands off my witness," Kiki ordered.

"I haven't even *begun* to get my hands on your witness," Connor promised. "How long have you been at this? And where are the Toxic Twins?"

"They went to the Sound. The drumsticks we have at the warehouse are shitty." Forest held up a photo of a graying, gaunt man. There was something definitely familiar about him, but for the life of him, he couldn't place where he'd seen the guy before. Passing it over to Kiki, he said, "I know him, but I can't tell you where from."

"You sure?" Kiki sat down on the edge of the desk, pushing her brother aside. "Think back over the past month or so. Maybe even before Marshall died. Could you have seen him then? Maybe at the coffee shop?"

"Shit, I don't know." He took the photo back and stared hard.

It was like he could almost hear the man's voice, a bitter, scalding high-pitched whine. Closing his eyes, Forest tried to imagine what the man could have been talking about—money? Drugs? None of that connected the dots, and he opened his eyes, shaking his head. He was about to toss the photo onto the desk when he remembered where he'd seen the man before.

"This guy—he was arguing with Frank. In the Sound, like a few weeks before—the fire? Maybe? I don't remember. I thought he was bitching about a studio session because he kept going on about lost time." Forest met the siblings' confused looks with an exasperated roll of his eyes. "Lots of people book studio time but never show up. Thing is, their deposit is nonrefundable, so they come in to bitch about it. Happens all the time. I just kept setting up and let Frank handle it."

"This is Gary Rollins," Kiki said softly, and Forest's breath caught. "You know who that is, right?"

"Yeah," Forest replied. "Shit, he looks so old. It's only been, like, ten years."

"Old's what happens when you go to prison as a pedo." Kiki shrugged.

"Who's Gary Rollins?" Connor cocked his head, studying the photo intently. "Name sounds familiar."

"He tried some shit on me when I first moved in with Frank. A couple of years later—my head wasn't on straight, and I got into the car with him behind the Sound, but Frank saw him. Pulled him out through the car window and beat the shit out of him." Forest whistled under his breath. "Fuck, I was—like, fourteen? Fifteen?"

"Underage enough to be tagged for a pedo. I remember now. Complaint was filed against Frank for assault." Connor frowned, picking the photo up to study it. "Good for Frank."

"Rollins pressed charges against Frank, but the pedo charge stuck on him," Kiki informed them. "He was caught with another teenager about a year later, and that sent him up. He got out about six months ago. Went straight into a halfway house, and about a month ago, Rollins slipped his leash, along with a couple of the others living there. No one knows where they are."

"So he's a good bet, then," Connor supposed.

"Yeah," his sister said. "He knows the Sound. Probably knows the coffee shop too. Had a confrontation with Marshall—maybe about ending up in jail. Marshall catching him with Forest started his record. Anything after that would put him behind bars."

"Hey, Morgan!" a uniform shouted from across the bull pen, and both siblings looked up. He pointed to Kiki and said, "Dispatch just came over with a 911 coming out of your murder scene down at Chinatown—possibly shots fired. They're sending a unit over but thought you should know."

Dropping his hands from Forest's shoulders, Con frowned. "Wait, did you say the guys went down to the Sound?"

"Yeah. But—" The memory of Frank's shooting hit Forest, and he paled. "Fuck. I'm stupid. I shouldn't have asked them to go down there. *Fuck*."

"I'm heading down there." Kiki pushed off the desk and reached for a phone. "Get some backup. If it's Rollins, then let's nail the bastard. Don't worry, kid. Miki and D will be okay. Miki's a tough shit."

"I should have thought—" Forest began, but Connor shook his head, brushing his mouth with a gentle kiss. "Con, if they get hurt...."

"No, babe." The man stopped him before he could say more. "*This* is not on you. Don't ever think you brought this down on any of us."

THE VERBAL scuffle'd been brief. There wasn't enough time to deliberate. Duarte came back from testifying in court just soon enough to be pulled into the unmarked he shared with Kiki. Over the inspectors' protests, Connor snagged Riley to take Forest home, then, after ignoring his sister when she argued against his coming, drove his Hummer to the Sound.

It was a very long ten-minute drive. Riding in the wake of Duarte's insane driving, Connor flipped on his emergency lights and followed close on the unmarked's tail. Streams of cars wove in and out of Chinatown, pulling up as close to the curbs as they could get to make way for the police, but the narrow streets left little room to maneuver.

Connor tried Miki's number, but it went to voicemail, just as it had the first ten times he'd tried. Kiki's voice was flat over the radio, informing the dispatchers of their ETA. His scanner crackled with information as dispatch cut into the chatter, giving the responders a timeline for everyone's arrival. Then in the middle of the muted noise, Con's phone chimed in, and he hit the Answer button, his heart sinking when Kane's voice cut through the calls.

"What the fuck's going on, Con?" His brother was furious. "Where are you? Dispatch said something about Miki, and I can't get him on the phone. No one's telling me shit. What the fuck…."

"Supposed shots fired down at the Amp." Con stopped his brother's rolling profanity. "Miki and

Damie were down there. I don't know anything beyond that right now."

"Oh God, Con...."

He didn't hear anything else Kane said. His brother's words were drowned out by a wave of sirens as another two police cars joined the stream. Connor rolled up the windows and cut off the undulating wails, hearing the panic in his brother's voice as Kane continued to swear.

"I don't know, K. It could be nothing. A backfire. Hell, it could be firecrackers. We don't *know*."

"I'm too fucking far away. Sanchez and I are near Oakland. *Shit*."

"I'll take care of this, little brother. I've got your boy covered. Keeks and I are heading down there now. As soon as I find something out, I'll tell you. Okay? I'll have Miki call you."

"Con, I can't... not him. Not now. I can't deal with... *shit*."

"We're almost there, Kane. I've got to go," Con said gently. "As soon as I can, okay?"

"Heh, and we're supposed to be the ones in danger." Kane's bitterness held little humor. "I'll wait to hear from you; then I'll call Sionn."

"I've got to go, K. Later." He flicked the phone off as he took a corner, the Hummer's tires squealing.

Something was burning. Wisps of smoke trails were beginning to seep out from between the far-off buildings, but the colors were off, more clownish than menacing. Even with the windows up, the scent of caustic smoke leaked into the Hummer's cab, and Connor blinked, trying not to rub at his eyes.

"Units responding to hazmat conditions," the dispatcher said calmly. "Please be advised to wear protective gear in area. Residents at scene report incendiary devices exploded, possible large-gauge smoke bombs. Caution is advised."

He was losing sight of Kiki's car. The smoke closest to the street's entrance was a thin, milky orange, and it crept out slowly, swallowing up most of the unmarked's flashing lights. Only a few sparks of red and blue in the plumes indicated where the car was heading, but Connor followed, gripping the wheel as he slowed the Hummer down to enter the cloud.

The heavy vehicle rocked when he hit a curb near the studio, and Connor corrected its swerve, taking one more turn to find himself in the middle of what looked like a war zone.

There was smoke everywhere, billowing up from the street. It choked the air, red and gray plumes thickening in the narrow space between Forest's place and the old apartment buildings across the street. The light breeze and damp air kept the smoke low, and Connor slammed on his brakes to avoid hitting Damie's parked Challenger. Visibility was poor—so poor he nearly missed spotting the people coming out of the apartments beyond. After throwing the Hummer into park, he shed his cumbersome outer gear so he could move easier through a tight space if he needed to. Connor opened the door, then pulled the collar of his T-shirt up to cover his nose and mouth, heading into the thick smoke.

The sting of chemicals burned Con's eyes, but he needed to find Miki and Damien first—both for his brother's and Sionn's sake as well as Forest's. He spotted the entrance to the Sound and headed over, coughing to clear his lungs of the burning smoke. Somewhere behind him, a car hit a post or one of the buildings, a terrifyingly loud shear of metal creaking through the air. The smash of glass soon followed, and then a scream rent the air as a woman began crying for help.

A fire truck crept down the street behind him, a pair of responders with face masks jumping from its open cab. Oxygen tanks rattled as the men disengaged them from the truck's equipment well. A second later, the woman's screaming turned to long, heart-wrenching sobs, and Connor lost sight of the men in the cloudy air.

The smoke around the Sound's door was thinner than in the street, and Connor pounded on the frame, shouting Miki's name. From what he could make out of the interior through the business's wide window, the studio seemed as full of vapors as the street, and he glanced down, searching for where the plumes might be coming from. Grabbing the door handle, Connor pulled, nearly yanking his shoulder out with his frustrated tugs.

"Miki!" Tearing his shirt from his mouth, Connor shouted again. "Damien!"

He coughed, sucking in a mouthful of chemicals, but he continued hammering at the door. There was movement through the window, but it was feeble, barely a flicker of a shadow against the dimness beyond. Swearing, Con tugged his shirt off all the way and wrapped it around his arm. He tested the door again, rattling it furiously, but it refused to give.

"Fuck this." Connor smashed in the window, ducking his head to the side to avoid the flying glass. Hitching his leg over the sill, he went in, coughing when a gust carried a fresh wave of smoke his way. Connor jumped in, then fought his way through the cloudy interior, stumbling over an upended trash can.

He heard coughing, a subtle whisper and hack under the continuing wail of sirens echoing outside. Ducking down to get as far beneath the smoke as he could, Connor moved forward quickly. Something moved to the left of him, and he cocked his head, searching for either man.

So intent on finding Miki or Damien, Connor didn't see the stool headed straight for his face until its edge caught him across the nose, and he went tumbling over, driven back from the force of the blow. He tasted blood and sucked in more stinging air, choking on his metallic-tinged spit.

The foggy air parted, and a shadow stretched over Connor. Blinking away the tears streaming from his abused eyes, he saw someone cross behind the counter. Suddenly, Miki stood over him, brandishing a heavy barstool. The singer wound up again, obviously intent on bashing Con's head in.

"Miki!" Connor shouted, throwing his arm up to fend off the blow. It came anyway, and Con felt his right arm shudder when the metal stool hit. A sharp pain shot up to his shoulder, and his hand went numb, his fingers tingling.

The barstool rose again, then faltered. Miki peered through the smoke, and Connor spotted a thin trickle of drying blood streaming down from a cut on the musician's cheek. The fierce look on the man's face eased somewhat, and he slowly tilted the stool sideways.

"Connor?" Miki's querulous rasp was broken by a series of coughs. "That you?"

"Yeah, you stupid—" Con cut himself off, remembering the mercurial singer still wielded a lethal weapon. "Are you okay? Where's Damie? We've got to get you guys out of here."

"Yeah, I'm okay." The stool dropped to the floor with a clatter. Then Miki bent over, grabbing Connor by the arm to help him up. "But fuck, I'm glad to see you. Damie's been shot."

CHAPTER EIGHTEEN

I don't know, Miki. The words… hurt too
  much, you know?
Dude…. Forest, trust me, man. I know.
And you still write them down. Why? Why
  the fuck go through it again?
So maybe someone else who's out there
  doesn't have to feel so fucking alone.
—Home Studio Session #5

"SHOW ME where he is. Then get out into the fresh air." Connor tried shaking the feeling back into his arm, but it was stinging from Miki's attack. Shit, his forearm hurt, all the way up to his teeth and into the base of his skull. "We need to get you guys out of here."

The studio was a mess of cables and equipment. If he hadn't known better, Con would have thought it'd been tossed, but the Sound's space became a storage area for the damaged coffee shop, and he dodged more than one stack of paper goods to get to the recording area's open door. The smoke was thinner in the recording studio, but the air was still cloudy and astringent.

Miki stumbled as he walked, and Con caught him by the shirt before he fell over. The man snarled softly, yanking himself free, and continued to pick his way through. His knee was obviously giving him trouble, and he was a bit unsteady as he wove through the boxes, but Connor kept his hands off the man. Miki kept his head down, coughing a few times as he went.

Connor was unfamiliar with the Sound. Other than helping Forest move a few boxes into the back room, he'd not been to the space. He got turned around once after losing Miki in the shadows. The lights in the Sound were off, and if not for the clatter coming through the broken window, the place would have been quiet. At some point, probably when the fire crews arrived, someone'd turned off the power, because the Studio's windowless interior was pitch black.

"My phone's broken. Guy jumped me, and I went down. Must have hit something hard," Miki said as Con was digging his phone out of his pocket. "Can you turn yours on? I need the light."

"Yeah, getting it out now. Tell me where he is and call out. Get us some help."

"Down the hall, to the right." The man's face appeared saturnine in the yellow glow coming from Connor's screen. "Come on. Reception's shit there. Too much steel and crap inside the building."

The hallway was clear enough. Certainly wide enough, but then Connor figured it would have to be to get equipment in and out of the area without too much difficulty. The door at the end of the hall was open a bit, and a very faint glow shone through the crack, nearly too faint to see except for the deep shadows in the enclosed space.

"Miki?" Damie's voice reached them, a soft, wavering call. "Fuck, dude. I hope that's you."

"Yeah, Con's here." Miki moved faster, then disappeared into the room with a quick slide of his body through the door.

Connor reached the door and tried to pull it farther open, but it refused to budge. A fast sweep of his phone's screen around the area told him why. The mechanism was damaged, and there were bits of wood planks hanging from the frame, thick, heavy nails poking out from the broken pieces.

He couldn't think about what could have happened to the men if they'd not been found. The smoke was bothering him, and he coughed again, his lungs struggling to get air. With each jerk of his breath, his chest burned, and the watering in his eyes blurred his vision. Blinking, Connor realized he was seeing double, and his face'd begun to itch, prickling fires spreading up from his nostrils and lips. He definitely had to get them out of there before they all suffocated from the spreading smoke.

The fog in the room was good for one thing. It refracted the waning light coming from Damie's phone, illuminating the man sprawled on the floor. He held a towel up near his face, and Connor saw water dripping from its edge, a drop hitting Damien on the throat. An empty Evian bottle crunched under Con's foot as he approached, and he kicked it aside, bending over the young man to check his wounds.

"Where are you hit?" Con asked as Miki appeared again out of the smoke. "We're going to get you out of here."

"My leg." Damien scrambled to grab his phone. Tilting it, he showed Connor the wet spreading over his calf. His jeans were soaked through with blood, and the fabric was torn. "Tried walking, but…."

"No, let me see if I can't get that door open more. If not, we'll have to squeeze you through." Connor looked around for something heavy to shove against the door, but nothing stood out to him in the cloudy darkness. He needed to force it open another few feet, just enough to be able to carry Damien through. "Maybe if Miki and I both shoved. Fire department'll have spreaders, but they'd have to call them down. You can't sit here in this shit that long."

"Yeah." Damien coughed. "Dunno how the fuck Sinjun got it open to begin with."

Miki was bouncing back and forth on the balls of his feet, a hot crackle of energy fueled by temper and fear. Even in the dim light of his phone, Connor could see the anguish in the man's eyes when he looked down at Damien. He reached for Miki, gripping his shoulder in a tight clench to reassure him.

"He'll be okay. Let's just get this door open," Connor said firmly. "Then you head out for air."

The guy was strong. Connor had to give Miki that. Leaning on the door, Connor tested its give and was disappointed to find it practically wedged in place. They couldn't do much. Too much exertion would strain their already compromised lungs, but he didn't want to do any more damage to Damien's leg. Miki came up with another thick metal barstool and wedged it between the door and the frame, nodding at Connor once.

"You push, I'll pry," Miki suggested. "Maybe we can move this thing."

His shoulders picked up the strain when Connor laid into the door. Miki wedged the heavy-legged stool into the opening and began to count. When he hit three, Connor threw his weight into shoving the door open. For a second it didn't seem like the door was going to budge. Then they heard a satisfying crash as the lodged mechanism gave way. The door flew forward, unhindered by its hydraulics, and slammed into the outer wall, rattling on its hinges.

"Go," Connor ordered. "Take my phone and get out. We'll be right behind you. D, get ready to light our way out. We're going to be moving fast."

By this time his voice was a mess and the edges of his eyes were swelling shut, but Connor made it over to Damien's side, tapping the man on the shoulder. Hitching his arms under Damie's legs, Connor lifted him up. His arms smarted a bit, especially the one Miki'd struck, but he cradled Damie's heavy body as well as he could.

"Just get me out the door, and I can lean on you. I'm too heavy," Damie said.

"Hold on." Connor hoisted him closer and led with his shoulder out of the room.

If anything, the smoke seemed to be spreading through the studio, reaching into the far recesses of the hallway and outer reception area. The busted-out window was hard to make out, but when Connor got Damien out from around the front counter, sunlight brightened up the space, outlining the punched-in opening. Shouts were coming from beyond the window, but Connor couldn't make out who was talking to him. His knee hit the wall, and suddenly there were hands reaching for Damien, and someone took the man from him.

A gruff-voiced woman grabbed Connor's arm and guided his leg over the edge of the broken window, gently encouraging him to lift his leg up a bit farther. He pulled himself out, cold air hitting his bare chest and back. At some point he must have hurt himself, because a spot on his shoulder blade seemed raw, and Connor felt the sticky tack of blood clinging to his skin. Once fully outside, he blinked, startled by the sudden flare of light in his eyes, but the rush of cold air in his lungs felt good, and he inhaled hard, coughing out as much of the smoke as he could.

"Sit down, Lieutenant," the woman ordered. "I'm going to wash your eyes out. From what we can tell, there's only a bit of capsaicin in the smoke solution, but it's enough to sting. I'm going to run a flush and check you over. When I'm done, I'm going to give you some electrolytes in some water, and I want you to drink it. It'll help your throat."

The flush was cold, or at least felt cold, and Connor sighed at the relief, trying to keep his eyes open under the rush. She repeated the flush twice, then handed him a towel to pat away the moisture. A bottle of water was shoved into his hand, and Con thanked the woman before sipping it. Wiping away the wash coming from his smarting face, he looked around him and grinned when he spotted Miki sitting a few feet away.

"Hey, St. John!" Con caught the man's attention. "Do me a favor."

"What?" Miki sounded worse than Connor felt, but the snarl was still there, and the sound of it made Con smile.

Leaning over the space between them, Connor pointed at the man's phone and said, "Call your boyfriend. I told him I'd give him an update once we found you. I don't do that, he'll come kick my ass."

"Fuck. I'm fine. He worries too much, but okay," Miki snapped back but took the phone anyway, his fingers flying over the screen. "Shit, I didn't even get the damned sticks!"

"I NEVER should have asked them to go down there." Forest tried taking a step forward, but pacing in the waiting room was next to impossible.

Mainly because it was full of Morgans—both cop and otherwise. He'd spent a couple of Sundays at the house, but Forest'd never encountered the clan en masse. Even in the large area set aside for waiting families, they were overwhelming.

He was pretty sure he now knew what it felt like to be a penguin in a kiddie pool full of leopard seals.

He just didn't have a glacier to hide behind.

"It's okay, kid," Kane said, patting Forest absently on the shoulder. It might have been meant to be a light tap, but the hit rattled Forest's teeth in his skull. "Damie's tough. And Miki...."

Kane didn't finish what he was saying. Instead, the large man paced off toward the ward doors, only to be turned around before he could push them open by a sharp word from his father. Kane glared back for a moment, then paced back off, hands on his hips and spine taut and firm.

"Worse than trying to keep them in their playpens," Donal muttered under his breath to Brigid.

"Yer the one who yelled at me when I tied them to the tree," she shot back, her voice rolling along with Donal's heavier accent. "It was good enough for my gran."

"Yer gran also taught ye how to spit chewing tobacco when ye were three." He rolled his eyes. "Thank God, yer mum put a stop to that nonsense."

"Now yer scaring the boy." Brigid reached out to snag Forest's hand. He let her pull him closer, grateful for her arm as it slid around his waist. "It'll be fine, love. All of them are stubborn bastards. Don't know what you were thinking when ye fell in with this lot."

"The boy's a lot stronger than ye think," Donal said, winking at Forest. "How are ye holding up, son?"

"They're a bit...." He searched for a word to describe the sheer presence of Morgan around him. "*Intense*, and I'm scared. Scared shitless."

"It's okay to be scared, son." Donal wrapped his arms around both of them, squeezing lightly before letting go. It was like being hugged by a redwood, but Forest thought it felt nice. "But I'm telling ye, they'll be fine. Injuries weren't bad, and the doctors just want to make sure they get their pound of flesh."

Forest was mollified, but the Morgans didn't seem to get the "they'll all be fine" memo. Even Quinn, the quietest of the Morgans, glowered and simmered from his place against the wall. A young nurse tried to move him to reach into a cabinet next to his elbow, and she was pushed back by the sharpness of his hard green eyes. Apologizing to the woman, Kiki dislodged her brother. Shoving him aside, Kiki aimed him toward a less trafficked part of the room.

The others were no less worried and certainly as fierce. He'd barely recognized Riley, who'd come to pick him up. Even though he'd gotten a phone call from Connor saying everything was okay, but they were at the hospital, Forest feared the worst when Con's younger brother showed up at the door looking like an avenging angel ready to reap his soul. As a collective, they were a force, a roaming tsunami of bristling nerves and snapping tempers.

"Who's here for Connor Morgan?" As one, the clan snapped around to face the man standing by the swinging doors. "He can have a visitor now. He'll be able to go home once we get the final tests back in, but everything looks good."

Kiki took a step, but Donal caught her gently. Nodding to Forest, he said, "It's the boy's time, darling. Go on, Forest. He'll be looking for ye."

Brigid squeezed Forest one last time and shooed him toward the door. "Tell him not to give the doctors a hard time, or I'll be back there to remind him of his manners."

"What about Miki St. John?" Kane growled.

"That's who I was going to ask about next." The nurse stood firm against Kane's looming form. "You can come back now too."

The walk down the hall wasn't memorable. He left the wave of Irish behind and caught a whiff of it in someone's voice in a room down the way. At some point along the noisy clatter of the emergency room, he'd lost Kane when the male nurse guided Kane toward one of the side rooms. Forest got a glimpse of a grit-smeared Miki, and then the man was lost from sight, swallowed up by Kane's embrace.

Shuffling behind the nurse, Forest was led to the next open door and left there, his heart lying dead under his ribs and his love choking him when he finally saw Connor.

There was no question the man'd been through a war. He looked like shit. His eyes were ringed a painful red, turning his blue eyes to a vivid iciness. Shirtless, he was an impressive sight, even with one arm wrapped in a cast and lines of paper tape striping one shoulder, reaching down his back. Con turned, breaking off his conversation with a female nurse to smile at Forest.

Forest's heart began to beat, and he could breathe again.

"God, you fucking scared the shit out of me." Forest exhaled, and Con grabbed him by the wrist to drag him forward.

Their embrace was tight and bruising, and Connor's mouth found his in a rough, hard kiss. The heat of the man's body seared away the chill the waiting room left on Forest's skin, and he sighed, opening himself up to Connor's assault. He clung, suddenly more frightened than he'd been outside with the group of Celtic raiders masking themselves as civilized people. Then the rage settled in.

Shoving off Connor's chest, Forest punched the man in the arm. Surprised, Connor yelped, and a piece of tape flapped loose, waving over Con's shoulder.

"Fucking asshole. Actually, all of you. Fucking *assholes*. You scared the *hell out of me*!" He refused to cry. Refused to sob. Hell, he wasn't even going to tear up because the female nurse Con'd been talking to was now trapped against the wall, cornered by Forest and Connor crowding the examination table. Moving out of the way, he let her out, then rounded on Connor before the man could fold him into another hug. "Dude, no hands. You get your hands on me—"

"I'm sorry, love," Connor whispered. "But hey, I saved your band."

IT WAS a small gathering of Morgans and lovers. Forest was glad for the comfort of Connor's fingers wrapped around his. Miki paced angrily back and forth, fury pushing his steps, his hands shoved down deep into his jeans. Kane watched him, his arms crossed over his chest while he leaned against the wall. Connor and Kane had convinced Sionn to stay with Damie since the hospital was settling the guitarist into a room, and they'd found a common space to talk about what they were going to do.

Duarte and Kiki joined them after a few minutes, with Donal close behind. Kane held his hand out to Miki as they approached, and the singer hesitated for a moment, his body vibrating with repressed emotion, but he stepped into Kane's space, placing his shoulders against his lover's chest.

"Okay, I'm going to break this down for all of you now so we're all clear on what's going on." Duarte nodded at Connor. "Your dad's here as a debrief. Got it?"

"Yeah, shoot." Kane spoke up, wrapping his arms around Miki's waist. "Mick said he IDed the guy who broke into the Sound."

"Miki IDed Gary Rollins as the man who cracked him over the head, shot Damien, and then closed them inside of the studio," Kiki agreed. "The lab's running prints to verify. We found a heavy flashlight on the floor in the reception area. Its lens was broken, and there was blood on it. We think that's what he used to hit Miki."

"Who the fuck else could it be?" Miki said it before Forest could. "I didn't know the guy's face before Forest tapped him out."

"It's just a precaution, son," Donal assured him. "And if there was someone else with him, it might help us find him."

Connor pulled Forest in, nestling against his back like Kane'd done for Miki. It felt… comfortable. Safe. Even the weight of Connor's cast across his chest was reassuring, a reminder that the man'd come out the other side of a shitty situation and was ready to take on the world. There was a brief pressure on the back of his head, and Forest smiled, now knowing the feel of his lover's kiss in his hair.

Connor smelled a bit of antiseptic, and he'd borrowed a T-shirt from Kane. The combination of unfamiliar laundry soap and Connor's skin confused Forest's brain for a bit, but the soft cotton was a damned sight better than the paper gown he'd been given to wear. It hugged every muscle on his torso, and Forest raised his hands to slide his fingers into Connor's pockets, glad for the warmth of their pressed-in bodies.

"Do we have any leads on where Rollins is?" Connor's voice rumbled through Forest's chest when he spoke. "Any known associates?"

"We're looking into people he knew before he went in." Duarte quirked his mouth ruefully. "Family too, but so far, no one's even wanting to admit they know the guy, much less be related to him."

"Look, we know Rollins is probably the guy. One of the men he'd run with at the halfway house is a demolitions nut. Those smoke bombs were huge, nearly twenty-five pounds each. Too sophisticated for the average DIY, and Rollins wasn't known for his science skills," the senior inspector informed them. "We found one that didn't catch. Rollins, or whoever's helping him, had them on low-end auto-fuses. Chances are, he broke into the Sound to lay the one we found there and was surprised to find St. John and Mitchell there."

"Most auto-fuses are good for, what? An hour? Two?" Kane asked softly. "Think he stuck around to watch his handiwork?"

"More than likely. We're asking around to see if anyone saw him or any of the other guys who bolted from the halfway house." Kiki glanced at her father. "Captain's given us leave to run up overtime on this. A lot of the uniforms are going door-to-door with photos."

"Hell, he might even be in the area," Duarte commented. "We're hoping for a hit. They had to have transported the cylinders in something. Probably passing them off as rolled-up rugs. So it'll be a van or something like that. There's some camera shots the lab's going through. That might help."

"Do we know why he's doing this?" Miki interjected. "Forest—you knew this guy for, what? Five minutes?"

"Little bit more than that. I did some—" He made a face at the singer. "—some really fucking stupid things when I was a kid."

"I still do stupid things," Miki shot back. "Any clue why he's stuck to your ass now?"

"Not a damned one," he replied. "I haven't thought about him in years. Rollins was some guy my mom's friends brought around. That's how I knew him. Frank knew him from before that, and it's not like he went to jail for roughing me up. Shit, I didn't even think he was arrested. Frank was the one the cops hauled in."

"Yeah, Rollins'd been tagged," Kiki said. "Then he had a few run-ins with parents about inappropriate behavior. Was logged in as a sex offender and was caught trying to molest a kid on a soccer field. That's what sent him in, finally."

"What about that kid's family?" Con shifted his arms tighter around Forest's chest. "You guys have an eye on them? If Rollins is after his past victims, he could hit on them too."

"We're in touch," Duarte said. "Family's left the state. So far, it seems like he's only lashing out at Ackerman. It might be Rollins didn't mean to murder Marshall, or maybe he thinks both of them are responsible somehow for his incarceration. I can't speculate about motive right now. It's not as important as finding him."

"So what do we do?" Kane looked at his brother when they spoke at once. Connor shook his head, and Kane continued, "Short of killing this guy."

"Totally an option." Connor tightened his arms around Forest's shoulders.

"I'd rather see him in jail, boys." Donal spoke softly. "Let the courts have him and walk away."

"Not that I don't agree with you, Da," Connor replied. "But I'm telling you, on this one, it's hard."

"I know. It's hard on us all. This man's hit at us, but we're going to hit back." Donal squared his shoulders. "In the meantime, go home. Take care of yer own and stay safe. And be on yer guard. No telling what this bastard's got up his sleeve."

"SIT DOWN," Forest ordered Connor for the third time that evening, pushing his lover back down onto the couch after he came back from the kitchen. "The drops go in its eyes or it gets the hose."

"I would pay money to see you try to beat me with a hose," Con grumbled back.

It was late, and Connor'd been lounging in the family room, debating if he should call it a night and sleep. A look at his bare-chested lover in loose sweats changed his mind. There were other things he could be doing besides sleeping, most of them centering on Forest.

"I wouldn't be the one doing the beating," Forest countered. "I'll call your mom and ask her to do it."

"Oh, wickedly unfair there, boyo." The man laid on his accent thickly, but he eased back, resting his head on the cushions. "Okay, do your worst."

"Hold on. I forgot a towel." Forest patted Con's chest. "Do not get off the couch."

He waited, still staring up at the ceiling, for Forest to return. When the man finally found a clean hand towel to use, he sat on the couch next to Connor, yelping when Con dragged him over to sit on his legs.

"Least you can do is ride me while you do this." He stroked at Forest's sides, spanning his hands around to the small of his lover's back.

"I'm not riding you for a while, dude," Forest reminded him. "Doctor said to rest. Your lungs took a beating. I'm surprised they let you go."

"Just a bit banged up. Miki did more damage to me than anything else." Con raised his plaster-wrapped forearm. "Bastard's like a goddamn ferret stuck in your pants. Watch your shit around him. Especially now you're their drummer."

"Yeah, I am. Aren't I? That is so cool. I can't—even. No words." Forest beamed, a crinkle of a smile taking over his face. *Tsk*ing humbly, he gripped Connor's chin and moved his face to the side. "Look up."

"You're going to get more in my eyes this time, right?" Con glanced at him from under his lashes. "The inside of my ear is still soaking wet."

"If you weren't such a dick about getting stuff close to your eyes, you could do it yourself," Forest reminded him. "Now stay still. Or better yet, talk to me while I do this. What did Sionn just say about Damie when you talked to him?"

"Damie's doing okay. Resting. They're sending him home tomorrow. Miki's growling at people, but I think that just means he's okay too. Kane's going to see if he can get Miki to go home in a bit." The first drop hit, and it felt like Forest shoved an ice shard down into his eye. Biting his lip to avoid yelping, Connor grabbed at his lover's ass. "Shite, that's cold."

"Four on each side." Forest moved the towel over and cupped Connor's cheek. "Hold on. Gotta do the other three."

He could stand the three, Connor told himself. He'd handled worse, but the second drop struck his eye and chilled him down to his spine. His ass clenched in response, and the twitch of his hips nearly unseated Forest.

"Really?" The man looked down at him, fingers firmly holding Connor's jaw. "You're being a baby. Damie got shot. You and Miki just have to get eye drops, and he's probably doing them himself."

"That's because he's a fucking ferret. I'm telling you, boy's inhuman." Connor settled down again, lightly resting his hands on Forest's thighs. "Hope Kane never pisses him off. Bastard'll gut him as soon as look at him."

"Nah, Miki's cool," Forest said as he quickly let another two drops go into Con's right eye.

"Shit, warn a man!" Con hissed, blinking furiously.

"Yeah, incoming."

He saw Forest shrug; then the towel covered Con's eye.

"Keep it closed. You're supposed to let the drops sit. You're one of those guys who's a big baby when he's got a cold, aren't you?"

Connor wasn't going to humble himself to answer the question. Sniffing, he tasted the drops in the back of his throat and made a face. "God that's like piss down my mouth."

"I don't even want to know who you've let pee into your mouth, 'cause it ain't going to be me."

Connor kept one eye—the unmolested eye—open and regarded his lover. Forest looked… settled. Maybe even happy. There was a crease of worry between the man's large brown eyes, but that was for Miki and Damien. He'd reminded Forest several times that the shot to the guitarist's calf hadn't been serious, and other than an overnight stay in the hospital and a keen watch for infection, he'd be as good as new. Miki'd been given the same drops and treatment as Connor. A flush of their systems and a few beeping machines verified their health.

And he thanked God for that because he had enough on his hands as it was—seeing as they were currently curved over Forest's ass.

"You know, once you get these drops in, I might be persuaded into being coddled a bit," Connor said gruffly. "You know, to soothe my self-esteem. I went into a smoking building for you."

"And I'm grateful for that," Forest replied solemnly, the worry in his face lightening a little. "Do you need coddling? What's involved in that? Foot massages? Hot towels after you shave?"

"I'll write you a list." Connor tangled his fingers into Forest's hair and pulled him down for a kiss. Cupping his cast to the small of Forest's back, he craned up and dipped his tongue past Forest's lips, tasting the soft heat he found there.

Forest made a husky mewling noise in his throat, and Connor was more than willing to forgo the drops. In fact, if he could reach the table next to the couch, he'd pull out the bottle of lube he'd tucked in there and show Forest point by point everything that *should* be on a coddling list, including a few he had in mind to do to Forest if the man ever felt like he needed it. He opened his mouth, about to suggest just that, when the house suddenly went silent.

Then they were plunged into a deep, heavy darkness.

CHAPTER NINETEEN

Sour mash and cheap wine
Smokestack lightning, bathtub gin
Took me for a slow ride
Damn woman 'most done me in
Popping corks in long black limos
Champagne giggles and lots of skin
Breaking hearts more than a million times
Just like my own has been
—Riding Low

"WHERE'S YOUR phone? I want you to call emergency while I check things out. Landline's in the living room. We might not find it in the dark." Connor grasped Forest's hips to slide him off. In the black, the world seemed to flow and tilt around him, but Con's hands were firm and steadying. "Can you get to it? Mine's dead. I've got it charging in the bedroom."

"In the kitchen. It's on the charger too." He tried to peer through the darkness, waiting for his eyes to adjust. "Maybe the streetlight's still on. The hedges are too high, dude. I can't see shit. Is it just the house?"

"Looks like it. Could be the fuses, but I'm not going to chance it." Con stood, a darker shape against the already dark shapes around them. "Grab a hold of my waistband. I want to make sure you're safe. Flashlight's in the garage somewhere. Shit. I forgot it out there."

Outside, in the distance, lights shone down the hill, and there was a bit of a glow coming from someplace beyond the high boxwoods lining the backyard, more than likely coming from a streetlight in front. Built on a cul-de-sac, the Victorian sat on one of the city's many serpentine tiers, its back facing an open view of the harbor and the streets below.

The rain made it difficult for ambient light to seep past the house's partially drawn heavy curtains, and Forest felt his way to the kitchen, keeping his fingers hooked into Con's pants. He was tired. Hell, Con was probably worn down to the bone, and he would love for it to be as simple as something inside the garage. His hopes were dashed when the sound of breaking glass came from behind them. Connor's back went rigid under the light brush of Forest's knuckles, and Con grabbed for the doorframe.

Con moved quickly, a silent rush of muscle, and forcibly dragged Forest along behind him. They hit the swinging doors to the kitchen fast, and Forest bit down a yelp when the shutter-style doors nearly struck his back. With its windows facing the side yard and its high fence, the kitchen was nearly pitch black, but Forest had a good idea of where his phone was.

The house moaned, creaking as the wind outside kicked up. The family room lights flickered a few times, then went dark, and over the kitchen's saloon-style doors, Forest caught sight of a tree branch scraping at one of the slender windows facing the backyard.

"It's okay, Con. It's a tree." Forest found his phone and turned it on, illuminating a small area of the kitchen. "Not much charge, but plugged in…."

A blast shattered the window over the sink, peppering the kitchen with shot. Something stung Forest's face, and a burn cut through his right shoulder. It was a deafening wave of terror and sound, fire flashing up from the side yard. He caught a glimpse of a silhouette before Connor dragged him down to the floor. Rolling him over, Con tucked Forest under the thick-legged oak table set against a wall.

Another boom came upon them, tearing through the kitchen. Wood flew from shattered cabinets, and some of the shot must have hit a stack of dishes because it began to rain porcelain and glass. The shooter wasn't alone. Moments later, there was a shout—a man calling out to someone else to get into the house and take care of things.

Forest's stomach knotted up tight around itself. He was probably one of those *things*.

He'd held on to his phone, but it'd been ripped from the charger when they'd gone down. Even though Forest could make out Con's mouth moving in the phone's pale light, he couldn't hear a damned thing. The ringing in his ears ululated, then died away, leaving his head with a deep throb. Up against the wall, there was nowhere for him to go, and a part of him—a long-buried frightened little boy part—panicked at being trapped between a warm body and a hard place.

Taking a deep breath helped. The fear receded, slinking off into the crevices it'd come from. The dark held something more than shadows. There was a malevolent stillness to it now. Even through the buzzing echoes in his ears, Forest felt the weight of something—something dark—pressing in on him.

"You okay?" Con asked gruffly. His hands were running over Forest's limbs and chest.

"My shoulder hurts. The right one." Forest kept his voice low and then bit his lip to keep from whimpering when Con's fingers explored his shoulder. "Not bad. Not until you touch it."

"Sorry, love. Okay, you call 911," Connor whispered. "I'm going for my gun."

"Dude—" Forest swallowed his protest. Connor was a cop. An injured one, but a cop just the same. "Be careful."

"Sure thing, babe," Connor promised solemnly, and then he was gone. "You too."

The bite of wind coming through the blasted window cut through Forest, and he curled up as tight as he could, crouching under the heavy table. Fingers shaking, he dialed emergency and waited for someone to answer.

WHEN HE'D converted an oddly placed half bath into a pantry for the kitchen, Connor'd wondered if he'd been smart to put his gun safe there. Now, standing in the eerie green glow of the safe's battery backup lights, he pondered if he shouldn't have built in an entire armory instead.

Because he really could have used an AK-47 right about then.

The trembling in Forest's body nearly broke Connor. The last thing he'd wanted was to leave the man, but shit had come to his door, and he was going to do his damned best to shove it right back out.

His arm was unwieldy, and not for the first time that day, he silently cursed Miki's kill instinct. The light set above the keypad was barely bright enough for him to see the numbers, and Con quickly punched in the code, letting out an unexpected sigh of relief when the safe door clicked open. Unthinkingly, he reached in with his right hand and winced when he banged the cast against the edge of the safe.

"Okay, beat the shit out of Miki," he muttered, grabbing his Glock with his left hand. Tucking the weapon into the back of his pants, he pulled out his spare piece, a Beretta his father'd given him. He slammed a load into the Beretta and headed back out.

Connor stopped long enough to grab his armored vest off its hook by the garage door. It was a short struggle to put it on, and when he glanced beneath the table, he was relieved to find Forest looking up at him, his lover's phone shining over his pale face.

"They coming?" he asked.

"Yeah, they told me to stay on the line," Forest murmured. "She also said to tell you not to do anything stupid."

The sound of more glass breaking reached the kitchen, and Connor growled back, "I'm not the one doing something stupid. Get into the pantry and close the door."

"I'm not leaving you out here," he argued.

Of course Forest would argue. Connor'd learned quickly the man gave in only when it suited him. Apparently, the situation didn't suit him.

"I'd rather you get into the bathroom and get into the tub, but it's too far. They're already in the house."

He didn't need much light to see Forest's stubborn scowl. There wasn't a lot of time, and Connor didn't want to waste it arguing. He had to find the men breaking into his house, and he couldn't do that while worrying if Forest was safe. Pulling a trick out of Brigid's guilt bag, he asked softly, "Please?"

"Fucker," Forest grumbled as he scrambled into the pantry, then closed the door behind him.

"Lock it from inside. And don't come out for anyone but me. Tell dispatch I'm armed." Connor pressed his hand against the narrow wall between the pantry door and interior hall. Casting his eyes up quickly, he beseeched, "Keep him safe for me, God. That's all I'm asking in this."

Rollins's actions didn't make any sense. Revenge? Killing Forest wouldn't gain him anything. Not any more than killing Marshall had. There had to be something else there—something broken inside the man that somehow gave the whole mess perspective.

At that moment he couldn't care about motive. Hell, Connor barely had the patience to hunt down the men coming for his lover. The only reason he didn't grab Forest and beat a path to the door was he couldn't be sure there wasn't someone else waiting outside to mow them down. At least in the house, he had the advantage. He knew every turn and hallway in the Victorian, as well as the areas he hadn't quite gotten to—like the living room with its creaky joists and iffy floorboards.

He'd thought about going into the garage to fetch the flashlight for Forest, but he didn't know if the pantry door sat flush to the floor. A strip of light would draw someone to his presence. No, Con thought, better he stay as much in the dark as possible.

Reaching the foyer, Connor was thankful for the soft ambient glow coming through the half-moon window above the heavy front door. Keeping his back to the wall, he let the shadows cover him, then called out to the rest of the house.

The interior of the Victorian was still a warren, a Z of a hallway with rooms connected to one another with nested doors. There'd been a plan to open up the space, eliminating as many of the jogs as possible, but for now they served as a baffle. There'd be bottles of whiskey sent to his brothers for being too busy for serious wall demolition.

"Rollins? That you?" His voice bounced, echoing around the enclosed space. "Tell me you brought more than one guy to take me out!"

From the sounds coming from the back of the house, Connor guessed his intruders were having a difficult time getting up over the window boxes built along the outer sills. A bout of heated swearing and pained cries followed by wood cracking lightened Connor's worry. The boxes wouldn't be able to hold up a full-grown man, but obviously Rollins and whomever he brought with him didn't know that.

"Hey, whoever's with that asshole, did he tell you I'm a cop?" Con slid down the wall and switched over to the short L in the hall, bringing him in line with the downstairs bedroom. Another few feet, and he'd be able to wedge himself into a corner at the back of the house and see into the long family room.

"He's a fucking cop? You came here to rip off a fucking cop?"

Con smiled, glad for the reaction. He heard another man cussing the first out, but no one else chimed in. The rain thickened, muting anything else the men said.

"Your friend Gary didn't come here to rip me off." Con risked peeking around the corner to see if the way was clear. Drawing his gun up, he slid forward another foot. "He came here to kill me. Like you killed Frank Marshall and everyone else who got in your way. You've got a lot to answer for, Rollins."

"I came here for that fucking faggot whore." A weedy male voice broke through the sound of the rain. "You can walk away from this!"

"Yeah, I don't think so." Another step and he froze. They'd brought a flashlight with them, and Con could see the powerful beam cut across the hallway opening. If he could make it past the doorway, he'd be able to get enough cover on the other side to bring the men down. "Kind of fond of Forest."

"Fucking bitch put me in jail," Rollins—if Con guessed right—screamed back. "He started this whole damned thing. A couple more minutes, and he'd have been begging me for my dick. Fucking Marshall should have minded his own business!"

Connor remained silent, watching the beam cut across the hall again. The second the light passed back toward the front of the house, he was off, his bare feet moving across the slick wood floor. Grabbing at the shadows on the other side, he pressed his shoulders against the bathroom door at the end of the hall. Bringing up his matte black gun, Con took a deep steadying breath and waited for Rollins to move into his line of fire.

SOMETHING WAS wrong. Forest could feel it. Or at least he guessed it was. There'd been some muffled scrapes coming through the walls, but after that, nothing. Not until he heard a loud thump.

"I'm going to put the phone down," he whispered to the dispatcher. "Just tell them to hurry the hell up, okay?"

He turned the volume down as much as he dared, mostly to drown out the dispatcher's increasingly aggressive orders for him to stay on the line. Leaving the phone as close to the jamb as he could without it being stepped on, Forest slowly eased the door inward and peeked outside.

Then he jerked his head back into the dark as soon as he spotted the large bulky shape crawling through the shot-out window.

Forest braved another look as the man nearly tumbled back out. The intruder grabbed at anything he could to anchor himself, snagging the sink's faucet handle. Water gushed from the spigot when he pulled on it. He grumbled in surprise, then slapped at the elongated handle until it turned off.

From what he could see, the guy crawling through the window wasn't Rollins. Not unless he'd gained a hundred pounds since he'd been let out. The phone's screen really didn't give Forest enough light to see by, and the safe's sickly green illumination barely extended beyond its own door. The man's bulk was going to be hard to take down, and Forest couldn't see if he was armed.

"A gun," Forest murmured, standing up quickly. "The safe!"

Ignoring the creaks in his knees from crouching on the hard floor, he scrambled to the safe and carefully swung it farther open.

Only to stare at a very disappointing emptiness.

"Not like I know how to fucking shoot a gun, but shit, Con," he grumbled. "Throw me a damned bone here."

Going back to the door, he peeked again, trying to see if the man's hands were free. Since they appeared to be mostly flailing about as he worked to get through the tight space, Forest thought they were empty. From the writhing and the man's windmilling arms, Forest suspected the heavyset man was stuck.

"Doesn't mean he can't have a gun on him." He chewed on his lower lip, trying to work out a plan. "Think, dude. What the hell am I going to do?"

A knife was out of the question. A wood block of blades was out on the kitchen counter, too far for him to snag one and defend himself against the intruder, and short of grabbing one of the spindly wooden chairs at the table, there wasn't anything he could really use to bash the man's head in.

"Crap, Miki can do this, and he's…." Forest trailed off his thought. "'Cause Miki's *psycho*. Okay, focus. Do something, Forest. And don't get shot doing it."

His phone was nearly out of juice. It'd been pining for the fjords when he'd plugged it in after he retrieved Con's eye drops from the fridge. With the line open, he'd soon lose not only the squawking dispatcher but any light it could give him. Bending down, he rifled through the partially full shelves lining the walls, looking for something heavy and portable.

There had to be something he could use in the pantry. A Roomba. A brick. *Something*.

His fingers closed over a thick-rimmed large gallon can on the bottom shelf. Picking it up, he huffed under its unexpected weight, and his injured shoulder whined a bit, but he sucked up the pain with a hissing breath. Unwieldy for sure but hefty enough to do some damage if he had enough leverage.

"Got one shot at this, dude." Forest braced himself and balanced the enormous can against his hip. "Okay. *Go*."

Barreling out, Forest hefted the can over his head. The pinprick of pain along his shoulder reminded him again about being creased by one of the shotgun pellets, but he kept going.

Forest didn't know who screamed louder—the man stuck in the window definitely had an elephantine bellow, but his own warbling pitch wasn't anything to be ashamed of. Either way, he rushed in close and slammed the can down as hard as he could on the intruder's head.

The man quaked in his prison, his torso twisting about and his arms flying around uncontrollably as he took the shock of pain. He lifted up, nearly perpendicular to the kitchen floor, and his eyes were wide pale moons in his partially shadowed face. Up close, his breath stunk of onions and beer. His body wasn't much better, and from the wave of aromas coming from his twitching arms, he held a grudge against deodorant in general. His ass wiggled as he kicked at the side of the house, and glass from the broken window fell from the frame.

Forest's shoulders shook from the hit, and it felt like he'd taken a sledgehammer to a solid granite block. But the can held, and the man groaned, his head lolling back and forth. Forest brought the heavy can up, then hit the man again, silencing his distressed moans.

This time, the can's thinner sides gave in, and it burst, sending a gush of nacho cheese down the man's unshaven round face. It pooled in his nostrils, bubbling up when he exhaled. Giving one final twitch, the intruder moaned once more, then slumped down against the kitchen sink. Blood dripped from his waist where he'd cut himself on broken glass, and a red river sprung up from a wide cut on his forehead, fighting the violently orange ooze for space on his stubbled jowls.

A shout of victory welled up from inside Forest's belly, and he almost let it go, but a chillingly harsh laughing came from the next room, cutting off any celebration and driving a spike of fear into his guts. The glow of a flashlight popped up over the kitchen's saloon half doors, hitting Forest in the face. Blinking against the harsh light, Forest could just barely see a dark, dangerous shape slicing up into the beam, aimed for his head.

"Shit." It was all he could get out. Then the gun went off and everything went black.

IT SOUNDED like someone let loose a pack of flying monkeys. There was a high-pitched screeching reminiscent of a hair band and a deep walrus-inspired howl. A mighty thunk echoed out of the kitchen, then a moment later, another weaker thunk. Connor couldn't imagine what the noises were. Then a thought dawned.

"Fucking Forest." He swore softly as a man he recognized as Rollins stepped into his line of sight. "God damn it! Forest!"

Rollins was unimpressive. He looked more like Riff Raff than anything else, but his rawboned face turned toward Connor, and there was clearly not a drop of humanity left in the man's eyes. They burned nearly black, even in the light of his companion's flashlight. Bringing his own lantern up, Rollins peered over the kitchen's swinging half door, and his deep chuckle set off every alarm in Connor's brain.

His Beretta was uncomfortable in his left hand, but Connor didn't have time to switch it out for the Glock. It wouldn't have made much of a difference. He'd practiced shooting with his off hand, but he wasn't a sharpshooter with it. He could hit a target's inner rings eight times out of ten, and he figured that was all he was going to need if he could get off a clear shot. Connor moved into position.

Spreading his legs to anchor himself, Connor took aim—just as Rollins raised a gun and pointed it over the doors. Its thick, heavy black body was menacing but not as evil as the man's cackle.

Tamping down the emotions roiling up to choke him, Connor shouted, "Police! Drop it!"

Rollins didn't even bother to turn. His finger squeezed, and the gun jerked in his hand, the barrel flashing bright in the uneven shadows. With the shot gone, the man twisted and looked over his shoulder, a curling thin smile reaching up to his ears.

Connor took a step into the room, glancing at the other man standing near the window just long enough to verify he was unarmed. Aiming straight for Rollin's forehead, Connor spoke around the lump of cold fear in his throat. "Put the gun down, Rollins, and get to the floor."

He couldn't think about Forest. Not now, but his mind wandered in worry. Connor heard nothing from the kitchen, and his fear grew, sinking its talons into his belly. Forcing himself to shake off his anguish, Connor repeated his warning.

"Drop the fucking gun, Rollins," he ordered. "Now."

Rollins responded by lifting his gun up, and Connor pressed the trigger, pulling a few shots out of the Beretta. The man's body jerked when the powerful round cut through him, one grazing his jaw. Blood splattered the family room's newly plastered walls, and Rollins stumbled back.

But he didn't fall.

"Get the fuck down, man!" Rollins's associate cried out. "He's a fucking cop! He's going to kill you!"

Somewhere in the room, the other man whimpered, and Connor tried to pinpoint where he'd gone, but Rollins brought his weapon up again, aiming for Connor's position.

"I don't give a shit if he's a cop. He can die just like his faggot boyfriend," Rollins replied, and he fired.

Connor slid to land on his knee a few feet in front of where he'd been standing. Anchored to the floor, he steadied his weapon with his cast and let go another burst. This time he hit Rollins square in the shoulder, and the man's head spun in an *Exorcist* imitation.

And this time, Rollins went down.

The man's flashlight bobbled about, then hit the ground, its wide beam catching on the kitchen's entrance. Rollins didn't come back up, and Connor rose quickly, bringing the Beretta around as he circled the couch he'd cuddled Forest on less than an hour ago.

The kitchen doors swung open, and Connor jerked his gun up, drawing on a new target. His heart stopped, fear grabbing it with cold fingers when he recognized who'd come through the door.

Forest blinked at him, his eyes widening in panic when he spotted Connor's weapon. Illuminated in the bluish-white beam, Forest looked like an avenging angel, his blond hair bleached silver in the bright light. Bloodied and worn, he held an industrial-sized can of jalapenos against his chest.

Kicking Rollins's gun away, Connor gasped in relief at seeing Forest. His lover started to move in, but

Connor shook his head and motioned to the scrawny small man quivering by the window. He had to keep focused, and if Forest touched him, Connor wasn't sure if he'd hug him or throttle him for leaving the pantry.

"Let me get that guy taken care of. Watch Rollins," Connor ordered. "You have my permission to kick his face in if he moves."

Rollins lay at Forest's feet, his eyes filled with agony and blood bubbling up from his torn-apart jaw. He writhed, senseless with pain. Clawing at the floor, Rollins mewled, his chest heaving with the simple act of breathing.

Somewhere off in the rain, sirens were drawing in near, and Connor eyed the man by the window before grabbing a roll of duct tape from a pile of building supplies he'd dumped on a side table earlier that week. He tore off a few strips and secured the man's hands and wrists, then patted his chest with a solid thump before pulling his Glock out from the back of his pants.

"I don't know if I should kiss you or beat the shit out of you," Connor muttered, settling for giving Forest a fierce one-armed hug as he kept one eye on Rollins's twisting body. "I thought I told you to stay in the pantry."

"Found out I don't like being told what to do," Forest admitted softly when Connor risked giving him a brief kiss.

"Yeah, we need to talk about that," Connor said gently. "You could have been killed."

"Sure, we can talk about it, and while we're at it, can we talk about what the fuck you've got in that pantry?" Forest hefted the can of jalapenos he'd been holding. "How much fucking nacho cheese does one guy need?"

CHAPTER TWENTY

We held on to each other
In the rain and at the dawn
People told us we wouldn't make it
Said we'd die off and be gone
I'm here for every step
Every inch of every mile
Down to our very last breath
Till it hurts too much to smile
—Every Mile

THE CONTRACTOR kicked ass. Well, and Jules kicked it as much as anyone else, Forest amended.

After three weeks of hard-core renovation and design fights with the decorator, they'd gotten Marshall's Amp back up and running. No small feat, considering the place looked like an Alderaan diorama by the time Rollins and his crew'd finished with it.

The damage to the outer wall had been extensive, and much of the old brick had to be tossed. Using what could be salvaged, they'd instead broken up the former- ly unrelieved wall with colored glass bricks and long windows. It lit up the inside of the coffee shop even before the wood floors and paneling had been stripped down and restained.

Now the coffee shop gleamed with the mod vibe Jules longed for. Deep pinks, greens, and chrome ac- cents, and miles upon miles of pale honey wood. Re- aligning the counter away from the kitchen door opened the space up even more and made it easier to flow take- out customers out of the shop without tangling with anyone seated at the retro-style lounge chairs Jules found at a discount furniture store. Reupholstered and arranged around low glass and wood tables, they were comfortable, and he eyed one, wondering if he'd been insane when he'd agreed to the pink tweed.

She'd practically begged Forest to let her blow a few thousand dollars on a lava lamp wall sculpture, a six-foot-wide rectangle backlit in changing neon lights. He'd agreed as soon as she'd brought it up, and now he was glad for it. Dominating a formerly dead space near the long wall, the modulating blobs looked... cool.

Nearly as cool as he felt.

They'd decided to hold a soft opening, a small gathering of friends and family as a kind of test drive. A freebie meet-and-greet with coffee and nibbles of pastries on an invite-only kind of thing. Forest figured no one would come by.

He'd forgotten his lover was related to half the po- lice force, and the other half seemed to drop by just for shits and giggles. Still, with the Amp's spacious interior filled with Irish lilts and laughter, Forest felt... content.

Fuck that. He was goddamned *happy*.

"Holy shit. This is what happy feels like." He looked around the shop, sifting through the sea of Morgans until he found Connor standing in a semicircle with a couple of his brothers. They were laughing about something, but Con must have felt Forest's gaze because he looked up and their eyes caught. Winking, Con gave Forest a small off-kilter smile, and the warmth in his belly kicked up a notch.

The espresso machines were doing a brisk business, and the smell of roasted coffee beans and sugary pastries drew in people off the street. Jules gave him a curious look, as if to ask if she should kick out the uninvited, but Forest shook his head, mouthing for her not to worry. They had enough food to feed five armies, especially since the cops and firemen the Morgans dragged in seemed much more interested in coffee and chatting than donuts.

Not something he'd ever thought he'd see, cops not interested in donuts—but as he glanced over at Connor, who was licking chocolate off his fingers, Forest was kind of glad he only had to keep *one* cop in ganache-enrobed pastries. The oldest Morgan boy definitely knew his way around a chocolate donut.

And Forest was more than happy to help him work off that chocolate afterward.

"Hey, Forest." Miki nudged him in the ribs. "You doing okay, dude?"

"Yeah, just kind of… things are good," he replied, glancing around the room over the singer's shoulders.

"Freaky, isn't it?" Miki leaned against the counter, brushing up against Forest's side. They'd come to be good friends—close friends. Bonding over a shitty childhood could do that to a couple of guys, but most of all, Miki was an all-or-nothing kind of guy. Still, Forest had hope he could bring Miki around to seeing Brigid as one of the best things to ever happen to them.

He wasn't holding out a lot of hope, but he was going to try.

"You get all happy inside," Miki continued softly in his distinctive raspy purr. "And then you kinda want to check yourself because it feels so fucking wrong. Makes you a little scared."

"Makes me a *lot* scared," Forest admitted. "You ever get used to it?"

"Dunno," he replied. "Haven't yet. I still get up in the middle of the night and touch Kane to make sure he's real. Sometimes I worry about being in a coma, and this is all bullshit my mind's come up with to keep me busy or shit."

"But I'm not in a coma," Forest snorted. "Shit, at least I hope not."

"Nah, maybe I dreamed this for you too," Miki said, pushing off the counter. "Or maybe Damie's doing it. You know, so we both have better lives. He's good like that."

The singer wandered off to find his brother, dodging a chattering pair of women walking away from the cream and sugar bar. Snagging a lemon bar bite, Forest popped the treat into his mouth and chewed, wondering if he could ever taste the tart citrus sweet without thinking of the lemon chiffon soap Con used. Or how good the man's skin smelled when they had sex in the shower.

A familiar shape appeared to linger just in view of the Amp's main picture window, and Forest frowned, wondering for a fraction of a second why he *knew* that indistinct form, when it dawned on him. It was Ginger, and the warmth in his soul crackled up quickly, turning to an ashen sourness thick enough to choke on.

"Are you all right, love?" Brigid came up to him and put her hand on his back. "You look like you've seen a ghost. Maybe you should sit down."

"No, um...." He stumbled over his own tongue, unsure about what to say—what to do, really. He'd not seen his mother in months, and when he'd paid her bail, she hadn't even come by to thank him. Now she hovered outside, obviously turned off by the show of police in the shop but wanting something bad enough to slink about at the perimeter, probably gathering enough of a spine to walk through the door. "My... mom's here. Outside."

"Do you want me to get rid of her for you?" Connor's mother asked gently. "'Cause I can, you know. It'd be my pleasure. I won't even use a knife to do it."

He looked down at her, startled but not surprised. For all her soft voice and sweet Irish tone, Brigid's eyes glittered with a fierce anger. She'd been a constant in his life since Rollins invaded Con's—their—home. Between cooking dinners and stuffing the freezer, she'd plied Forest with cookies, hot coffee, and most of all, a constant chatter to fill the quiet he often found himself falling into.

She'd gone with him to buy a car, working the salesperson down to the bone in price. Then they'd spent the afternoon making ice cream with a bemused Damien and a wary Miki. When Brigid finally wrangled a wide smile from the singer with an impromptu game of throwing chocolate chips at his mouth to see if Miki could catch them, Forest felt his first tingling awareness of a life outside of what he'd known. Of what he'd expected. Sitting in the Morgans' kitchen, surrounded by decades of family and love, Forest found himself not *longing* anymore.

It was the weirdest day of his life—the most *normal* day he'd ever had—but it was weird.

When Connor came by to ooh and ahh over his newly purchased Honda SUV, he'd let the man lead him up to the widows' walk and sat there in the waning sun, holding Con's hand as Donal readied a massive BBQ for the family's Sunday gathering. It was perfect—sitting between Connor's raised knees and basking in the sun.

The moment became sublime when Connor leaned over Forest's shoulder to kiss his ear, then murmured, "Love you, *a ghra*."

Forest couldn't let his mother—wouldn't let his mother—ruin this for him. Not when he'd not even let himself *dare* to dream of living a life he'd seen others lead.

Shaking his head, he replied, "No, but thanks. I've got to—this is something I've got to do myself."

"I'm here if you need me, honey." Brigid's growl was a soft mewl compared to her son's rumbling whiskey of a voice, but it bore as much of a bite. "You go and tell her what you need to, but when she tries to pull any shit, you remember I'm there with you." She tapped his chest, right above his heart. "In here. No matter what, I've got you, son."

"Thanks, Bridge." Forest kissed her cheek, and one of her curls tickled his nose. "Tell Con where I'm at if he asks."

"SO ROLLINS is sick?" Captain Leonard frowned over his coffee. "What the hell is porphyria? And why the hell didn't they find it when he was in prison?"

"It's genetic," Connor explained to his boss. "He had records of migraines, but they figured it was bad eyesight or something else. Why look for zebras when you hear hoofbeats? Doctors went after what they thought was the problem. It's not common. They don't know if they can cure it either. He's too far gone."

"Mad King George's disease," Kiki said. "Makes people delusional. Even hallucinate. They don't know if he's ever going to be really okay. It was left untreated for too long. Some talk of suing the prison docs, but shit, those guys are risking their lives to give out flu shots. They gave him the best care they could. The court's going to have to see what they can do for him. DA's still pressing him for murder. That's not going to change."

"So he's nuts," Leonard stated. "They're going to let him walk."

"Can't. He's a danger to himself as much as to society," Connor pointed out. "They put him on suicide watch. No matter what the doctors say, Rollins isn't coming out again."

He spotted his mother moving through the crowd, and Connor looked past her, searching for Forest. He missed something Leonard said, and rather than ask the man to repeat it, he nodded and let Kiki take the conversation as they moved on to talking about the police department's new rugby team and its slim chance of winning against Fire and Rescue's brutes.

"That bitch who gave birth to him is outside," Brigid muttered at her oldest son, her voice low enough to carry up to his ears but not much farther. "Bring the Hummer around. I'll grab a knife from the kitchen and take care of her. We can dump her in the bay. Maybe there's enough crabs left down by the bridge they'll eat her body."

Connor excused himself from his conversation with Captain Leonard. Grabbing his mother by the elbow, he led her away to a more secluded corner. He saw his father's eyebrows raise in question, but by the expression on Donal's face, Connor knew he was feeling more sympathy than curiosity. After all, the man had several decades of dealing with the Finnegan he'd married. If anyone knew when to get out of Brigid's way, it certainly was his da.

Connor just had to figure out if it was one of those times.

"What do you mean, she's outside?" Connor bent his head down to hear his mother over the rumble of conversation in the shop. "Here? What does she want?"

"She wants to destroy him," Brigid growled back. "God, I hate her. I want to stab her eyes out with a fork. I'd do it, too, if I wasn't sure your da would arrest me. What's wrong with that man? Sometimes I think his mum dropped him on his head."

"Forest?" Connor tried to follow his mother's heated rant. "You think he was dropped on his head?"

"No, your da! Donal," Brigid sighed. "Pay attention, boy. Focus. What are we going to do about that woman?"

"What's up?" Damie edged in. "Something wrong with Forest? Where'd he go?"

"Probably too many people. I'd duck too," Miki cut in, and Connor sighed, wondering how he'd ever thought he'd have a private conversation with his mother anywhere near Forest's band mates. Catching the look he got from Con, Miki frowned. "What? No?"

"Unlike you, freak, Forest likes people," Damie snorted, then nodded to Brigid. "No, seriously, what's up?"

"His mother's here." Connor held up his hand to ward off the rounds of suggestions on how to deal with Ginger Ackerman he knew would be offered up. "Mum just wanted me to know."

"Why's she around?" Miki cocked his head. Jerking a thumb toward Brigid, he said, "He's got a new one. Mom 2.0. Much fucking better."

The interruption was worth it just to see Brigid's emerald eyes glittering with tears at Miki's casual remark. Her arms lifted, and the singer found himself caught up in a fierce hug. To his credit, he didn't wriggle free immediately, and it took a second or two for his shoulders to stop being stiff, but eventually he hugged her in return, patting her back awkwardly until she let go.

"You should go see if he needs some help." Brigid turned to Connor, wiping her face with the back of her hand. "Maybe run her off into the street where I can hit her with a car."

"Gotta love you, Bridge." Damie grinned.

"I'd kill for any of you." She sniffed back. "God, that woman just boils my teeth. Connor, you've got to...."

"I'll see if he needs me," he promised as he clasped his hands onto his mom's shoulders. "But Mum, he's a strong guy. He can take care of himself."

"But he shouldn't have to," Brigid shot back. "That's your job. Just like he takes care of you. It's how a marriage works. Good marriages."

"I haven't asked him to marry me, Mum. Too soon. Probably scare him off. Hell, scares the shit out of me just thinking about it," Connor admitted, holding up his cast-wrapped arm. "I'd like to get this piece of shit off of me first. It'd be nice to have hot rock star sex without worrying if I'm going to bash his head in."

Miki eyed Connor and snorted softly. "Dude, if you're worrying about bashing someone's head in during hot rock star sex, then you're doing it *all* wrong."

IT WAS hard seeing her. Not because of the changes in his life, but because a part of him ached to see his own mother shuffling back and forth on a street corner, her arms wrapped around her too-skinny body. Even in broad daylight, she scanned passing cars, looking for something—someone to take her in.

He'd done that with her. That looking. That hoping for a trick so he could get something to eat. Have enough money to stay someplace warm.

Then he'd spat in Franklin's face when the man gave him what he'd wanted, what he'd needed. But Forest couldn't abandon her. Not then, when he'd still held on to the lingering belief she'd always been there for him.

Only to discover she'd abandoned him long before Frank *ever* came into the picture.

"Hey, Mom." She turned when he spoke, startled for some reason to find him staring down at her.

Ginger looked like shit. Worn and scrawny, he caught her lighting a cigarette off the end of another, puffing furiously to get the thing going. A couple of burned-out stubs lay at her feet, their smashed filtered ends a fan of greasy brown and white.

"Hey." Her eyes, so much like his, flicked over his shoulder. "You alone?"

He looked around, wondering for a half second if someone'd followed him out, but other than the stream of people coming in and out of the Amp, it was just the two of them. Handing her the cup of coffee he'd brought for her, Forest nodded.

"You want to go inside?" He regretted asking as soon as the words left his mouth. Asking opened him up to her rejection, and Forest didn't know if he was ready to deal with *that* on top of the already long and trying day.

"Nah, not my thing." Ginger took the coffee and sipped at it, making a face. "Not enough sugar. You know I like things sweet."

"You're welcome," he replied wryly. The refusal didn't sting as much as it had in the past. So *much* had changed in the past few months.

"I didn't know this was going on." She waved her long press-on nails at the store. "Or I would have come by some other time."

"No, it's good," Forest said. "I'm not here as much as I used to be. I don't live above the studio anymore."

"The cop putting you up?" Suddenly her eyes narrowed, and he could see her brain ticking away. "Shit, good job. He's got some money. I've seen that car of his. Milk *that* for as long as you can."

"Mom, it's not like that," Forest began to protest, but Ginger's face grew ugly.

"It's always like that, you fucking idiot," she hissed at him, glaring at a woman who glanced at them as she passed by. "Get what you can and get the fuck out. Hell, leave him wanting your ass and work him. Shit, you can keep him going while I hook you up with a guy I know. Play two guys if you have to. Haven't you learned that by now?"

"Mom, I love him," he told her in a quiet voice. "He loves me. It's not like *that*."

"You are so fucking stupid." Her hiss turned hot, scalding his face when she exhaled a vodka-soaked puff of smoke at him. "You're nothing but a piece of meat. You're fooling yourself if you think you're anything more than a hot hole for him to put his dick in. Take what you can get and leave before he decides to take his shit back. *Jesus Christ, you're stupid!*"

He had to look away. It still hurt. *She* still hurt. He had to feel around the edges of his pain, searching through it like he'd done a broken tooth once, probing at it to see how bad it was and if he could stand the pain just a bit longer. Frank'd paid to have that tooth filled, then coughed up even more money to get it capped when it went all dark side. It pretty much described their entire relationship—that tooth—and Forest's heart echoed with regret he'd not thanked the man sooner.

Through the sting of his tears, Forest saw Connor standing by the door, his thumbs hooked into his jeans pockets as he watched them from a distance, a silent sentinel waiting—just waiting for Forest to indicate he was needed. Their eyes met, and Connor smiled, melting away the choking cold of his mother's words.

"I'm not going to live your life with you," he finally said, breaking through the muttered rant Ginger'd worked herself into. "I can't. I don't want to. Yeah, Connor might hurt me. Hurt my heart. It's a part of life, and we're going to rub each other the wrong way sometimes, but the good of it is so fucking worth it. He trusted me to love him. And I'm going to do that. For as long as he'll let me."

"You're—" Ginger started, but Forest cut her off.

"If you need something, like—to help to get off this shit life you like having, I'll help you," Forest promised. "But you're not going to take me with you.

I won't *let* you do that to me. I won't let you do that to what I have with Connor. You've got my number, Mom. I'll always answer it for you, but that's all you're going to get out of me."

Then he turned and walked away. Toward Connor. As his mother screamed behind him.

"She's a piece of work. And not in a good way," Connor said when Forest reached him. Wrapping his arms around Forest, they kissed lightly, briefly, but it was enough to set Forest's insides on fire. Pulling back, Connor asked, "You okay?"

"Yeah." He nodded. "Better. With you."

IF SOMEONE'D asked him if he'd be head over heels in love a year ago—*hell*, six months ago—Connor would have said love needed time to grow and build. He'd never thought a single moment would change his life. Sure as hell not on a raid and never in a million years in the form of a blond drummer with a quiet voice and a fierce soul.

Forest didn't just turn his life upside down. No, the man'd turned Connor's soul and heart over, forcing him to take a good hard look at himself and admit he could find happiness in a place he hadn't ever dared to imagine before.

Yeah, Connor thought, life was better once he had Forest in it. Much better.

"I love you, you know," Connor murmured, rocking Forest in his arms. "Never ever doubt that. No matter what."

"I love you too. Hey, you took a stool to the arm for me." Forest grinned at him, their noses touching. "Not every guy can say that about their boyfriend."

"Boyfriend," Connor repeated. "That's good. For now."

"For now?" It was Forest's turn to pull back but only enough so he could peer into Connor's face. "What the hell else do I call you?"

"Yeah, about that." Connor bent his head down to kiss the corner of Forest's mouth. Throwing caution to the wind, he said, "I was thinking maybe sometime in the future, you might be wanting to be calling me something more."

RAFE ANDRADE lurked in the corner of the coffee shop. He'd been introduced to the members of Sinner's Gin before, and while Sionn was his best friend, he still felt a bit weird talking to Damien Mitchell as if the man was a normal part of everyday life.

He wasn't starstruck. Not by a long shot. They'd been peers of sorts, but Sinner's Gin had been on the rise while Rafe was working like hell to bring his own band down. His downward spiral into drugs had been spectacular, a nearly cataclysmic fall from grace, and he was still smarting from it.

Rafe was pretty sure if he reached back and touched his shoulder blades, he could feel the smoking remains of his wax and feather wings.

They'd been nice. Kind, even, but Rafe felt the sting of their wariness. Although to be fair, Miki St. John was known to be reticent, and Damie'd been more than happy to fill up any silence with an ongoing babble about music and musicians they all liked.

It felt *good* to talk music with another guitarist. Even better, when the conversation drifted away from modern music to rock's Southern roots. Damie thrummed with excitement as he began to talk about old-school blues and how he wanted to build more of his music on that platform. It must have been a much-discussed point, because Miki rolled his eyes at Rafe, and they'd laughed, sharing a moment of amusement at the man's fervor.

It felt too damned good, and Rafe had to walk away before he emasculated himself and hugged the men in relief.

His disastrous fall left him a pariah among other musicians, and even after a couple of years of hard sobriety, many of his contemporaries still treated him like a leper.

"Shit, burn down *one* hotel room," Rafe muttered darkly. "No one got hurt, and I put it out."

He'd slunk home to San Francisco in disgrace and licked his wounds. It'd taken him nearly dying in a pool of his own vomit for Rafe to pull himself out of the gutter, and he'd be the first one to admit he'd fucked up something bad.

Still, wasn't like he deserved being shoved into a wicker man and used as a sacrifice.

Rafe was about to go find Sionn in the knot of Morgans he'd last seen his friend in when his eyes settled on the one Morgan boy who made his heart race.

Quinn Morgan, Rafe mused, the odd duckling born into a house of griffins.

Unlike the other Morgan men, he let his hair grow to a wild mane down past his jaw. It curled a bit at his nape, thick black waves around his strong, lean face. There was something hypnotic about the man's dark green eyes and how they could stare right through a man.

Rafe'd spent his teenaged years avoiding Quinn Morgan. The third Morgan son had been too young, too weird, but most of all too pretty. Of course, Connor and Kane would have beaten Rafe's face in with their meaty fists if he'd even lifted an eyebrow in the direction of their younger brother.

And he'd wanted to do much more than lift an eyebrow at Quinn Morgan.

Especially now, since the scrawny, bony boy'd grown up to be a hot, smoldering young man with graceful hands and a full mouth ripe for kissing.

"Shit," Rafe muttered when Quinn spotted him staring. Grinning cockily back, Rafe swallowed his apprehension when Quinn began to work past his siblings and headed straight for him. "Fucking hell, now what are you going to do, Andrade?"

"Hey," Quinn said softly. "Just the guy I'm looking for."

"Yeah?" He played it cool. If it was one thing Rafe knew, it was how to be cool in the face of a firing squad. He'd faced them often enough. Hell, he could give lessons if he wanted to. "Whatcha need?"

"I needed to ask you a question." Those long black lashes fluttered once, shuttering Quinn's emerald gaze for just a moment, and then Rafe found himself drowning in green once again. Taking a deep breath, Quinn looked around first, then leaned in close to whisper into Rafe's ear. "I kind of need to lose my virginity. And I was wondering if you could help me out."

BOOK FOUR OF THE SINNERS SERIES
RHYS FORD

SLOE RIDE

"Rife with mystery and intrigue." — Fresh Fiction

Sequel to *Tequila Mockingbird*
Sinners Series: Book Four

It isn't easy being a Morgan. Especially when dead bodies start piling up and there's not a damned thing you can do about it.

Quinn Morgan never quite fit into the family mold. He dreamed of a life with books instead of badges and knowledge instead of law—and a life with Rafe Andrade, his older brothers' bad boy friend and the man who broke his very young heart.

Rafe Andrade returned home to lick his wounds following his ejection from the band he helped form. A recovering drug addict, Rafe spends his time wallowing in guilt, until he finds himself faced with his original addiction, Quinn Morgan—the reason he fled the city in the first place.

When Rafe hears the Sinners are looking for a bassist, it's a chance to redeem himself, but as a crazed murderer draws closer to Quinn, Rafe's willing to sacrifice everything—including himself—to keep his quixotic Morgan safe and sound.

www.dreamspinnerpress.com

PROLOGUE

Got shadows on my ass
Time's not on my side
Life came to give me a kiss
Then Death took me for a ride
—Riding A Pale Horse

A Couple of Years Ago

RAFE ANDRADE couldn't shake off the black tendrils wrapped around the base of his brain. Whatever he'd taken the night before lingered, dragging him down, and there were stretches along his back and legs where he couldn't seem to get warm. His bones ached from the cold, a brutal, icy seep into his marrow. Rafe didn't think he would survive if he didn't stop it soon. Moving didn't seem to help, or at least not when he tried to shift about. For some reason he couldn't get his arms and legs to work properly, and his balls were pulled up someplace beneath his destroyed liver. After a moment or two of flailing about, Rafe realized he was trapped, contained in a small, hard box he was painfully banging his elbows and shins against whenever he moved.

"Oh God." Panic and fear set in when he opened his eyes and found nothing around him but a darkness his vision couldn't penetrate. "They buried me. Oh God, they thought I was dead and buried me. God, *no*."

He fought against the box's solid, icy sides, his elbows and heels shocked with pain with each glancing blow. The air in his chest grew hot, and his lungs folded in, tightening until Rafe couldn't draw in another breath.

"Think, dude. I'm naked. Who the fuck buries someone naked? Up. Push. Up." His feeble brain sparked a thought from its murky drowning. Shoving his hands up against the top of the box, Rafe felt… nothing. His arms shot straight up into the air, momentum carrying him off the cold bottom an inch before gravity slammed him back down.

"What the fuck?" The box wasn't covered. "Where the hell am I?"

Rafe slowly sat up, ducking his head in case he hit a top as solid as the walls, but once he got upright, he found he could grasp the thick sides. Moving was still a problem, and his foot struck something solid at the bottom of the box. Feeling around the space's slightly rounded sides, he found a spigot sticking out of the short wall by his foot, its metal surface as frigid as the slick walls around him.

"I'm in a goddamned bathtub." His relief nearly made him sick. Sucking in heaving breaths, Rafe tried to figure out exactly where he was. There wasn't a whisper of memory in his confused mind. Nothing to pinpoint where he'd been before the tub's high walls held him in. The air was warmer once he'd sat up, although his ass was still freezing, and Rafe blinked, waiting for his eyes to adjust.

Nothing. Not even a sliver of light coming from under a door.

"Okay, Andrade. You can do this." He carefully tried to stand up, but his legs didn't seem to be connected to whatever part of his brain he normally used to move him around. It took what felt like forever before he could hook a leg over the side of the tub and then another long hour or so before he felt the floor with his toes. Stepping carefully, he lowered his foot to the solid tiled surface, then gripped the tub tightly until he could get his other leg similarly untangled.

Being upright was a significant challenge. The dark didn't help. Rafe couldn't tell which way was up or even how large the room was. As odd as his blackened prison was, his body seemed to be in a very familiar state.

He ached from sex, and a sour rankness poured off his body, a combination of drugs, vomit, and come filming over swathes of his skin. Rafe wasn't exactly sure if he was on the upswing of drunk and stoned or coming down. It was too soon to tell. He'd have to give it a few minutes to see if he got happier or sadder with healthy doses of belligerence and anger if whatever he took hit those spots in his brain. Thinking hurt. His skull felt boiled solid by his muddled thoughts, and as he stumbled forward, looking for a wall or a doorknob, Rafe heard his subconscious whisper for him to crawl back into the tub and wait for death to take him.

It would be easier than actually killing himself. And sure as hell less painful than how he'd been at it before.

"Fuck the pity party, Andrade," he grumbled aloud. "Just find the fucking door."

The knob seemed to appear beneath his grasping fingers, and he lunged for it, using one hand to slap at the wall nearby. Feeling up around the frame, Rafe found a switch, then flicked it up, hoping to finally see what he was doing.

A simple click, and suddenly he was blinded by floodlights bouncing off of white marble. A turn of the knob, and he was free, blindly stumbling into a bedroom he didn't remember but knew its stench. It was intimate and cloying, just like the odor bleeding out of his pores. There was a pounding coming from somewhere, but Rafe couldn't figure out if it was his head or the anxious tap of his heart in his chest.

"Hotel." He carefully looked around. Double doors, one hanging off its hinges, led to a living room off of the bedroom. "And I've trashed it. That's par for the course. But where the fuck is the hotel?"

The king-size bed was a mess, and something'd leaked on the floor near an overturned nightstand. It was standard high-star hotel fare, slithery duvet crumpled up and probably full of dried come. Somehow either he or someone else got all the artwork off the walls and thrown into a pile of torn canvas and frames in a corner of the room. Burn marks on the wood pieces were a hint at an attempted bonfire. The water-soaked carpet and an empty ice bucket set on top of the pile spoke of at least a panicked success.

Oddly enough, the bedroom was empty. Rafe's bedroom was never empty. Hell, even if he had to sneak a piece of ass around Jack once in a while, his bed was always filled.

"Okay, so somewhere, I probably lost a boy." He rubbed at his face, shivering in the air-conditioned room. "God, I could use a good fuck. Better than coffee."

His balls were still AWOL, and his dick was limp between his legs. He was thinking about sex, and nothing. Not even a stirring want churning up in his belly. Common enough. The drugs were taking their toll, and for the umpteenth time in his life, Rafe promised himself he'd cut back. A few little blue pills took care of any nonsense his body decided to toss back at him, but au natural was definitely a better way to go. Looking down at his cock, Rafe suddenly realized the chafing on his skin had less to do with fucking himself senseless and more about the condom rolled down his shaft.

"Jesus Christ." The sheath was hard to get off, and he tugged at it, snapping it clean off, then tossing it into the failed bonfire. Rubbing at his temple, the pounding continued, a muted thump-thump echoing across his skull. "Okay, forget the guy. Where the fuck am I? I don't even know what city I'm in."

Panic was starting to set in. He felt like he'd missed something—a birthday or even maybe a show. It wouldn't have been the first time he'd slept through a gig, but Jack'd been harsh on his ass the last time he skipped out. The band wasn't going to take much more of his shit, but for the life of him, Rafe couldn't recall if they were on tour or if he'd just gone someplace all by himself and got stinking-ass wasted.

"No, not on tour. Come on, where's your stuff, Andrade? There'd be a bass in here if—"

He found the guy he'd been looking for in the living room.

Unfortunately for both of them, he was as cold and lifeless as Rafe's cock. A pretty blond, barely old enough to know better than to let a rock star lure him up to a hotel room, or maybe he hadn't cared. Either way, it was a decision he'd never live to regret. His lifeless brown eyes stared up accusingly at Rafe, a froth of vomit speckled with something black drying over his parted lips and long throat. Sprawled out naked on the floor, his fingers were covered in dried blood, the carpet near his thighs streaked a dark brown where he'd clawed at the pile. Shock closed Rafe's throat, and suddenly the pounding grew louder, shattering the silence.

Then the door flew open, and Rafe's world broke apart.

"Police! Hands up! Clear the room!" There were a ton of cops, too many to count. Hell, too many for Rafe to even see. It was a tidal wave of uniforms, some blue cotton while others wore the red-gray livery of a Los Angeles hotel he'd stayed in before.

And in the middle of it—Jack *fucking* Collins, lead guitarist and Rafe's mostly-on-sometimes-off lover, staring him straight in the face. Jack's handsome face was curdled with rage, and the white light coming from the hotel corridor formed a corona around his broad shoulders, gilding his sun-streaked hair.

"Fucking Christ, Rafe. What the *hell* did you do?" Jack accused, a hot spit of words and anger pouring from his lanky body. "You're out of the band. Missing last night? Too fucking much, but—*this*? I just—God, Rafe. What the *hell*?"

Naked, cold, and hungover, Rafe did the only thing any rational bass player would do when standing over a stiff corpse and being surrounded by cops. He leaned over and vomited all over the dead guy's body.

Nine Months Later

REHAB TOOK everything out of him. More than two hundred days of white walls, porridge, and singing "Kumbaya My Lord," and Rafe'd been about to kill himself just to get free. Sobriety sucked, and even worse, he'd spent his birthday craving a blow job and some coke. What he'd gotten was a cupcake and a call from his mother.

He'd clung to her voice. In an instant he'd become a little boy again, curled up around a plastic headset and crying, deep, jagged sobs violent enough to tear him apart. They'd been the longest five minutes of his life, too short for his brain to grasp and too long for his soul to take.

It would be the last time they spoke for months.

Thank God for Brigid and Donal, or he'd have gone mad.

Rafe's skin didn't stop itching until three months into his sentence. As court orders went, he'd gotten off easy. Locked up in rehab on a suspended sentence was nothing compared to jail time, and despite a grumpy judge's opinion of Rafe failing the course, he'd done pretty good. Despite what everyone'd thought of him, when he sobered up later that fateful evening, the horror of what happened in his hotel room haunted him.

He also couldn't seem to get his feet clean of the dead blond's—of Mark's vomit.

Now he was slinking home, worn through and torn apart by his own demons. Despite the cleaning service his former manager set up, his Nob Hill penthouse smelled stale and dead. The doorman'd been friendly enough. Once Rafe established he actually belonged in the building and once security reassured themselves of his ownership, the property manager scurried out from his office and handed Rafe his new keys.

"There were some issues, Mr. Andrade," the beak-nosed man simpered. "Some very hateful things paint-ed on the side of the building, but it was taken care of. Have no worries. We rekeyed the penthouse as a precaution."

There was no good-to-have-you-back nonsense from the sour-faced man. Rafe knew if he hadn't actu-ally bought the penthouse outright, there'd have been a fight to get him out. No matter what anyone said, life was always just like high school. Fuck up royally, and people were more than happy to rip his ass to shreds and hand it back to him piece by piece.

This time, he didn't blame them.

Set on one of San Francisco's steep hills, the build-ing had gorgeous views of the city and bay. When he'd first seen the penthouse, Rafe knew he had to have it. It was the furthest thing from the shithole he'd grown up in, a symbol of how far he'd climbed from being a char-ity case begging for scraps of education and food. He'd always wanted more—wanted what his friends Connor and Sionn had, longed for a time when he didn't have to look at price tags and juggle food against electricity or snatch cigarettes off the back of a truck to sell in a Chinatown alleyway for a bit of extra money.

The water glittered off in the distance, and the city's spires below hadn't quite shaken off their fog-gy veil. On a clear day he could see Finnegan's, where he'd washed dishes for Sionn's grandmother, wanting to be too proud to take the day's leftover food home, but he hadn't been stupid. He'd taken everything any-one offered and sometimes without permission. He'd sucked out what he could from the private school ed-ucation his mother'd gotten him and charmed his way out of shit he'd fallen into.

Oddly enough, the penthouse and its million-dollar view meant nothing now. He owned it. He owned a lot of things. Stashing money and hiring people to keep ev-ery damned cent he made was the best piece of advice he'd gotten from Donal Morgan. It was a pity that was the only advice he'd listened to.

Despite the months he'd spent in Malibu soaking up sobriety, his place looked almost exactly the same as when he'd left it. Rich, warm buttery walls and com-fortable furniture with a few dashes of art the decora-tor tossed in warmed the empty apartment. A sparkling kitchen armed with gadgets he had no idea how to use and bedrooms with beds soft enough to sink into lay off the main entrance. He'd paid for a room to be sound-proofed and set up amps and a soundboard, intending to blow out his own ears while staying up all hours of the night with Jack.

That bit of life never happened, and Rafe won-dered if it ever would have to begin with.

To the left of the front door, unread books lined a bank of cases, and the view from the midcentury mod-ern living room was heart-stopping, the Golden Gate Bridge poking up through the far-off mist. His favorite part of the place was the guitars hanging from a long wall separating the rest of the house from the long living space, bright spots of color splashed up against white paint and what he'd used to pull himself up out of perdition.

Some of which were now gone, taken by the man he'd built his escape on.

There hadn't been love. Not the love he felt for Quinn Morgan—the love he'd tucked away deep inside himself so it wouldn't hurt—but a casual affection, a kindred musical spirit he'd not found in his other relationships.

Fuck, Jack dumping him out of his life *really* hurt.

The gaps in the guitars hurt the most, and Rafe stumbled to sit down on something before he fell to his knees and cried. Of all the things Rafe'd fucked up in his life, losing Jack Collins's friendship left the biggest hole. It was more than hurt, he realized, staring at the white spaces where Jack'd once hung some of his favorite instruments. It was losing parts of his life Rafe knew he'd never get back. The band was gone. Jack was gone. There was no one he hadn't fucked over, including the person he'd thought he'd always have, his own mother. As empty as he felt inside, Rafe knew he'd run out of excuses. Reality came back and bit him hard because he'd been the one to set it all on fire and laughed when it burned to a crisp.

A note was tucked into one of the wall mounts, and Rafe debated leaving it there for the housekeeper to clean up. His resolve lasted about a minute before he snatched it out of its perch. He wanted a drink, something to steady his nerves, but the stint in rehab left him with a sour taste for numbing his brain when things got rough. While anything chemical was now off-limits, alcohol hadn't been his problem—wasn't his problem, Rafe corrected himself.

"Shit's not going to go away just because you want it to. Always going to be there." He sat down on a fluffy armchair he didn't remember owning. The whole place looked odd, unfamiliar in so many ways, leaving him to wonder if the guitars weren't the only thing Jack took with him.

From the look of the handwriting on the folded paper, Jack at least left him a Dear John letter.

"More like a fuck off and die," Rafe muttered, opening the note.

It was everything he'd imagined. Clear and strong in black ink, Jack left Rafe with no delusions he'd ever be welcomed back into Jack's band or life. There'd been too many times, too many disappointments, and one too many deaths for Jack Collins's liking, and Rafe Andrade could go twist in the wind for all he cared.

They'd not been in love. They'd fought as much as they'd fucked, bound by rhythms, words, and a shared hardscrabble past. Rafe wasn't a fool to think Jack cared for him more than he liked a good piece of steak or a fine bottle of tequila, but they'd been friends. Hell, they'd gone through so much together. Rafe'd created the band with Jack, and despite it all—or maybe because of it all—he hadn't fought Jack when he'd been pushed out. It was all over between them except for the legal wrangling as lawyers and record companies untangled Rafe's half ownership of a band he'd help put on the map.

"I should fuck them all up and refuse to sell." Even as the spite gushed from the sourness in his belly, Rafe knew he wouldn't do it. He owed Jack. With as much shit as they'd been through at the start, it'd been Jack who'd held it all together once Rafe began to destroy it all in the end. "Hell, Jack. I wish you'd just let me say *I'm sorry*. Would you fucking at least give me that much?"

He'd fallen so damned far, crashing down on sharp rocks and tearing out the wings he'd built for himself to get away from who he'd been. And now Rafe was back where he started. Alone, unwanted, and most of all, scared down deep into his soul.

"Damn it, Andrade." Rafe swallowed around the pain hitching up through his throat. "Should have just done the shitty world a favor and taken one last handful of fucking pills. 'Cause after all of this crap, no one's going to fucking want you around."

RHYS FORD is an award-winning author with several long-running LGBT+ mystery, thriller, paranormal, and urban fantasy series and is a two-time LAMBDA finalist with her *Murder and Mayhem* novels. She is also a 2017 Gold and Silver Medal winner in the Florida Authors and Publishers President's Book Awards for her novels *Ink and Shadows* and *Hanging the Stars*. She is published by Dreamspinner Press and DSP Publications.

She shares the house with Harley, a gray tuxedo with a flower on her face, Badger, a disgruntled alley cat who isn't sure living inside is a step up the social ladder, as well as a ginger cairn terrorist named Gus. Rhys is also enslaved to the upkeep of a 1979 Pontiac Firebird and enjoys murdering make-believe people.

Rhys can be found at the following locations:

Blog: www.rhysford.com

Facebook: www.facebook.com/rhys.ford.author

Twitter: @Rhys_Ford

RHYS FORD

SINNER'S GIN

"A raw, sexy read..." — *USA Today*

Sinners Series: Book One

There's a dead body in Miki St. John's vintage Pontiac GTO, and he has no idea how it got there.

After Miki survives the tragic accident that killed his best friend and the other members of their band, Sinner's Gin, all he wants is to hide from the world in the refurbished warehouse he bought before their last tour. But when the man who sexually abused him as a boy is killed and his remains are dumped in Miki's car, Miki fears Death isn't done with him yet.

Kane Morgan, the SFPD inspector renting space in the art co-op next door, initially suspects Miki had a hand in the man's murder, but Kane soon realizes Miki is as much a victim as the man splattered inside the GTO. As the murderer's body count rises, the attraction between Miki and Kane heats up. Neither man knows if they can make a relationship work, but despite Miki's emotional damage, Kane is determined to teach him how to love and be loved — provided, of course, Kane can catch the killer before Miki becomes the murderer's final victim.

www.dreamspinnerpress.com

BOOK TWO OF THE SINNERS SERIES
RHYS FORD

WHISKEY
AND WRY

Sequel to *Sinner's Gin*
Sinners Series: Book Two

He was dead. And it was murder most foul. If erasing a man's existence could even be called murder.

When Damien Mitchell wakes, he finds himself without a life or a name. The Montana asylum's doctors tell him he's delusional and his memories are all lies: he's really Stephen Thompson, and he'd gone over the edge, obsessing about a rock star who died in a fiery crash. His chance to escape back to his own life comes when his prison burns, but a gunman is waiting for him, determined that neither Stephen Thompson nor Damien Mitchell will escape.

With the assassin on his tail, Damien flees to the City by the Bay, but keeping a low profile is the only way he'll survive as he searches San Francisco for his best friend, Miki St. John. Falling back on what kept him fed before he made it big, Damien sings for his supper outside Finnegan's, an Irish pub on the pier, and he soon falls in with the owner, Sionn Murphy. Damien doesn't need a complication like Sionn, and to make matters worse, the gunman—who doesn't mind going through Sionn or anyone else if that's what it takes kill Damien—shows up to finish what he started.

www.dreamspinnerpress.com

BOOK FIVE OF THE SINNERS SERIES

RHYS FORD

ABSINTHE OF MALICE

"From the get-go I was absolutely enthralled." — *Novel Approach*

Sequel to *Sloe Ride*
Sinners Series: Book Five

We're getting the band back together.

Those six words send a chill down Miki St. John's spine, especially when they're spoken with a nearly religious fervor by his brother-in-all-but-blood, Damien Mitchell. However, those words were nothing compared to what Damien says next.

And we're going on tour.

When Crossroads Gin hits the road, Damien hopes it will draw them closer together. There's something magical about being on tour, especially when traveling in a van with no roadies, managers, or lovers to act as a buffer. The band is already close, but Damien knows they can be more—brothers of sorts, bound not only by familial ties but by their intense love for music.

As they travel from gig to gig, the band is haunted by past mistakes and personal demons, but they forge on. For Miki, Damie, Forest, and Rafe, the stage is where they all truly come alive, and the music they play is as important to them as the air they breathe.

But those demons and troubles won't leave them alone, and with every mile under their belts, the band faces its greatest challenge—overcoming their deepest flaws and not killing one another along the way.

www.dreamspinnerpress.com

BOOK SIX OF THE SINNERS SERIES

RHYS FORD

SIN AND TONIC

"The perfect ending to a spectacularly touching series that meshes mystery, romance, and family." — Mary Calmes

Sequel to *Absinthe of Malice*
Sinners Series: Book Six

Miki St. John believed happy endings only existed in fairy tales until his life took a few unexpected turns… and now he's found his own.

His best friend, Damien, is back from the dead, and their new band, Crossroads Gin, is soaring up the charts. Miki's got a solid, loving partner named Kane Morgan—an Inspector with SFPD whose enormous Irish family has embraced him as one of their own—and his dog, Dude, at his side.

It's a pity someone's trying to kill him.

Old loyalties and even older grudges emerge from Chinatown's murky, mysterious past, and Miki struggles to deal with his dead mother's abandonment, her secrets, and her brutal murder while he's hunted by an enigmatic killer who may have ties to her.

The case lands in Kane's lap, and he and Miki are caught in a deadly game of cat-and-mouse. When Miki is forced to face his personal demons and the horrors of his childhood, only one thing is certain: the rock star and his cop are determined to fight for their future and survive the evils lurking in Miki's past.

www.dreamspinnerpress.com

415 ☆ INK • BOOK ONE

Rebel

RHYS FORD

415 Ink: Book One

The hardest thing a rebel can do isn't standing up for something—it's standing up for himself.

Life takes delight in stabbing Gus Scott in the back when he least expects it. After Gus spends years running from his past, present, and the dismal future every social worker predicted for him, karma delivers the one thing Gus could never—would never—turn his back on: a son from a one-night stand he'd had after a devastating breakup a few years ago.

Returning to San Francisco and to 415 Ink, his family's tattoo shop, gave him the perfect shelter to battle his personal demons and get himself together… until the firefighter who'd broken him walked back into Gus's life.

For Rey Montenegro, tattoo artist Gus Scott was an elusive brass ring, a glittering prize he hadn't the strength or flexibility to hold on to. Severing his relationship with the mercurial tattoo artist hurt, but Gus hadn't wanted the kind of domestic life Rey craved, leaving Rey with an aching chasm in his soul.

When Gus's life and world starts to unravel, Rey helps him pick up the pieces, and Gus wonders if that forever Rey wants is more than just a dream.

www.dreamspinnerpress.com